Copyright © 2021 by Eric Shepherd

All rights reserved. This book or any portion thereof may not be reproduced or transmitted in any form or manner, electronic or mechanical, including photocopying, recording, or by any information storage or retrieval system, without the express written permission of the copyright owner except for the use of brief quotations in a book review or other noncommercial uses permitted by copyright law.

Printed in the United States of America

ISBN:	Softcover	978-1-64908-965-6
ISBN:	Hardback	978-1-64908-966-3
	eBook	978-1-64908-964-9

Republished by: PageTurner Press and Media LLC
Publication Date: 05/04/2021

To order copies of this book, contact:

PageTurner Press and Media
Phone: 1-888-447-9651
order@pageturner.us
www.pageturner.us

DEDICATION

I would like to dedicate this book in loving memory to Vicky Shepherd who has recently left this world and gone beyond the looking glass. I also like to thank her sisters Cindy Shepherd and Kathy Shepherd for sticking by me when reading and giving advice on how this book came about. But most of all I would like to thank my Anunt Margert and Doris Shepherd my grandmother. For without them this book and series would have never been possible, as well as the Downing family.

Book 1 What's Behind The Looking Glass??

EJ Stewart is caught between two worlds searching for The Five Keys Of Destiny that can control the outcome of not only his world, but the worlds behind the looking glass. He must relive his past and find ways too change it with the help of his new friends, which are in desperate need of his help; before the evil wizard Morgan and his master Hess destroy the worlds behind the looking glass as well as his own. Most of all stop Morgan and his Dark Prince and their master Hess from gaining the five Keys Of Destiny that will lead them to the ultimate prize. Or be forever lost inside the Look Glass.

The question is… Are you brave enough too take the journey of the young boy and help him with the help of his friends. Battle Evil and rediscover what is behind the looking glass…? Or loose your soul forever?

What's Behind the Looking Glass?

Written By Eric Shepherd

Square Peg

A square peg and a round hole it's only right that the two don't fit. So Why? Do people think it's me who always needs to be fixed even thou nor so easily mixed?
Too long I've tried to mold my way through life anxiously like a fool with nothing to say. But if by chance my words and thoughts flow like unto a raging river into the far depths of the sea, or if my words and thoughts you decided to keep. Then I will know that the sea is not so distant nor so deep.
Then for the rest, can ponder and dream wherefore life is but a dream. For they will never understand my kind except for old father time, who's Life has no beginning nor end like the sands upon distant shores.
As the stars in the heavens gaze brightly down upon the depths of the sea, time will pass but yet never fade, except for those who have gone before me and those who have joined me on this mysterious crusade.
May the stars forever guide us on this journey that I haven't yet made? For time will pass us yet never fade like the darkest night or the brightest sun nor the shimmer of the moon, for life is still forever young and those who survive and are among.
Here's to you who have fought and won, and to those that are still gazing out upon the battlefields of time and here's to those who can still hear so ever faintly the battle cries of the fallen old and young.
For hear me now and forever my beating heart, my whispering words, upon the wind, hear my thoughts among the rustling of autumn leaves. See me truly, see me who I really am nor what you want me to be for I am my own eagle and with hopes of my own that soar among them in the heavens endless sky.
See me for who I am nor what can you make me be .I have my own dreams that come alive upon a new springing awake for the first time after cold hard winter.
Listen, quietly listen, see without eyes and be amazed yet not afraid, feel not with not what you can not touch with flesh of hand nor bone but with only true , mind and strength.
For I will never again live in fear of fitting in as a square peg into a "Round Hole."

By Eric Shepherd

Some may it finds disturbing, but for the facts and truths that lie behind these pages are true even though some may it find fictional.

I question you this what is real scope of realty? The realty you understand that exist now or the reality you that you thought exist or hoped exist?

There are worlds out there today which have not yet been explored or mysteries yet solved into today's world. Who knows what lies beyond our world and exist in and out of our own world? Just because you have never seen them or it, doesn't mean it does not exist. Remember a hidden path or entryway can still be discovered or culture of people you thought never existed or thought existed only in fairy-tales can exist. They are just hidden behind the looking glass unseen by you until now.

Reality or Time has no meaning or scope nor existence. The question is do you really yourself exist at all or perhaps your the one they perceived as the fairy-tale? It all depends on what side of the Mirror you are on.

THE EARLY DAYS
CHAPTER 1

It had been many lonely years since Derrick stood in the fields on His families farm as a boy near the town of Zueqinten. A place so far away among the stars and many of its galaxies from the young planet known as Earth, which had just reached its modern era and still unseen by many… unless you are a wizard or had been born or given the gift of "Sight" to see beyond the shadows of time and behind the looking glass. Its golden fields of wheat and corn that grow beneath the dark rich soil and warm sun above known as Tala and her three brother's moon shone brightly by night. Syrian was the color of reds and yellows. Railen was blue and green as the oceans of Tahar and Dole the color of molten gold. He had always enjoyed the sweet scent of Serine Pine from the hills of Gladern, and the cool glacier water that still trickled down the path in front of his onetime home.

His parents died when he was young during the last wizard's war nearly three hundred years ago. The anger still burned deep within him the day Hess… Morgan's master annulated the entire village. The only thing that consoled him, are the memories and the voices of his family laughing around the dinner table. Even as a boy of fifteen he was tall like his father and older brother Nathanial before he joined the ranks of **Council of Light** as a member of Death a Grim Reaper to some, but something more entirely. A title is worthy of any warrior whose purpose was keeping the balance of Light and Darkness. "Evil vs. Good" and helping the lost souls find the light and freeing them from the darkness.

Sometimes he missed his brother like now as he bent down placing white lilies upon the grave of his mother and his father. Wiped an escaped tear, remembering the last words his father said to him. 'Never give up hope, for the truth and the light will always prevail over the darkness. You must have faith in the **Council of Light** as they watch over every man, woman, and child. Even though they may not see you or know that you fight for their very lives,

What's Behind the Looking Glass?

you must do your best to protect them from the darkness.' Derrick sighed heavily. "I will do my best father." It is hard to believe that it had been nearly four-hundred years and he still grieves for them. Remembering the comfort of his mother's arms and the sweet scent of jasmine in her long brown hair, her deep blue eyes the color of the ocean Leona and hearing her voice reminded him of a voice of an angel when she sang a lullaby when he was merely a babe.

Derrick stood between the graves and took one last breath feeling strengthened as he listened to the voices of the dead around him and ready to make the hard choices for the realms he is in charge of protecting. Taking his ivory staff and slowly tapped the ground six times as the air around him shimmers and reformed around him as he entered his own private chamber given to him and his brother Nathanial. As they work together in saving their world and the worlds beyond.

No. Being the man called Death was never easy like now, sifting through the lives before him as he gazed at the stars in his chamber; trying to find that one single spark that could change the balance of time. That could win this war that is coming as the darkness gains another foothold in the realm of "Time" behind the looking glass. Like the man before him now... a man that has given up on all his dreams and passion. Who has put aside finding love for fear of becoming like his parents? Wondering if he could face the world alone, or simply give up and die quietly into the darkness to escape the nightmares of his past and unloved and forgotten by the world he lives in.

His light slowly dims like a candle flickering in the wind as he draws his last breath. A man, who had fought for the rights of others like himself that have been abused, beaten and discarded like common trash, preyed upon by so many. A boy shaking in fear of his own shadow, but a man who would still help a stranger or another child in his desperate time of need. A man asking for nothing in return accepts to find an escape from the pain and the memories of his past.

Could this be the man, if given the choice to fight on the side of the light? Could he be the one to bring others to their cause if given the chance? The man called Death like his brother Nathaniel so many centuries ago hesitates as he puzzles out among all beings before him. Their stars so brightly burned with hope, so many lives could be held in the balance and destiny's altered forever as he chooses the path they walk. Like a God of old, yet he is just a caretaker of their souls; a simple man with the duty sworn to protect this cluster of stars before him from the darkness that has engulfed the land once more.

With his right hand, he slowly encircles a few thousand and looked deep into each person destiny and with slight movement alters their path according to their needs and strengthens their very will… by providing them a choice to walk the path before them or different path entirely, other then the one they were on. The man called Death aka Derrick makes the hard choices to extend their life or remove it or alter the path they are on. And with a simple wave of his staff, he stands in the shadows and waits and watches the man before him knowing his time is at hand.

Chapter 1-1

In the distance, a small house sat on a hillside, where an old man sits in his rocking chair gazing at the clear night sky. The evening had befallen the old man, and in the coolness of the breeze, his gaze had turned toward the shimmering stars above...

The old man sat alone on his porch, his face is weather-beaten and his hands marked from the years of hard work. The old man lets out a slow heavy sigh and looked down at his only loyal friend. The long barrel of the shotgun shines silver in the night. He pats the redwood butt that has his name burned into it, and rocks in his chair, his mind remembering the past.

He fingered his name on the butt as he rocked softly in his chair in-tune with the gentle breeze. He dreads these night as his eyes swept across the land. His family gone and the few friends he does have never come calling. Only the old nightmares call and the old regrets of a wasted life; it didn't need to have been wasted; if only something could have been changed!

He sighs. "I'm an old man now, looking back on old memories," he says to Betsy his shotgun. "Just like all old men do. Yep, isn't that right old girl?" He pats the redwood butt. "Just need maybe one or two shells for the task at hand. Should have done it years ago to tell you the truth old girl; me alone with nothing to do except look at the stars?" He sighed. "Death been playing hard to get. He's never home when I come calling."

"Is that so?" Says a warm voice, "I'm so sorry I was late." The man called Death takes a seat next to the old man. His eyes are gentle, and he rocks with the old man, eyeing the shotgun in his hands.

The old man looked upon at the man called Death sighed with relief, yet not surprised by his arrival. He pats old Betsy, rubbing shells between the nubs of his fingers and looks up with his eyes without so much as a simple nod. "You know I've been waiting a long time for you?"

"Like I said, I'm sorry," Death says his voice calm and warm, for he has seen the old man's possible future. Knowing now the time has approached and he has readied the man's mind for what is about to take place. For Death himself is the one keeping the old man alive. Just barely his eyes drawn upon the shotgun, knowing if he was any later everything would be lost to us all. The time has come as evil has stretched forth its hand touching his world beyond the very stars themselves and this man's world as it lays dying, corrupted by Morgan's evil and his master pushing the course of this old man's doom. Dooming us all by simply waiting in the shadows and has reawakened in the old mans mind the horrors of his life and future realities. *"No! Morgan and his master must be stopped."* His mind reeling with the thought of this man dying, but first, he must save the old man and the boy within him. His eyes soften as he gazes into the old man's mind.

"Yes, I heard you," he says as he leans further back in his chair. "Me and Betsy here were wondering if you were ever going to show. I've spent the last twenty years miserable and alone with nothing, but the nightmares to keep me company."

"Like I said," said Death putting a gentle hand on the old man's knee. "I'm sorry, I really am. I've come to you now though, providing you are ready to leave?"

The old man laughed. "I'm sitting here alone at night holding a gun! Either I go with you, or I'll go with another. I'm not going to spend another twenty years in this living hell alone."

The man called Death smiled, slowly taking the gun from the old man's white-knuckled hands. "I have a proposition for you, I think you'll like in the end." He says as the old man's eyes fix upon on the gun at Deaths feet. Wondering how it got there… his mind seemed tired as if it was already asleep. The Darkness lightened in his mind dulling his senses.

What's Behind the Looking Glass?

"What kind of proposition you got in mind?" He asked, as he shifts and lifting his eyes to look upon Death... his mouth dry his mind buzzed, wanting to fall into a deep sleep. He tries to shake awake, but it was already too late.

"Oh, you'll see," Death, said eagerly, taking his right hand and with a simple wave a shimmer of air before them as it formed a circlet of air then an object appeared as it the air before them became shaped itself into a large squire mirror. But not made of glass, for it had no sides nor back, it held no reflection.

The man called Death grins with a wave of his hand a cool breeze picks up the old man up from his chair and threw him towards it as he tried flail or grasp the post off at the top of the steps, as the wind gently strengthens around him as it pulled him towards the mirror itself. The old man screamed as he was forced to let go of the post he passed through its shiny silvery skin like water watching it swirl around him until his entire body was inside looking out at his house and the clear night sky while mirror slowly started to shrink into nothingness.

It was if he had fallen through time, images kaleidoscope around him. Faster and faster, he twisted and tumbles. Images of his miserable life engulf him and unfold before him. All the pain and sorrow of his shattered dreams, the result of one wrong choice, the wrong choice spreads like cancer. Which had became several wrong choices that have ultimately led him to this moment of unbearable suffering? Heavy chains of burden suffocated him, making him gasp in despair and pray for an end.

He hits something solid; the wind is knocked out of him. He lies still, gasping for breath in a body that felt broken, his mind swarming with old and distant memories. He is trapped and alone, unable to move anything, but for his eyes. He loses track of time, lying trapped within his own body waiting for the images to fade. He felt compelled to speak his name but is unable to breathe but a whisper.

The room around him is not very big, and yet has halls leading from it. The light in the room is soft, barely enough to see by. It seems to have no point of origin, as though the very walls themselves were producing it. The light is pale in color, yet not a color at all. The room is eerily silent; no sounds can be heard coming from anywhere. The place has an unnatural feel, as though the laws of the world don't apply here. The old man panics from its strangeness. "Help! Can anyone help me!" He screams. His screams are suppressed by the places unnatural nature. His pleas for help; muffled by a strange force, as though he were shouting through a pillow.

Feeling weak, he laughed at himself. "Fine mess I got myself into this time. Thought it was hogwash, thinking Death was going to help me and give me some peace at last. Great, now we're talking to ourselves. Well I don't like it here and I want to get out," he said to himself rising to his feet slowly and painfully, feeling all the aches and pains of being old he hated the fact that pain was only another reminder how old he had gotten and how alone he truly was in a world that doesn't want him.

But was worst was the nightmares from his past… and then there were these other nightmares of people from strange lands he had never heard of and other things he weren't sure if they either people or monsters out of some fairytale calling out to him begging him to save them from the everlasting darkness or sickness that was covering their land. Whatever it was, it seemed just as real as his own waking dreams, and that bothered him the most because he couldn't help them… Just like he couldn't help himself, as he screams begging the images and the pain he was feeling to stop.

The feeling of being trapped is stronger with each step he takes and despair and loneliness were getting stronger by the minute. His heart was racing like was it going to beat right out of his chest. "I am doomed," he said, and about to give up. He turned around he sees a tired-looking young boy wearing a look of bewilderment. "Asking where did he come from?" Having the question forms in his mind; "I would have known if someone else were here he thought." But that wasn't important right now. "Who are you? How did you get in here?" He asked the young boy in hopes he might know the way out.

The tired young boy just looked at the old man as if he should have known who the boy was, fell to the ground in a nearby corner with his head in hands and begins to cry. The old man ponders this in his mind while he gathers his strength and some courage. Went to where the boy is sitting. He tries again… in the hope the boy might now the way out.

Taking a closer look, he sees how frail the boy is as if he had been through a war - though of a different kind of battle he couldn't be any older then 12 or 14. Mossy brown hair badly in need of a hair cut and comb. Blue eyes, still having a baby face quality with puffy cheeks and small squarish chin, He wasn't tall by any means and it looked like he was nothing more than skin and bones, in many ways he reminded him of his younger self when he was about his age. Just for a fleeting moment, his mind remembers something then just like that it was gone as if it was on the tip of his tongue or the edge of something then drawing a complete blank.

He's dirty, but so is the old man, he doesn't care at this point. He's shivering and not sure from the cold. The old man quietly removed his jacket trying not to startle him and puts the jacket around his shoulders. The boy flinched but does not lookup. He tries to make him feel more at ease, plus to contain the excitement that there might be a way out and he must have come in a different way then he did. There was also this nagging feeling that he is the key, but the key to what, the images and the dreams had repeated it that he must find the key… yet they never said where he was to find it, or what it might look like or most of all who had the key they were telling him he needed to find.

He also knew from experience that now is the worse thing is to do is frighten this boy more, he cursed because the images and the dreams of people begging him to help them and feeling the pain they were feeling as it weighed heavily on his mind and in heart, driving him towards nearly to madness, to the point he can't sleep, he can't eat. All he could think about was the darkness and what will happen if this darkness traps him. He shook himself as he focused on the strange boy, he started to introduce himself, but he couldn't remember his name.

The image of him sitting on the porch not more than a few moments ago was the only thing he could see, yet the difference was this time. He could see his own self loading the shotgun and pulling the trigger as his body falls dead to the ground. The sound of the gun deafened him as he covered his ears, hearing the ringing of gun fire as he fell to his knees begging the images to stop watching the darkness creep over him engulfing his mind and body. Nothing he did seemed to help, feeling the coldness seep through his body as the darkness was covering him as if someone had snuffed out a candle…

Suddenly all was quiet all but the quiet sobs of the boy are almost at peace now, finding his small little hand in his hand, feeling the darkness lessons, and the images that were tormenting his mind starting to fade. All he could hear is the soft sobs of the boy, but his touch of the boy wakened some sort of peace, he gave a slight sigh opening his eyes, feeling strangely alive, and in no pain. Then again if he was really dead why was he here? And where did he go on from here? Yet he still couldn't remember his name, but he could remember everything else. Most of all the feeling that said Time wasn't on his side.

The question is. "TIME… does it exist here? Does anyone know that I am even missing, or if I am dead? Does anyone even care? Does it even really matter anymore?" The old man thought of old Betsy sitting alone by the side of the house his only friend these days. "Or does Time exist at all?" All is quiet where he is at the moment even the boy is silent. "Strange, did I do something? Did I say anything because I am alone with my thoughts, unless?" The old man thinks for a moment.

Noticing the boy's eyes staring back into his, somehow they were warm, friendly yet they seemed full of pain, sorrow and loneliness, the same sorrow and loneliness he himself had seen when he looked at his own reflection in a mirror. The old man just realized something. *"He must have brought him here. He is also the key to this strange puzzle, but why?"* His mind screams pounding inside him as he gasped feeling the pain and images return at full force, he screams pressing his hands to his head. "Will the pain of sorrow ever end?"

All he wanted was just to die, to forget the nightmares of his past and the world dying around him. Worlds and dreams that are not his own and nightmares of everlasting darkness caused by some evil man named Morgan. Things seemed to just get worse, not better. The old man thought as he rubbed his head with the back of his hand. "We need to find the way out and soon." The pain lessened again feeling the boy retake his hand causing him to look at him as the pain and darkness lessoned with his touch. Here he was trying to comfort the boy and in turn, he was comforting him.

He looked down at the tired young boy who seemed to be bewildered and lost meeting his gaze as their hands lingered motionless as a loving father would hold it, something he had long forgotten what that simple feeling felt like ... This time lying beside him was a set of old keys. They both looked at the keys lying beside him. He gave the old man a quirky little smile handed them to him, without so much as a thought as if their minds on some level were linked.

The old man looked into his deep tear laden eyes, as he is about to turn and ask his name. The young boy gripped him with all his strength that he has left to him as he began to stand and helped him up by taking his other hand, as his own strength had been transformed to the boy as the boy lifted him off the ground to walk with him. He turned suddenly as strange tingling of air had changed something so quick like a blink of an eye to finding a door that he was sure wasn't there before. The old man thinking, *"I don't remember any doors or windows, just walls that go nowhere."*

The old man turned to ask his new friend about these keys and why he never used them seeing the door that had seemed to been there, noting the solidness of it and the frame around it as if had been there all along, but couldn't have because he could have sworn it was just nothing more than walls in the long endless hallway they were both standing in and walking trying to find the way out. Or the more important where are all the doors for these keys? The old man turned on his right to ask, just to discover his friend is gone. His jacket lay on the ground where he and the boy used to be, but moments ago. "Where could he have gone? I need him. Please don't leave me not now, not here, not in the dark, where are you? Who are you?" The old man calls out.

The old man wondered if he should go on alone, he began to search the corridors for the doors as it seemed that one he was sure was never there in the first place was now gone and once more the wall was solid once again. Most importantly where did his missing friend go? He never heard him leave, he was there right beside him holding his hand and then in a blink of an eye like the door he was gone as if he was never there, to begin with. Once again the feeling of fear and the everlasting darkness was creeping around him; the pain and the images were slowly taking hold of him, making it hard to think. The old man can barely hear anything except for his own heartbeat and the dull sounds of clinking of the keys in his hand twisting beside him. "I must be mad; I never saw any door's in here, where could he have gone? It's so dark in here. Wait I see. Yes, I think I see something just up ahead, a shape? WAIT? DON'T LEAVE!!" The old man screamed.

His heart raced faster as he got closer to the shape, he saw a small figure the same size of the young boy. "Yes. It is the same boy pointing to the same door?" He asked himself; running, tired, but knowing he must get there, afraid he might leave him here alone. "I hate being alone especially here. I was right," the old man said nearly out of breath. "It is the small boy." And once more the thought came back that he looked somehow familiar to him as if he'd had seen him somewhere before perhaps in a dream? The old man noticed the same sad, wanting eyes. The young boy looked up at him, gave a little smile and pointed at a little keyhole at a rusted lock in the door. The door is old, black and tarnished. The old man turned and asked. "Is this the way out?"

The young boy backed away from the door quickly. Fear was shown on his face and all he could do is point with his little fingers, shaking them at the door. The old man looked back to where the little boy was standing and watched him fade into the background with the door as the old man opened it using the first key of many on the large ring of keys you would find on jailer in an old prison movie.

Once the door was opened he stepped through finding some sort of light, so bright he couldn't see much other than the shapes or shadows of shapes and nothing more other than bright white light that was blinding him as he walked towards it down the same type walls he and the boy had walked along. He looked back once more and watched the door close, even the air is different, the colors the sounds started to change as he got closer to whatever was in front of him. Yet the one disturbing thought was. "But why was that boy so afraid? Why did he look so familiar to me yet so sad?" More questions. "Why am I here? I wonder how old that boy was. He could have not been any older than ten or perhaps eleven."

Just for a moment, the old man thought he was left alone again with his own thoughts as the white light had shimmered or as if he walked through some sort portal like the mirror that brought him here in the first place. He was now in someone's backyard again it seemed so familiar to him, yet he couldn't quite place it. Even the house before him seemed like some forgotten memory. The red brick and large overhang porch on the side of the garage the large cinderblock wall dividing the house from some church parking lot, which that too seemed so familiar. Yet again the moment he thought he had it, that memory was gone, just like his name. All he could remember was the feeling he had been here before and the sense of loneliness and the everlasting cold darkness, most of all the pain… so painful it was like his heart was being ripped right out of his chest.

The old man looked around noticed questioning the time of year. "It feels like it was September or early October," he whispered. The leaves had just stopped falling and the winter cold was just settling in. There in the yard was a young boy playing in the leaves. Much like the one he left behind, behind the door now closed as he watched him for while unseen. He wondered what it would be like to be that young again. Not to have adult problems, not having too suffered the things that he has suffered. Forgetting about the boy… for the moment, for in that single moment, he becomes that boy…

* * *

The old man never felt so alive the autumn leaves touched his skin as he threw them into the air watching them fall to the ground around him. The wind ran through his hair, "I am FREE!! The pain is gone," he shouted. He ran through the yard, down the road as fast as he could and yelled into the wind. "How long would it last? Run, run, and let nobody catch me, I won't tell a soul. All it matters is that I am FREE from the world. I am a kid again at last. Run, run don't let them catch me… don't let them find me. I' am FREE to LIVE, to LIVE AGAIN!" As the old man ran trying to escape himself in the boy's body he was overpowered with the boy's memories and emotion, his mind slipping into a distance fog. He becomes trapped in the boy's world…

* * *

"The only problem with running was there is nowhere to run to. After all, I am only 10 and it's getting cold now, except for this nagging feeling that I am supposed to do something be somewhere, besides play in the leaves. Wishing is great and all besides running around its lots of fun too. I want to go home," the boy said to himself coming back into the backyard wondering why he left the yard in the first place, since the last thing he remembered was raking up the leaves and playing in them, even though he was told he was supposed to rake them up and put them into the garbage. The thought bothered him for a moment hearing more sounds as someone was in the house.

Instead, his thoughts were that his foster brother Jeff must be home early from work today; he's 18, he's getting ready to go on a mission and works at a local welding shop. We don't talk much… he's always busy. He gets the feeling he hasn't been here very long. Something tells him he doesn't stay anywhere very long. Some sort of a nagging feeling like being tugged towards the house as he looked around hearing more strange noises angry noises coming from the house hearing smashing and things breaking. He questioned it hearing it from the outside of the house or was it just the sound as if the wind just made something fall at the back of the house. It made his skin crawl as he searched with his eyes… Noticing there was no car in the driveway and it really bothered him being as the noises were getting more frequent.

He decided it must have been Jeff. Never did know when he was coming or going these days. The folks left for the weekend won't

What's Behind the Looking Glass?

be back till sometime tonight. Better make sure the dishes are done before they get home or my ass is grass that's for sure. They won't care who left them. Jeff's their perfect little angel. I'm everyone's gum on their shoe or yesterdays garbage. His feet guided him towards the house with on the last glace seeing a strange darkness coming over him and the house. He paused at the door before opening it leaned the rake beside the porch.

He couldn't help his thoughts as the noise in the house was making him want to run away as thoughts of his parents entered his mind hearing the loud screams of anger that sounded like a lot like Jeff who was supposed to be at work today and wouldn't be home for another couple of hours so he could go on his date tonight with his girlfriend. He had tried running away couple of times, always ran into a few problems; money, age, cops and food. During the winter… it's cold during those months. He hated parks; burr spent enough time living in trees when he was younger. The cops are really big about you sleeping in the park and if they catch you they bring you back because you are not old enough to go to juvie. Then you can expect the biggest beaten of your life then they wonder why you wanted to run away. My question always would be the same, "why would you want to stay?"

Yet things were getting a little better. Heck, he might actually get to go home; there is talk about sending him home for good, that's hard to believe. Course he hadn't lived at home more than, let's see counting 1,2,3,4,5,6 maybe 6 years of his entire life at home since the age of 10, which usually is not more than 3 to four months at a time. Well, but look at the possibilities… Never leaving again. Maybe it is a mistake? Maybe they do want him… they? Or he does, meaning his father and possibly his mother? There's that noise again. Somebody is in the house. Jeff must be home. Funny he didn't hear his car. The young boy walked through the house. There was an odd feeling, its cold against the boy's skin. It was a feeling or a presence of death in the house like as if he was walking through a graveyard at night. The source of the noise was coming from Jeff's bedroom down the hall.

The boy's legs felt like they are made out of lead he could barely move them, slowly reaching Jeff's room. The boy slowly turned the doorknob and opened the door, very quietly so not disturb anything including the dust. The boy puts his hand to his mouth to scream no, but no words, no sound. Nothing came out of his mouth. The young boy felt paralyzed to move as his eyes within those short few seconds locked with Jeff's.

In that last instant, the gun fired. The young boy watched him fall to the floor. He could see the blood-forming a puddle on the rich blue carpet around his head. He gazed upon him for the last time. He could see his dead cold eyes staring back at him as if they were holding him hostage. The room was silent now except for Jeff's last breath leaving his limp body. The boy turned to leave the room leaping through the closing door as if being pulled by some unseen force as he legs moved as his body felt it was being pulled apart looking back seeing himself standing in the open doorway of Jeff's room as a man who was his neighbor was holding him in his arms forcing the boy he was looking at too look away closing the door not only of that world but the world he was currently in,

He looked down finding an old man laying down on the ground in the hall where he must have come from moments ago have gone and transformed back into the strange forbidding room behind the looking glass. The boy fell to the ground, as the world around him covered him in complete darkness as the images of his life, and the pain and the nightmares overwhelm him giving a loud scream as the pain became unbearable. Then there was nothing but darkness and pain.

Chapter 1-2

The old man blinked awake as if he had been in some sort of dream, or nightmare like the ones he was having. He remembered clearly what had just taken place he remembered one name which was Jeff, yet for his own name he still had no memory of that name, it was at the tip of his tongue and just out of reach as he sat up finding the same set a keys laying near him reminding him where he was and what had just transpired said out loud. "I hate this place, but right now I don't know what is worse, images or the memories and those horrible feelings that the boy and I had experienced." The old man stood still shaking, not sure what he could have done asking himself. "Would I have made a difference if I was there with the boy watching his foster brother die in front of him like that? The question is and still remains; do I make a diffcrence? Is there still time to help the boy? Can I help the boy? I now understand why the boy would not go inside there. We must be on our toes in case "Time" itself, in our mind, decides to lay traps for those with wandering souls, like mine." He remembered something he had written in not more then lifetime ago it seemed; a small poem that was more of a thought every time he woke from a bad night wrestling with a nightmare of his past.

<u>Fear</u>

Written by Eric shepherd

"For they, are those that need to fear are those that fear, fear itself. For Darkness waits for no man… even light has its shadow, which hides deep within itself. So when Death comes so eagerly to some, rebirth will come on the Morning tides.

For fear has nothing to hide for shadow and light is one, meaning death and rebirth is equaled to life. For fear has no fear without understanding fear itself. Few will soon discover fear will go away, leaving a rebirth of something else instead of being and living in fear forever."

"Is this what Death is purposing, that I help the little boy?" The old man whispered softly to himself.

The old man realized that he must push on and find a new zeal and reason too move on; knowing that fear could be waiting at every door he opened behind the looking glass. The old man could sense deaths nightmare and bated breath, the same one he has been living with for the last twenty years or so and knowing soon it would come sweeping down upon her wings to crush him.

The old man laughed silently. "Maybe, at last, I will die. Or maybe I am already dead? If that is the case why don't I feel any peace? There are no angels, no heavenly light or personages waiting to take me into their arms and embrace me. Yet there is no devil or suffering souls except my own. All I see is an endless tunnel of nothingness as far as the eye can see. No doors, not windows. Not a single sound of a person voices except my own." And once again we find ourselves in that dreaded horrible looking hallway, in the search for that missing little boy. In hopes of finding that the way out is near or better yet he will soon provide the answer that will change his past before "Time" runs out for both of them or die in here forever.

The old man pushed himself down the hallway not far. He begins to hear distant whispers. But unsure because everything is so muffled here and he really had to strain his ears and eyes, which are just getting used to the lack of light here. Once again he thinks he sees two images. "But how is that possible?" He asked; "and how did they get in here? I can't even get out. Am I losing my mind?" The old man said running towards them feeling angry as he watched them as they began to walk away as if they hadn't even noticed him. "WAITE, WAITE, WAITE, WAITE FOR ME! ...WHO ARE YOU?" He screamed.

The old man yelled again, thinking that would get their attention, but they paid him no mind. They kept walking away and faded away as quickly as they came. So tired and angry, he falls to the ground with a loud slump. The keys chimed hitting the ground beside him; rubbing his eyes with the heels of his hands, trying to remove the tears of anger behind them. He yelled with all his might…. "What in the hell am I supposed to do now?"

He yanked his head back letting out a blood-curdling scream. In hopes of frightening some poor defenseless chickens too death, causing them too lay all their eggs at once and when they hatched. Be they hard-boiled, scrambled, or doubled yoked. Go figure, the chickens had a rough day.

His head rebounded back against the wall; instead of feeling the hard cement wall with the back of his head, it felt hollow with a soft thud. The old man placed his right hand behind his head to feel it, making sure what he felt was real. His eyes widen with surprise and dismay at the same time. Fear crept over him as his heart began to race with excitement and fear after what had happened last time he had gone through a door here.

Caution was needed as he remembered the pitfalls of the last door he opened. Yet at the same time, he wondered what could be lurking behind this door? After he gathered some courage and dusted himself off his feet, he said "let's see this door. I am sure this door wasn't here before? Question is where did it come from? Where is that little boy? Who is he talking too? Where did he go?" The old man wondered in his mind what lies behind it.

The door was cold too the touch, bore ugly scarred markings like its heart had been torn out of it. Not really sure he wanted to go in there, he wondered. *"Could it be the way out? Which key fits the lock is the question?"* The old man looked down amongst the keys, feeling each key one by one. Noticing each one had a different, but odd feeling about them; it was hard to describe the feeling as he felt each key. He closed his eyes tracing each with his fingers afraid it would be the wrong key.

He mumbled to himself. "At least the boy could have given me instructions. Even a map would have been nice, especially if he was going to run off like that." He said as he allowed his mind to drift thinking of the boy and the person he was with; then he laughed at the mere thought of how to use a set of keys. "Well, it still would have been nice." He said as he decided on the key he had chosen.

For some reason, the strange odd-shaped key felt like a twisted tree in the wind felt right in his hand. Finding the keyhole, he placed the key into the lock and slowly turned the key, hearing a small "click." As before, another room opened. The old man stepped through it and the door closed behind him quickly the moment he had walked maybe 5 feet blending into the background as the same white light like before dissolved all around him. Finding himself inside a small trailer sitting in a metal folding chair tied up, but this time he was the same boy again.

He was different somehow unlike last time yet the same, images quickly swirled around him. Old memories intoxicating out of control, something or someone in the room immediately grabbed hold of him. He gazed about as if in a daze about to awaken, his body now felt so small, cold and trapped, hurting from the pain of the wounds incased on his now small body. Like before his mind swimming as he becomes the boy in this body as it takes hold seeing and feeling like a tidal wave of emotion, that pierced his inner soul, leaving the old man behind as he becomes that boy once more, like a flicker of a candle the old man he was faded away like as if that image was but a dream leaving him only the memories of the old man and now the boys memories.

* * * *

The sounds in the small room were angry and hostile. The boys left eye was swollen; he could barely open it enough to see through the bottom of his eyelid. Looking around he noticed he was indeed tied to a metal folding chair with a chain wrapped around his unclothed body. He could hear a small child crying nearby. A mother was screaming at him at the top of her lungs as the boy was being beaten by a wooden spoon on his bare bottom, trying to do dishes at the moment, trying to find a way to escape the blows. There are smiles on his sister's faces while they played with their dolls on the other side of the room as they watched. The boys minded stated their names were Peggy and Dona and the boy being whipped was his brother Danny. Then it was like a bolt of lightning had just struck him. He knew who he was, his name everything was flooding back

What's Behind the Looking Glass?

he was Eric Stewart, the small boy was him more than a lifetime ago. Somehow he had forgotten this, but then again he did his best not to remember it and now questioned if this is what the man called death had in mind to help change his past so he did end up lying dead on his own front porch alone and forgotten, by the world around him. With no friends, no family to call his own; nothing and no one to care about him.

He said without thinking out loud. "How can you help him? Right now I can't even help myself? The question is who am I? Where am I?" he whispered as he gazed down upon his cold, naked feet, asking. "How did I get myself into this mess?" As if he was asking the little girl named Peggy across the room, playing with her dolls these questions?

She looked up, turned and laughed. "Look mommy it asked a question. It thinks it has rights to ask question's now!" The little girl named Peggy, with long brown hair and picture-perfect doll-like quality who was no older than 8 or 9 a year younger than him at that time. With the same blue eyes yet cold as they looked at him with such hate and that stated that hate was all she ever had for him. Her sister name was Dona more reserved and so different in likeness with dishwater blond hair and pigtails. Blue eyes and Barbie doll patterned after her sister yet so different it was hard to believe they were related other than the same hate, the same meanness, the same quiet anger and she was only 6 or 7, known as the baby of the family.

His brother Danny was so small compared to his older brother and his two sisters and for a boy of 6. He had the same mossy brown hair and the same blue eyes; he looked a lot like him. He hated the fact that just like him everyone here that consider him family hated him, he hated the fact that there was nothing he could do or had tried to do made no difference, maybe he could change that, maybe he could not only change his life, but his brothers as well, but the question was how.

His mother Linda quickly came over placing herself in front him as if he was nothing but dirt under her fingers nails yelling to his brother Danny not move from that spot or she would whip the tar out him if even think about moving, said. "He does, does he? That ingrate little brat. After he tried too run off and tell everyone how he got all those bruises. He nearly got us all into trouble again. We all know girls, how he fights all the time, he got them at school or fell off his bike, him and his brother. After all your father and I would never ever lay a hand on him, we love you all." She said standing in the middle of the room with her hands on her hips holding the wooden spoon which had seen better days.

"How many times have I told everyone? ... Boys will be boys. This is how you train them if you want a good one these days. Besides these boys are always in trouble! People need to mind their own damn business. If it ain't broke don't fix it… if it is, there is always a new one down the street on sale; right girls? And you boys are going to learn that lesson if we have too beat it into your little stupid heads. Oh, look your brother needs to go the bathroom. Can you take him outside Peggy? After that put him to bed for the night, I don't want him disturbing anyone next door." She said as she pointed to his brother at the sink, dancing trying not to wet himself.

The girls laughed as something struck them funny, as she said smiling; "anyone ready for round two?" his mother asked. Eric wasn't laughing, the pain was nearly unbearable already as she came over to pop him a couple more times, because she thought he was being smart,

He yelled. "STOP IT!"

His father came into the room and took off his belt and swung it across his bare legs and feet. "Don't ever talk back to your mother like that you worthless little brat! Why did you come back in the first place? They didn't want you? Nobody wants you!" He replied with anger in his voice as his knuckles turned white. His father wasn't a large man by any means, in fact, he was barely 5 feet tall if that, but still taller and bigger then he was, and twice as scary. He hated him and his brother more then words could possibly say. No one understood why other than they stay away from him.

All that he and the boy could remember was that Jim his father had hated him and his brother Danny since the day they were born. Plus the fact he not once claimed to be their father or grew angry if we called him that, and he seldom if ever called them by the name they had given them. His father was always angry, and his face showed nothing but hatred. Even his face was made of stone other then the red blotches on his mostly bald head and in hard cold blue eyes said he hated them with every fiber in his being. He didn't walk or run like other men since the car accident, leaving a hard limp in his right leg that never healed right. Yet it never really slowed him down either, as he took off his belt and started to swing it back and forth as it whistled in the air. The belt was deadly as his fist because he kept the metal buckle sharpened to cause the most damage.

At that moment his father was punching him and hitting him with the belt in wild uncontrolled anger at the same time his mother was also beating him with her fists and her favorite weapon of choice known as the wooden spoon, even though she also favored the metal pancake tuner or anything she could reach. The wooden spoon broke in two as she hit it him across his already sore shoulders wincing with pain. The sharpness of the blow must have loosened the chains that wrapped around him snapping a link in the chain and freeing him. Without thinking he quickly dived for the door, he was cold, hungry and did not care as long as he was away from there, for that was a living hell. The pain that he felt was great, but right now it was a blanket of warmth.

He was never going to return to that and to think a small boy could or ever think that could be called home. He knew that he had to find some shelter for the night. Lucky for him there was an old barn not far from the house, just right for the night. He found an old horse blanket for covering and hid behind an old hay wall to keep the wind and prying eyes away until morning allowing him to fall into tearful, deep sleep…

* * *

The term love, home, and family will always be redefined in different ways to the young boy and others like him and added many of its factors to his life. Like the terms or words <u>disposable</u> or <u>replicable</u> are more or less have come to new terms known in today and in some social circles as true Family and Factions. For they are and have become terms to a contract as slavery for this young boy and others; some would say White Slavery or Back Door Slavery. The government knew about it but went on regardless even though they were hidden and well guarded. Few knew they existed or even cared; some found it easier to ignore the problem after all was said and done. 'It was not their problem; best to pass it on' or 'I don't have the time right now, maybe later.'

Remember deniable ability is everything according to any rules could be traps that lay before him. The next best trap of them all is love. It can be just another lie and can be well hidden. Played upon the innocent; then smashed, crushed or ripped apart. Done enough times, you can become numb. Yes, love and family is one of the best-laden traps the world has ever known. Some people say it is given freely, but there's always a price to pay. What is the price of man's own destructions? Ask the boy now asleep underneath the old horse blanket in a simple barn, forgotten by the governing world of men and their so-called government. The question is raised will this boy be one of the forgotten souls that time has hidden away? Is his life among the different hidden realms of reality? Does it exist in your world and you have chosen to ignore it and its many Factions?

* * *

The older man of the boy in questions wonders in his subconscious as he stood alone in the veil of shadows as he watched the boy sleep as if he himself was in a dream, that only he could see and still be apart from the boy that lay before him. Hearing the soft sobs of the small boy as he falls into everlasting sleep and after seeing, after feeling and knowing the choices made long ago, some against his will. Watching his very hopes and dreams die with the boy his past self, it was obvious that this little boy, "was, as, he is now." Remembering it was he, himself; for he was this boy long ago and soon he too will just stop feeling as he relives his past like a broken, tired old man that nobody wants or has forgotten about because he no longer matters.

What's Behind the Looking Glass?

He has no family, no friends or close relatives that care for him. Everyone he did know, are long gone leaving him to suffer, not caring if he lives or dies. To them, he was nothing more than stranger, nothing more than someone that didn't deserve to be loved by them or anyone. In the world he lived in was nothing more than hate and avoidance.

"Was this Death's design and purpose? Or was this a joke that Death himself is playing on him?" The old man asked as he himself becomes trapped inside the boy's mind at the end of his subconscious.

For beware of cupids poison arrows. It tricks him; hope is something he cannot have, nor ever have. For if he does this simple act of love for that small nameless boy knowing that this is his only hope… and he might be able to save him before he becomes the man he is today as he stands alone in the veil of shadows.

* * *

The man called Death aka Derrick smiles as he looked down upon the boy, sleeping in the barn as he slowly gazed deep inside the old man's subconscious standing alone in the shadows veil. Death watches the old man fight a war he could no longer win; he shushes his mind, letting the two minds come together as the child mergers once more. He gives them both one last hope from a new sense of reality behind and beyond the realm of the looking glass "I wonder? Yes, my boy, I wonder?" He said, leaving a small kiss on his small, tear laden cheek, whispered softly in his ear; "go find them, help save the boy and yourself." Brushing away his soft brown mossy hair, a teardrop falls from Death's own cheek. "I am sorry I was late, but I am here for you now. Not as Death, but in life, I give you this gift of a new chance at life." In a whisper of the wind, he was gone and the boy and old man are one…

* * *

If you think back to the 1970 generations it was common practiced back then almost as it is now too find a small boy easily fallen through the cracks. Children back then were easily not seen through the public's eyes nor heard from. They were known as society's cast-offs or for a better word, garbage. The generalized government or social services during that period of time assumed the role and standard. If it doesn't work, it's ok, not our problem. Ignore it until there is a real problem. Then lets us know until then fill this out and wait six months and then come back to check on the progress after you waited 1 year?

The words of his mother and the mothers and fathers like them could still be heard over the years even today feeling a sense of regret or the fear of getting caught for what they had done their own flesh and blood as they speak to the cops or family services to some caseworker that doesn't care about boys or girls that they are in charge of other than the fact they get paid or that might be overworked for such little pay. The human factor with many of them is such unreachable and uncaring when dealing with the world in general. "What was the problem? I see. Did you fill out the paper work? I see. That program changed; did not someone from the department tell you? So how can I help you? Yes I can help you with that. Just fill this out and send it in. It will take about six months for a reply back. What was that Mrs. Stewart?"

"Your son is missing, he dove out the front door last night and has been gone for? You don't know why? Oh I see, he got into another fight at school, does that a lot and you think he might be in some sort of trouble. Not to worry we know how to handle that sort; remember there's a saying my grandmother used to say 'in for a penny in for a pound.' Plus; when they get hungry enough they'll come home with their tails wagging then feed them and put them right to bed."

Chapter 2

The new dawn, a strange word for a new day as the boy slowly awakened from a restless sleep. With images and fragments dissipating when he slowly awakened. When he stretched he felt stiff, and sore. Sitting up he wiped and noticed the straw, which was stuck to his back. Held on by the dried blood against his skin, where the chains dug in and pinched him. The chain link edges were sharp as they twisted and turned against him when he moved the night before, leaving marks and cuts. It gave him chills thinking about it and a new resolve with new reason too escape another house of horrors and a father's whip.

EJ is the name he liked going by mostly because it was the name his grandmother had given him. It angered his parents every time he or she used it, his mother Linda most of all. Yet in truth, it meant Eric James, two names he hated more than anything because the name Eric came from a dolls name his mother played with growing up as a constant reminder that he was her plaything to do with as she pleased. The middle name James came from his father. Not too honor him, but to remind him he belonged to him like a piece of property, which they reminded him often than not, even though his father mostly never called him that.

He always usually calls him boy or some degrading name or a cruse word. He was found of swearing, and he did so often, regardless of who he was talking to or the company he was keeping. It angered him when people used his name in his presences, and he paid the price for it either by beating him with his fist or whipping him with his belt. He even did so in front of them sometimes not caring or daring them to turn him in. Telling them it was their word against his, and he had been doing it since the day he was born and nobody has yet to stop him.

EJ looked outside through the cracks in the wall to see where he was, said. "It looks like I am on some old abandon farm, a good mile from the house. Good, hope they're not looking for me because

I am not looking for them that's for dang sure. I am only glad this time I chose to leave in the summer or I would have frozen to death last night," EJ said as he laughed at himself. "That would make them only happier. Considering they thought this would keep me from running off; since they locked all my clothes away except my faded boxer shorts," as he remembered the home he left not so much as feeling of regret.

There was shining glimmer that caught the boy's eye. Over there in the corner under a tarp, an old cracked mirror. Finding it like a prize for a king for him. He just needed to uncover it. "One, two, three aaachuu and aaachuu," he sneezed as he rubbed his nose because of the dust. Then tossed the old tarp covered with dust in the corner. "Now let's see if I can lean this against that wall and have a gander."

He unwrapped the horse blanket around his waist, the boy stepped in front of the mirror. "Well at least I still had my boxers on, hope nobody saw me last night; might have given them the wrong impression that I was streaking through town. Need to find some clothes, can't go anywhere just like this, people might notice, a 10 year old boy with blue eyes brown hair only wearing striped, torn boxers, barefoot and no shirt and little beat up." He looked quite skinny some would say it aged him or he was on a hunger strike.

He looked down at his left and right side of his rib cage he noticed two huge bruises "Looks like I will be leaving with a matching set. Thanks to a parting gift from good old Dad and couple on my legs where the belt struck across. Ouch still stings a bit." He said taking a closer look at his face in the mirror he noticed that most of the swelling had gone down from his left eye and few little cuts and bruises on his feet and a fat lip. "All in all I say chaps I've been in a prizefight, that's what they would say in an old English pub. Well, times a wasting need to find some clothes and see about springing my brother from the grips of hell and the noose."

The old barn had many things that would interest a 10-year-old boy. Odd gadgets and gizmos of yesteryears gone by, but none he had a use for, but out of the corner of his eye. He thought he saw a shape, a human shape. Fear crept over him and held him tight, he dared not speak. His ears listened for every sound, every tiny hair a quiver, his mouth dry, unable to swallow. He tried not to make any sound at all. His mind raced, his heart beating fast, he crept forward placed one foot in front then the next. Stops... His heart beats faster, eyes strained for the tiniest movement. EJ crept forward again placed another step closer. Beads of sweat began to form on his forehead and the palms of his hands. It was just a few more steps, as he crept forward again taking another step, thinking. *"If I can just make it back to that wall, I can peek over it and see them or who they are and they won't see me."*

EJ winced a little from the pain still fresh; the boy's anger pops into his mind, which in turn overrides his fear, *"I know one thing. I am not going back,"* he said firmly in his mind.

EJ crept forward, springs for the wall and huddled into the corner where the darkness is like a mother's protective blanket. His ears listened to every sound, his eyes open for any movements beyond this wall; wondering what dangers lay on the other side of this wall. Pressing his body flat against the wall, he winced now and again because of the pain, slowly and carefully; he slid towards the figure that was sitting in the shadows, which seemed to be waiting for him.

The boy's heart beat was fast every second as if it was going to jump right out of his small chest at any given moment. EJ got closer he could see an old farmer sitting on an old haystack.

"I thought I was alone out here. What's he doing sitting in a corner, sleeping drunk I guess? The misses must have put him out here tonight. Just great how I am going to get out now with him by the door looking like this in broad daylight? I can just see it now walking down the street in only my boxers. "Hi ya folks how ya doin" and not to mention the cops they'll have a hay day." He replied softly to himself thinking of the reply they would most likely make.

"Hey boy, did you know you are not wearing any pants and by the way what about those bruises." Then they'll grab ya take you back home so they can beat you some more, no thank you, well I have had enough. Maybe I can wait till he leaves, he's bound to wake

Eric Shepherd

up sooner or later after all the misses will be calling him home," he said under his breath.

EJ sneaked back to the corner where he had a good view of the farmer and felt fairly safe. He brought his knees up to his chest to keep him warm and huddled in the corner he drifted off to sleep. When the boy awakened, the sun was setting in the later part of the evening, not yet dark. Irritated that he allowed himself to fall asleep in the first place, he glanced over to see if that old farmer was still there, shocked and dismayed struck.

"I can't believe it. He still there, will he ever leave? What's keeping him here?" He said softly in a heated whisper. Anger was building up inside due to feelings of being trapped like an animal. Thinking, he needed too leave. "Maybe I can distract him long enough to escape, then run, if he is drunk he won't be able to catch me. If I wait long enough it will be dark soon and I can I hide in the shadows where nobody can see me."

EJ finding some small pebbles along the wooden planks along the bottom of the old barn, the small boy puts them in pile near him. Hoping the farmer would just leave and he could just make a break for it, but as time went on; the day was slowly turning into night. With one last sigh, it was time to strike. The first pebble missed its mark and hit the ground just below the old farmer's feet. EJ heart leaped right out of his chest as he sprang for the corner as he waited for certain doom.

He waited, and waited, not even a sound, no shuffling feet. No voices, nothing not even a grunt or a stir. His heart raced and his eyes squeezed tightly shut. EJ gathered enough courage to peek. Finally, the boy peeked underneath his eyelids to see if there was any movement at all. Nothing had changed, the farmer was still there setting on his perch fast asleep. EJ irritated and mad "stupid old farmer," he said softly irritated.

EJ realized he needed to get closer. With a hard swallow before bending down, he slowly gathered his pile of pebbles then slowly crawled along the wall towards the old farmer. His eyes never leaving the farmer as he slowly laid the pebbles next him not daring to blink an eye or barely breathe. One by one he slowly adjusts the pebbles according to their size. The boy examined the next pebble in his hand looked up at the old sleeping farmer now nearby.

He aims the pebble then tossed it; "kerr plunk," missed again. This time right above his head. EJ ducked; quickly behind the wall as he waited to be caught for sure this time. The boy peeked through the small cracks in the wall. He could still see the old farmer has not moved, not even an inch. Relived yet at the same time he felt angry and frustrated, thinking either that farmer is deaf or so drunk he doesn't know he is even there. The small boy kicked the dirt with his big toe. EJ decided what to do next. "Either he's leaving or I am; one of us is leaving that's for sure," he said softly to himself.

Nighttime had now fallen once more, leaving him clothed in darkness and moon giving off her guiding light. He thinks to himself. "Stupid old farmer, why won't he leave for home? Do you not, have any food waiting there or a bed to sleep in?" He said underneath his breath.

EJ sees the horse blanket nearby; slowly he reached for it with one eye on the farmer. Carefully EJ slid along the wall not to draw any attention then quickly crawled back into the darkest to the deepest part of the shadows, the boy thinking this gave him an idea and he smiled then rubbing his bottom lip, "Ouch that still hurts a little."

EJ placed the old horse blanket around his shoulders and then looked over at sleeping farmer. "Maybe I'll play a little hide and seek;" he said smiling, and then grinned, "ouch that smarts" touching the side of his lips. "This time I am going to sneak up and see how drunk he really is or enough to sneak past him right under his nose," he said very softly.

Again carefully not to make a sound EJ began too crawl against the wall, then keeping to the shadows with the horse blanket on his back as he used it to hide under while crawling on his hands and knees. Stopping every few inches to listen, while lying on his belly slithering slowly through the shadows like a snake, with his eyes open and ears poised for any signs of life on the figure set before him. Quietly, ever so silently EJ reached the nearby corner where he could almost touch the old farmer.

This is the closest he has ever been to him all day, yet he still does not stir nor does he make a sound. The feeling of fear nearly filled the boys' mind, yet excites him at the same time; blood is pumping through his veins feeling his heart beat faster. EJ wanted to turn back, but now knowing he must go on to survive. He told himself. "I have made it this far and we are not caught yet, we must go on."

EJ stayed well hidden under the horse blanket, he could see there's a small pillar of light beaming down from the adjacent windows above the old farmer. The old farmer was wearing one those old red and blue checker shirts, bib type overalls with a ten-gallon hat to boot; "I wouldn't be surprised to see if he was wearing cowboy boots," he replied with a soft snicker.

All of sudden a noise was heard "BANG" he heard something move from the outside, the small boy jumped back into the corner, his heart raced a mile a minute EJ made sure that he was covered completely in darkness. Seeing lights flashing through cracks, his thoughts raced… "*Oh no! They have found me, I've been caught!*" Quickly hiding under the horse blanket…not daring to come out, he waited for the lights to fade. It was just a car backfiring going down the road.

The lights and sounds slowly returned with the darkness and shadows are where they belong with him at the moment. EJ peeked underneath the horse blanket towards the old former he noticed he never moved. "Strange? There's something very odd about him. I wonder what he looks like under that old ten-gallon hat," he said very softly.

Finding a twig nearby the boy began to carefully lift up the corners, trying very hard not to disturb the sleeping old farmer. The boy knew one false move and he would be caught for sure, his very survival depended on it. All of sudden he slips… the twig "snaps" in two and the hat falls, crashing to the ground. With a startled scream, EJ fell backwards, sprawled upon his back. Scrambling quickly, backing into the far reaches of the corners of the barn. His heart

What's Behind the Looking Glass?

pounding, knees, pressed hard against his chest, quivering with fear as his eyes gazed towards the old scarecrow, not wearing his hat dressed as an old farmer as the boy's shivered in the dark. After a few minutes the boy; smiles, falls on his back laughing at himself for being scared of a stupid old scarecrow.

After feeling so humiliated, EJ went over to the scarecrow. "Hope you had a good laugh today, now it's my turn." He said as he gazed down upon it, he poked his fingers at him making sure it was made of straw, then rubbed his chin and smiled then shaking and nodded his head with amusement.

"Humm this shirt a little bit big, but it will do for now, what do think old Mr. Scarecrow?" He said as he puts it on. "Let's see I'll try on those overalls too if you don't mind. Ya see I am not that picky at the moment how about you? No? Good. By the way where's your hat?" The boy said as he looked on the ground to where it fell. "I'll be needin that hat too if you don't mind?" He replied as he placed it on his head, "I would take your shoes, but you aren't wearing any. I guess scarecrows don't need them or can't find your size." He replied as he laughed at the old scarecrow and himself.

"Now then let's see how I look in the mirror? Not bad, not bad at ta'l." He said rolling the legs up a little tucked in the shirt, "I almost look like Huckleberry Fin going to a western. Maybe I'll put some that peroxide crap in my hair to bleach it out a little and grow my hair long. Nobody would recognize me… What da ya say to that Mr. Scarecrow? They'll never find me." He said as he rubbed his chin stood in the mirror. "That reminds me if and anybody comes a callin I wasn't here… got it? Time find some grub, see ya later," he said with a simple wave of the hand.

The moon had resin above the treetops giving off her wonders-us guiding light. EJ slowly reached the door, made sure the coast was clear before making a break for the nearby trees. Fear and excitement filled him with a watchful eye for any approaching lights. Wondering the possibilities if he was part rabbit with his eyes, ears, and noses twitching as he listened for every sound, every smell; as he weaved in and out between the trees. Scouring long quickly across the ground, crouched in thickets of a nearby underbrush, not far from the ditch bank there's was a cornfield. Trying not to make any sound that might alert even a dog to bark in his direction. He broke off three patches of corn then quickly hurried back to the nearby underbrush to eat them.

While eating he never realized how hungry he truly was and devourers the corn eagerly, but not being greedy either, yet mostly the fear being caught drove him not to go back for more. For he knew very well the hell his brother must be going through and if there was a chance he must try to break him out. Provided he could break him out at all. EJ also knew he had to least try or he could never leave without knowing without the guilt that he had at least tried or at very least said goodbye. Cutting a path through the field was the easiest way to get there without being seen. Now the hard part choosing which path to take…

"I could go around the cemetery or through it? Let's see, the road is lit near the houses? Bad idea, ghosts and old bones which don't seem to say much when they're dead, well at least sometimes, he said; "humm I'll take the ghost's any night at least they don't try to beat me to death. Hey maybe I should have brought old Mr. Scarecrow, but right now he doesn't' have a thing to wear to the party." He laughed to himself, making a dive for the cemetery. The boy noticed a car coming up the road, a cop car. "Oh no it's slowing down, great this all I need." He said with anger in his voice remembering a time of yesterdays.

The cop's searchlight searched the area where he dived into the cemetery. His body quickly flattened to a tree, he tightly closed his eyes, hoping, and dared not to breathe. The cop's searchlight slowly scanned the tree nearby and around the area before driving off. EJ let out a gasp of air and sighed with relief. "That was close, thought I was a goner for sure. Now I am glad I did not take the road by the houses that's for sure." He said very softly to himself that only a few ghosts might hear.

EJ leaped from one tombstone to another as he crisscrossed in between some more trees. It soon became a game for the small boy. After a while he was through the cemetery, not a single ghost was seen nor heard this night. For they figured he had or was going to have enough problems of his own to be bothered or play with a poor little boy. He was nearly there; just over the next ridge around the corner was where his house and brother waited for him.

Getting there would be easy. "They most likely won't be expecting me. Now getting out again that's the real problem. The other problem is to where to go next when I leave. The old barn is too far away for my little brother, he would never make it on foot not without his bike and we can't take it because they locked it up inside the shed. Hope they lest put his breeches on because I don't have spare with me. Just because he still wets the bed now and again, even though it's his sister's fault getting him in trouble on purpose, by spilling warm water on the bed while he is asleep is not fair. I swear one day she'll pay the price. I don't know how, but she will," he said to himself.

Chapter 2-1

A dog barked as he took cover under a nearby hedge. He waited to see if a porch light turned on or if everyone was asleep. EJ paused for just a moment in the shadows. Feeling safe he moved on towards a large thicket of weeds nearer his home, and then gazed about using the moonlight as his guide for direction. He noticed an old shack sitting in the corner of the empty field among the high weeds. Thinking that it might be just what he was looking for the escape out. *"Best to investigate it first."* That way, he would leave no unturned surprises in his awake when you are leaving in a hurry. *"I have a gut feeling I will be,"* he thought.

As the boy made his way over to the old shack, a car turned the corner. His only cover is the weeds around him. The small shack was out of reach; he tried not to panic, as the car got closer. Fear was strong and it nearly engulfed his senses, with nowhere to run, nowhere to hide, they are coming. Without thinking the boy hit the dirt, laying flat on his stomach he awaited for almost certain doom to ascend upon him. The car speedily drove right passed him and turned the corner. Again he was covered in total darkness. The boy's heart raced as he turned over on his back, his breathing hard, but with a sigh of relief, sweat poured off his face.

After a few minutes, he looked up at the stars, with the house and his brother being so close and yet so far away. "I sure hope he knows all trouble he has put me through tonight," he replied softly. EJ swallowed hard then blew hard through his mouth then gets on his hands and knees. EJ not taking any more chances as he crawled over to the shed. With a quick look, he thought to himself. *"It could work. Humm…if I lean a few of those old boards on the outside against the shack and pry a couple these boards off for a door and make a possible escape out the back,"* thinking to himself. The boy remembered how old Mr. Farmer little trick made him feel trapped still seemed to haunt him. With one last look and quick nod of his head, the boy puts on his ten-gallon hat. "The Calvary's a comin little brother with guns a blazon, saddle your horse's men, we ride," he said into the wind at his back.

There was a large oak tree towards the end of the road; the boy quickly weaved in and out of the shadows, which now become child's play for him. Just four more houses on this lane with a large empty field across it. He could see the house his brother is being held in. It is the third one down. His palms are sweaty, realizing that the tiredness is setting in. He arched his back and shoulders and winced a little from the pain, stretched his arms and gasped.

"Oooohh, bad idea," he said. The bruises quickly reminded him why. "I'll try little stretches for a couple of days, won't hurt as much." He said though no one, but he could hear.

EJ raced quickly down towards the empty field. The boy had never felt so nervous in his life and excited with adrenalin running through his veins. He could see the bedroom window where he and his brother usually slept. All the lights are turned off except the one in the living room.

He noticed the bedroom window had been left open ajar. "They might have thought I had left the county by now or lest hoping and therefore not expecting me to return anytime soon. They got that right, but they might have forgotten one small detail. Never leave a man behind enemy lines they always say." He said softly only pausing for a second. "Now the question is how to get into that room? Humm looks like they moved all the stuff from underneath window so climbing up there not an option, plus it would have been too noisy anyway," he said softly.

While he looked around the yard, the boy was getting a little discouraged, but he refused to give up when an idea popped into his head. "Where did I see that old ladder last?" Taking his hat off, he scratched his head and retraced his steps. "There it is?" The ladder was leaned up against a tree, busting wide open he yelled. "Yahoo!" Too quickly and a little bit too loud.

Quickly EJ covered his mouth realized his mistake. A dog barked and the porch light came on with someone standing in the doorway. The boy's heart leaped into his throat, he dived into the nearby bushes just in time before being seen. Just then, he heard someone yelling in his direction. "Anyone out there? Me an old Clive here are itching for some action, George grab the scattergun, dang kids are at it again," the woman yelled.

EJ thought this time for sure he was going down with no doubt in his mind this time he was done for until he heard. "Lorain come back to bed, there's nothing out there; you are just hearing things you old bat." A man yelled through the house. With the porch light turned off he dived from the bush grabbed the ladder, placed it under his under his arms, held on to his hat and made a mad dash for the empty field.

Falling to the ground, dropping the ladder on the ground, EJ rolled onto his back, his breathing was hard and fast; sweat just poured off his forehead. EJ wiped the sweat off onto his pants; still panting he sits up for a minute to catch his breath after that last run. The boy stood up. "Glad to have two bare feet right now because shoes would have just slowed me down tonight. Not that I liked shoes in the first place rather go barefoot all the time. Except for winter, given the choice. I hate shoes," he said to the wind dusting off his feet.

Thinking about the clothes he was wearing from Mr. Scarecrow and judging by the size of his baggy clothes, which were a little hot for this time of the year. While undoing some of the shirt buttons in the front and looking down his pant legs and re-rolled them backup then re-tucking in the shirt, the boy puts back on his hat, picks up the ladder, looked towards the house where his brothers is. "Let's do it, boys," he replied while checking to see if the coast is clear.

The boy carefully crossed the road with the ladder by using the cover of darkness. EJ slowly lowered the ladder to the ground underneath the bedroom window. He decided to check to make sure the coast is clear first, before attempting the rescue before he climbed into the window. His body tense as he flattened it against the house. EJ slowly gliding along the side of the house. Eyes and ears listening for anything, any movements throughout the house as he crept along the sides, being careful not to disturb anything that would call attention to his parents.

The TV lights are still on in the living room. "They must be up late, should be going to bed soon." He thought to himself. EJ noticed the kitchen window is open and heard voices and decided to eavesdrop on their conversation which could provide him some insight on what's happening. "I wonder if they are looking for me or not?" He asked in his mind.... he listened...

"That boy! That dreadful boy! I thought you said he would never try running off like that," his mother said in semi-angered voice... EJ mother has always been strong-willed. A plump woman with short brown hair so she would not have to fuse with like most woman her age do. It always looked choppy and short like a boys with a bad haircut. Some would say fat and lazy, but she could move quickly when she wanted to for a woman of her size just under five-feet and had a nose like a bird of prey. It looked like that ever since she'd broken it in three places. For a woman, she was not considered pretty but average. She had always claimed she got this way after baring four kids and her figure never returned to what used to be when she was younger or before she met his father.

Linda had a strange temper. One minute she could be all calm, gentle and collected and the next wild anger would come out of now where. She looked like a mad bull running through a china shop. Her face would implode with red blotches as her blood roses to her face. She could be a good mother when she wanted to, but that was only when she had something to gain. At least that's the way EJ thought of her most of his life. Being sent out of the home so often, you would think he was a military brat. Which was not the case... for he was a kid like so many that bounced around through the foster care system like a yo-yo, only spending very little time in either place since the age of six.

Most of the time was due to his father hatred towards him and his brother Danny. Other times people found out was really going on in the home, not that bruise sent up red flags. And because of the bruises, he's parents did whatever it took to hide them; coming up with excuses, very believable lies, and excuses.

His father growled angrily. "Linda you are worrying over nothing. We will deal with his disobedience as we always have. No one will be the wiser. Trust me, who cares about such a worthless boy that nobody wants. Stop worrying I assure you he's fine, and if isn't who cares. I know I don't I should have killed him, if it wasn't for these damn laws and no good God damn neighbors and caseworkers breathing down our necks every time they find a little tinny bruise. I could have done so and we will be free of him and his God damn brother once and for all.

"I promise you the next I see him he will not live to see another day. I am sick and tired having to explain to those God damn people that have been raising hell, and causing problems and sticking their God damn noses where it doesn't belong. Trust me having them dead and gone once and for all. People will stop butting in where they don't belong; including his grandmother. Now stop it, I am tired of listening to you gripe about how worried you are about people finding out. When the truth is people just don't give one tinkers damn about him, and you know that. Considering when he isn't here, no one even mentions he's name."

His mother shadow stood up as she turned around to face his father. "Yes, but its too late for that. It's been almost two days and who knows what kind of lie's he is telling people. We beat him and his brother pretty good this time. Already people have been calling, and the State caseworker is coming to do an inspection to make sure what they heard wasn't happening. His grandmother too is demanding to see him. If he is dead and someone finds him before we do. We are going to look pretty guilty after the neighbors heard him and his brother screaming and now that boy has run off and you have yet to find him or refuse to go looking for him.

"What are folks going to say when they see him like that? You know how they are about sticking their noses into other peoples business." His father said nothing not even trying to resolve the issue without getting into another argument with her. Thinking he will come home on his own after that. His mother started crying as he placed his arms around her as she pushed him away said pointing his direction. "Even the cops will be on our doorstep if they find him all

What's Behind the Looking Glass?

beaten up. You know it." Her voice trembled a little as her shadow walked away further in the house, passing the kitchen window hearing the phone ring, his mother picked up and said. "No I think you have the wrong number, and if you call here again asking about that boy after I told you he doesn't live here anymore, we will sue you for harassment." She slammed down the phone and walked back into the living room and sat back down on the couch.

His father followed her seeing his shadow move towards her as his mother said. "I know dear... They said he would come home when he gets hungry; it's almost been two days. Where's he going to go dressed only in his boxers, not even his best pair? People have begun to talk already, as you can see the phone hasn't stopped ring. People are already getting suspicious about his constant disappearance," his mother said.

"About what dear," His father asked. "It's not like he actually lives here, as a member of our family. Trust me, the phone calls and the questions will stop, they always do once people realize that boy isn't here, we will just tell them we sent him to some distant relatives or placed him with the state again for obedience problem. Like I said nobody cares about a worthless boy that nobody wants and that goes for his brother."

Just too say his father Jim had an anger problem when came to his boys, would not even come close. No. He literally hated them, why only he knows. It was worse when he came home for serving two years in the war. He served in the American Air Force as a plumber on base. He never actually fought in the war, but somehow he came back as a changed man, according to his grandmother.

EJ was never sure of the reason behind it unless it was because he was not as fit like other men that served. Or was it due to his size being four feet five inches tall, dark brown hair slight bald on top and cold blue eyes that left you wondering if there was a soul behind them? His jawline pointed as it is drawn down his face. Jim was a muscular man in his early thirties, yet was not a bodybuilder. He had a slow limp in his right leg which showed more when he was angered which was more often than not. He once told him. He too would lose his hair by the time he graduated from High School.

Providing he lived long enough, providing he didn't kill him first. Yes, there was no love lost between them.

His mother said. "They are starting to ask more questions about all the fights he gets into. The bruises on his arms, legs, and face and why he's never here? Always gone months at a time and years sometimes? I do know one thing if we don't do something soon, his brother going to be just like him. If only he would keep his mouth shut. Just look at the girls, they are angels. They barely cause a fuse anymore." The thought of killing him and his brother never seemed to register with his mother, yet she never disagreed with it either nor had she ever tried to stop it. In fact, she had come close herself in doing so, more so when he was a baby and would have succeeded if it wasn't for his grandmother stopping her from drowning him or suffocating him with a pillow.

The boy EJ under the window nearly lost it after hearing that. "Angels right? Devils more like it," as he whispered to himself.

Peggy was just a year younger than EJ at age nine. Even though she always liked to claim she was the oldest by default, considering EJ seldom lived at home. Therefore he was considered an unwanted visitor, not her actual brother, blood nor genes had any bearing. She would prefer him nonexistent, again no love lost there. She had the same bearing as her mother. Except some would say more often than not, considered her pretty unlike her mother she wore her dark brown hair long so it hung loosely at her waist. Blue-eyed beauty like a porcelain doll. Almost four-feet, three inches broad shoulder like her father button cute nose with fair complexion. Some would say calculating as a chessboard, mean and spoiled. Takes after her father, but has her mother's disposition being strong-willed and cunning like a snake on steroids.

Her younger sister Dona, age eight. Born in the month of May had always claimed she is the prettiest due to her dirty dishwater blond hair. Which came from her mothers' side of the family; not sure if that was true or not, EJ had never met them in person but has seen pictures. But unlike her mother's straight hair, Dona's hair curled as she kept it shoulder-length, blue-eyed dyed blond. Pretty as a picture her mother would always say "perfection." One of her father's favorites, just like her sister Peggy. She had the same disposition as her mother when it came to temperament. She could be playful one minute and mean as a snake in the next second but had always been dumb as an Ox's.

His mother said continuing the conversation after a moment of silence. "Well, all I have to say is bad genes." His mother said with a sour smirk on her face that he has pictured seeing many times, not for the first time she has blamed him for having bad genes.

"What do you mean by that?" His father said.

"Your mother," his mother said.

"My mother! What's that's got to do with it?" His dad turned to face her more openly.

"She's never liked me and you know it." His mother replies back without pause.

"You know that's not true?"

"I've heard the stories about her, she's a real spitfire that one, part of gang I heard." His mother said almost sitting upright to face him.

"Don't believe everything you hear dear, but my father always did say, life was never dull around her, I think that's why he married her… It seems while growing up, she could control the wind out of the strongest hurricane according to my father. He used to say that all the time. I think I might of wittiness it once when I was very young, buts it is hard to remember, which was a long time ago. She's mellowed out now after Dad passed away, having to raise all of us on her own ever since then. I hear people say she's the salt of the earth. Nothing to fear… She is just a sweet little old lady with barely a little kick in her. Except for a little humble pie now again, other than that you have nothing to fear." His father said slowly standing turning off the TV.

"Somehow that doesn't make me feel any better," she replies standing up. "Well it's getting late, let's go to bed."

His Grandma Stuart was strong-willed woman in her early fifties according to his grandfather who passed away when he was six and soon after went into the foster care system not long before his body was even cold in the ground, but with him gone there was nothing he could do stop them, not anymore now that he was dead and his grandmother too didn't even try until it was too late thinking it was only a mere threat or perhaps the best thing for him rather than having to worry that he would end up dead lying in some gutter. So she let them, and kept tabs on him, making sure he was well taken care of or need to be placed in a home that would. The home was one place he would never be safe, she did everything she could to keep his brother safe, but without his grandfather support, she couldn't do much other than a surprise visit or a phone call.

She served in the war as a nurse. Her hair silver-white now and had warm blue eyes, while his grandfather's eyes were brown and warm. Whenever he looked into his eyes he felt at peace and at home. He was EJ's best friend and always looked up to him. His grandma would always tell him stories about him when he worked on the Pacific Railroad. Seeing the world as a train engineer, that always put a smile on his face when times were hard. EJ would always thumb through the photographs and look in the mirror standing tall on a stool next to his grandmother as they compared his likeness to him.

Grandma too was short like his father Jim barely over five feet, but her attitude always made up for her size. She seldom talked much about herself, but when he was down and out with his parents, she always made him feel better. She would listen to his problem and sometimes provide him with good advice. Telling him every time she saw him he reminded him of his grandfather, being able to think on his feet, by always learning new things and keeping an open mind when comes to reasoning. He always knew without a doubt she loved him.

Yet life was hard. Even harder still ever since his grandfather died, she seemed to hold back when it came to interfering with his parent's choices. Telling him 'things will get better, they always do.

What's Behind the Looking Glass?

He needed to stop running away every time things got out of hand. And perhaps they will if he would put in just a little more effort into things that don't make his parents so angry.' It was always the same speech. Why could she not see that it was tearing him apart inside as the beatings continued regardless? Yet he loved her very much and always wondered why she had changed so much after his grandfather died.

Thoughts of the morning filled his head knowing things need to change and if no one was going to come he would need to do himself one way or another he needed to make sure his bother was taken care of, he said in a low whisper. "I'll strike while they are all asleep." He whispered to himself. The boy in anticipation as he rubbed his hands together; "serves them right." EJ slowly went back to the bedroom window with as much care as before. Looked up at the window and sees it still left open just ajar from the last time he checked.

After a while the lights went out in the living room, he waited until he figured they were fast asleep. EJ sat on the ground under a nearby tree watching, waiting in the darkness. All is quiet, everything except for some crickets chirping in the background. Every once in awhile you could hear a dog barking in the distance other than that the world seemed to be in a night of rhythmic sleep. Grabbing a nearby branch he pulled himself up. "Well boys we have work to do," he said softly.

EJ went back to the open window, carefully picked up the ladder and gently laid it against the house. Making sure that everything is still and quiet. EJ climbed the ladder and slowly opened the window and stepped inside the room. In the bedroom, he could see his brother fast asleep. EJ looked down the hall where his sister's room was. The urge to play a trick on them was strong, but he resisted because this night of all nights is all about him and his little brother. He does not know how or when, but under his breath, he whispered in the darkness. "Someday the price will be paid. I promise you that." He said with anger, eyes flashing if they could burn holes through steel beams...

EJ stepped carefully over the windowsill into the room. On tiptoes as he crossed the room where his brother is sleeping. Carefully EJ removed his hat then gently set it on the bed beside him, so his brother would recognize him. He gently tapped him on the shoulder and whispered in his ear. "Danny, Danny wake up it's your brother."

EJ's brother Danny was the spitting image like him. Mosey brown hair, blue eyes and the cutest six-year-old on the planet according to EJ and his grandmother whenever they visited her. He was short for his age and too skinny unlike most kids his age. He too was picked on or bullied because of his height and sometimes the clothes he wore were mostly rags. Unlike his sister's nice dresses and well-kept hair and makeup. He did his best what he had to work with. Even though his hair was kept stub short so his mother wouldn't have to fuses keeping his hair comb. Danny was EJ's best friend next to his grandma Stuart. They had always done everything together. Through thick or thin, he was always there for him. EJ missed him more whenever he was away.

Danny stirred realizing it's his brother. His eyes open with excitement and not realizing his brother wanted him to be quiet, shouted. "EJ, where have you been?"

"Shush, Quiet," EJ putting his hand over his brother's mouth, whispered. "Please, I don't want to wake anyone," Said while holding a finger to his lips. "Keep it down." Tip toed back to the hall to check and make sure everyone was still fast asleep.

His little brother whispered. "Sorry," rubbing the sleep out of his eyes. "The folks are really mad."

EJ shrugged his shoulders. "That's nothing new, they are always mad at me for something."

"Ya, I know. Me too, they thought they had you for sure. They weren't expecting you to leave just with your skivvies on. By the way, where did you get those cool clothes anyway?" Danny softly giggled.

"Let's just say from an old friend," EJ said smiled back putting his fingers to his lips.

What's Behind the Looking Glass?

Danny looked down at the old cowboy hat. "Can I try the hat on?" He asked.

EJ reached down and placed the hat on his brother's head. "Looks real good on you partner," he replied in a whisper.

Danny with a grin that lit up his entire little boy faces said. "Grandma called while you were gone, everyone got to talk to her. They are really hush, hush about the whole thing. They said you were at a friend's house having a sleepover… They wouldn't let me talk to her very long though." EJ sat on the side of the bed next to his brother. "I haven't wet the bed for two whole days see? I am even wearing one of your old shirts," his brother said.

"Well, that's one less thing I have to worry about," EJ said as he smiled back and carefully watched the bedroom door.

"Whys that?" Danny whispered back.

"Because we're busting out of here," EJ said putting his hand on his brother's shoulder.

"We are?" Danny responds gleefully.

"Yep, but you got be real quiet," EJ replied.

Just then a hall light turned on. One of the girls was coming down the hall to use the bathroom. Quickly EJ ducked into a corner, but not soon enough before his nosey little sister Peggy poked her head into the room and looked right at her little brother Danny still sitting up in bed with his brother's hat on.

"What are you still doing up Danny?" Before Danny could respond, she noticed the hat on his head. "Where did get that hat Danny?" His sister seeing EJ standing in the corner flipped on the bedroom light. "Coming back to gloat have you now? MAMA, DADDY, Eric's HOME!" She screamed at the top of her lungs. "You are going to get it now," she said as she rubbed her two little hands together with an evil twinkle in her eye.

"I swear Peggy someday there will be a price to pay and I'll make sure you pay every last penny," he said.

Peggy laughed. "Says you, but that won't be today I think," she said. Hearing noises coming quickly down the hall from his parent's room. EJ frozen in place, his mind raced. He looked over at his little brother with terror in his eyes; Danny began to cry. EJ looked down at his brother then looked at his sister with fear and anger in his eyes. He realized that he needed to leave without his brother. He stepped out of the corner, his sister panics and she immediately stepped in his way. "And where do you think you're going?" And yelled. "COME QUICKLY, HE'S TRYING TO ESCAPE!" EJ felt like a trapped animal with nowhere to run. EJ pushed Peggy out of the way at the same time his father entered the room with his mother right behind him.

His mother gasped at the mere sight of him, almost speechless. "How did you get in here?" She said as she stared at the open window and then eyed him up and down. "Where did get those clothes?" She asked with a surprised tone in her voice.

His father, on the other hand, was not speechless you could see the anger building in his eyes and face and his back of his knuckles turned white as he closed his fist. "Your mother was worried sick about you boy as if she had enough to worry about. It's bad enough having to explain to everyone and coming up with excuses for you when you won't keep your mouth shut." He spat as his saliva dripped down his chin as his face turned red with anger.

"These things are family matters and that's where they need to stay boy," his father said while glaring down at EJ with heated breath. "Sooner or later you are going have to learn that boy and I would suggest real soon. Because we can't keep telling people why you are gone all the time… and you can't keep running off as you did either. People are talking and it keeps upset your mother and me." His father said while his father started to grab the belt off the wall.

Chapter 2-2

EJ knew he had to leave or he was going to get another beating of a lifetime. EJ's father said in a very gruff voice. "Boy, we can do this the hard way or the easy way?"

Peggy calmly moved over towards her little brother and sat down beside him and yanked the hat right off his head. "Look, mama, look what Eric stole." She said seeing the opportunity of getting a few extra licks in herself.

Danny looked up at his big brother. "You didn't steal it, did you Eric?" He asked.

EJ seeing the hurt in his little brother eyes and on in his little face, anger builds. EJ responds back as gentle as he could muster as he looked down at his brother Danny. "No, I did not steal it."

"I don't believe you!" Peggy said as she turned and looked back at EJ hoping to make matters worse.

Danny looked up at EJ. "Well, I do." He said with beaming confidence.

EJ smiled, while his other sister Dona walked into the room. "Well, well looks like the gangs all here, hi Eric, see that you are in trouble again, not surprised really you always was a troublemaker, most likely always will be," she said.

"That's enough girls! It's time for you to go back to bed. If you wouldn't mind, please take your little brother with you." His mother said trying to control the situation from turning into mayhem as she watched Jim from the corner of her eye.

"Oh, momma!" Peggy cried hoping to see some action as she glared at EJ standing in the corner.

"Just spread some blankets on the floor. This is between your father and Eric and I. Now get going and let him keep his hat for now. Go on, get with it, and get back to bed." She said her voice sounded shaken as she watched her husband Jim.

It was tough as he watched his little brother leave. For as they were leaving Danny grabbed his big brother too give him a big hug. Peggy seeing this immediately grabbed him by his little arms dragged him out of the room. "Come with me you little brat if know what's good for you!" She said angrily and disappointed.

EJ said under his breath, "one of these days I swear." As his eyes met hers as they left the room.

"Now then," his father said with a growl. EJ heard the belt smacking against the palm of his father's hand. "What did we decided boy, the hard way or the easy way?" It was the first in a long time. EJ thought he might have felt a little compassion from his mother.

"Do really have to do this tonight dear; after all, we have been…?" But she never got the chance to finish the words before his father began the first strike of the belt "SNAP" the belt missed him by a hair. EJ sprung like a cat on a hot griddle, sprang into the air and began to climb the room like a caged animal.

EJ; headed for the open window where he came in earlier, his father yelled. "OH NO YOU DON'T!" Swing the belt high in the air as it whistled through the air "SNAP" went the belt right across his legs. EJ screamed as he jumped up headed towards the other window.

The belt whistled in the air as his father swung it again with such force. "SNAP" it swiped across his back. EJ screamed in near agony, his mother nearly in tears. EJ jumped up on the bed towards the window and tried to open it. Finding it jammed shut panics. His father swung the belt back and forth wildly "SNAP" "SNAP" once more across the back of his legs and the other side of his back feeling not only the leather but the sharpened belt buckle he was famous for.

What's Behind the Looking Glass?

EJ screamed again. His body shook, his legs buckled do to the force of the pain. His mother finally yelled. "ENOUGH!"

EJ turned, looked straight into his father's eyes. All he saw was anger. His father got ready to swing again. EJ looked at his mother with one last hope. Hoping she might stop him, but did not see any hope in her face either, animal instincts took over. "I must survive, to do that I must escape."

EJ dived through the window. The glass shattered all around the ground around him with a loud crash, not remembering to tuck and roll as he fell to the ground he landed on his left side. His mother ran to the window seeing EJ lying on the ground. There was blood everywhere around the windowsill; she knew he was badly hurt.

She turned to his father for the first time. "Look; just look, what we have done to him!" Taking the belt from him and throwing the belt across the room. She turned with shock and horror on her face. "Quickly, we must help him, he is badly hurt," she screamed.

Porch lights turned on all around them, you could hear people yelling, "WHAT'S GOING ON OUT THERE?" Fear for the first time was on their faces and in their eyes. How are they going to explain this? By the time they reached the spot, EJ was already gone. He had gone far enough for the moment. Before they could drag him back inside to cover their tracks.

* * *

Let's just say a fly on the wall had a pretty good seat that day and the next. After all, they tend to live a long time, at least long enough to observe what going on in the Stuarts residence.

Porch lights and house lights were being turned on around them. The noise of shattered glass and shouting had awakened the nearby neighbors. EJ's parents were still staring at the ground where their son had landed, mystified beyond thoughts and belief. "Where could he have gone? How could he have moved?" His mother asked mystified, with very little regret. For they believed they had done nothing wrong. Yet a nagging feeling tugged at her mind. She dismissed it and whispered. "That damn boy and those damn bad genes."

The why was never a question for they knew the answer, for them a new change was in the wind as the man called Death aka Derrick stood by in the shadows wiped an escaped tear for the boy and the old man. Watching as his life begins to change. He hoped he has done the right thing. Not just for him and his people, as he tries to save his world from Morgan and the realm of shadows where the light is already fading. But he hoped the boy and the old man will be at peace in their heart and his mind. He questions. "Did I do the right thing? Is there still hope for us and him? Time will tell."

The old man remembered it differently. The time before he had never came back for his brother. Instead, he left and soon was caught a week later hitchhiking along the freeway heading towards Las Vegas with new hopes and new dreams for a new life with no family ties. Yet he had regretted that he never at least tried to free his brother from all the abuse. And ever since then they had been come estranged until he died at the young age of thirty from brain damage from all the abuse. He could never forgive himself for at least trying always wondered if things would have been different his brother would still be alive. It nagged at him constantly and he blamed himself for his death. It was the first of many mistakes he had made.

Perhaps now things will change as he tries to encourage his now younger self into making the right decision now. Not knowing what the new future will bring, but felt at peace for the first time in his life. As him and the boy lay in the weeds he tries to block the pain from the boy. Slowing the blood pumping to the ground, the old man pauses seeing Death stop before the boy, his right hand glows as says "ner'a bon'say ter gon," and draws a healing rune on the boy's shoulder.

He wasn't strong enough to heal him completely but he done so too keep the boy alive until he could find some help, hoping that people he had in mind would open their hearts and take the boy in and in turn bring help to others, until they were ready to learn the truth why the boy and them are so important. God he hoped he had done the right thing by changing the boy's destiny before Morgan finds him once again. The old man and the boy within him began to glow and he was trapped once more inside in the boy's mind, the pain dulled.

EJ's father seeing the ladder on the other side just below the window pointed to it. "Look dear, that's how he got into the house." He said as she nodded her head with a sigh.

"I see a lot of your father in him." She said with a small smile, her voice still shaken from the horror that took place in the room above, not more than an hour ago.

"What do mean by that?" He growled.

She tried to smile and poked him in the ribs. "Your father always was cunning like a fox and quite resourceful if I remember right." She said as she tried to make light of the situation as she swiped a loose hair from her eye.

"Great, some those bad genes again... I also remember him getting into a lot of trouble when he was younger, according to his grandmother."

"So where do you think he went? I know he's hurt, you beat him pretty good this time and you scared the hell right out of me tonight." Linda said cocking her eyes back toward the broken glass on the ground.

"I couldn't explain it was like the anger... I felt... like it just had total control over me. It was... it was if... like I... it had to be let out." The words sounded jumbled as anger still burned within him. His mind lingered on the anger as his fist tightened, nearly drawing blood. Jim whispered silently as if in prayer. *"Why me? Why can't everyone just leave us alone? That damn worthless boy, he's nothing but trouble."*

EJ's father picked up the ladder and threw it into the old field like it was old firewood to cover any of the tracks that would lead anybody to them. After a long while, his mother urged his father to go look for EJ. Knowing he is badly hurt and more worried if anybody but them found him. There would be a lot of hard questioned they might have to answer. She also knew they could not afford that. She would go look for him herself, but leaving right now with her three scared kids behind was not an option, especially without a plan in place.

What would the neighbors say if she asked them to watch them? *"Can you watch these kids while I look for my son... he's hurt?"* Oh, then they would ask *'how did he get hurt?'* There was no way she could tell them the truth. *"My husband and I were beating him and he jumped through a plate-glass window..."* Not on your life. *"After all we did nothing wrong,"* Linda said to herself as she gazed back towards the neighbor's houses around her. Yes, she needed a plan before confronting them.

After going back into the house the girls and little Danny came running out of the room expecting to see their older brother EJ; Danny with tears in his eyes looked into his mother's face and anger in his fathers face when he looked at him. "Where's Eric? What have done with him?" He cried with tears as they ran down his cheek. That was it; his mother broke down and cried.

"Gone," Peggy said gleaming. "Gone, runoff or dead." She said with an extra bounce in her step with new hope. She always felt she should have been the only child or the oldest. No matter what and whatever it took, it was the same result in her book.

Linda was in tears. "How can you even suggest such a thing?" She asked in a choked voice. Even thou she had wished it was true often her self from time to time.

"Well, I just wanted to know," Peggy said back snootily.

Linda tried to sooth little Danny. "Shush, it all right, no your father didn't kill him," she said. But in her mind, she was not so sure she was all that convinced herself. "Your father was about to go out to look for him," she said putting a little steel back into her voice.

What's Behind the Looking Glass?

"Right dear?"

EJ's father lost in thought did not respond right away. He could not get out the images left behind. Behind those eyes, *"Eric's strange eyes, they weren't a boy's eyes. They seemed older somehow. No. How can that be? But those eyes, when they stared back at me as if they could burn right through my very soul."* His mind raced with his thoughts. "What, what was that dear?" He asked.

"You are going to go look for him now, right?" Their mother asked.

"Yes, yes of course dear, where's the flashlight? It will be light soon." Their father said trying to snap back into focus.

"Think you might need some help?" Their mother asked finding the flashlight handing it to him.

"Help? Why? No. No, after all, like you said he's hurt now. How far can he be? Couldn't have gone very far," he said trying to instill positive hope. Thinking if anyone finds him they could be in a lot of trouble. *"Nosey neighbor, this is a family matter. They should stay out of it and leave us the hell alone. Why can't they mind their own damn business?"* Things seemed very bleak at the moment. "Oh while I am gone dear if you wouldn't mind. Try not to cut yourself on the glass and for heaven, sakes keep them all away from it as well. I'll be back as soon as I can," he said taking the flashlight from her.

"Ok kids mind your mother; she has a lot to do today. So if you would please bring your blankets and pillows out here you can all sleep all day in the living room." He said at the last minute before leaving.

Linda tried to smile. "Then later Peggy and I will make some pancakes to welcome home Eric. How does that sound? Danny you can help." She said trying very hard to control her emotions.

"REALLY? Pancakes?" Danny said jumping up and down with excitement. Mother nodded her head to Danny. Peggy and his sister Dona was not all that enthused with the idea.

Eric Shepherd

* * *

They were right about one thing. EJ was not that far and he was badly hurt. By sure will power and determination, he managed to escape. He was not more than thirty feet from where his father threw the ladder where it landed. He knew he needed to get somewhere safe and quick before sunrise, but he knew running was not an option. He could barely walk feeling weak. His sides hurt, his left shoulder hurt too bad to even move it. His back felt warm and wet with blood. He looked down toward his hands and feet picked out the little pieces of glass instilled in them. He cringed as he pulled out the little shards that he could see, the cuts stung on his feet and hands.

"I need to get to the shack. I don't think I could ever make it back to the barn, not like this anyway." EJ said trying to ignore the pain. He slowly moved, nearly crawled through the thicket of weeds towards the old shed. It took sometime hobbling about. He found an old rotted tree branch to use as a crutch and made it to the old shack feeling dizzy and nearly passed out. The sun was just peaking over the mountains. A new dawn was rising. EJ too hurt to care slid into the old shack. He propped up the old boards for the door, too tired to do anymore. Exhaustion and the loss of blood had won; he fell into a deep sleep and slumped into the corner of the shack.

* * *

We can only assume EJ's father was in deep thought, while he searched for his boy, but his mind has always been cloudy when comes to his own sons. While he searched the area he noticed traces of blood now and again; most likely thought if someone was in hiding like his boy. He was not hiding his tracks very well and smiled. He could see where the boy might have laid for a while together strength; seeing the evidence of leaving the shattered glass with his blood still wet on dry weeds. "Looks like he was headed west," he said to himself, what he could tell. "It might not be too late after all," Jim mumbled as he looked towards his house then rubbed his chin. Hoping it was too late to save the boy, oh how he hoped had been wanting him dead for a very long time. The excuse would be easy. They could say he ran away and turned up dead looking as someone had beat the boy. No one would be the wiser, all he needed was time, and then led them to find the body or what was left. Yes, that could work in his favor, he thought rubbing his chin.

His head turned towards the sound of someone walking towards him; he could see old Mr. Johnson walking this way. "Hi Jim what's ya doin?" He asked.

"Not much, Mr. Johnson," Jim said while he looked back at the spot on the ground.

"Heard there might have been a ruckus at your place last night?" Mr. Johnson said as he tries to study Jim.

Jim tried not to look at Mr. Johnson without fear in his eyes, or sound of a quiver in his voice, "what do mean?" He asked.

Mr. Johnson stared at the same spot where Jim was looking at then pointed towards the house with his finger; "broken winder over there and here." He said as he noticed.

"Oh, that?" Jim said thinking quickly. "Most likely kids planning games, you know how they are these days? Always doing something to cause trouble, besides I found a dead dog here and was just finished burying him," he said in hopes of explaining the fresh blood on the ground. He hated animals and everyone knew it. Who was to say he didn't kill the dog himself? He smiled seeing the lie working in his favor.

"True, true how's your family?" He asked. Jim started to really get nervous, "I haven't seen your oldest boy around much, got him locked in a cage somewhere? Never see him riding around town with the other boys, strange?" He replied as he looked at the spot that Jim was looking at then stared back at broken glass by the house noticing the blood trail, the dog story didn't sit well with him, but without proof he couldn't call the cops to come and take a look, but he would call them even they just do a quick sweep. "Oh well, tell the misses hi for me, got my chores to do or they'll be a price to pay come supper time. If you know what I mean?" He said with a slap on the back Mr. Johnson walked away.

Jim pulled out his handkerchief and wiped his brow, whispered. "That was close," putting it back into his pocket. "Where is that damn boy?" He asked and gets back on the road to find him. It's nearly noon and EJ father still has not found him. He has gone up the road and down the road, searching all the ditch banks and weeds with no signs of him. Not far from his path lead him to an old abandon shack where EJ was.

* * * *

EJ stirred and groaned due to the pain. He tried to sit up, but it was to hard move, in the small shack, he pushed with his sore feet to sit up. In the distance he could see his father not far from the shack as he walked up the little dirt path; fear gripped him. He knew he would not live if he finds him here.

He told himself he must remain quiet. His father looked up at shack and wonders. "I should take a look."

He began to walk towards the shed. EJ looked at escape hatch. *"I think I can use it; he must escape at all cost."* The feelings of being trap pressed down on him. Just then his father turned back around, EJ could hear his father talking to himself then watched him sit on a nearby log outside the old shack, EJ mind raced, his heart beating fast, *"questioning why would he choose to sit there?"* Covering his mouth not letting any sound out, not daring to breathe in case of being heard; he could hear his father mumbling just a few paces away.

"Why would he be in there at all? It's boarded up, after all his badly wounded. No one could make it this far not after that? He might be closer to home, he might have gotten help, oh God I hope not," he replied as he walked away.

Chapter 3

EJ; without seeing his father's face he could almost feel his father's fear. "Who would help him? What would he say? Damn the neighbors why can't they just leave family matters alone? I better get back home. She not going to be very happy, I never will understand that damn boy. Hope we have better luck with his brother, bad genes is all I can say, she was right." He said as he walked away. EJ watched his father move back down the road where he came from. It was a sigh of relief to him as he drifted back into a deep sleep.

Arriving home, EJ's father opened the front door. Danny raced up to greet his big… "Daddy where's Eric?" He asked.

His father fighting the urge to hit him across the face, he hated when his boys called him that worse because used the name EJ his own mother used when addressing the boy. Too him they would never be good enough to be allowed that simple pleasure of acceptance. They would never be his sons, what his older brother Steve saw in having sons he could never understand. To him they were nothing, but a disappointment just like he was with his own father. Jim eyes locked as he looked deep into his wife's eyes. "I couldn't find him," he said his head bowed.

She said softly. "Or he didn't want to be found… Not after what we have done to him," began to cry. Feeling remorseful, yet she could not figure out what they had done wrong. *"No… we did nothing wrong. Then why are you crying? Because I am scared that I, we might have, could that be? No, we did nothing wrong!"* Her thoughts and feelings betray her. As she argues with her inner self, so angered that she slammed her fits on the counter as the children looked wide-eyed at the sudden burst of anger. Linda wiped an escaped tear still wondering why she is crying over nothing. And why is everyone staring at her? *"SHE DID NOTHING WRONG!"* She screamed in her mind, trying to control the panic she was feeling, feeling the walls closing in all around her. *"Breathe damn it, breath. You did nothing wrong! But what if I did?"*

Peggy seeing another opportunity to move in and strike another blow while the fire was still hot, Peggy put her arm around her. "It's ok mama, it's not your fault. We all know he's always has been a trouble maker," she said her voice as sweet as poison honey.

"What do you mean it's not our fault?" Mother asked her mind struggling as she tries to ignore the panic. Breathing slowly and holding her breath and letting it out slowly, slowly gaining control. *Yes, we did nooothing wrooong* " the voice echoed in her mind.

Peggy avoids the question and answered. "After all you still have me." And tried to swallow really hard, "and Dona? Dona and me are your girls."

Little Danny jumping up and down, "what about me?" He asked.

Peggy snapped. "What about you?"

Little Danny standing there smiling, "she has me." He said trying to be heard.

Peggy not sounding convinced. Her voice barely audible and snidely at that, "yes momma there's still Danny." She said as she turned her head; so nobody, but her could hear. "For the moment anyway." With an evil smirk, "one down two to go."

"Well children, it's time for you to get dressed and go out and play." Mother said drying her eyes with the back of her right hand.

Little Danny looked up at his mother. "What about pancakes?" He asked.

Danny's father looked into his mother's eyes and says. "I think cold cereal will be fine today, we have a lot to do today Danny, with your bother gone someone needs to do his chores." Danny knew who the chores would be done by, seeing his father nod in his direction without words knowing he meant him and not his sisters. It didn't matter he was almost 7 he would still be doing them. Age meant nothing to his parents or his sisters. In fact, every time he told his grandmother or his friends the few he had they didn't believe him how cruel his parents actually were and when they did ask they simply lied telling them he was making up stories; that all they have chores to do.

Peggy couldn't resist as she looked down at little Danny. "Eric's fault, causing us problems again. You see Danny boy; he's a bad apple. Do you know what happens to bad apples?" She asked as Peggy looked at Danny. "They spoil and we have to throw them away."

Danny looked up at his sister and screamed. "EJ is not an apple, he's my brother," and began to cry.

His mother looked across the room at her crying boy. "Peggy? Why is he crying now?" She asked wishing for a bottle of aspirins as she rubbed her temples.

Peggy shook her head and shrugged her shoulder. "I have no idea, maybe he's mad about not getting pancakes. Who knows?" Peggy got down the box of cornflakes, trying not to smile and whispered in Danny's ear. "I would suggest you do whatever I say from now on, you little brat! It was easy getting him out of the way. Your turn could be next! Just remember who's really in charge around here and we will get along. If you don't, well, you can ask your big brother… Oh, you can't, that's right he's not here is he? Now be quiet and eat your cereal!" She said as she dragged Danny onto the kitchen chair and slammed the spoon on the table in front of him.

EJ parents are cleaning up the glass in the back bedroom near the window where he leaped for his life. "Well, there's at least one thing you won't have to worry about dear," Jim said trying to look on the bright side.

"What's that?" Linda asked as she looked up from making Danny's bed.

"You won't have to worry about what's he's wearing anymore," Jim said chuckling.

"Where on earth do think he managed to find those clothes? They were nearly two to three sizes too big for him, and that hat. If I wasn't so mad at him, I would have been busting with tears of laughter." He said in hopes of cheering her up.

"Like I said time and time again dear; there's a lot of your father in him and that's the truth and that goes for little Danny," Linda said with a joking smile.

"That's what worries me the most, we never saw eye to eye either. We better get this cleaned up soon or people are going to be asking questions. Then I need to go downtown and buy another window. Normally I take it from his hide." He said thinking he still might when he finds him and more for running off again and sighs.

His wife swept up the room and noticed the discarded belt still lying on the floor. "Jim? Jim, what do you want to do about this?" She asked.

He turned around and looked at the belt lying on the floor, hands shaking, falls to his knees whispered. "Never again." He turned to his wife, "go find a shoebox."

"A shoebox?" She gasped, "what on earth for?"

"Just do it, woman," Jim said his voice shaking.

She ran, dropped the broom on the floor, ran through the house, turned to look at the kids "Your father wants a shoebox," she said.

"A what?" Peggy gasped as she turned and looked back down the hall where her father was.

"A shoebox!" Her mother said dashing to her bedroom.

Linda ran into the bedroom, rummaged through the closet. She finds a box full of old shoes and dumped them on the ground. She ran back to the bedroom where her husband was finding him still on his hands and knees. She handed him the box. The box is marked EJ shoes. They never paid any attention to the markings on the box at the time. The box lay open on the ground near the belt as she watched Jim stand. "While you were gone," he said not looking up at her. "I made a promise a few moments ago. That we are never going to touch that thing again, not in this house."

Linda with tears running down her cheeks, "I am glad. Can you wait here just a moment dear? I'll be back." She said and ran to the kitchen where the kids are eating, opened a few cabinet doors and drawers.

Peggy turned and asked. "Mama, what are you doing?"

"Oh nothing, just eat your breakfast, me and your father we are just talking and are going over a few things that's all." She said trying to hold back the tears in her eyes. She grabbed all the wooden spoons including the metal pancake turner. Think twice about that one, but decide it to needed to go too. With arms loaded she quickly returned to the room down the hall and shut the door behind them so they could be alone.

Jim turned with a look of puzzlement on his face. "I only hope you brought a big enough box for one more item," he said looking at the items in her arms. "But can you wait a few more minutes dear?" He asked his wife as she sets the items down on the bed beside her pondering. "Where is he off to now?"

Father now passed the kids in the kitchen. "Daddy?" Peggy asked.

"Yes?" Dad stops and turned around to face the children.

"Is everything ok with you and mama?" Dona asked as she glanced at her sister Peggy.

"Yes, yes everything's fine now, finish up and go outside and play, but stay in the yard and away from the broken glass, ok?"

After going to the bedroom and retrieved what remains of the broken chain. He carefully wrapped it into an old rag and quickly carried it back to the bedroom where his wife waited for him. He looked at her than the box, "as I was a saying." He said now taking her hands in his and looked into her eyes. "I was making a promise. That I was never going to use that or anything like that on any of our children ever again, but I see that I am not the only one that feels this way."

Tears now streaming down her cheeks, Linda with her back of her right hand, tried to smooth the aging lines among his left cheek. "No dear, I too have something to say, we both need to make this promise together. For we might have lost one already… we cannot afford to lose another so I too make this promise; this same promises with you this very day," she said.

On the floor laid the box, it is now filled to the top, as they closed the lid together. To remind them of their pledge they made together. They placed a few bits of broken glass. Which is now stained with EJ's blood in the box with a note on top of the box: "**Never shall we let anger find this box opened, for our pledge has been made in our son's blood this very day."** It read.

* * *

The smell of bread baking nearby stirred EJ to wake in the old shack which caused his stomach to rumble from hunger. When he moved, he groaned from numerous pains surrounding his body. He tried to move but was very weak. His survival instincts or strong; he knew he must leave and find help. The only question is where and who can he trust.

Going back is not an option. He must go forward to survive. For the first time, EJ realized he must learn to dig deep within himself to find the strength and the courage. If he is going to survive as he watched the sky a storm was coming. The winds were beginning to blow and the clouds are darkening in the sky. He also knew his little shack will not protect him from the rains or the winds.

The only option to him remained to find safety before the storm, but he is also badly wounded and needed food and supplies. Luckily Danny's and his little tree house is nearby; less then ½ mile from his home. Along the canal, road was an underpass, if he could just make it there. He could weather the storm there for awhile. With plenty of orchards and farming gardens, he might be able to find some food and water and do something for his wounds.

EJ slowly with one good arm grabbed the side of the shack and leaned his sore body against it, with a lot effort he makes it. Pulling away from the old boards from the door he slowly stepped out of the old shack. It is late in the afternoon. The shadows are not going to help him much, he groaned with every step. His body throbbed in pain as he looked towards the open path. He stops; his head is pounding and still dizzy, he paused just for a moment then looked back down the road towards his house before he moved on across the road.

"Best not to be seen, if it can be helped." He thought as he saw someone coming his way. Quickly as he could he ducked behind a tree and waited for them to pass him by. "Almost there. Just little further, need to rest before going on," he said to himself. EJ decided to sit underneath the tree. Coming around the corner a lady and gentleman came strolling by, fear nearly grabbed hold of him with nowhere to hide. Thinking fast; he greets them with a smile. "Howdy, fine evening were having, looks like it's about to rain, better get inside, you don't want to get wet do you?" He said

"Sounds like a good idea, you do the same lad," the man said with a simple wave.

"Planning on just doing that; Good day to you and have a good night," EJ said and waved them on down the sidewalk.

"Thank you, son, such a good boy," and walked away.

EJ gave a sigh of relief as he watched them walk away, thinking. *"That was easier said then done; imagine if I was still in my underwear."* EJ grabbed the tree branch crutch behind him. He struggled a little getting up as he hobbled a couple of times getting up to catch his balance and headed on down the road. EJ looked up into the clouded darkening sky, arrived at his and Danny tree house and realized that neither of them had been here in quite some time.

Eric Shepherd

Remembering how they used to keep a box of keepsakes up at the top of the tree until the winds kept blowing it down so they built a little cubbyhole at the base of the tree. Finding the spot where they put their little treasures, he dug into the dirt and pulled a piece of flat stone they found from a nearby creek bed where they would swim on hot summers days. And wondered if they would ever be able to do that again together someday? He did not know if he would ever see his little brother Danny again.

Chapter 3-1

Opening the little wooden box of keepsakes was his Swiss Pocketknife that his grandmother gave him for his birthday last year. He found some strings, a notepad and pencil, some fishing hooks and a bandana his grandfather gave him when he worked on the railroad and other cool stuff. EJ took the bandana and spread it out. He laid in the pocketknife, string, fishing hooks, and notepad and pencil. Then tied the corners together into a knot and stuffed them into the front of his shirt. Before he could reach the underpass it began to rain.

"Just my rotten luck," he said as he looked up at the sky.

The rain was coming down hard and fast as it soaked him to the bone. EJ grabbed some apples off a nearby tree sees the clearing of the underground underpass. The mud is very slick and made it nearly impossible for him to reach it, but he pushed on. Safety was near and he must get out of this storm. He was cold and wet and hungry, the underpass is dark, but at least it was dry. Finding some wood, he remembered his Cubs Scout days on how to make a fire.

EJ removed the bandanna from his shirt; uniting the knot he pulled out the string then found a flat rock and strong stick and a flat piece of wood to make dry kindling to make a fire. At the entrance, there was enough wood built up to make a fire from the orchard from the discarded tree limbs that have not yet been removed or burned. He sifted towards the bottom where they were still dry.

EJ tied the string to the stick then wrapped it around so it would spin when moving it back and forth on the flat board. Soon he had a small fire as he placed more wood on the blaze. Firelight danced around the shadows of the underpass. Eating the fruit from the tree, EJ sat and watched the rain outside while he huddled near the fire to get warm as he looked out into the storm. He wondered about his little brother and decided to leave him a note in hopes he would find it.

Eric Shepherd

***

He writes:

Dear Danny: I am sorry I had to leave you behind. Please forgive me, but I needed to do this on my own and hope someday you might understand. Please do not let your sister Peggy push you around either. Remember three things: To be a good boy plus there are no such thing as bad genes, but most important I will miss you.

Big E...

***

Linda watched the same rain outside her kitchen window. His mother pulled back the curtains worrying as she watched the rain fall then slowly closed them with a sad sigh. While her husband Jim down the hall covered the broken window with plastic to keep the rain and the weather out. "Do you think he's all right?" Linda asked, trying to sound hopeful in spite of the rain and the gloomy sky.

"You are the one that keeps saying he's resourceful now," he said as he placed the last of the tape against plastic. "Humm, that should do it. Tell you what. In the morning if it's not raining, I'll go back out and look for him, if that will make you feel any better? Who knows he might come home by then," he said. Hoping if they find him their trouble would be over. Then if he is dead then the problem would be solved all together and in their favor.

***

Meanwhile, EJ curled up near the fire, fell back to sleep; while the rain outside silent subdues him in the middle of the night as it rocked the small boy EJ to sleep. Upon the next morning, sagebrush birds chirped happily as they looked for worms after a storm. A warm gentle breeze gently nosed EJ with its soft touch, while rays of morning light peeked through the clouded sky upon his face. EJ opened his eyes and could barely move his muscles. They were so stiff and sore from the previous day, his clothes felt damp and heavy from the night before. Trying to sit up it nearly took all his strength. He now knows he cannot do this on his own. He can't turn to his parents they have abandoned him, nearly beat him to death. He had very few friends and they were young as or younger than him. He had this tugging inside of him as it pointed north, he assumed at the time it meant his grandmother.

The one person clearly in his mind who has shown any love or care was his grandmother. If only he could make it to her, she might be able to help him. She would never send him away and she might be able to help him or least give him some answers or where to go to find some help and to help Danny too. With new courage and determination, he gathered his wits about him.

"I must find her; she will know what I should do. The problem is," he laughed at his banged-up self. "Is the mess I am in right now, plus she lives clear over in Springville and we are on the edge of Santaquin which is nearly 30 miles away. How in the world am I going get there especially like this?" EJ said as he looked down at himself thinking. "Time to patch me up I think, she would say and 'stop a groan and start moving.' He said smiling as he thought of her loving face and great big hug she would give him providing he could reach her at all.

"Well let's see, the first thing I need to do." EJ winced with pain as he turned his head. "Is too sees about these wounds. These clothes are soaking wet and stained in dried blood. And try to dry these clothes. Its good thing I learned little first aid to because." Lifting the edges of his shirt he could see bloodstains where his shirt was sticking to his skin. "Better find some kind of clean bandages too." Trying not too grimaces with pain as he dropped the shirttail.

EJ decided it was best not to look at the rest of the wounds until finding a way to patch them up first and afraid he might have only enough strength to do it this one time with none too spare and afraid to ask for help would raise too many questions as he remembers past events with the authorities. Did not turn out so well the last time; seeing the note he made for his brother an afterthought came to his mind.

Eric Shepherd

* * *

Dear brother:

PS.

If you wouldn't mind; Please stock the tree house with extra supplies like bandages would be nice, can goods and dry matches. You never know when you might be needing them. Thanks again.

EJ.

* * *

EJ slowly got up and put out the fire he made and made sure he had enough stock to make a new one when he got back. After all, he figured he was going be here for at least a couple of days to recover before he was well enough to travel. Never knowing who might show up, it's best to clean up as if you were never here. EJ placed the note he made for his brother back into the box, he covered it back up. Then folded up his little knapsack with all its items and slipped it back into his shirt for safekeeping, with EJ's eyes on the road and crutch in his hand, he began once more down the road towards where the source of this strange tugging was. The difference being he had the desire to survive rather than escaping from his captures as they were now in the distance.

Not far down the road, EJ could see some wash being hung out to dry. The only problem was EJ believed in not stealing anything without paying for it first. The problem was he had no money and he was in no shape to earn it. And he was not about to go up to the house say. "Hi ma'am, I noticed your nice clean white sheets, may I take one and tear it up for bandages?" He had a feeling that might not go over so well.

EJ decided the best thing to do is to write her an IOU, that way she could collect from him later what was due at a later time and they both get what they want. Thinking he might have heard about it in one of the ads in the stores once "buy now pay later," something like that. Right now he needed those bandages more than she needed those sheets he figured.

What's Behind the Looking Glass?

Going round the old barn he wrote the note for the IOU writing the address and phone number was a little harder because he didn't want to use his home address. After some thought, thinking his grandmother's address might be best; considering that's where he was headed. Nodding his head in agreement and quickly wrote it down. Checking to make sure nobody was around which was good. Since he was doing this in broad daylight, and he did not want to get caught.

EJ hobbled up the best he could and got ready to take down one of the dry white sheets, as he was undoing the second clothespin. EJ stopped and noticed, seeing a shape bending down humming to herself. He stopped, frozen in his tracks. Knowing it was too late to go back. Stoops down just in time when she turned her head, seeing nothing continues on with her work as before.

This gave EJ an idea, by copying her every movement. He carefully unfastened the clothespins and re-hangs them with the bottom of the sheet from the other side. Leaving what appeared that all sheets are still left hanging. While he dropped the sheet he planned to take for bandages on the ground. Then leaving the note hung on the line next to the sheet. He carefully picked up the sheet, wads it up and placed it under his arm and stopped and waited for her to stoop down and quick as he could, hobbled back behind the barn. Hoping she never saw him.

He felt strange the moment he got far enough that he needed to turn back, but the feeling soon faded. The man called Death aka Derrick cursed wanting to scream "you idiot go back," but he had already interfered too much already and **Counsel Of Light** were already breathing down on his neck for what he had done. Yet nothing said he couldn't work a little harder convincing these people to go after the boy as he smiled waving his hand causing a breeze to stir just enough towards the woman to turn and look at the boy making off with her sheet.

On his way back to the tree house he realized he still was going to need some food. Thank goodness it was harvest time in the area or he would be in trouble, thinking *"fish for supper would be nice change tonight from the nearby creek."* And picked a couple more apples along the way and stuffed them in his already bulging shirt. "You know Mr. Scarecrow," he said hobbling down the road. "Your clothes ain't half bad when comes to needing room to put things, but they sure do stink," as he puts his nose to the sleeve, "PEWU! You stink," he said.

After he arrived back at the tree house the sun was high in the sky, somewhere around noon he was guessing. The morning chill was still in the air so was the overcast skies. EJ laid down his loot for the day by the tree. "Well, if we are going to be here a while to mend up a bit, we better set up camp." He said after having spent a lot of time out here camping or running away, it always looked the same. A hobo's camp they would find.

His and Danny tree house had a long rope to hang the wash on, even room to hang a fish or two. A number ten can to cook or boil water in or make a pot of squirrel or rabbit stew and a spare one if he needed two. After spending an hour setting up his little tiny camp, he made a pit for cooking and a fire by gathering wood from the entrance of the underpass and some water from the nearby creek. Dipping both his cans into the creek he filled them with the water then placed the two cans into the fire pit around hot coals to heat the water. "I think we need to make a paste for the wounds," he said not relishing the idea at all.

Knowing how to do it and doing it was going to be a whole different matter entirely. For he was only taught this at one time at Scout Camp, never in his life thought he actually be doing it. The paste he made was out of firewood ash and hot water and red clay; it was used to help seal the wounds according to the Scout Manual he once read and was taught.

The problem was he didn't have red clay so this was going have to do. EJ took some of the dirt from the ground. While the water was warming up, EJ brought over the white sheet and set it down beside him then leaned up against the tree for a little support, Taking out his pocketknife and began striping the white sheet into long strips, "RIP," thinking. *"If that poor lady could only see what he was doing to her nice clean white sheet she'd kill me."* RIP. Sticking his finger in the can to check the paste, making sure it was nice and thick. "I am really dreading this part," he said.

What's Behind the Looking Glass?

EJ looked down at himself not trusting the paste. He puts a little on his finger and placed it on a small cut on his hand. He winced at the pain, "ok, ok it stings a little." He said getting mad at himself for being such a big baby. Decided if he does it real fast like ripping off a bandaged maybe he could do it. Another thought popped into his head. *"What if it really does hurt a lot more than this and I yell really loud, will somebody hear me?"* Not willing to take the chance either way and wondered if he should get just a little further away just in case.

He decided to go down by the creek after all the clothes did need a good washing. They did smell pretty bad as he put his nose close to them. "I don't think Mr. Scarecrow has ever had a bath in his life," he said crinkling his nose. "I hope he doesn't scare all fish away either because I am hungry." After he banked the fire to very low burn so it wouldn't go anywhere and go out until he returned. EJ gathered his newly made bandages and paste and hobbled down to the creek.

Arriving at the creek he could see where he and Danny had built a little dam to hold back the water just for them. It was their private swimming hole, where they would spend hot summer days swimming and fishing together, thinking about how he wished Danny was here right now. Thinking this he remembered the pain, the torment they lived in and how he must survive if was going to make a difference for Danny not just for himself. With that thought in mind, he knew what he needed to do. "I must fight through the pain and get to my destination to find help for me and Danny," he said. EJ set down his roll of bandages, paste and with his crutch in his hand, he eased himself to the ground.

Undoing the overalls was painful as they went over his legs and his feet. The marks on his legs were horrific say the least. His right leg was swollen where the belt struck and there was a small piece of glass still embedded in some of the cuts that he could see. Other then that, they were both badly bruised with large gashes in his legs and the side of his left hip. EJ decided to deal with one problem at a time.

EJ finds a good clean sturdy stick, stripped off the bark. EJ then grabbed the Swiss Pocketknife and opened the pliers. Taking a deep breath removes the overalls sets them to the side of him as he sits down near the waters edge. He then took the pliers and plucks the glass right out of his leg. Biting down hard as he could on the stick as he screamed between his teeth, breathing hard due too the pain. Blood poured out of the wound where he pulled the glass from out of his leg.

EJ began to stick his leg into the water to wash the wound, again biting down hard on the wood as he screamed between his teeth. The cool water numbed the wound. He pulled his leg out of the water to check the wound. The pain was agonizing but he knew he wasn't even close to being done.

EJ daring only too rests for a minute; just long enough to gather strength and courage with sure will power. He reached once more for the stick and again placed it into his mouth. EJ began to unbutton the left cuff of his shirt first then the right, biting hard as he lifted the corner of the shirt, slowly he peeled it away from his skin. He screamed between his teeth, feeling the skin tearing, ripping from his side. Afraid to look that he might stop, he squeezed his eyes tightly shut and bit harder on the stick while he screamed. Be sides the agonizing pain. He could feel a warm sensation going down his left side. Not sure if it is was the blood or sweat or both at this point. His left arm free, but the shirt is still stuck on his back. Thinking there's got to be an easier way than this.

Opening his eyes he looked down on his left side, he noticed it is puffy and swollen and there is fresh blood from the huge gash of torn skin. "Looks like I might possibly have cracked my ribs when I fell, no wonder it hurts like hell when I move. Glad I don't have a mirror, I would have been a fright to see. I don't think I'm ready for the paste yet or the water. Just in case there might be some glass still inside," he said as he looked at the bloodstains on the right side of his shirt.

EJ's body shook with pain, it hurt like hell. Thinking if his right side hurt like this he can't image what his left side is going feel like, not too mention the large cuts on his back? But for some reason, the pain was dulled or he would have been screaming and unable to move at all. For now, he couldn't think of the reason as if from the corner of his eye he noticed a strange mark on his left shoulder, but when he looked directly at it was gone. *"Strange? As if was just a dream."*

EJ grabbed the stick still breathing hard from the last one. "Can't do it, my left side hurts too much to bring it over; I needed some help to remove the other side. I need to get this shirt off me." He said as the sweat of pain ran down his face.

He looked around for any ideas or solutions. "No other choice, we have to get into the water," EJ said thinking the water would help loosen the rest of the shirt and numb the pain as well as help cool down the fever from his wounds, he wasn't sure how high it was and didn't think twice about it because of the pain and it was starting to be another hot day. Yet the water could help him enough so he could remove the shirt to put the bandages on once he gets out of the water and worry about the fever later realizing he should have gone straight to Mr. Stringum at his store, but the thing was this place was closer.

He could tend his wounds now then make his way back if he had too and perhaps talk him into taking him to his grandmother, considering he had said he was close friends with her and his grandfather. Besides, it wasn't the first time he had to patch him up after a beating from his parents he was the closest thing he had to a father. Making sure he had a warm place to sleep, and food in his belly, and warm clothing when he needed it. EJ put the stick into his mouth grabbed the crutch to help him pull himself up. The pain in his legs felt like they were on fire, as he bit down on the stick, dizzy as his head pounded.

EJ tightened his fists and bites harder while he planted both feet into the water. "Oh that's cold," the pain searing his legs. EJ started biting harder on the stick between his teeth, as he waded in closer toward the dam. The water deepened and slowly it was up to his waist, the shirt slowly rose to help him to remove it just like he had planned.

EJ bit harder as he waded deeper into the water as it reached his chest he screamed. The pain was so bad he lost his footing. The stick rippled back to the shore with the lapping water. EJ went under the water. The pain was unbearable, but he tried to swim anyway. The dam broke as the swift current grabbed hold of him, holding him under the water. EJ tried to surface while he tried to swim at the same time he took a long gasping breath. The pain and the loss of blood had weakened him severely. EJ went under this time losing cautiousness. When two arms grabbed him turned him over and pulled him to shore.

Chapter 3-2

* * *

A father and two of his two boys, Robert and Will stood on the shore. "Pa that was close," Will said.

Pa looked down at the boy on the ground, shaking his head as he looked at his boys Robert and Will.

Wayne Downing always had a gentle side to him, but you would not know it unless you met him and looked into his bright blue eyes. Soft brown hair with a tan complexion from working on a farm and the fields as he provided for his family with traded goods hand made wooden furniture and crops from the fields. Taller than any average man standing seven feet ten inches, built like an oak tree and had arms of a bodybuilder. His face chiseled by arc angel Michel himself, his wife Martha quoted to him on occasion or two. A farmer and woodcrafts man by trade. Gentle as they come, but had a stubborn streak true to any mule alive.

He was the type of man that would go out of his way to help a neighbor in trouble and not ask for anything in return. An honest loving man and father of five children three boys and two girls, who he loves more than the earth itself. Wayne strongly believed in honesty and hard discipline, not in the use of anger or words, but in deeds to fit the punishment and well-placed handshake when taking someone's word or a promise when striking a deal.

"What on earth do you think he was thinking? It was a good thing for him we were following after our mothers flaming sheets." Robert said, Pa still shaking his head at the boy on the ground at his feet.

Robert is the type of guy that takes life seriously when comes to making a hard decision. He has always looked up to his father and knows without a doubt he can talk about anything with him without feeling embarrassed regarding any subject. He too like his sister Julie was very mature for his age of a fourteen-year-old teenager. But he feels that time has slowed down as he watched other kids his age go out and do things that neither his Pa nor his Ma would approve of while he could just grow up to be an adult today instead of waiting. Which was fine sometimes any away because he had plenty to do right here helping his Pa take care of the farm and helped him with his brother Will with his Pa's woodworking. If it was one thing he learned it was responsibly and be responsible for your action or suffers the consequences.

Robert resembles his father regarding his broad shoulders and hair color of soft brown hair and blue eyes or should he say one blue eye and one green eye depending on the light. He stood tall at an average height of five feet six inches. Lengthy and sprite when he moved and considered doing nothing more than being with or playing, or teasing his two brothers Will and Sam. Yet some times he did not agree on things regarding his sisters Julie and Anna, but no matter how hard they made him blush or teased him. He loved them and held them in high regard when asking for advice.

Will went over to the pile of white on the bank of the creek. "Well Pa I think we found those sheets," he said with a chuckle. "But they are not what I would call sheets anymore," he said bringing them over to his Pa.

Will was 13 just a year or two older than EJ. Still very much a kid at heart getting in trouble whenever he could, but he was not considered a bad kid wanting attention. Yet it was true he acted out more for the fun than question the consequences. To say he was a handful at times would be stating the true nature of his fun-loving self. He too took life seriously like his brother Robert, just not as serious as he would have liked. He preferred to play in the sun and fish and swim in the pound here near the house more often than he did his chores and has been grounded more times than he can count.

Will was still waiting for his growth to kick in like his brother. Not just because his brother Robert and his friends at school tease him about enough. He tried to stand tall a four-feet eight inches, to his size six feet, unlike his bothers size nines. It was true he'd never be a basketball star or make the team playing football, but there was always track. After all, he has to outrun his sisters from time to time.

What's Behind the Looking Glass?

Will liked to wear his hair long just barely over his ears and enough to keep it out of his deep blue eyes like his mother. He was proud of his lengthy stride and his high cheekbones like his Ma. He always had a smile for girl whenever they would wave to him in the hallway or the classroom as he watched his brother roll his eyes often because girls liked him more than him so it seemed. He was known as the jokester, yet he could be the sweetest guy around when he chose to.

Pa taking one of the corners of the sheets and examined it then looked down at the boy on the ground then turned his head towards his boys Robert and Will and rubbed his chin. "Boys we have work to do. This boy is hurt bad and Ma would kill us we don't get him home so she can stitch him up."

Will and Robert saying at the same time. "And fuss over." Which was true, their Ma was the type of mother that hovered over them at the slights cut, or smallest fever or cough, but that only made them love her more.

"Now boys!" Pa said staying serious as he gazed at the boy in front of him, Pa thinking fast. "Boys this no time too wrap him or clean him up, he's hurt too bad and full of a small piece of glass by the looks of it. Grab those logs. We will make a stretcher you Will, go to the wagon and get the horse blanket and the quilt from under the seat," Pa said taking charge.

"Pa have you ever seen such a sight? This boy is cover from head toe with lashes and bruises and such like he has been through a meat grinder." Robert said shaking the water out of his hair and ears and ringing out his shirt and jeans then adding them to brother Wills as he was lacing up shoes.

"Only once in my life Robert, "Pa said with a tear in his eye. Back in the war, you would not believe what men can do too other men when anger rises. I shudder to think about what has happened to this poor little boy."

Robert watched his Pa finish the stretcher and stares down towards the unconscious boy at his feet. "Pa?" Robert asked.

"Yes, Robert?" As he tied the last rope on the log.

"Did you hear anything just a few minutes before we got here? I could have sworn I might have heard him scream."

Pa turned. "I know son. I believe it was the scream of courage." He said, as he looked down into the water lays the stick with teeth marks on it. Pa hands it to him; Robert could see where EJ had bit clearly by the marks indent in it.

Robert lifted it in his hand; about to throw it back into the water, his father stopped him. "Son, don't! That stick is his and it belongs to him. Nobody has the right to take it or discard it. He has earned it this day, someday son you to will understand." He said as he takes the sticks and lay's it next to EJ's unconscious body. Will returned back from the wagon with the horse blank and quilt. "Ok boys let's lift him on to the stretcher 1, 2, 3, heave."

"Oh my, look at his back," Will said as they turned him over on his side. Will grimacing "ouch."

"Come on Will, no time for that now. Ok put the quilt over him and give me some of those bandages for a pillow," Pa said as he covered the boy.

"Pa, why didn't we just bandage him here?" Will asked.

"You know your Ma; she'd skin us all alive if we try to do it ourselves. She'll go over him with a fine toothcomb and then some and more before and after the Doc looks at him. No son… trust me… its better this way. Someday, when you get a wife of your own, you'll understand; never cross them, just nod." He said as they laughed.

Pa turned to the boys. "We need to clear the camp for the boy's sake. Robert, you and Will think you can manage to back the wagon back down here closer to the creek? I don't want to carry him further than we have to. While you are doing that I'll gather the rest of his things here by the creek and break down his camp. We don't need anything blowing way and ruining anything for him until we hear his side of the story."

What's Behind the Looking Glass?

The boys walked back to the wagon talking about the boy. "Robert, have you ever seen this kid before?" Will asked.

"Not sure, I think I might have once or twice. He might even have a brother. They come down here sometimes to play in the old tree house. I don't even know his name or where he might live?"

"Robert, why do you think he looks like he's been through a war?"

Robert not answering Wills question. "We need to get this wagon back to the creek before Pa thinks we got lost. So if you can guide me it would help? The sooner we get this done the sooner we will have answers, besides I'm getting hungry," Robert said.

The boys backed the wagon to the creek just like their Pa asked. "Ok boys; let's get him into the back. It will be suppertime soon and Ma will be getting worried," Pa said.

"This time she'll have more to worry about than loosening a sheet or two," Robert said.

Pa joined the boy in the back of the wagon. He watched the sleeping boy rubbing his chin. "How true that is boys, how true that is."

Pa turned to Robert. "Be careful of the rocks we don't need him bouncing around like crazy back here either. He's been through enough I think." Pa feeling the boys head, not sure what all the damage was. "He has a fever, I can tell by the sweat on his forehead and arms. We need to hurry and put this kid to bed." He said with concern on his face and voice.

Pulling a handkerchief from his back pocket he wiped the boys head, removing beads of sweat. Pa looked up sees the house sighs with relief. "Will quickly, get your Ma and then find your brother Sam. Robert, help me with the boy we need to get him into the house quickly," Pa said with urgency. The man called Death breathes a sigh of relief as he stands nearby watching says. "I have done all I can, for now, go my son and may the stars and the heavens watch over you here." He vanishes after saying a few words placing some protection over the house to hide the boy from Morgan and his spies knowing, if they find him they will do everything in their power to take him preventing him from stopping him and the darkness that is covering their lands. If that happens everything they have done will be for not and the world like this one and beyond will cease to exist.

The farmhouse wasn't far as the boys made their way home. It was a large homemade of old logs cut from large trees. From the front, you could see three large windows. One from the kitchen, one from the bedroom their parents slept in and a third large window was where the large family room was looking over the farm itself. Just up above the farm was a large red barn where they kept the animals like pigs, and horses when the weather is bad. Plus the large work wagon and the family pickup. Plus it was where Pa and the boys worked on building wood future to sell in the stores as part of the farm's income.

The farm sat on nearly 160 or so acres with wheat, corn and hay fields and plenty of room for their three horses. The rest was apple and cherry orchards. Very few houses were nearby enough to be called neighbors. Santaquin was more of a farming community then actually town like Provo, Springville or even Spanish-Fork. The further south or west you went you found smaller towns just like this one. Some as old and forgotten copper mines and coal mines; finding more fruit orchards and fields like this one.

People spoke broken English like words you would here from time to time. Backwoods was known as hillbillies or such. Yet more so here than in the other towns unless you were born and raised here known to some as the down south or southern area of Utah. Nothing much happened other then people knowing everyone's business or get excited over the little things like the man with the largest pumpkin. Or some rich dude came through in a limo and pulled up at the local restaurant known as the Family Tree where they sever these homemade scones that were so big your eyes popped out of your head.

The town itself had a doctors office, a hardware store known as Stringum hardware and goods, a small drugstore and one bank. The county office was nothing more than two large houses connected together with another house as its city library. Across the street was a small post office in the red brick building where most of the people picked up their mail; since they didn't have mailmen delivering curbside delivery. We had one big school which was known as Santaquin Elementary. And were the process of building a new one about half a mile up the street. All the kids that were grade 6 through 8 were bussed to Payson Jr. and High school for grades 9 and 12. Payson was the closet thing to a much larger town compared to Santaquin and the four or five smaller towns further south and west.

Once the boys and Pa reached their little farm, Will ran into the house yelling. "Ma, Ma come quick! Pa needs you out front by the wagon." Ma dropped her bread on the table, making a mad dash for the front door seeing her husband and Robert carrying a small boy on a homemade stretcher.

Will looked up and smiled. "We found your sheets too," he said.

Ma looked at both of them, "sheets, this no time for sheets. Wayne; quick, quick get him inside," Ma yelled at the top her lungs. "Julie! Where is that girl?" She said. Martha a loving wife and mother of five children and a husband, some would say she was very beautiful with her long brown hair tied into a nice neat bun. Her deep blue eyes and her soft cheekbones which seemed to make you smile and feel safe in her arms. She also had the voice of an angel whenever she sang to her children at night when they were younger or sick in bed.

It is true what they say regarding her status when came to things that need to be done around the house. She wore the pants in the family and her husband Wayne would not trade it for the world. Her cooking was one of the best to be found next to her husband if she allowed him in the kitchen at all or near her stove. Martha had a heart of gold when came to her children needs, but she always expected more from them when it came to discipline. She always helped them choose what was the right thing to do and never encourage bad behavior or tolerated fighting.

She was a stay at home mom by all counts that are important, to be there when her children needed her. Plus she always had her husband Wayne closes by if she needed him. Martha has always lied heavily on her gut instincts when comes down to strange occurrences or making hard decisions, regarding family matters. You also learn to never cross her when she wants something done bad enough to expect it to be done come hell or high water.

"Here I am," Julie replied. Coming in from the barn after doing her chores.

Julie was the oldest of the five children at the young age of nineteen and took after her mother with the same hair coloring, but wore her hair down slightly below shoulders and put flowers in her hair. Julie had deep blue eyes like her mother and her brothers except for Anna and Sam the youngest of her three brothers. She had a small petit frame and was considered very mature and pretty for her age.

She loved all her brothers and her sister Anna, considered them her best friends. She was a tomboy at heart and loved to tease and wrestle with them on the floor or in the dirt. Had done so often enough when they and she were younger while other girls went to parties or played with their dolls. She'd rather stay home and spend time with her family. More so since she graduated from Payson High School two years ago and never looked back while her friends went on to college. Family was her most important goal.

Her Ma turned her head said. "Good. I need you to go and turn down Wills bed, we will put him in there, and it's the closest. Will, do you mind sharing a room with one of your brothers tonight?" She asked as she looks at the boy lying on the stretcher.

"No Ma. That will be ok with me." He said knowing when it's best not to argue with his mother.

"Wayne; you and I are going to talk, but right now we have work to do. Now set him gently, set him on the floor," Ma said taking charge.

What's Behind the Looking Glass?

"Don't you think we should put him to bed first?" Pa asked.

"What; in that?" Ma said as she pointed to his bloody clothes or what's left of them. "Not without least a quick bath. Set him... Set him down, boys." Ma said as she turned to Julie. "Julie I want you to go in the kitchen start heating some water, not to hot mind you, I don't want to burn him. Will, go down the hall and grabs some towels and I think a lot, not a few washcloths," she replied as she shook her head. Ma said closing the door which Wayne was heading for. Ma stepped in front of the door, "And where do you think you're going Mr.?" She asked.

Wayne swallowed hard. "Just checking to see if they needed any help," he said.

"Help you say? Why there's plenty to do right here." Ma said as she pointed at the boy on the floor. "That I can see. You are hiding something aren't you?" Ma asked and Pa looked down at boy lying on the floor. "I have eyes, I can see he has a fever and a bad one at that. You are afraid what I am going find underneath that blanket aren't ya Wayne? That's why you don't want me to see? Well after raising three boys and two girls and a husband. I have seen it all. Nothing you or in this world is going scare me... and clearly, this boy needs my help. So let's get to it. For he is not going get into my clean bed until I clean him up. Is that clear Mr.?"

Wayne also knew better than to argue with his wife. "Martha just don't say I didn't warn ya," then letting her pull back the quilt. She could have never prepared herself enough for what she was about to see. Ma dropped the quilt and gasped, puts her hand over her mouth and uses the other to steady her balance against the wall.

Wayne quickly steadies her in his arms; she turned to Wayne, with tears streaming down her face. "This poor boy, he is hurt so bad. How can anyone or any....?" She could not finish her sentence. Quietly almost whispering; "tell Julie to bring lots of clean bandages, and my sewing kit. Bring it here when the water is ready. Then call the Doc and bring him here if you have to and have Robert bring some soap and more towels and the extra cot and a chair dear if you wouldn't mind. It's going to be a long night." She said as she sat on the bed and looked at the boy on the floor and Wayne gently closed the door.

The little boy EJ groaned on the floor underneath the quilts, due to the pain and delirious with fever. He laid and remained unconscious. The mother in the in the room knelt down beside the boy, with tears in her eyes and a quiver in her voice. "Its ok son, go back to sleep." In her heart, she whispered a soft payer. "Please stay asleep my child you are going to need all your strength," as she smoothed his small face with her hand.

Pa; raced into the kitchen. "Where's Julie? How's the water coming?" He asked.

Julie stuck her finger in the water to test it. "I was just about to take it down to her; do think that's it's going to be enough?" She asked.

"I would say yes, but knowing your Ma, I would start some more and keep it coming," he said.

Sam walked in the door. "There you are!" Julie replied.

"I saw Will on the run, tried to ask what was going on, but said I shooould seee you first," Sam said as he looked at the all the pots of water on the stove, with a puzzled look on his face.

Sam was the youngest of the five children age six and a half. He has the most adorable puppy dog brown eyes. That would make you melt when you look at him. It was true he was short for his age at three feet and two inches. He had a tendency of jumbling his words when he got upset or nervous and it worse around strangers. His thick brown hair would curl at the ends when it needs to be cut or comb, and still had his cute baby face where his strong jawline was just shaping like his Pa's and his brothers.

His favorite thing to do was to play in the dirt or wrestle with his brothers and sisters. Sam like most boys his age hated bath time and would run until caught. But once he was in the tub. He would play with his little sailboats while his brothers or sisters would bathe

What's Behind the Looking Glass?

him. If he had a favorite chore on the farm it would be feeding the chickens and the horses. The pigs always seemed to be too smelly for his taste, but he could see the advantages of playing in the cool mud as he dug his toes into the dirt.

"Well don't just stand there, grab a bucket, I can't carry all this water without spilling it all over the place, Sam?" Julie said.

"Where's your sister Anna?" Pa asked.

"She was right behind me Pa," Sam said.

"Here I am," Anna replies with a wave as she entered the kitchen with a basket of eggs from the chickens.

Anna to was a tomboy at heart and could feel comfortable wearing jeans rather than a nice farmer dress like her sister Julie and her mother. She was considered short for her age at five feet "two, but that didn't stop her from beating her brothers when came to wrestling. Her eyes were a soft chocolate brown which went well with her light brown hair that when the morning sun shined on it turn golden honey.

Anna was known for her stubborn streak that matched her mothers. Some times she worries that her family hid things from her because she does not act as mature as her sister Julie. Thinking they need to always have to handle her with kid gloves. If only they could see her who she really is, not a little girl anymore but a young woman. Perhaps after she graduates from High School this coming year, things will change for her as they did for her sister. There is nothing more she loves than having her bothers around her all the time and being with her sister and mother. She hopes when she grows up she can make them proud of her.

"Good, go find your mother's sewing basket the one she uses for First Aid."

Anna, Sam's eyes open wide "Who's hurt? Is Ma ok?" They asked.

"No, everything's fine… well not exactly, now stop dawdling, we; have work to do, so mind your sister. After that you are going have to help her with dinner, your Ma going to be busy for a while." Pa said picking up a cot from the closet headed back to the room.

Sam and Julie bring a bucket and Anna with First Aid kit; they headed for Wills room where we find Will and Robert who had changed into some dry clothes, helping Pa placing a cot in a nearby corner of the room and a big chair for Ma to watch over the boy. Ma turned around seeing the crowded room. "Ok, everyone out except for Pa and Will. The rest of you go down and help with dinner. Pa did you call the Doc?" She asked.

Chapter 3-3

"Oh, the Doc!" Pa replied.

"Never mind, I need you here." Ma said, trying to remain her motherly calm self. "Robert, will you go down to the kitchen and call the Doc, please? Tell him we need him here straight away, if he gives you any flak at all. Tell him that Pa, if need be, will drag him by the coat tails himself if he needs to get him here. Now I got work to do." She said as they were leaving and about to close the door. "Thank you, dear sweet children, I would not know what I would do if anything would have happened to any of you. Julie if wouldn't mind dear please put some more water on and a strong hot cup tea would be nice thanks, dear."

Julie closed the door wept silently as she went down to the kitchen for the boy she didn't even know. Who has already touched her deeply in her heart? She wiped her eyes on her apron and put on the water and remembered to put the tea on for her mother, checked on the food for dinner.

Robert picked up the phone and dialed for the doctor, the only doctor here in Santaquin and who still made house calls only to be told by he was out doing what he does best helping someone in need and was told to call him there if someone needed him. "Hello Doctor Hatfield this Robert Downing, yes ...Wayne Downing son, that's right. We need you to come out to the farm if you can, right away... No, the family's fine. Why? Hard to explain really. It's; easier if just come and see for yourself.... It's a boy, he's been hurt. No, we don't know who he is? Buts it's bad, really bad. Ma says if you don't come, Pa will come get ya drag you by your coat tails and you know she'll have him do it sure as shootin. Ok, I'll tell her the best you can do is first thing in the morning. She won't like it, but I'll tell her. Thanks, Doc." Robert said hanging up the phone.

"Julie?" Robert asked.

"Yes, Robert?"

"Needs some help with that?" He asked

"Thanks, Robert."

"Robert?" Julie asked.

"Humm?" Robert replies as he looked towards the hall and his mind on the hurt boy.

"Tell me about the boy, how bad is it? I overheard you talking to Doc Hatfield and the way Ma was acting it must be pretty bad," she said asking him.

Robert put his arm around his sister. "Pa said he has seen something like it in a war once. But he never talks much about it or what happened when he severed. I hope the boy is ok; he looks like a nice kid."

"Well, Ma will need this tea and the water, mind helping with it?" She asked him.

"What are brothers for?" Robert said picking up the bucket of water.

Pulling back the quilt, Ma takes another look at the boy. She tries to hold back the tears shaking her head. "There is no easy way to do this is there? The only thing I'm glad for, that is. At least he is asleep and not aware what's going on, least for the moment, we can take some small comfort in that and we need to keep him that way for now. Wayne can you bring me something that will help keep the boy asleep, we don't need him waking up and finding strangers trying to help him." she said and he nodded and quickly did what she asked.

Ma knelt down beside the boy on the floor while other two watched with loving care as she helped the boy sip small sips of water that contained the sedative that she had grounded up and mixed so he wouldn't wake, he was have out of it, calling for his grandmother she pretended that she was the one caring for him as he took small little sips choking down the water.

Then once the sedative started to work she went back to her work, cursing silently to whoever did this to him. The question wasn't how he got most of the injuries. The question was why, and how the glass came into play the other wounds were obvious seeing the long thin strips of a leather belt that could be seen. They watched her work with such a mothers love washing a newborn baby; cleaning and washes his poor bruised little body.

With EJ stirring, moaning due to the pain and fever now and again, she softly whispered. "SHHH now, SHH now. Its ok son, sleep. Just sleep." With delicate care and fine seamstress eye with needle and thread. She removed the shards of glass that still remained in his torn flesh of his body. And then cleaned the wounds with loving care then stitched them up with a surgeon's skill the best she could. Will watched his mother work and had gained a new respect for her that day as he sat and watched with his father the sweet tender mercy of angelic care, for a small boy she never knew. "Will?" She asked.

"Yes, Ma?"

"Would you mind getting some more water and tell your sister, Julie, I am ready for that tea. I need to take a break for a minute. I am afraid the works only half done." She said feeling just a little tired. "And I haven't even seen his back yet. While you are out, can you find him a clean pair of shorts? I believe yours should be the right size, but they might be just a little small, just until Pa can get into town and buy me a few things? Thanks, dear," she said as she sighed tiredly.

Ma covered the boy carefully with the quilt and sat back in the chair. "Pa I need you to go to the closet, and bring me a couple more sheets and couple more quilts and another pillow for his head," she asked. Pa not daring to ask why she needed more sheets, "I believe I am going need more bandages and then find Robert and Julie for me. Then I need you to go headed without me have something to eat with the children. Anna and Sam can clear things away; by then

I will need you and Will to help me finish and put this poor boy to bed." Ma said as she wiped the soft tears with the back of her hand.

"What about you dear? You haven't had anything to eat yet? I am sure you are tired."

"I am fine. I'll have something after he's in bed and fast asleep when the Doc gets here," she said.

"Martha, didn't Robert tell you? He can't make it until morning, buts he is coming," Pa said.

Martha frowned and mumbled to herself. "Go on, I can't do anymore without fresh water and bandages."

Pa leaned down near to his wife kissed her gently on the forehead. "Do you know how much I love you?" He whispered. "The sky could not contain the sun which could not shine bright enough to show it when I watch you care for someone else boy. This is just one of the reasons why I love you as I do." He said and then he gives her another kiss and closed the door behind him.

Martha not turning wiped the tears from her eyes whispered. "And I love you to my dear, sweet man." EJ moans not aware what's going on around him; He tried to open his eyes. Ma leaned down carefully lifted up his head and puts it in her lap and whispered softly. "You are safe my little one." Wiped the sweat from his head and cheeks then stroking his brown mossy hair and gently rocks him back to sleep.

Pa; down in the kitchen with his family at the kitchen table, tries to bring back some order back to the farm with his family at the table. While Ma was down hall caring for the small boy, Pa decides to have a small family meeting during dinner. "Ok then," as Pa clears his throat. "As you all know by now. Ma is busy in Will's room with the boy and he is badly hurt."

Julie asked before he can say another word. "Yes Pa we know this, however, Anna and I would like to know… you might say, have more details on this subject. All we get are vague answers because

What's Behind the Looking Glass?

everyone's in such a hurry." She said as she passed down the rolls and butter.

"As I was saying Julie," Pa said taking a roll and buttered it. "It is time everyone was on the same page as it were before I was interrupted."

"Why didn't you just say so Pa?" Julie said with a smile as she tossed her long brown hair back and bats her big blue eyes around the table as everyone smiles back at her.

"Sorry darling, I'll try harder next time, as you already know. Ma sent us looking for her missing sheet and thought she saw the boy hobbling down the street and thought we should go after him. Afraid he might be hurt or in trouble." He said as he passed down the summer peas.

"You all know how your Ma is about things like this, well anyway she told us not to startle him. Just see what he wanted with her sheets and if he was going to be all right, after all, it's just a sheet. I asked her about that she just looked at me and said 'I have an odd feeling about him.' Taking a bite of chicken, Pa sets it back down on his plate. "Now I have known your Ma for a long time, not to question her, besides she'd pester me tell I did it anyway," he said. The children trying not to giggle knowing how true that was when it came to their mother. "So me and the boys loaded the wagon and followed the boy's trail. On our approach, Will and Robert thought we might have heard a scream down by the creek. Not sure we hurried a little faster; up ahead not far we found the boy in the creek."

"Pa?" Sam asked with his mouth full.

"Yes, Sam?"

"What was he doing in the creek?" Sam asked still chewing with his mouth full.

"What we could tell, trying to clean the wounds he had himself," Pa said taking another bite and wiped his chin with his napkin.

Anna said. "That's why he wanted the sheet to make bandages silly."

"A hum," Pa said as he cleared his throat. "When we reached the creek the dam broke and the boy slipped and fell into the water. The currents were too strong for him in his current state. Seeing this Will and Robert went in after him and brought him to shore. All we know is he has been beaten up pretty bad and I don't think it was from the creek mostly. I think he is in trouble and needs our help. So that's what we are going to do, any questions?" He asked as glanced at each of his children at the table.

"Yes, Pa?" Julie said.

"What's your question, Julie?"

"Do you know who he is or where he came from?" She asked scooping up some peas with her spoon.

"At this moment, no, but I assume he might live close by. Where? I don't have a clue. That is why after everything is settled and the boy is in bed and after the Doc has seen him. Will, Robert and I are going into town and do some looking around to see if anybody is looking for a missing boy. Until then nobody is to say a word regarding him. I have feeling that if he wanted to be found he would have chosen to be, got it?" He asked.

"Yes Pa," all kids answered.

"Now then, let's finish supper and get our chores done, Sam," Pa asked.

"Yes, Pa?"

"Will's going to be sleeping in your room for a while if you don't mind," he said.

"Sure, Pa."

"Robert?" Pa asked.

What's Behind the Looking Glass?

"Yes, Pa?"

"Ma says for you to bring by a change of clothing for the boy, you are about his size, but I have a feeling he not going to be needing it for a while and might need something bigger after she gets done bandaging him," Pa said with a smile crossing his face.

"Ya, when Ma done fusing over him, he may think he is mummy; better take the mirror out the room so it doesn't frighten him," Robert replied and Will slaps him on the back in agreement.

"Ok Boys," Pa replies trying to keep things under control. "Julie before you put up supper, fix your mother a plate and I'll take into her… thanks, dear. Will; I believe she ready for us to get back. Mind bringing in the water and I'll bring the sheets?" He said. Pa and Will opened the door where Ma and little EJ was still on the floor resting his head in her lap. "How's he doing?" Pa asked.

"He opened his eyes for a minute, but I rocked him back to sleep. He has a really bad fever and the wounds are only half cleaned. I need some help cleaning the rest of him boys and get him off this floor into that bed." Ma removed the quilt below the boy's waist Ma looked at the boy's sides sees the large gashes of torn flesh and feels his ribs.

Ma looked at Will and Pa as she turned her head. "I am no Doctor, but I say their cracked and at least two maybe three. We are going have to cut these off to remove them. His legs are too swollen and I don't think we'll not be able to put on another pair seeing how far the wound goes down his side of his hip. Will, can you hand me my scissors please," as she asked for help.

Will hands her the scissors and looked down to where she about to cut. "Oh Ma, I don't think we should?" He said.

"Shouldn't do what dear?" Ma asked not looking away from her work.

"You know," Will said almost turning red with a strong blush of his cheeks.

Ma turned around and looked into Will's eyes with a motherly calm. "You are old enough to know that there's nothing I haven't seen on you boys; after raising and washing you, all your lives, but if it bothers you that much. Just close your eyes. I promise I am not going to care and I'll be gentle and I won't stare. For me, there's nothing to see." She replied with loving care.

Ma carefully slipped the scissors down the side of the boy's leg and gently cuts them off avoiding the wound. The wound is deep. The gash is long and deep in his thigh. She could still see some more pieces of glass embed deep, "It's going to need stitches all along the side. I'll have to think of something else for britches," she said as she leans him up on little on his other side. As she carefully rolled him on his back then with a folded sheet places it over his waist. "Can you boys first help me? Let's remove and get rid of this filthy, bloody quilt," she said.

Will grabbed his legs and feet while Pa put his arms under the boy's arms. "Ok, lift him up 1, 2, and 3 heaves." EJ moaned, but being heavily sedated and with a fever stayed asleep. Ma pulled the old dirty and bloody bedding from underneath him and placed the clean sheet and blanket underneath with a better pillow for his head. "Ok set him down gently," she said all out of breath. Ma took a minute to catch her breath. "I will need some help to turn him over on his stomach," she said.

Chapter 4

Will, looked down at horse blanket and bloody quilt and rags now piled in the corner. "Ma, if you would like. I can take them out?" He asked.

"Its ok son, I need you here with me and your Pa. Can you please have Robert come in and have him remove these things? They're not worth washing or mending, the smell could scare fish a mile away. It might be a good idea just to burn them if you know what I mean?" Ma said turning to Pa. "Did he have any other clothing with him?" She asked.

"No dear, just these overalls and what remains of this shirt that we fished out of the creek," he said.

Not daring to hold them close to her nose, she instead put a hand to her nose and mouth in disgust. "You can burn those too, their not even fit for a burial, put them on the burn pile," Ma said. Ma leaned down towards the sleeping boy, covered him with another clean sheet then leaned back into the chair. "I think we all need a break." She said as she looked down at the sleeping boy. "Tell Julie to bring my tea and make it extra strong. Then come straight back dear."

Pa left the room seeing Robert helping Julie in the kitchen asked. "Where's Sam and Anna?"

"Helping with their chores, she figured that's the best way she could help at the moment," Julie said.

"You've got to hand to your sister she always thoughtful, never asking what needs to be done, she takes after you and your Ma you know."

"Thanks, Pa, you need something?" She asked putting the last of the dishes away.

"Ma's ready for her tea now."

"I know, and she wants it extra strong. I know Pa," she said.

"That's just what I mean, the spitting image. Robert, Ma needs you to take the old bedding and clothing out to the burn pile and burn it straight away."

"But her quilt?" Robert asked.

"Never mind that, I'll get her a new one, just do it!" Pa said.

"Yes, Pa."

Julie entered the room carrying the tea like she was asked. "Here's your tea Ma, I made it extra strong just the way you like it," Julie said as she looked down at the sleeping boy. "How's he's doing Ma?" She asked. "He looks really bad and very sick."

"I think he's going to make it. He's going to be here with us awhile I am afraid. The wounds are nasty and he has a bad fever, we're going have to watch him very closely," she said.

"Mind if I sit with you a while? I have more water heating on the stove for you and a plate of food when you are ready for it."

"Thanks, dear, I would love to have your company."

Robert walked in the door. "Pa says you wanted me to take the old bedding out behind the barn and burn it, is the right Ma?"

"Yes that's right son, after that I want you clean yourself up really good, we don't need you kids getting sick either. I think I'll have enough to do with watching after this poor boy than having to worry about all of you," she said.

"Ma, will help you with him," Julie replied.

"I know you will. In fact, I am counting on it."

Robert gathered the old bedding and clothing into an old

gunny sack as Julie visited with Ma as they watched the sleeping boy, "Ok I believe that's everything. Come on Julie? Ma's got work to do," he said.

"Julie, will you be a dear go and find Will and Pa?" Ma asked. "I need to finish and it is getting late."

Will and Pa entered the room as they sat down the fresh supplies of water and sheets Ma once more knelt bedside the boy then reached over and wiped the boy's forehead with a cool cloth and lightly brushes his mossy brown hair with her hand. Then without a pause leaned over and kissed his warm cheek.

As they watched, it brought a tear to Pa and Will's, eyes. Pa turned to Ma and put a hand on her shoulder trying to control his own tears from strolling down his cheek. Pa; turned to his son, "its ok son if you want to cry. Just let it out. It's too hard to just to hold it in son and is it not meant too as we look down upon the savior son." Pa said and they both embrace as the tears flowed down with love for each other and for their Ma's tender care.

Ma said with a chocked voice. "We still have work ahead of us and this poor boy is waiting on us." They removed the blanket as Ma settled into her work, gently washed and stitched the tares of his skin as she instructed them to tear up her good white sheets into long strips for bandages. "Ok boys let's turn him over so I can finish please, watch his head now." Ma seeing boys back is almost bad as the front. She doesn't dare ask anymore but just goes on about her work; pulling the bits of glass and the remains of the old shirt.

She carefully stops the bleeding and stitches up the cuts, finding fresh patches of new skin against his somewhat tan skin that said he spent a lot of time out in the sun. Noticing that the skin seemed recently healed because it was slightly pinkish white compared to the rest of the boy's soft tanned skin.

Wondering how that was possible when the rest of the skin in some areas were so badly bruised or the cuts that weren't as deep, but enough to need stitches. That it looked like that someone or something tried to heal the boy just enough until he could find help again. And not for the first time today she felt someone was telling her to help this boy and brought him here, but the questioned seemed not as important for now, but it bothered her none the less. She turned and faced Pa and Will. "Ok let's turn him back around and sit him up."

EJ moaned with each movement, she just whispers, "shush now its ok lad, we're almost done, go back to sleep." Praying that small sedative she had given him keeps him asleep long enough so she could stitch him up. Taking the sheet, she rips it into thirds and binds it around his body tight and carefully pins it in the front. Then laid the boy gentle back down and gently put the blanket back over him and propped up his head on the pillow. With her right hand, she brings it to her face and wiped her brow, looks down at her self then turns to Pa and Will, "I am a bloody mess," she said. Then turned to the nearby chair by the boy. "Mind turning down the bed for me why I catch my breath?" She asked.

They smile as they looked at her. "Of course, and by the way Ma you look like an angel to us and we love you just the same," Will replies.

With a tired smile, Ma said. "Thanks, I think. I will feel much better when he is in that bed and were all asleep." Noting how late it had gotten. Pa and Will turned down the bed then lifted EJ gently into Wills bed, "Careful now, I don't want you two ripping out his stitches."

"Yes Ma," they said.

Ma put the blanket around the boy and lovingly tucked him in. Then leaned over with a gentle kiss on the cheek and stroked his hair, Whispered in his ear. "Now sleep my little one. Sleep. I'll keep you safe my dear sweet angel son."

Chapter 5

Turning out the light and halfway closing the door, Ma turned to Will. "If you wouldn't mind, keeping an eye on the boy for a while for me. Your Pa and I need to talk awhile." Will knowing better than to argue sat outside his door as he watched the boy sleep as his Ma and Pa walked down the hall.

Pa slowly gazed upon his wife's face as their eyes fell on small boy sleeping in now in Wills bed, for a mere second, without hesitation. Pa could not understand this strange feeling he had as he gazed at the boy, as if there was something important about him, he whispered. "Strange? First, let's get you cleaned up then we'll go out on the porch and talk."

Martha turned round to face him; "Wayne, what about the boy?"

"What about the boy? You have done all you can for him at the moment and Will is watching him."

"What about the rest of the children?" Martha asked feeling just a little overwhelmed as she looked at Wayne.

"The children are fine, Julie has everything under control and before you say it, Sam and Anna have finished all the chores. Now scoot. Go get cleaned up. I'll go find Robert and check on Julie and put the children to bed. Then you and I will go out on the porch and I'll explain and answer all your questions, while I'm stuffing a plate of food down you. Now go, scoot," he said.

With a puzzled look on her face, she gave her husband a kiss on the cheek and shook her head. Not easily, but finally gives in. For she to knew and knows when he is right and has to admit not often that he was. While she was in the bathroom cleaning up; she saw the bathtub and thought a hot bath would feel so good right about now. She could feel the sore muscles in her shoulders right down to her toes. "Now is not the time for this sort of thing, perhaps later when things have calmed down a bit more." She said to herself with a longing sigh of regret.

Taking off her apron and setting it aside, she looked down at her clothing in disgust laughing to herself. "What fright I am." She looked at her clothing then looked into the mirror. "Angel indeed, ha." Then with a heavy sigh turned again to look at the tub, "I'll just wash up a change out of this." Looking at the discarded clothing, "I doubt it will ever come clean." She said shaking her head as she fixed her hair and washed her face and hands.

She picked up her dirty clothes as a small piece of paper floated to the floor. Setting down the pile of clothes into the hamper, she bent down and picked up the small piece of paper. It read.

IOU 1 sheet EJ, please collect at... Springville. Sorry, please forgive me I had no choice.

Putting a hand to her mouth with a small little gasp and tear in her eye. She whispered the name, "EJ, that poor little boy." She gently folded the paper back up and put into her new clean apron, only thinking it was her heart. Sitting on the edge of the tub with her face in her hands, she wept while thinking of that poor little boy, right in Wills bed. Trying to gather her composer and wiped away the last of her tears she walked out into the hallway seeing Will and just nodded her head quietly. "Is he still asleep Will?" She asked.

"Yes Ma, everything's fine. Pa says Julie is putting Sam to bed and Anna is getting ready for bed too. Robert is just finishing up and tying up the horses for the night and I have set up the cot in the room. Ma if you don't mind I like stay with him tonight?" He said holding back a yawn.

Ma looked at Will seeing his caring eyes. "All right son, if there are any problems..."

"Don't worry Ma, I'll come get you?" Will said as he looked at her worried face. "Don't worry Ma, everything will be alright." With that Will stood and went into the room and laid on the cot which he has set next to EJ as he watched him sleep through the night.

"Martha. There you are, for a minute I thought I was going to have to drag you out by your heels away from the boy, so he could sleep?" Wayne said.

"You wouldn't dare?"

"No, but the thought did cross my mind, the way you fuss over us. This is another reason why we love you, even more, my dear! Now eat, I had Julie warm it for you and you are going to eat every last bite," he said.

"Wayne?" Martha asked.

"Yes, Martha."

"Did you ask Will to stay with the boy tonight?" She asked.

"Actually no, I thought he was going to share a room with Sam. If you want I can ask him to move in with Sam?"

"No, it's fine. Will sure has grown up a lot. I see a lot of you in Will and Robert." She said taking a small bite of food.

"Funny, I was just telling Julie the same thing tonight, strange?" He said as sat down next to her on the porch swing.

"No. What's strange is that boy in there. There is something about him… Yet for the life of me, I can't put my finger on it." She said taking another bite. "I know his name," she said playfully.

"You what?" Wayne asked looking down at his wife. "Say that again, you what?"

"I know his name dear?"

"But how?" Wayne asked feeling little more puzzled by the minute.

"You first tell me the details after I sent you boys after my sheet. I need to know, but I think I already know the answers." She said as she wiped the plate with a roll and shoved it into her mouth.

"You know the answer?" He said looking a little dazed. "You are hiding something from me now aren't ya?"

"Just call it a mothers IOU… yes that's it."

Wayne felt a little flustered. "That would be an understatement!" He said. Nodding his head told her how they found the boy and the missing sheet. For the first time, she didn't even bat an eye. Knowing most likely the how's, just did not know the whys. But now just knowing he is safe from harm's way because she's already patched and stitched the boy asleep down the hall in bed, she felt a little more relaxed…"Well? Are going to tell me the boy's name?" He asked seeing that she got him by the shorthairs.

"Only on few conditions," she said. Seeing and knowing that he lost the war and agrees.

"First of all, we both know he is no shape to go anywhere and will remain in that bed until I say so. "Agreed?" No contest there and agrees as Wayne nods.

"Next when he does wakes up. He will not be pressured into telling us what happened to him or anything unless he wants to and I don't care how long it takes, got it?" She waited as she tapped her foot on the ground.

"Agreed!"

"Now after Doc arrives in the morning, I want him to give him a good going over, even if I have to stand over him and believe me I am going to."

Wayne knowing better not to argue that point either says. "Agreed!"

"Next when you go into town, you are just going look around, that's all. Don't get too nosy, I have a hunch you won't find anything there, but if you do, be careful who you talk to. Something still doesn't feel right and I think you know what I mean. There's someone I want to talk to first anyway." She said polishing off the last of the food.

"Who's that?" He asked.

"Just idea, nothing too concern yourself about," as she smiles. "But that can wait. I am tired so let's go to bed." Martha starts to get up from the porch swing.

"Darling?" He asked taking her hands in his as he helps her up out of the swing.

"Yes, Wayne?"

"Dear did you think I was going to forget?" Slowly he takes her by the hand and puts them around him.

"Forget what? I'll wash the dish in the morning," she said.

Wayne slowly takes in her scent, staring deep into her deep blue eyes, whispered softly in her ear. "You were going to tell me the boys name," as he kissed her softly on the forehead.

Martha giggled. "Oh, I almost forgot... His name, his name is EJ."

"Do you have a last name, my little sweet angel?" He asked.

"No just EJ," she said.

"Well, that will do for now, let's go check on him and the rest before turning in. I have a feeling we're going to a have very busy day tomorrow." With that, he pats his wife on the bottom then grins. "I just love that little devil in you to you know." Martha smiled back with a twinkle in her eye. Wayne followed his wife down the hall.

Wayne and Martha opened Wills door just a crack to give them room so the light of the hallway doesn't disturb their son Will, Martha went over to the bed were EJ is sleeping. Taking her hand gently lifted the covers over his bare shoulders and leaned down to kiss his cheek. Then walked over to where Will is sleeping with his hand out as she carefully lifted his hand back underneath the blankets.

Will stirs and looked up at his Ma's loving face sleepily. "Everything ok Ma?" He asked.

Ma leaned down gently pushed the hair away from his eyes. "Everything's fine son." Kissed him gently on the cheek then whispered, "now go back to sleep." Then leaving the room she paused for one last look before going down the hallway, closing the door and turned to her husband.

"He'll be fine, remember we're just across the hall," Wayne said taking her hand.

The next room they turned to is Roberts then Sam's seeing their small children all sleeping like little lambs. One by one she gave them a warm motherly kiss and whisper of mother's love, for her, they are her greatest joy. The next rooms are her daughters she calls them the jewels of her eye. She paused and gazed at each one of them knowing them best to her they always shine. Coming full circle they paused once more at their bedroom door. They never thought for a moment in their hearts if they had room for one more. As they gazed into each other's eyes, they knew what the boy needed, but at that moment they did not dare to ask for more.

* * *

Not so far away in EJ's home, there was a different picture. For if they were worried they really did not show it, except maybe one. A little boy named Danny had put on a long T-shirt that once belonged to his brother EJ." Mama when's EJ coming home? I am worried about him. Peggy tells me Daddy killed him. That's why he's not looking for him, is that true?" Danny asked.

"No, Danny, Daddy didn't kill him. We figured he will come home when he's ready. Peggy, please put Danny to bed. It's way past

What's Behind the Looking Glass?

his bedtime. Make sure he goes to the bathroom first that way he won't wet the bed," she said.

"Oh, Mama!" Peggy whined.

"Just do it!" She said sounding cross and tired.

"Come on you little brat, and don't take all day about it either," Peggy said.

"Daddy, Dona won't do what's she told and I had to do the dishes again," Peggy whined.

"Girls just go to bed! I have had enough of you guys fighting all the time! Can't I get any peace around here anymore?" Their mother nearly screamed.

Dad shouted. "Everyone! That's enough! Just go to bed! So me and your mother can have some peace and quiet without you guys always whining about something!"

"FINE!" Peggy yelled back.

"And close the door! We don't want to hear another word out of you tonight!" Her mother said listening to door slam down the hall. They give a heavy sigh.

"Jim, are you sure that was a good idea we had now about not lying finger on any of them again? Because I could just kill every last one of them… By the way, your mother called again, she wants to know about those clothes for school. If the children needed any help picking anything out and she hasn't heard anything from Eric for a while. I told her he was out playing with his friends and would be out camping for a couple of weeks on a Scouting trip. That is what you have been telling the neighbors too isn't it? In your walks to work, have you seen any signs of him?" She asked.

"No dear, I am sure he's all right or he would have come home by now. He can't last out there much longer. I'm sure of it, no use getting worried over nothing. The glass will be in tomorrow; I'll go by the store and pick it up. Now let's go to bed, we have a long day tomorrow," he said.

* * *

Will was wakened as EJ stirred from his restless sleep, his fever was breaking and the pain has settled in. Will, could hear EJ moaning as he tries to stir from his restless sleep. There is only a couple's of hours till dawn he figured, he better get Ma before he wakes. Will swiftly crossed the room where his Ma and Pa are sound asleep. Will gently taps her on the shoulder "Ma I think the fever is breaking... Ma, come quickly, his in an awful lot of pain and about to awake."

Without hesitation, she rushed to the bedside of the sleeping boy. Ma puts her hand on his head and looked at Will. "Will dear please go wake your Pa for me."

Will rushed back across the room where's his Pa is to wake him but sees he is already awake. "Pa?"

"I know son, your Ma needs me, am, I right?" He asked.

"Yes, Pa. The boy is stirring and is a lot of pain," Will says.

"Ok son I'll be right there," he said.

Will and Pa hurried across the hall where the boy was. Ma turned to Pa. "I believe the fever is starting to break and the sedative I have given him has worn off, can you watch him for a minute? I need to get some medicine to ease the pain and see if I can find something to help him sleep." Ma ran down the hall to the bathroom medicine cabinet to get the pain medicine and the last of the sedative.

"Let's see, I need to get this medicine down him somehow. "Humm, now what was that my mother used," as she thinks a moment. "Yes, I remember now, if I mix it with some broth it should work? He most likely hasn't eaten anything for a day or so. I like to give him some kind of food as well, that should work if he's asleep?" Let's see, humm where did I put my mother's recipe? Oh here it is, this should do the trick." She mixed the broth with the medicine and brought it down the hall. "Can you boys help me set him up? While I see if we can get this down him." She said as she placed a towel under his chin and slowly poured it and closed his mouth and held his nose and waits for him to swallow.

Will turned to his mother. "Now that's a neat trick. Who did you learn to do that from Ma? He doesn't even know he took that horrible stuff."

She giggled. "Oh, it just something my mother taught me for stubborn boys and men," not even glancing in their direction. Finishing the last of the broth she wiped his face and smiles. "We'll give it a few minutes and should start to work. Now then speaking of work we might as well get started."

Pa turned to Will. "If you want, you can stay with him a little bit longer while he falls back to sleep, but then I need your help later, ok."

"Alright, Pa."

"Why that's settling, I'll start breakfast. Plus I need to make a list of supplies I need from town. Wayne dear you might as well wake the children. We have a big day ahead of us and I want you and all the children ready when the Doc gets here," she said without pause.

Pa turned to his wife with another puzzled look. "I thought he was coming just to look at the boy?" He asked.

"Oh, he is. No question about that dear! I was just thinking while he was here and all, that he might as well make it worth his while and have a look at all children and you dear." And with a quick kiss on the cheek, she left quickly with him standing there.

Pa stunned as he watched his wife leave out the door, rubbed his chin. "That's your mother for you Will. She's always full of surprises and that just another reason why I love her so." Leaving Will with the boy, Pa awakened his sleeping children nestled in their beds. "I know it's early, but Ma needs you so dress quickly. Breakfast will be waiting after early morning chores." After giving his boys a warm smile and gentle a nudge then going into his daughter's rooms and giving his girls a quick kiss on the cheek," he whispered, "good morning my darling angels."

Chapter 5-1

Meanwhile, Ma down in the kitchen was preparing the morning meal. Thinking about the boy and wondered if she needed to find out more about him. Or tell anybody about him, but who would she tell? Or should she tell? She wiped her hands on the apron and felt the note, she had folded into her apron the previous night. *"Could it be? I hate to simply presume or imply, but he is hurt really bad."* Thinking maybe there's a way she can do this without doing more damage to the boy? "I'll just ask a few questions, that's all, I just need to know?" Ma turned around and noticed her daughter Julie. "Good morning dear, thank you for taking care of things for me last night. You were such a big help," she said.

"Glad to help Ma, how's the boy? Is he going to be ok?" She asked.

"He's hurt real bad and in a lot of pain, he has a fever, but it has come down a bit during the night, he should sleep most of the day."

"I am so glad. I like him already and don't even know his name."

"Julie, would you mind finishing the meal for me while I do a few things?"

"Sure Ma."

Ma went into the living room where she can have some privacy, pulled out the note of EJ's. "I am just going to ask questions. That's it, nothing more." Then she picked up the phone.

"Hello, I am sorry to be calling... I am not waking you, am I? But this is important," she said as Grandma Stewart gives her name.

"Early? No dear its fine, how can I help you?" The women on line replied.

"Do you know a little boy by the name of EJ?" Martha asked.

"Yes. He's my grandson, can I ask who calling please?" Grandma asked.

"Oh I don't want to alarm you ma'am, but I just have a few questions."

"What's this all about? Who is this?" Grandma asked.

"My name is Mrs. Downing, do know where EJ is?"

"Yes, his mother and father tell me his away at Scout Camp at won't be back for a couple of week's dear. Do you need him for something; you can call him at … Wait just a minute dear. How did get my number? …There's something you are not telling me, dear. I can tell it in your voice…"

Martha voice starts to quiver to a panic, pausing…. "What do I do, what do I say?"

"Come on dear, it's just easier if just tell me. I am not fool you know, which by the sounds of things I have been." Grandma said as she waited for the answer.

"Mrs. Stuart I don't know how to tell you this over the phone, but he has been badly hurt and has had a very high fever," she said as calm as she could muster.

"Oh My…Do you know how he was hurt?" Grandma asked.

"My husband and I have a pretty good idea, but we don't want to run to any conclusions."

"I think I understand dear, it can wait dear. You never did answer my question, how did you get my number?"

"I believe EJ was on his way to you, but he didn't make it."

"How long ago was that dear?" Grandma asked.

"We found him yesterday afternoon, Mrs. Stuart."

What's Behind the Looking Glass?

"I see... well, there's only one thing for me to do then dear." Grandma said.

"What's that?"

"I'll be there about an hour; don't worry about a thing, dear. His Grandma Stuart is coming and then you can tell me all about it."

"What about his parent's?" She asked.

"Don't you worry about that either. They won't know until we're ready. I have some conclusions of my own. You just take care of my grandson you hear? Now give Grandma the directions and she'll be off."

Martha said. "Down the old canal road then follow the old dirt road. You will see a farmhouse with a big red barn, that's it... come right through the old gate. That will be us."

"Thanks, dear, don't fret. He's tougher than he looks and if he wakes just tell him Grandma's comin and you take care of my grandson and I'll take care of the rest. See ya in about an hour."

* * *

Grandma Stuart hung up the phone her voice shook with anger as her mind calculated those conclusions, "What have they done now? My poor boy... Richard?" His Ma called.

"Yes, Ma."

"Pullout old Harley Davidson and hookup the sidecar then set it out along the side of the house. While I pack the saddle and change into my old leather duds, Grandma got some hell to raise," she said going into her bedroom. Pulling the trunk out of the closet and she lifted the lid and pulled on her leather boots, Grandmas slipped them on with the rest of leather duds and rummaged through the trunk. "Where did I put my Old Thompson knife? Oh here it is and it is still sharp," placing it in her boot. "Well, son stop gawking."

"But the neighbors Ma," Richard replied.

"Damn the neighbor's boy. I never cared what they think in the first place, now get to it times a wastin Boy. They hurt my grandson and its time for a little thunder. I feel a storm comin and I'm bringing it," she said throwing the bedroll onto the bed then putting clothes into the saddle.

"Couldn't you just take the old Ford?" Richard asked as he looked out the window of the kitchen.

"Na." grandma said shaking her head. "Can't do it," as she pulled out her leather jacket and put it on. "I think it has a flat." She patted down her gray hair. Robbed the wrinkles around her deep blue eyes then took the time to add a just a little rose color lipstick. She looked sharp in her old leather jacket as it brought old memories of yesterdays gone by. Oh, how she missed her husband, who has been dead going on six years now. Oh, what glorious memories. Now it was up to her to set things right as she watched her youngest boy Richard from the corner of her eye.

Richard looked shocked and somewhat amazed. But knowing he was beaten goes out and does what he was told to do. Passing the old Ford just as it sat in the driveway. He turned and shrugged his shoulders as he looked at the tires, shaking his head. Thinking to himself, *"I don't see any flat."* Once when he was a young boy he could only remember seeing his mother dressed like this, but that was in pictures. He had heard rumors from his father, but the bike he knew all to well was a hobby of hers.

She liked to tinker with it and sometimes would ride it, but that was years ago. Things changed after he passed away. She had mellowed he thought. His Ma comes down the stairs in her finesses leathers. He was almost praying the neighbors would not see this as she loaded the bike with her saddle and bedroll.

Ma just turned to Richard. Sticks her left fingers in her mouth and pulled it out to test the air, turned. "Richard?" she says.

"Yes, Ma."

What's Behind the Looking Glass?

"The winds blowing to the south," put on her leather gloves on climbs on the bike. "Oh Richard, before I forget. You mind setting up a bed for little Danny and call my sisters to meet me in Santaquin in about three or four hours or so in front of Judge Parker's place, please? No one else minds ya, and keep it under your hat. Very important and I stress this for EJ sake and little Danny. Don't let the cat out of the bag just yet. For now at least until Grandma Stuart has had her say, is that clear?" She asked.

"Yes Ma, how bad is it?" He asked.

"It's really bad son so I've been told," she replied. With a final nod of her head, she put on her helmet, slings her blue scarf behind her then she jumped on the peddle bring old Harley to life. With rumbling roar as she rives the handle, with white smoke blowing out the back of the mufflers; black streaks on the road as she peeled out of the driveway. She popped a quick wheelie on the bike and off she went down the street.

Richard quickly looked around as the noise and dust settled. He could see some of the curtains and doors closing. With a smile on his face, he yelled. "Gock all you want, for that's my Ma and she taming the wind today!" He would have never thought he would ever see the actual day his mother tamed the wind of yesterday.

Richard went back into the house wondering what's going to happen, but knowing he better do what his mother said. For they tricked her now, they made her really mad and the storm was coming. Richard stood alone in the kitchen thinking what in the world is he going tell her sisters? He looked up at the clock. "I better do it soon too because she will be awaiting and she will not be in the mood." Richard picked up the phone...

"Hello aunt Lizy this Richard," he said.

"Yes, Richard?"

"Ma wants you and your sister to meet her in Santaquin in about 3 hours in front of Judge Parker's place."

"Did she say why Richard?" She asked.

"I can't go into details. She says, she will explain everything when you get there... All I can tell is this though, she's dressed in her old leathers and she has taken old Harley with her." He said looking back at the clock on the wall.

"Did you say Old HARLRY? OH MY! Old HARLRY! You did say?"

"Yes?"

"OOH MY! This is serious. All get Mary. Richard, did she give any other instructions?"

"Yes..."

"Then I would. OH MY! I. I just can't believe it! I better go dear the Harley."

* * *

Ma yelled down the hall. "Will, Robert, Pa needs you out in the barn to help finish loading pickup then you can pull the old pickup to the front of the house. Then you are to go out to the horses and feed the chickens before you leave ok?"

"Ma, what about the boy?" Will asked.

"Is he still sleeping?" Ma asked as Will looked over as he finished tying on his shoes.

"Yes Ma, it looks like he's doing better."

"The medicine I gave him should work, let him sleep then we will check in on him in a little while... Anna you and Sam finish your breakfast then help me clear the table." Ma said taking control of her house once more.

What's Behind the Looking Glass?

"Ok Ma," Anna replied.

"What do want me to help you with Ma?" Julia asked.

"You dear get to help me make the list of things I want your Pa to pick up in town then we will go check on the boy, alright," she said.

EJ awakens from his restless sleep, still heavy with fever and the sedative he had been given to keep him asleep. He heard strange noises all around him. Confusion is lost among the pain. He tried to move but felt confined. Fear builds in his mind and not knowing where he is frightens him even more. He opened his eyes and finds himself in a strange room." Where am I?" He muttered.

He can barely see, he tried to move, but every muscle is strained and his vision is blurred and little confused. Thoughts of being captured of being taken back home, he felt he must escape. With all his will power he could muster he managed to slide himself onto the floor.

"Ma did you hear something?" Julie asked as she looked towards the hallway.

Ma, Julie paused. "No, must be the boys outside." Ma said and returned to their work of gathering their list of supplies.

EJ noticed his wounds had been dressed. He looked around the room to see if by chance if Mr. Scarecrows clothing still lay around the room. But not wanting to wait for the final surprise, fearing they might check on him at any moment. Thinking it will be his last. He must escape his captures. EJ slid over to the dresser and finds a large shirt. Not the one he lost. His head filled with dizziness, the pain was agonizing. "I must at all cost escape, I can't go back. And I won't be able to help little Danny if I get caught." His mind worked feverously.

Gritting his teeth, he put his arm in the shirt and pulled it over his left shoulder. His breathing heavy and hard, fighting the throbbing from his side. EJ gritted his teeth once more as he put his right arm through the other side. He needed a moment to catch his breath as he leaned against the bedpost, wondering where his captures had him and who they are.

"I need to get out of this room and find my grandmother. She's only one who can help me now, but to do that I must escape." His mind says as it worked as thoughts of only escape. Opening another drawer he finds a pair of pants, "I am glad their big because I can't bend my left knee." He looked down. He noticed a large bandage around his thigh it's very painful to touch. Thinking of little Danny and his grandmothers awaiting arms, he gritted his teeth, groaned and laid back on the floor.

EJ scooted himself into the pants. He rested a couple of minutes more. To gather his remaining strength, the sweat poured down his face from the fever and the pain. He was so dizzy and in so much pain he wanted to scream. But knowing that would give him away. EJ covered his mouth against his arm to silence the sounds of pain and heavy breathing.

He knew he couldn't walk or stand up straight not without help. He looked around the room to see if at least the crutch is in the room, not finding it. "The only option is for me to try, is to crawl out the door on my stomach. And find some support outside the home and make a break for it before they come back." As EJ approached the voice grew closer than he would have liked. "I hope they can't hear me," he stopped at the edge of the hallway and listened.

"Julie dear, how are you coming?" Ma asked.

"Just fine Ma."

"In just a bit, I think about 10 min or so that broth should be ready and we can give it to the boy. Do you mind helping me with him dear?" she asked.

"No, I would like that."

EJ knowing his time was nearly up needed to hurry if he was going escape being captured.

"Julie?" Ma asked.

"Yes, Ma."

"After the list is made just set it on the table so I can go over it before your Pa takes it into town. They are loading the pickup out front now," she said.

"Ok, Ma."

Chapter 5-2

EJ listened, his mind and thoughts working as one against the pain. *"I am not going back, I can't go back,"* thinking. *"Maybe there's way out of this mess, the pain I must fight it, and she said town, escape, escape, must leave, Grandma."* Sweat poured down his face, blood started to seep through the bandages. EJ scuffs down the hall as he gritted his teeth putting the back of his hand to his mouth to hold back the groans as he carefully slid across the doorway as he looked into the kitchen unseen. He reached the porch and saw the old pickup parked in front.

The tailgate is still down. EJ looked across the yard. He can see his captures getting ready to load things for going into town for trade. EJ knew his only chance to escape unseen is hitching a ride. *"If I can just make it."* EJ looked down at the blood that has started coming through the bandages and leaked through the shirt.

"Nothing I can do about that now. I must get out of here and find my grandmother she will know what to do? I will call her when I get to town." Fighting through the sweat and the agonizing pain and fever made it difficult, but he kept the hopes of little Danny in his heart and his survival the number one goal. EJ pushed himself towards the truck. EJ looked and thought the best way to get into the back is to roll, fall off into the bed of the truck.

EJ landed on some of the hay near the back. He could feel the stitches tare, but now it no longer mattered because the pain becomes warm and numb. EJ could almost feel the dizziness slipping over his eyes as the blackness took over as he fainted from the pain and fever.

"Ok boys. Will grab the list from Ma and Robert you can close up the barn. We need to get to town and get back before the Doc gets here." Pa said as he closed the tailgate, without so much as a glace due to the extra stuff in the back they were taking with them. They never even noticed EJ under the hay behind the sacks of grain as the three of them headed off with their little stowaway as they went into town...

What's Behind the Looking Glass?

* * *

"MAMA! Danny wet the bed again," Peggy yelled.

"Did not!" Danny said.

"Did too!"

"Did NOT!"

"Did too!"

"DID NOT!" Danny screamed breaking into tears.

"Then how comes your bed's wet ha?" Peggy said knowing full well he didn't while holding the empty glass behind her back.

"All right that's enough Peggy! I swear Oh... Never mind. It's time to get up anyway. Danny you are getting too big to be doing this, you know that right?" She asked.

"I know, but I didn't do it, I don't see how!"

"What do mean you just got up went to the bathroom a few minutes ago?" His mother asked.

"I came back it was wet Mama."

"See Mama, he is already starting to fib just like his brother," Peggy replied hiding the grin on her face and the glass.

"Peggy I am not! I promise. I don't know how it got wet?" Danny said as he wiped the tears from his eyes.

Danny's mother stared down at him with her hands on her hips. "Maybe you just thought it was dry," she said.

Danny feeling hurt began to cry. "EJ would believe me. I know he would," he said.

"But he's not, is he?" Peggy said gleefully.

"Peggy stop picking on him!" Her mother said.

"Mama, he just needs to grow up that's all." She replied and stomps off with a little smirk on her face carefully setting the glass in the sink.

"Danny go change your clothes have Donna help with some cold cereal," she said.

"But I want pancakes Mama, when are we going to have pancakes for breakfast?" He asked.

"Maybe you can get Dona to make them for you."

"She can't cook."

"Then I don't know what tell you, go now do what you are told and stop being such a baby."

"Mama!" Dona shouted from her bedroom.

"What now Dona?" She asked.

"All my dresses are dirty and I can't find anything to wear. Can you help me find something to wear?" She asked.

"Peggy can you please help Donna find something to wear." Her mother said as she growled between her teeth.

"Jim remind me again why we wanted to have kids again? I feel I am the only one that does anything around here, can you least help me do something?" She asked.

"I am dear if you ever want me to fix that window today? The glass should be ready this morning. I need to swing by and pick it up at Stringum Hardware Store on Main. Is there anything you need why I am at the store?"

"Yes, a maid would be nice! And a large a bottle of aspirins," she said as she looked at the kids down the hall.

What's Behind the Looking Glass?

"The maid will have to wait, but I can get you those aspirins if would like?"

"Jim?" she asked.

"Yes, dear?"

"I am worried?"

"Worried about what?"

"Eric."

"Oh, I am sure he's fine. He's mostly likely moping around somewhere feeling sorry for himself. When he gets tired and hungry enough, I say let him get out of his system. He will be home on that doorstep before you know it and we won't have any more problems. I'm sure of it as long those damn neighbors stay out of the way and he minds us. Never did understand that boy. Kinda reminds me of my father. We never got long either and look how I turned out. Of course, things changed after the war. After all, he can't last out there much longer. I think now, no I am sure of it," he said.

"If you say so dear, he was hurt pretty bad."

"Maybe and maybe not, I never did find him and far as I can tell nobody has found him either. At least in the ditch banks anyway so I wouldn't worry, most likely his hold up somewhere having the time of his life. I wouldn't jump to any conclusions just yet. Like I said we never found him and so far neither has anybody else that I can tell," he said in hopes to change the subject as a thought pass through his mind. "Damn that boy."

"But you haven't asked anyone either!" she said.

"No, but they have sure been asking me." He said thinking of Mr. Johnson just down the road apiece.

"That Scout Camp story getting old, if he doesn't show up soon we're going have to think of something mighty fast; more so when family services arrive." She said knowing she's not going to get any more out of him.

"Now, now you are the one that's always telling me how resourceful he is remember?" He said.

"I know." She replied trying to convince herself with hope.

"Well if I am going to get that window fixed today I better get going, see you in a while," he said leaving quickly before she can pester him some more.

* * *

"Hello Jim," Mr. Stringum said.

"Hello, Mr. Stringum is the new window I order come in yet?" Jim asked.

"Hum let me see. Dave is Jim, Stuart's window in yet?"

"I'll go check," Dave replied.

"So Jim. How's the wife and kid's these days?" Mr. Stringum asked.

"Fine. Girls are growing like weeds. Can't seem to slow them down much these days?" he said.

"And your boys, how's little Danny?" Stringum asked.

"He's six you know and taking after his big brother," Jim replied hope to get away from answering more questions about his boys. Never did like to talk about them much or at all if it could be helped.

"Can you wait here, Jim? I just need to grab this order," he said as he watched Wayne Downing walk into the store.

"Sure Mr. Stringum. I am in no hurry," he said.

What's Behind the Looking Glass?

"Thanks, Jim. Why Mr. Downing the wife said you were coming and wanted to make sure you stopped over at drugstore before you left town. I'll have Dave here fill your order in a couple of minutes and then help your boys load it out to your truck ok?" He said as he watched the boys bring in the things to trade.

"Thanks," he said.

"Just wait here at the counter Dave will back in just minute," Stringum said.

"That's fine, can I also have some that penny candy as well?" He asked.

"Sure, sure. Oh, Jim, I was going to ask about EJ. I haven't seen him around lately and I was wondering if you could have him swing by here, I have few odd jobs for him?" Stringum said turning to Jim at the counter.

"Sure I'll have him do that, but right now he is away at Scout Camp and won't be back for a week or so," Jim said with the same lie he and his wife been using the name EJ made him growl. "Well, when he gets home. I'll tell him to stop by," containing the lie.

"That will be fine Jim. Oh here's Dave with your new window, if it is not the right size, let me know I'll get the right one," Stringum said.

"Thanks, Mr. Stringum," Jim said leaving. Groaning as he had to carry it all the way back to down the street, since he couldn't drive anymore; wishing he had asked his wife Linda to drive him up and back, yet there was no one he could trust to watch the kids, and bring them would only result in more questions he didn't want to answer.

Wayne was not sure what he just overheard as he carefully eyed other items on the shelf, while he watched Jim walk out the door with the window. "Dave almost done loading your items, is there anything else I can get for you today Mr. Downing?" Stringum asked.

"Well come to think of it, my wife could use some more sheets and a couple more quilts." He said keeping his thoughts of the boy in the distances.

"How many sheets would you like?" Stringum asked.

"Well knowing her I would say about a dozen. She wanted new bandages and took all the old ones to make them, what could I say?"

"True, true," Stringum said.

"Well have you heard anything odd going on around here lately?" Wayne asked keeping out what he has already learned to himself.

"Let's see, there was Mrs. Wilson scarecrow? She says one night she could have sworn she saw it leaving the barn just the other night as if it might have decided to take walk. We all figured it was a couple of kids playing tricks on her. Never did find it though," he said.

"Maybe it decided to take a dip at the creek?" Wayne replied half amused.

"Mr. Downing, why would it do that?" Stringum asked.

"Just call it..." Wayne rubbing his chin then grinned. "Just thought being how hot gets now that is summer." He replied knowing now where the boy got the clothes from and why they smelt so bad.

Mr. Stringum had a funny look. "Funny thing is someone did say they thought, some kid that looked a lot like Jim son EJ was wearing them. But I asked Jim Stuart about it? You know the fellow who just ordered the new window who was just here? I asked him a few days about it. Anyway, he said EJ was out of town at Scout Camp so it couldn't have been him. Plus he had some sort of crutch; well I can't put my finger on it." Stringum said checking off the items to order.

What's Behind the Looking Glass?

"What's really strange I thought the Scouts were back from their trip three weeks ago? Oh well. Just nothing but gossip anyway fills my head up sometimes. I need stop meddling gets me into trouble, besides none my business anyhow. Well, Dave got your truck all loaded and your bills all taken care of. See yea next trip and say hi to the misses for me, Hey have some extra candy for those kids of yours on the house." Stringum laughed with a wave.

"Well, boys we just have one more stop to make. Your Ma wanted us to stop at the drugstore first before we head back. She needed some supplies and she's already called in the order, all I have to do is pick it up. Can you boys make sure the tarp is covering the goods, we don't need anything blowing out?" Pa said as he headed down to the drugstore on the corner just two shops down from Stringum Feed and Hardware.

"Yes Pa," Robert replied.

Will and Robert headed back to the truck talking among themselves. "Robert?" Will asked.

"Yes Will?"

"Do think the boy is going be ok," he asked.

"I sure hope so."

"Did hear what that man said, what do you think he was talking about?"

"I'm not sure, Pa going to back in minute help me with this... Will, go get Pa fast." Robert pointed to the back of the pickup seeing the boy in the back.

"Pa! Pa! Pa!" Will ran down the street towards the drugstore, yelling at the top his lungs "Pa!" Will nearly out of breath. "It'sssss the theeee boy heee's!" Will tried to reply out of breath.

"Slow down Will," Pa said as Will pointed to the back of the truck.

Pa thunder stuck as he saw the boy lying there in the back of the pickup just uncovered from the tarp. He throws the drugs and supplies to Robert, Robert catches them tossed them on the seat. Pa leaped into the bed of the truck, he checks the boy yelling to Robert and Will. "We need to get home fast, his burning up and looks like he has torn some of the stitches and the blood has seeped through bandages. What on earth was this poor boy thinking? Ma going to kill us, mind the ruts Robert we need to get there in one piece." He said with urgency in his voice.

"Yes, Pa."

"But fast," Pa said once again.

Chapter 6

"Anna. You and Sam mind playing in the living room for a few minutes while me and Julie go check on the boy to give him some more of this broth." Ma said as she placed the cup of broth on the tray.

"Ok Ma, come on Sam," Anna said.

"Julie, while we're at it put some more water on for some tea, I'm expecting company soon," she said.

"Yes, Ma."

"Now let's go check on that boy, and bring some more that broth."

"Ma, what's that sound?" Anna asked.

"What sound Anna?" Ma asked.

"That loud rumbling sound outside?"

"I hear too?" Julie replied.

"So do I," Sam said.

Anna and Sam ran to the window. "What the world is that Ma? Somebody's coming and I don't know who it is!" Anna said.

Ma walked over to the window to take a look, seeing someone on a motorbike contraption. "I don't know who it is either! Well, it's not polite too stare, move away from the window kids." Ma said as she went over and answered the door. "Hello, can I help you?" She asked.

"I am not sure. I am looking for a Martha Downing!" Grandma Stuart said.

"Yes, that's me and you are?"

Grandma took off her gloves fold them up and placed them in her back pocket. "Believe or not, I am EJ's Grandma Stuart," she replied.

"Oh please come in." Ma said about to close the door when she looked up the road for a brief moment and saw their truck driving fast, barreling down the road. It pulls in and up to the porch.

She heard Robert calling. "Ma, Ma, come quick!"

The first thought that went through her mind was another boy down. "Oh no!" But saw Robert then Will. "Where's Wayne? Not him. No, I can't bear it," Ma not turning to face Grandma Stuart as if in a daze. "Could you please excuse me?" Martha said paying no attention to her new guest. Grandma Stuart turned to see what all the fuss was about as Martha ran out of the house towards the pickup. Ma turned to Robert, "Where's your Pa?" she asked.

Wayne yelled, "I'm right here Martha, it's the boy!" He said.

"It's the what?" Martha said taken back with surprise.

Wayne jumped out of the truck. With one sweep he picked up the boy and carried him in his arms. He turned to Martha, "I don't know how he did it? And I don't know why? He's burning up Martha."

Martha was taken back. Even more, mystified as she looked at the boy in Pa's arms. "How on earth?" All she could get out.

Grandma Stuart came strolling back out of the house. "I am his Grandma. By the look of things, this is no time for pleasantries neither, let's get this poor boy into the house," she said. With Pa leading the way back to Wills room they gently lay him on the bed. "What a mess this boy has gotten ourselves into. Ok boys clear the room. Your Ma and me have some work to do." Grandma said as she removed her jacket and gloves then tossed them to the nearby chair in the room... "But before you go? You boy what's your name?" She asked as she pointed to Will.

What's Behind the Looking Glass?

"Will, ma'am," he replies.

"You can call me Grandma, everyone else does. I want you to run a cold bath? Can you do that son?" She asked.

"Yes, ma'am." He said making a dash for the door.

"You girl what's your name?" Grandma asked as she pointed to Anna.

"Anna," she replied.

"Fine name, call me Grandma too, go find me some ice and put it in the tub. Pa I want you to take everyone else and clear the room. Pa before you go I want to have your strapping young boys if they wouldn't mind bringing my bags in. It looks like I'll be stayin awhile, then get back here pronto, now go! Well, what ya stand-in around fer catching flies for Martha? This boy needs to be cooled were going to do the coolin. I hope your boy's not too particular about these because their history when I get done."

Grandma pulled out her knife out of her boot. "Well grab your scissors; oh don't worry about me. I'm tamer than an old bobcat and we will have him cleaned up slicker than a whistle. I was a nurse back in the day, learned a few tricks that's all," Grandma said.

Martha's just little taken back as she watched Grandma work. Grandma looked at Martha and laughed as she began to cut. "Don't fret so much dear. These Stuart boys are stubborn, as an ox's sometimes, but also tough as nails. This child here, I think he might be a part of different stock all its own, reminds me a lot of my late husband. Well, I do declare look at that, you were not kidding, looks like Grandma is going to be staying awhile dear if don't mind me saying he is a mess. I've some questions of my own and Grandma knows exactly where to start. I do have to admire your handy work Martha, I'll you give that," she said as Pa walked in the door. Grandma turned to him. "Is everyone clear?" She asked. Pa nodded his head.

"I don't wona expose him to just anyone you know and you can call me Grandma to everyone else does, let's go." She said as

Pa picked up the boy in his arms and carried him quickly down the hall, he placed him gently in the tub. "Ok Pa stand back, I got to unwrap some those bandages and see what this boy has done to your mother's handy work." She said undoing the bandages around edges of his waist, Grandma shook her head and mumbled under her breath.

With Ma's sewing kit and thread, she stitched him back up. Then leaned back to look over her handy work and tightened the knot with her teeth. "I believe that's last of them." Then turned to Martha; "Martha when this kid wakes up. I'm going to give him a loving kiss and a piece of my mind." She said as she looked them straight in the eye. "No, I think you know what I mean."

They both looked into her sweet loving face as she gave them a wink. They perfectly well knew what she meant. "With that being said, I believe we can dry him off and put him back to bed where he belongs," she said after she rubbed the hair on is head. "Why we are doing that...You mind having your oldest girl... I am sorry I didn't ask her name?" Grandma asked.

"Julie," Martha said, Grandma looked at Martha with a new pair of eyes. "She is the spitting image of you, what a doll. Anyway, think she mind changing the bed and turning it down?" She asked.

"Then we'll put him to bed... then I think nice hot cup tea would surely be in order while we all get reacquainted." She said as she smiled and shook her head at the boy. "You stubborn ox, stupid, fool headed boy; just like my husband and just like some boys that I know." She said gently rubbing his cheek with the back of her hand as to test his temperature and temperament. "Just about right," she said as she nods.

Pa enters the kitchen and finds all the children visiting among themselves talking about all that has transpired, seeing Pa, they all try to ask at once; "what's going on? Is she really EJ's grandmother? What's going to happen to him now? Is he all right?" They all asked.

"Yes, she is and I will answer your questions later, but first they need to get him back to bed where he belongs." Then he turned to

What's Behind the Looking Glass?

Julie. "Would please go change Wills bed? I am afraid we made a mess in there dear, Anna you can help if you would like," he said.

"Yes Pa, I am glad he'll be ok," Julie said.

Pa looked outside the window, "Oh I complete forgot," he said.

"Forgot what Pa?" Robert asked.

"The supplies we brought back from town."

"We already put those away, we figured you had enough to do and all," they said.

"Thanks, boys, what would I ever do without you?" He said as he put his arms around them.

"We put all the things from the drugstore on the table," Will said.

"Thanks again, boys. I better get back to your Ma. Would ya mind bring EJ's Grandma Stuart things in? It looks like she going to be staying awhile," he asked leaving them.

"Well, we are all finished here, just in time. Let's get him back to bed Pa. Before the Doc gets here." Ma said.

"Doctor, Martha, we have done more doctoring to this boy then he will do in his entire lifetime," Grandma said.

"I know Grandma Stuart," she said.

"Just call me Grandma please child."

"As I was telling my husband before all this started; what I was thinking was that was before I called you... Anyway, it seems like a lot has happened since then," she said.

"It does get that way sometimes doesn't it? Go on didn't mean to interrupt," Grandma said.

"Anyway, I was thinking since I was doing all his work and since he was coming out this way anyway. Why not have him look at all the children and my husband, that way, he at least earned his pay," she said.

"You know Martha, I really like you. Are you sure that you don't have any Stuart blood in you? Martha, who is this Doctor that's coming out?" She asked as she wrapped the towel around EJ.

"Doctor Hatfield."

"That wouldn't be Doctor Richard Hatfield would it?" Grandma asked.

"Why Grandma Stuart?"

"Please, just you call me Grandma everyone else does."

"Ok, Grandma ...Why yes?"

"He and I used to serve together. I was one of his nurses, nice fellow. When he gets here you tell him that's my grandson in there and I'll be checking in on him. Ok, Martha?"

"But I thought you were staying?" Martha said confused.

"Oh, I am… There's a storm comin dear and after you tell me what's this boy been up to. Grandma got a little business to take care of and then she will be back here sure as shootin, plus 1."

Pa entered the bathroom. "The girls tell me that they have changed the bed and they have the tea ready. Julie says the broth is still warm for EJ if you still want to give it to him." Wayne announces as he walked in the door.

"What broth is he referring to Martha?" Grandma asked.

"It's my mother's recipe, too give for pain and plus put some nourishment down him. But it also supposed to keep him drowsy too." She said still amazed on how this boy pulled it off.

Grandma rested EJ's head on her shoulder.

"Remember dear, I told you not to fret any. Mind if I have look at that recipe dear?" She asked.

"Sure Grandma," she said still stupefied.

Pa turned around. "Actually I am not saying anything. So far I have seen him do some amazing things," he said shaking his head.

Grandma lifted up her head towards Pa. "And I can't wait to hear them, so let's get him back into bed before he catches a cold," she said.

Pa picked up EJ carefully carried him back to bed. "Be careful Pa, don't ya dare tare out our stitches; he won't have any skin left to stitch up at this rate," Martha replied.

Grandma laughed. "Not to worry Martha, if I have to we will bolt the sheets down to the floor and the nailed door shut too so he can't go anywhere without us knowing about it first. But I have a feeling he won't try it again, after a good old hug and kiss for me." Grandma said as Pa laid EJ gently on the bed and watched his Grandma tuck him in.

"Now my darlings, before that Doctor gets here sit down and join me and have a cup of tea and tell me about my grandson? But I already fear the worst, but tell me anyway. Because there's a storm coming and old Grandma Stuart here, she is the wind and the storm? Oh, that's much better," she said after taking a couple of sips of tea.

"Martha I have to hand it to ya, now that's a fine cup of tea. Sit, come on the both of ya. I might look little rough around the edges, but I am no fool. Well, then maybe, I might have been. To look of things," she said as she looked at her grandson sleeping in a strangers bed. "Now tell me Pa, what is your name son? I can't keep calling ya Pa now can I? You are not old enough for me," she smiled.

"Wayne, Grandma Stuart," he said as he as laughed.

"Please dear call me Grandma everyone else does," she replied.

"Ok, Grandma it is."

"Here is that recipe Grandma Stuart, sorry, Grandma," Martha said handing over the recipe.

"That's better dear. Just add little more of this and you'll be just fine. I think the problem was not the recipe dear, but I'll tell you why in a minute," she said.

Martha tells her about how she found EJ's IOU and how she sent the boys after her missing sheet. Wayne, tells her about how they found EJ to the point they are now.

"Well, that's quite a story I have to say. When that boy wakes up, he's got a story of his own tell I bet. Grandma here is going go right to the source and believe me child questions are going to be asked and answers I am going get. Now for as that recipe is concerned dear; nothing wrong with it; except for fear, courage, the heart of a lion and stubborn and determination of a Stuart. I think after he wakes up and he realizes he is safe and with a hug and kiss from me of course. He will stay in that bed. Now give him that broth, I need to meet all your sweet children before I go, because my sisters are waiting for me." She said as she stood with another look at EJ.

"You dear have Doctor to see, but I'll be back in a while after I have taken care of some business in town. There are some little packages I have to pick up and one I have to bring back with me. One of those little packages is for him to see. Then after that, I'll leave him in your care. I really think that's best for now. You see dear, Grandma is not a fool, its plain as day. They might think she was, but that's until they played with the wind and made it look like a fool. Now then let's go meet those children of yours," she said waiting for Wayne by the door.

Chapter 6-1

Pa took Grandma Stuart down to the living room to meet the children. They're eyes nearly popped right out of their heads with amazement.

"Are you really EJ's Grandmother?" Sam said busting with excitement.

"Yes dear, I am. Tell, me your name little one?"

"Oh, my name is Sam,"

"And mines Anna."

"Well, then I bet you never have seen likes of me before have you dears?" She said laughing.

"No, ma'am."

"Don't be frightened dears. I do not usually look like this all the time," she said referring to her outfit. "But Grandma just got to blow off a little steam," she said as she looked at their Pa.

"Grandma this is going to be a day to remember for them I hope?" He said, referring to EJ's parents as she nodded that it won't be a lesson they won't forget.

Grandma looked outside at her bike sitting in the middle of the farm then stood up "Downing Family hold on to your hats, it's going to be a whopper of a storm." She said as all children looked outside the window, turning to Grandma asking.

"How can there be a storm Grandma, there's not a cloud in the sky?" They asked Pa and Grandma laughed at the children.

"Dear sweet children, I am the storm. Wayne, I'll be back soon," she said as she looked at the clock as the big hand points 15 min to

3. "I believe am running just a little late, take care of my grandson, if EJ wakes up. Tell him to stay put while I run a few errands, but I'll be back. Oh and set an extra place for dinner too, for that small package that I am bringing is for EJ, but I want it to be a surprise. The package is going to be staying with me for a while if you know what I mean?" She said with a wink.

"Yes Grandma Stuart, sorry Grandma," he said.

"That's better dear," she said waved back as she left.

With that Grandma Stuart put on her gloves and helmet, tied her blue scarf around her neck and step on the peddle and just for fun for the children, she did a couple of wheelies just to hear them scream with delight as she pulled out of the Downing Farm.

"Well, I do have one thing to say," Pa said.

"What's that Pa?" Robert and the rest of the children asked.

"There is certainly not a shortage of surprises around here. Not with EJ in the house," he replied. Watching Dr. Hatfield drive into the yard and pull up to the house as EJ grandmother left in a cloud of smoke and dust as Ma came into the room bring in the tray and the plates of cookies.

"Hello Dr. Hatfield, it's about time you got here," Martha said.

"Martha, what's this all about a hurt boy? I want you to know I was nearly run over by some old lady that looked a lot like someone I used to know."

"Oh, that? She was in a hurry that's all, that was Grandma Stuart. Her grandson is the one that's hurt," she said.

"Stuart you say. Had nurse with that name once. No, it can't be? Could it? Well, let's go see this boy then." The moment he walked into the Wills room he tsked. "Tsk, tsk Martha. I have never seen such a mess. This boy is lucky to even to be alive. You are right about those ribs Martha there cracked alright and possibly broken need an x-ray to be certain but that can wait. Just look at that swelling too. Oh my, he's got a fractured left collarbone as well. My dear poor boy, this wrist looks sprained too. Let's take a look under these bandages shall we," He said as he pulled the pins out.

"I do have to give you credit Martha nicely done. Those are some nasty gashes on his back and the front of his legs and that left hip. Nasty wounds around his waist and I don't like the look of those cuts on his back either. Some or quite deep, tsk, tsk; this boy been through a meat grinder. He's got more colors on him than a rainbow. That fever still worries me too. He's not out of the woods yet I am afraid. That Stuart woman you mentioned earlier. When I look at this boy he reminds me of a Betty Stuart. I wonder if she could be the same one." He said as he rubbed his chin as he looked at the boy.

"She said she served with you back in the war as one your nurses," Martha said.

"Well looking at those sutures she got to be the same one. Ya know I would have traded 10 good nurses for her back than. Then if this is her grandson dear, I better take real good care of him, or she will come and hunt me down. Unless that was her firing a warning shot," he said as he rubbed his chin. "Let's get him covered up and tucked back into bed Martha, he going to need lots of bed rest. And some these pills to keep away the infection, and something stronger for the pain, and something to help him sleep."

"Now remember to change the bandages often, to keep the skin from drying out too much. I want you to apply some this ointment on those large nasty cuts, but you know all that. He's staying here isn't he or is going home?" Doc asked.

Martha looked at Wayne for conformation. "His Grandma Stuart says he staying here," she said.

"Good, now as far as clothing," he tried to reply.

"Yes I was thinking of an apron to go around the waist, but larger with sides so it folds behind him," she said.

"Martha that's… That's a great idea," he said.

"Well, I have raised three boys and a husband you know?"

"How true that is, after being a Doctor so long, modesty I seem to forget. Then after that when he heals more and stitches and bandages are gone. Winter will be here soon enough I'm afraid. When he heals and the bandages are gone a long sleeve nightshirt will do fine. For now, I recommend he not be moved.

"I'll head over to the Judge Parkers and file a petition and giving you temporary custody of the boy so nobody can bother him or you while he's on the mend. Unless Martha you think different?"

"No, no he's not leaving Doctor Hatfield. How could you even suggest a thing like that after seeing this poor boy? I am not fool," she said.

"Never thought you were Martha…Well then." He said as he rubbed his chin again and took another look at the boy. "I'll be by in a couple of days to check on things since you have everything well in order," he said as he closed his bag.

Martha put her foot in front of the door preventing him from leaving. "Dr. Hatfield?"

"Yes Martha," he asked as Wayne swallowed hard.

"I am not done with you just yet. Wayne, do you mind staying with the boy since you are going to be last." Not waiting for an answer he sat in the chair next to EJ.

Dr. Hatfield looked like a cornered mouse waiting for the cat to pounce on him at any given moment. "Martha was there something else you needed from me?" He asked.

"Yes, while you are here and all. I have decided since that I was so kind to do all your work for you while I was waiting for you. That it would be such a shame, that you should come out all this way for me and his grandmother just to admire all our work." Martha said she looked at EJ sleeping in the bed.

What's Behind the Looking Glass?

"We were thinking we would like you to take a look at all our children and my husband before you leave. That way his poor wife and grandmother won't have to worry about them. So if you wouldn't mind, please follow me. I had Julie set up a room for you down the hall and the children are waiting for you there." she said taking his bag from him.

Doc turned to Wayne for help. "Wasn't my idea," he said as Doc looked at Wayne sitting next to EJ. "I learned not to argue with her."

Dr. Hatfield took one more look at EJ, grabbed his bag with a shake of the head, he turned and quickly followed her down the hall to take look at the children. For the first time, Wayne was alone in the room with EJ since he has been here. The room is quiet now except for the sounds of soft moaning sounds of EJ stirring in his sleep. It is restless sleep still do to the fever and the pain of the inflected wounds. He gazed upon the sleeping boy's face, which he has carried in his arms as if he were his own child.

Words randomly go through his mind. *Why would they? How could they? Why would anyone?* Taking his hand shaking not with fear or anger, but with love reached above EJ head brushed the hair away from his face that wasn't there then brushed against his warm cheek laden with fever. With a tear in his eye, his voice cracks softly, "my sweet little child. I must keep you safe, you are safe." Then taking his little hand in his, holding it as he pressed it firmly into his at his bedside. Wayne listened to him sleep. He watched his small little chest rise and fall as he breathes.

Martha walked into the room where EJ was sleeping, seeing Wayne holding EJ's hand. She did not want to cry. For her this she will always remember this tender moment. But she could not help it. "Wayne dear he's not going anywhere, I'll hold it till you get back," she said as she wiped her eyes. With a quiver in her voice, "do it for me. I can't have any more of these surprises." She said as she looked at EJ then looked to her husband with tears still in her eyes. "He's going to need all of us, even if he knows it or not. There is a storm coming remember?" She said.

"Yes Martha, so I have been told."

"Now get down the hall get looked at, we have things that need to be done before his grandmother gets back. While you are down there please send the children in here, tell them to be quiet. So they can see EJ if they want to. Ok, dear now go on," she said and pushed him out the door.

"Yes dear." With a quick peck on the cheek and another glance at EJ, Wayne shuffled down the hall to see the Doctor while mumbling to himself. Upon seeing the children "Ma; was wondering if you children would like to see EJ for just minute?" There was open excitement in their eyes and on their faces, "I'll take that as a yes, but you are going to have to be very quiet understand?"

"Yes, Pa; how long is he going to be here with us Pa?" Robert asked.

"According to the Doctor, awhile, He going to need lots of bed rest for along time though, it could be weeks, maybe a month it's hard to say."

"Then what Pa?" Will asked.

"Will have ta' see, your Ma's got some things for you to do since his grandmothers will be with us a while and I go see the Doc," he said.

"Well, Wayne come in, come in, what a day, what, a day. I never did get a chance to explain to your misses why I was so late. Not that it would've matter none, knowing how Martha. Once she gets an idea stuck in her head, you might well just figure on you have of already lost."

"Doc, you don't know how true that it is. That's just another thing why we love her so."

"Well the reason I was so late, and would have come sooner if I could, but I was knee-deep delivering babies; triplets as it were. All of last night and part of the morning and I just finished up a few hours ago, all boys yep, yep, that poor boy. Tsk, tsk. What a mess, that's for sure. Wayne, I've known ya for a long time, heck Wayne I delivered all ya kids too if it serves my memory right," he said as he examined him.

"You have the nicest bunch of kids around these parts. Good strong boys, healthy as a horse, girl's fine. Fine young women just like your wife; they got the same fire to… A fella gonna have' ta be on their toes when the time comes, that's for sure. What do know about this boy Wayne?" He asked.

"Nothing really, heard about something in town about he might have been in some fights in school and around town with kids, never saying which kids though. Local people don't believe it to be true. Too much speculation in town, they say he's too nice of a kid and gets along with everyone. Then what I saw down at creek…"Wayne said then pauses.

"Well, what do you believe?" Doc asked.

"There's something going on? Pieces just don't fit, Doc."

"Yep, I knew you were no dummy. The wounds were mostly man-made yes sir'ery bob, but I don't need to tell you that now do I? Well I've done my job. You are as fit as horse other than a few sore muscles from old age. Yep like I said earlier, for the time being, he stays here. I'll see to it, Doctors orders. Personally, I couldn't think of any better place, but that's not for me to decide is it? I am just a family Doctor. Well I'll see ya in a couple of days or you know who will come hunting me down. It's bad enough having one woman come looking for me, but two your wife and his grandmother; watch out for her, she's got claws." He said as left with a wave of his hand.

Chapter 6-2

"Ok kids; now be very quiet. I don't want you disturbing him. We just got him back into bed where he belongs," Ma said.

"Yes Ma," they replied softly.

"Now EJ; is going to be here for a while so that means Will."

"Yes, Ma."

"You are going to have to move in with Sam since he has the bigger room or you could move in with Robert," she said.

"Yes, Ma."

"Robert would you help Will gather his clothes and some these things. Julie, Anna girls I want you to gather all the old sheets you can find around the house we're going to make bandages for him. My sweet, dear children he's going to need all of you when he wakes up?"

"You don't have to tell us Ma, we already know. We'll help you," they all said.

"I know you will dear and thank you. Ok, his grandmother will back soon; Robert after you boys clear out the room will setup the extra bed in here that way someone will be with him all the time and will bring in the big sitting chair. We will set in the corner as well. I'll have your Pa find us a small table and well have a private little room just for him." She said taking charge once more as Pa walked in.

"Well then, Ma; looks like you been busy as a beaver," Wayne said as he walked into the room.

Martha looked around the room. "Oh just tidying up some, little here and little there that's all dear. I didn't want his grandmother to come back thinking I was a slob, now did I?"

What's Behind the Looking Glass?

"Oh, I don't think for a moment she would call you that dear, how's he doing?"

"Still sleeping, the Doc gave him some stronger medicine to help him sleep and for the pain. He thinks the fever should show signs of breaking most likely by morning."

"Well, that's good."

"I also had Will move in with Sam, they're just finishing up."

"Then I'll go check on them. Oh, Martha dear, I did tell you his grandmother said to set an extra plate for dinner for a package she's is bring back with her ...Didn't I dear?" He asked with an amused smile.

"Dinner! Oh my. I nearly forgot with all the things. I, I, I can't believe I forgot. Julie, Julie," she called.

Wayne just smiled and kissed her on the forehead. "Sit my dear, it has already been taken care of as we speak," he said.

"How could you?" She asked. Wayne just smiled placing another kiss on her forehead.

"I am not completely helpless you know. Besides I do have two very fine daughters to help me and three strong boys remember." He said as he looked over at EJ. "And could be four boys soon, now sit. I have things under control."

"Wayne?" She called.

"Yes dear."

"I just love that big devil in you sometimes." Then without warning, she kicked his butt out the door. Wayne, with a big grin on his face, goes on down the hall. Martha turned to EJ and smiled grabbed a washcloth and wiped his forehead whispered to him, "EJ my little one, what have you gotten yourself into?" Then placed his little hand in hers and sat in the chair beside him whispering to herself. "I wouldn't trade it for the world," she said as she watched him sleep.

"Robert?" Will asked.

"Yes Will?"

"Do think EJ going to be ok?" Will asked.

"I think so, I guess so why?" Robert asked, "Why do you ask?" He said moving the dresser in the room.

"He's kind of banged up and all, that's why. I know Ma, sure worried about him and they know something. I can see it in his Pa's eyes, he won't tell me about it, but he knows?"

"Knows about what Will?" Robert asked.

"I don't know. Well, you are going to have to ask him. Help me with this bed." Robert said.

"Will?" Robert asked.

"Yes?"

"You are standing on my foot."

"Oh sorry, is that better?"

"Yes thanks, could you believe that was his grandmother, I thought I was going to die when she did a wheelie out on that thing, scared the chickens and horses to death," Robert said.

"Ya that was something, that's for sure. Now help me hang up your clothes or Ma will kill us both if she has to wash them again. Speaking of which, Robert do you know why or how he got into the back of the truck?"

"No. But knowing Ma, she'll make sure that's not going to happen again. I wonder though what he was thinking about." Robert asked.

What's Behind the Looking Glass?

"I'm sure we will know soon enough."

"Are you boys almost done in here?" Pa asked as he peeks into the room.

"Yes pa," they replied.

"Good, because I'll need your help in the kitchen in a while, but first get the chores done. The livestock still needs to be feed."

"Ok Pa," they said.

Pa and Robert on their way out to the barn Pa stopped Robert as he put his hand on his shoulder. "Mind if I talk with you a moment son?" Pa asked.

"About what Pa?"

"Oh, nothing much, just something on my mind that's all."

"Ok, Pa."

Pa and Robert walked a few paces as Pa gathered his thoughts "Robert?" he said.

"Yes, Pa?" Robert turned to Pa seeing the warm gentle look in his eyes that he has seen so often.

"Thanks, Robert for picking up the slack for me and your Ma. We haven't been around that much too help, it really means a lot to us son."

"I know Pa, glad to help."

"Pa?" Robert asked.

"Yes, Robert?"

"Is EJ going to be ok?"

"Yes son, I think so. You know son. I have a feeling he is going to need a big brother to look after him and I can't think of a better person for the job."

"Pa, he's not even awake yet, how do even know he needs one?"

"Because son, we all need a big brother once in a while too lean on from time to time and for the time being son," Pa said as he put his arms around his shoulders. "Robert my boy it couldn't have happened to a nicer guy I think. Now I need to find your sisters and get dinner started."

"But Pa, I didn't know you could cook?" Robert said surprised.

"What did you suppose I did before I meet your Ma? Starve to death? Hardly son, don't worry it will be eatable. After all, we do have guests tonight and your sisters will help me. Now let's get these chores done. Times a wasting and see if you can help me find Sam."

"He should be feeding the chickens and gathering the last of the eggs for the day Pa," Robert replied as walked towards the horses.

"Hello Pa," Julie said as he walked through the door.

"How are my two beautiful daughters doing?" He asked as he gave each one a squeeze and twirled them around the kitchen as they giggled.

"Pa what has gotten into you?" Julie asked.

"Shush, don't tell your Ma."

"Are you sure the Doc said that you were fine?" Anna asked.

"Yes dear, now can't your Pa have a little fun once in a while with his daughters?" He said as he twirled Anna one more time around the kitchen as she giggled.

"I suppose so Pa," Anna replied with a laugh.

"Now then how's the roast doing and how can I help?"

What's Behind the Looking Glass?

"Well, first of all, the roast is doing just fine. Sam just brought in the eggs for the rolls and he is on the porch peeling the carrots and potatoes if you want to help him you can. Then you can take this tea and broth into Ma." Julie said as Pa reached over to taste the gravy and with gentle "slap" on the wrist…"Now Pa," Julie said giggling waving the spoon as she was pretending to be Ma. "It's not done yet," she said.

"I was just testing it. Alright, alright; I'll go, you know," he said trying to look hurt. "You are as bad as your mother sometimes." But grinning from ear to ear as he went out to the porch where Sam is. "Well Sam," Pa said as he picked up a potato.

"Yes, Pa."

"Looks like we got our work cut out for us," he said as he pulled out his pocketknife.

"What do you mean Pa?" Sam asked.

"Will and Robert are in the barn doing all the work and your sisters kicked me out of the kitchen.

"What about Ma?"

"Well, she busy with EJ and she kicked me out too. So I thought maybe I'd come here whittle with you a while if that's ok? Because your Pa here doesn't have anywhere else to go, if that's alright with you?" He said while looking into Sam big brown eyes.

"Oh, Pa you mean it?"

"Of course I do son. Now let's see if we can get these peeled," he said.

"Pa?" Sam asked.

"Yes, son."

"I was thinkin?" Sam said.

"Yes, son I am listening…Thinking about what?" Pa asked.

"What I would, if I knows where's to go?" Sam tries, but the words don't seem right as he says them.

"Yes … go on." Pa knowing how nervous Sam is let's him speaks.

"I don't know… I don't where's I'd go, never been anywhere. Pa? Do you think maybe I could? Na, it stupid." Sam said changing his mind.

"What son?" Pa asked.

"I'm younger than Will and Robert. What can I do?" He asked.

"First of all son, nothing you do is stupid. I am sure whatever you do will be just fine. For right now just try being his friend. He's going to need someone to talk to. It's going to get pretty dull lying in that bed all the time or anywhere else for a while. Do you think you can do that son?" Pa asked smiling, putting his hand on his shoulder.

"Yes Pa," he says.

"Now let's take these into your sisters ok?"

"Ok Pa," Sam said grinning.

Chapter 7

"Sorry I am late girls, but I had a few things that needed to be taken care of. Well don't just stand there looking stupefied and gocking at me with your mouths open, Yu'll catch files that way, so close your mouths and listen up. My grandson is hurt really bad," Betty said. Her sisters looked back and forth from her to the bike still bewildered...

"Sorry Betty what did you say about your grandson?" Lizy asked. Lizy Dragren; Betty Stuart's younger sister still a young woman at heart, married young too a sailor who died in the Korea war years back, never remarried nor had any children. She was known at one time a redhead now her hair was more auburn grey than red. Blue-eyed Barbie doll figure. Average height at five-feet seven inches, had the backbone of a mule when comes to getting her way like her older sister Mary.

Smart as a whip when comes to books or movies and has always had a soft heart when comes towards children even thou she had none of her own due to a hard miscarriage. It had always saddened her when she found out that it would be a magical occurrence if she ever bared a child. So, for now, she had given up hope and lives alone, teaching middle school.

"As I was trying to say he's is hurt bad, Lizy... Before you interrupted me."

"Sorry, do you know how it happened?" Mary asked. Mary Fillmore likes too think she's the wiser woman of her two sisters Lizy and Betty. Despite her hair has turned gray and dyed to the color of blue silver. She considered a high society woman of her age. With her lengthy built as she towered over her two sisters gaining the advantage from her fathers' second wife. Whom she regards as a hideous witch of a woman as she had hope growing up waited and hoped a house would fall on her. Yes, you could say she was spoiled because she always got her way one way or the other and forbid her two sisters beat her to it.

She never got along with her younger sister Lizy when they still played house and with their dolls, her green eyes sparkled as they set off her long aristocratic nose and drawn down chin into a petit triangle. She had never married or likely will as she considered the possible candidates of today or will ever likely fall in love, heaven forbid. Never saw the point when she was younger. Again using the phrase: 'It would be a magical occurrence.' Yet now she has regrets now that she is alone in a small apartment built for two. Her livelihood a librarian going on thirty years, until this day she never believed in true romance. That somewhere out there is a man of her dreams and all she had to do is wait for him. *No dark-haired, blue eye man or chiseled body for me.*

"Yes, I do, well I am not exactly positive, but I do have my suspicions. Mary, that's why I am here at Judge Parker's place, I need to do some paperwork and get it filled out to make what I am about to do is legal." Betty said her fingers tightened into a fist as she thinks of all things Jim and Linda have done to her grandchildren. She unclenched her fists when Mary wiped an escaped tear with her handkerchief trying not to ruin her mascara.

"Betty you didn't bring us all the way out here to file some paperwork and you simply did not get all gussied up in that to do it either. You are up to something, now sit, spill the beans and tell us both what you have in mind. Or we are going to hogtie you to that bench until you do. So start talking sister." Mary said, placing her arm around her, walked them towards the bench sitting under the tree near the courthouse.

Betty filled them in on what has taken place down at the Downing Farm while she watched their mouths drop and eyes pop nearly out of their sockets. "Oh my, that poor child and those poor children… what do you think is happening to them right now?" Mary gasped her hand reaching up to capture the quick-release breath.

"I have no idea, but we are going to find out Lizy and Mary, that's why I need you two here. I figured that I could take care of his brother Danny, but if you girls would take care of his two sisters. Then maybe we might have a chance to save this family." Betty felt the anger and release of the guilt of not doing anything sooner and sighed heavily. EJ had barely been home not more than a couple of months when his foster parents the Steeds moved out of state, and his parents and she refused to let him go with them. A mistake on her part, for when he came home, she didn't think anything could have gotten worse, but apparently, they had.

"What about EJ?" Mary asked regaining her composer and brings her sister back from her dark thoughts. With her hands sitting neatly in her lap, but her leg and foot tapped the ground giving her away. She was on pins and needles thinking about how she could manage a nine-year-old or better still her sister, and the problems that came with it. Her thoughts of unruly children in a library could not compare.

"I am going to leave him with the Downing's for now. He is hurt too bad to be moved and I have a really good feeling about them. It would far better than putting him back into the system. Now let's get those papers filed, the Judge is an old friend of mine," she said. Slowly getting up clutching her purse as she takes two steps to the door, almost afraid of what's inside. Her last thought was going to a spring dance with the boy now a man who was now inside those doors all grown up as Mayor of this small town of Santaquin.

"Betty?" Mary asked.

"Yes, Mary?"

"You can't go in there dressed like that; he'll think that you lost your marbles." She said stopping her in her tracks trying to keep it together. *Me alone a child too raise, I have never...* taking a hard swallow felt something stuck in her throat.

"I suppose you are right," Betty said laughing. "I am a sight ain't I? But I left all my clothes down at the Downing Farm." She implied gazing back at the Harley sitting there its silver chrome tailpipe gleaming in the sun, begging to ride off into the sunset.

"Well not exactly, we stopped by your house after speaking with Richard and grabbed some extra clothes; he wasn't sure what you took so I picked some for you," Lizy said getting up from the bench. And opened the car door too rifle through the outfits and deciding on the green skirt and light blue blouse with white ruffles along the front. She picked up the black heels and handing them over to her sister Betty

"That's my sister's, always thinking for me. I'll go change, but I am not taking off the jacket, or the boots" she said and tossing the heels back into the car. Her biker boots seemed right even though they did not go with the outfit, but she was not in the mood to play dress up.

The girls laughed at her stubbornness. "Glad to see the fire's back! We kinda missed it! But did you have to bring Old Harley?" Mary asked.

"Oh Lizy, Mary you know the grandkids love it, besides I get such a kick out hearing them squeal with delight and you are only young once. So let me have my fun." With that Betty left to change her clothes.

"You know Mary," Lizy said.

"What's that Lizy?"

"Betty sure knows how to kick up a storm that's for sure. Imagine that?"

"Imagine what Mary?" as she leaned against the front of the building.

"Oh I was thinking how EJ parents manage to hide this from her all this time," Lizy said joining her on the other side while they waited for Betty.

"Well they're certainly in for a surprise and I don't want to be in their shoes. Isn't that…? No, it couldn't be." Mary said watching a man she once knew and dated if she recalls; placing another checkmark in the not possible or her type of man she was looking for.

Doctor Hatfield known as Doctor Richard Hatfield, He was elderly gentleman perhaps in his early seventies the last of his breed known to make house calls in Santaquin county. His office stood at 113 main street, three stores down from Stringum Goods & Hardware and right next too the Santaquin Pharmacy. If you ever been in Santaquin you'd blink and you'd miss it, but Doc didn't mind. He loved small towns where everyone knew everyone and their business. He loved the gossip and had been known to spread some himself. He lived alone now going on twenty years when his wife died in the early sixties of hermetic fever.

Heck, he's birthed and raised half the county for going on sixty years. Some would say back in the days he was a ladies man. With his dark brown hair now white as snow right down to his handlebar mustache and bushy eyebrows holding up his green bluish eyes. Most people would think he could be an imposter to Kernel Sanders if wasn't for his height just below four feet and seven inches. He served in Second World War taking and trained the best nursing staff a hospital could find.

He may be old fashion, but no doctor could beat his bedside manner and his temper. Known to toss a gurney or the nurse on it through the door, but all said and done; he did his job and he did it well. Better than most Doctors today. He always looked his best with a smart bowtie with different colored spots to get the attention of his cliental. Man or beast paid him sometimes in coin or sometimes in whatever they got or made. All he cared about was their welfare not his own. When comes to riches or well being of his patents, patents always came first.

It was still warming up to be a very hot day as Mary and Lizy fanned themselves as they waited for Betty to return. It wasn't long before Doctor Hatfield slowly made his way towards them as they sat on the nearby bench.

"Couldn't be who Lizy?" Mary asked.

"Old Doctor Hatfield, what's he doing here?"

"Who's Doctor Hatfield?" Her hand waving the cooler air to her face and dabbing the sweat with her white handkerchief along the back of her neck.

"He was the Doctor she served with when she was a nurse. Hello, Doctor Hatfield fancy meeting you here." Lizy said, putting out her right hand to shake.

"Well, I'll be. Is that Lizy? It is. I didn't think I'd be running into you. So what brings you down to these parts?" He asked releasing his hand.

"Oh, my sister Betty has got business to attend to down here. Oh look here she comes." Lizy said seeing Betty coming around the corner fixing her hair.

"Well, I'll be a cooked bird on Sunday dinner, if that's not Betty Stuart. I thought you were in town. You nearly ran me over back there with that contraption of yours," he said eyeing the Harley on the side of the road.

"Sorry Doc, but I was in a hurry? Did you have a look at my grandson?" Giving him a quick glance over as she ran her eyes over him. Thinking how he has aged over the years, but so has she come to think about it as her lips tightened. *Is he shorter or is just me?*

"Yes, I did," shaking his head. "Tsk, tsk. What a mess my dear, what a mess. Actually, that's why I am here. It's my professional duty and obligation to make sure that boy stays in that home to recover. Unless of course Betty, you think he shouldn't be, but I've known the Downing's a long time. I can't think of a better place at this very moment, but I don't know his parents like you do. For right now looking at those wounds, I have a pretty good idea that's not such a good idea.

"I have just gotten off the phone with child services they say that this grandson of yours has been through more homes than any boy they know. That this isn't the first time this has happened, and they are concerned that if he went back into the system it will be tough to find a home for him. More so because he is very good at running away and other problems I am sure you are aware of. I told them that Downing's would be a better fit for him. That is my opinion that shouldn't be moved at this time. Depending on a medical and child psychologist evaluation is done, before he goes back into the system giving you plenty of time to deal with the matter at hand."

Betty nodded and agreed with him and said. "Doctor Hatfield, I am not as dumb as most people think." She said taking him all in from age's past it seemed. "I agree... That's why I'm here as well, but there are three more children in that home and I have no idea what's going on without my knowledge," she said the worry lines shown on her face.

"Yes I am aware of that, yet for the moment I am more concerned about your grandson EJ at the moment, and I plan to stop by his home and see to his bother and his two sisters the moment I am done here today?" Shaking his head." He eyes her up and down discreetly *she seems taller than I remember.*

"Yes, so you see my job is only part done. EJ my grandson may be safe for the moment and out of harm's way, but what about the others? That's why I am here, to see if I can help them too. My sisters and I that is, could use all the help we can get, that is if you are willing?" She said seeing that extra sparkle in his eye and mischievous smile remembering days gone by.

"Well, it looks I'll be a dog going on a coon hunt. Let's see if we can get Judge Parker to get that boy of yours a piece of safe heaven and those other grandchildren of yours to higher ground. It sounds like too me you are planning on paying them a much need visit. Well then batten down the hatches because Betty's in town and she's about to blow." They all walked inside the mayor's office.

Betty went up the reception desk. "Yes, we would like to see Judge Parker please, he's expecting me. Just tell him it's an old friend and she's bringing the wind with her. He'll know what that means," Betty replied at the reception desk.

The woman nodded and quickly went inside to announce them. "Judge Parker there's a woman out here that clam's that you know her," the reception said. Judge Parker aka Brad T. Parker: Judge and Mayor of Santaquin county. A fair man and considered to be an honorable man in his late sixties. Graduated the top his class at Harvard University at the age of 26, Married Mildred F Swanson soon after. Raised ten children, seven boy's three girls; his youngest child off seeing the world and studying to be a lawyer for defenseless children, and married a congressman. A Republican running for mayor somewhere out north last he heard.

"Yes, yes tell her. Tell her I am busy, please. Please have her come back later," he said going over a mound of paperwork… running his fingers through his sandy brown hair or what's left of it and mostly gray towards the ends. His clear blue eyes peeping through his wired rim reading glasses as he works on case file after case file, with the paperwork never-ending even in a small town like this. Shaking his head at the outbox and the high pile in his inbox.

"She says she brings with her the wind and Doc…"

"The Wind!" You say I haven't heard that in… Tell me is she wearing a leather jacket?" he asked slipping his glasses off and folding them in front of him.

"Why yes." She said with a confused look, standing in the open doorway.

"Oh dear, you better send her right in then."

"What about Doctor Hatfield, I believe he is with her?" She said getting ready to leave.

"Send them all in, don't just stand there," he replied as he pushed aside his work for the moment and rubbed his tired broad shoulders and straightened his bowtie and crosses uncrossed his short legs that allow him to stand just under six feet.

"But…?" She tries to ask.

What's Behind the Looking Glass?

"But nothing, you don't keep the wind waiting. Trust me, send her in," he said with urgency pushing his brown leather chair way from his desk.

"You can go right in now." The reception said as she opened the door and stepped aside and closed it when they were all through the door.

"Well, thanks to be my lucky stars. Betty, Betty Stuart it has been a long time, how have you been?" He asked getting up and offering her and her companions a chair. *She still looks good after all these years.*

"Brad, I would love to catch you up on old times, but this isn't a social call," she said setting her purse to the side and taking the offered chair and introduced her two sisters as they take the couch on the side and Doc taking the seat next to her.

"I didn't think so. Not when you dress like that Betty and drop by announcing yourself at the door as the wind... You have something on your mind, let's hear it. Plus; I see you have Doctor Hatfield with you as well. I am not going to like it am I?" He asked.

Shaking their heads, "no, I am afraid not," she said eyeing Doc from the corner of her eye.

"Humm," as he sighed. "Then have a seat and some tea then tell me what's on your minds." Moving over to the table near the door and begins to pour.

Betty sits down her foot taps the floor as she tries not let anger boil and stay calm as she tells him all that she knows which is not a lot. But enough for her to get what she's after for now anyway. Taking the teacup and sipping it. Cringes at the biter taste of too much lemon then she likes sets it down and holds it in her lap.

"That's downright shocking, to say the least, but Doc I'll need some kind of evidence. Pictures or something Doctor Hatfield," the mayor said after hearing the news. Setting down the tray and returned to his seat listening to it creak. *I need to oil that* making a mental note.

"Well I thought of that and I took some. If you need more, you can see the boy down at the Downing Farm for yourself," Doc said. Opening the green olive folder with EJ's name on it and shoving it closer to Judge Parker to read.

"Brad I am on my way to his parent's house to ask a few questions of my own, I feel a full investigation is in order," Betty said.

"Do you agree with Doc?" Brad asked placing his glasses on his angler nose and adjusting them to see better as he reads and seen the pictures, grimacing thinking *Ouch that poor boy.*

"Yes, something smells bad, very bad. I'll know more when things settle down I am sure, but right now that's boys safety is my concern. Not to mention his brother and sisters as well I might add. I have already contacted child services and they agree that the boys parents are known as abusive parents and hopped that things had gotten better, but apparently they haven't and are planning to stop by and ask some questions of their own and possibly suggest they both see psychologist, as well as their children and a marriage counselor before the children, are returned to them. Yet their grandmother had stated clearly that she and her sisters could take the children temporally before they are forced to put them in the system, and have agreed that her grandson EJ remain where he is until they can do a further evaluation of his home and give him time to heal."

Judge Parker nodded said. "I see, and I agree with you more so seeing these pictures. Well, Betty as much as I don't like breaking up a home I see we have no choice. I hereby give him to you and full custody of the boy EJ after seeing the pain inflicted by his parents. I also give you permission to remove the other children from the home. You and your sisters will be their legal guardians until this matter is completely resolved.

"The parent's visitation rights I leave up to you, as I know they are young children and may not completely understand what is happening. Though I would advise that you keep your son Jim and his wife as far away from these children as possible...." He said writing up the document and making a copy. "Now I have work to do and you have grandchildren who need their grandmother right now. Do what you came to do Betty, Betty blow," he said, laughing, as they parted.

Betty turned around. "So Brad, do you think this is a little too much? My jacket I mean for kicking in a few doors?"

"Oh no, not all... I just wish I could see their faces when you pull up at the front door with old Harley. It's going to be a gas for sure," as he leaned back on his chair as it groaned. "By the way, sorry about your grandson. I am sure he'll be ok. Good family the Downing's. Nice bunch of kid's too." He said fingering the fine oak desk that Wayne Downing and his boys made him for winning the last election.

"Thanks, Brad."

"Now blow, I have work to do," he said, watching the door close behind them.

"Hey, Doc...?" Betty asked taking him by the arm as they walked.

"Yes, Betty?"

"Thanks for all your help?"

"It was my pleasure, you where always my best nurse you know," he said. Turning around and patting her hand on his arm.

"Doc, do mind taking a look at the rest of my grandchildren? I am not sure what kind of shape they're in. I haven't seen them yet. I'll have my sister's drop the girls by at the office, but his brother will be with me. I'll be with EJ for a little while until he wakes up and until I get him settled in."

"Oh, that will be fine. I was planning on stopping by in a day or two to check on him so I'll look at him then unless... I hate to even think about it. If anyone is like that or close to it, you call me you hear?" As they parted company and Doc walked back to his office for his bag and a few more files.

"You can count on it, thanks again," she said. "Well girls, everything is in order. I have the papers. Let's start this little showdown. I got some hell to raise," Betty said climbing on the bike and starting the engine as she primed the gas. She has always loved the power of a machine like this between her legs and the wind blowing through her hair. Oh, how she missed her husband, but this was a closes second.

"Oh my Lizy, look at her go, she's going to kill someone on that thing, but you do have to admit?" Mary said watching the dust and smoke clear while she stood by the car door before going inside her blue 1970 Toyota know as Marilee.

"Admit what Mary?" Lizy asked getting in and rolling down the window before turning the key.

"She got style," she said as she climbed into the car Green 1965 Chevy know as the bomb listening to it as it backfired with black smoke and followed her down the street towards EJ's parent's house. *Man, I need a new car...*

* * *

"Mama, what's that noise?" Peggy said as she looked out the window.

"What noise Peggy?" Her mother asked. fumbling with her Tri-Chem paints as she changed colors for a red robin for the roses as she was painted a new print tablecloth.

"That noise?" Peggy said hearing a motorcycle enter the driveway.

"MAMA! MAMA!" Dona screamed seeing a strange woman that looks like grandma and two cars pulling up right beside her.

What's Behind the Looking Glass?

"What Now! Dona?" Her mother asked frustrated about being interrupted. *"Can I get any peace, Why Jim did we have kids instead of a nice quiet life?"*

"Somebody's here?" She said.

"Who's here?" Her mother asked. "Stop yelling! I just got your brother down for a nap."

"They're coming to the door, three-woman one looks a lot like Grandma and I don't recognize the other two," Peggy said closing the curtain and going to the door.

"What on earth would your grandmother be doing here? She never leaves the house and she would call first. Where's your father?" She asked feeling angry and annoyed to put up with her crap. Especially because EJ's run off again and has been gone for nearly four days, which is not unusual for him. He always running to who knows where, but to have her come here and rub it in her face she got the nerve. *"After all I…we did nothing wrooong. No.* she tries to shake the echo out of her head she must get control. *"Damn it to hell kids I never wanted any."*

"He's not back yet mama," Peggy replied.

Grandma knocked on the door, Peggy opens the door…"Hello sweetheart," she said.

"Grandma, what are doing here? How? Where? When did you? What are you wearing?" Peggy said her eyes glued to her.

"Surprised to see you to my dear. Well, are you going to give your Grandma a kiss and squeeze?" She doses unsure of herself. "Now then may I come in? Me and your mother and father have some business to discuss… I see your mother, but where's your father Peggy?" She asked trying very hard to stay calm.

"Oh he's not home right now, but should be real soon." She said standing aside to let grandma in the two people she remembers seeing at family reunion ages ago as she tries to smile at them.

"Fine dear, would you mind going with your Aunt Lizy for a while down to the drugstore for some Ice cream?" As she gently handed Peggy too Lizy, "where's your sister Dona?" She asked.

"Here I am Grandma," Dona replied coming in from behind Peggy.

"How have you been dear? Come give your Grandma a squeeze. Would like some Ice cream too?" she asked.

"Yes Grandma," she said after giving grandma a hug.

"Then go with Lizy dear," as she gently handed her to Lizy. "Now then," she said as she watched the girls leave. "Linda why don't you and I have a seat while we wait for that son of mine to return home… Linda, where's Danny?" She asked.

"He's taking a nap," Linda said trying to overcome her shock noticing grandmas outfit and her two sisters besides her. Her head hurts just thinking about all the possibilities why they are all here in the same room. *Why me? Why Now?*

"In which room my dear? I thought maybe he might like some Ice cream too? That way we can talk without being disturbed. Don't worry, the children will be fine. Their aunts will take real good care of them and give them a chance to get to know each other." She said keeping her voice polite as she could as the storm of anger builds inside.

"Mary if you wouldn't mind? Would you please wake him and take them down for some Ice cream? Don't worry, I'll be nice," she said. Mary turned to look at Betty before walking down the hall to where Danny was sleeping.

"Now then I would like to take EJ down for some Ice cream too, Oh yes where is EJ Linda? Is he still sleeping over at friend's house or was it a Scout Camp. That's right you told me that a few days ago didn't you? Now I remember. It's such a shame too. I really wanted to see him. What a shame that I missed him, my memory not as good as it used to be." She said trying to be the fool that they think she is.

"Grandma, Grandma is that you?" Danny said as he ran down the hall towards her.

"Yes, my boy it's me, oh how I missed you." She said as she picked him up and gave him kiss on the cheek and a big squeeze. "I've got a big surprise for you my dear boy, but for now I need you to go with your Aunt Mary down to the store and she'll buy you the biggest Ice cream you can eat, can you do that?" She asked.

"Grandma, what about EJ?" Danny asked standing beside her as he yawned as she helped put on his shoes and socks.

"Shhh later," she said and whispered in his ear just so he can hear. "He's the surprise."

Danny turned." EJ, he's alive?" He said to himself.

"Shush later." She said trying to contain his excitement and pushed him towards the door where Aunt Mary was waiting.

Then Danny whispered to himself as he went out the door." I knew it," he said with the biggest grin on his face. Danny reached the driveway and saw the Old Harley. He looked up at Mary. "Did Grandma drive that?" He asked.

"Yes she did, and you little one get too ride in that little motorcar. That it is the second surprise just for you," she said as she rubbed his hair.

"Wow!" He said his eyes as big as saucers going over to check the bike out.

"Wow is right, Danny boy! Your Grandma is something else! Oh, look! Here comes your father now and I sure don't want to be in his shoes when he gets home. You know, Danny. I think I'll have two scoops of ice cream, too," she said as she opened the car door for him so he could sit in the front seat.

Chapter 7-1

* * *

Passing the driveway Jim noticed his kids in the cars waving goodbye. He wondered where they were all going than seeing the Old Harley Davidson, which he has not seen in years. With shock and dismay crept up inside him, his face nearly white. *"No, it can't be? My mother, she has not ridden that thing in years. Besides, she mellowed out and what would she be doing her in the first place? It can't be her. We told her EJ won't be back for at least another week."*

Jim rubbed his chin, grabbed the new window and starts to bring it into the house as he climbed the old wooden stairs that so badly need a paint job, he heard his mother's voice. Jim swallowed hard, but noticed she is calm; just shootings the breeze with his wife as if it was a Sunday dinner. *"Maybe nothing is wrong? Must remain calm… Yea that's it, she doesn't know."* He came into the house setting the window glass to the side.

"Oh there you are son, come in and shut the door if you wouldn't mind. What have you got there? It looks like a new window to me." She said calmly feeling the fool and almost felt sorry for him and his poor wife of the bomb she was about to drop.

"Yes, Ma, the other one needed to be replaced." He said wondering how much she knows as he looked over at Linda and placed the window in the corner for now.

"Oh, I see. Come, come in and sit down." She said as if she was a spider and they were the fly, spreading a new web just for them.

"Now then, that's better. Nice and comfortable?" She asked. "Can I fix you a nice hot cup of tea my, special blend?" The air in the room started to change when she stood. "Why I am up because we were going to be here a while." Trying not to change her voice, but

What's Behind the Looking Glass?

kept it pleasant, but stern. Linda started to stand... "SIT! ... My dear, now! ... That's better," she said calming her self down just a little... while she waited for the water to steam. She looked over the small three bedrooms home. A housekeeper Linda is not as she frowned at the state of things, taking her finger across the countertop wiping the dust from the corners. Shaking her head as she quickly washed her hands.

"So mother," Jim said as Linda turned to look at him as they both swallowed hard, mouths dry and shaking a little. "What's on your mind? I noticed the Old Harley outside and your old jacket." He said with a puzzled look on his face, taking another swallow as she looked through the cabinets and fridge. He winced knowing there was old and stale food that should be thrown out weeks ago watching a mouse scurry along the living room baseboards and disappeared behind the stacked boxes that he had meant to cover with a sheet. *Too late she noticed.*

"Oh. This old thing? I was just thinking about you son." She said as she came around and takes a chair across from them to see their faces better, watching them squirm. "Is there something you would like to tell me?" She asked as she clicked the teacup with her fingers and eyes blazed as if they could burn a hole right through his head... Linda and Jim squirmed like a mouse caught in a trap.

"What do you mean Ma?" Jim slowly replies looking down at the ground refusing to look at her.

"Oh. Son!" She said as she leaned forward from the chair, placed one hand on his knee looked him straight in the eye. "Don't you dare play coy with me? I am not the fool you think I am!" Then slowly turned looked straight at Linda. "Do you know where your son EJ really is?" She asked pausing... "Well I do ... and he is not... Oh no ... Not at any Scout Camp, that's for sure," she said pausing again to let it sink in sitting back in the chair before them.

Linda's voice cracked as she asked. "How do you know this?"

"Because... I have seen him!" Fear swelled in their eyes. "And I know where he is too." Then she glanced at the new window lying against the wall. "And I have a pretty good idea what's been happening around here too." She said she could hear them swallowing hard, but wanted to wait before going in for the kill... "You haven't tried the tea yet." She said almost teasing. Like it didn't matter, but it did to her.

"No. Thanks, Ma." Jim said with half a whimper in his voice. They never really cared for tea. It was like drinking toilet water to them, but they kept the tea kettle and the cups just for her whenever she decided to visit.

Linda shaking, takes the little cup, tried to take a sip and slops it down her front, she sets it back down and wiped her chin. Grandma doesn't say a thing but was smiling inside. Knowing it was now time to stoke the furnace and light the match. "I've just finished patching him up again and saw all his wounds; there is not a question in my mind. On the hows and the where or the whose?" She said wanting to strike while the iron was white-hot. "Now then I need minute so just sit there and reflect, what I am about to do." She said coolly letting it sink into them. Eyeing the clock giving Doc and several of police time to inspect the property outside and question the neighbors before she informs them they are here and why.

"What do you mean… about to do?" Linda asked, as her voice is about to crack again.

"I said a minute dear!" She said gets up and pours her some more tea and then sat back down as she gazed back at them as she sipped the tea slowly. She gazed some more and back at the window by the door then back down the hall towards the boy's bedroom. She slowly reached into her pocket and pulled out a copy of the paper from the Judge and handed it to them. Allowing time for them to read it and waited for it to sink in; thinking now it's time to let it burn and simmer, as she stares at them clicking the teacup with her fingernails. Her eyes hard as steel as she gazed down upon them not one eye blinked.

"Mother, mother you can't, you can't do this!" Jim said shakily reading the paper in his hands. His fist tight and knuckles turned white as he made a fist as he reads the court paper. Granting his mother full custody of his children, and allowing her to take them out of his home.

Grandma waited. "But I can and I have done it. Now I am sure you are going to have some questions, but I see now is not the time to ask them... Have you noticed? Not once did you ask me if he was ok, or what was going to happen to your other children now that they have been given full custody to me since it is obvious you can no longer care for them after what you two have just done to your oldest boy, thinking nobody including me would ever find out.

"He hasn't even been home for two full months and the state said you were making such progress again it's obvious that none of that were true and just another lie. I want you to think about that for a while. They are being cared for by someone else for the time being. Why you seek some help and I strongly suggest you do it. I will send back my sisters to pick up their things, please have them ready. For now, I need to go sit with EJ my grandson and Danny, since they need me the most right now.

"I won't be home for a few day's, you can leave a message with Richard if you need to." She said. Grandma turned back towards the door to face them. "How could you?" As she looked right at Jim then leaned back into the chair eyes tearing up. "Why, would you both?" She thought of EJ down at Downing Farm as she sat there sipping her tea to regain her Grandma composed self.

"Linda if you wouldn't mind? I will need some of Danny's clothes to take with me. If you can gather them I would appreciate it. I will send for EJ things later. Now, now don't pout dear. It causes wrinkles you know and I am trying so hard to be nice. If you feel that you need help, please feel free to ask. They are just right outside." Linda and Jim looked shocked. "Oh. I didn't tell you, dear!" As she looked at them pleased as punch and sees the terror in their faces and watched them turn white. "I almost completely forgot. My memory these days... Well then... While I was down at Judge Parker's place. You know me and him go way, way back, in fact, I remember the time."

"MOTHER!" Jim replies in an angry and impatient voice.

"What son? If you want to say something, you don't have to be rude about it. Anyway, it was decided that a full investigation should be done… So, Doc Hatfield, you do remember him, son. I served with him as one of his nurses, nice fella. During the war remember?" She asked.

"Mother!" Jim replied as he gritted his teeth.

"Yes, son?"

"I know who he is, get to the point." She forgets that this is a small town, everyone knows Old Doctor Hatfield. Yet this did not bring a smile to his lips, just thinking of the gossip and scandal she has caused. His father wouldn't have been proud. No, not of him, he has not been proud of him in a long time ever since he married Linda without knowing her folks and family as he announced coming back not more than two-three months after his LDS mission they had gotten married. *"It was his choice not his or hers for that matter, Steve married young why can't I? Besides what more could he look for in a wife? So what she can't cook or keep a clean house. At least she doesn't complain when I don't pick up my clothes or make the bed or even leave dirty dishes in the sink. That's what we have children for I thought, to do those meaningless things. Besides I am too busy working to put food on the table and pay bills, I don't need a distraction."*

"Yes, son. I was just about to do that if you would stop interrupting me. Anyway, Doctor Hatfield has seen EJ already and is planning on seeing the rest of the other children. He and an officer from the Court House are outside. If you would like I can bring them in to help if want dear? Now, where were we? Oh yes. Danny things, Linda would you please. I really need to get back. It seems you two have a lot to do and you need time to be alone." She said standing up to say they were through for the moment as she waited for Linda to squeeze by her before sitting back down.

"Yes. Grandma." Linda said sounding very angry as her eyes glared back at her.

What's Behind the Looking Glass?

"You dear can call me Grandma Stuart or Grandmother Stuart, but not Grandma dear! Now Danny things please; I have a grandson to get back to," She said trying to control the anger.

Linda carefully nodded her head, which is about to explode of the events that just unraveled in front of her. Eric has indeed been found and, he has been badly hurt, what's worse she knows. In fact, everyone knows it was their fault. *"Her fault, her fault her fault..."* She shakes her head to clear the echo. Right now she has a hell of headache more than one as she looks at Eric's grandmother sitting across from her husband Jim. It reminded her of a black widow spider, *"I hate spiders,"* thinking too herself. *"She never did like me. Just look at her gloating over there. My question is, how did she find out in the first place?"* She thought as she walked to Danny's room seeing the empty beds, gazed over where Eric would normally sleep. "Too many of those bad genes if you ask me," she said.

She grabbed a pillowcase off the bed and stuffed some of Danny's clothes into it and throwing in that cursed old hat. She said walking past the broken window where Eric leaped for his life. With a tear in her eye, she whispered, "What have we done?" Turned down the hall toward the girl's room and sees their empty beds. "My little angels, there still might be hope for you still." Then turned and walked with pillowcase in hand back to the living room. She sees the spider waiting, sitting with her husband in the web she has just spun about them; getting ready to prey upon its meal... *"Sweet mellow mother in law... phew, I was right all along, bad genes. Lot's of them in spades if you ask me."*

"Now then Jim as I was saying," Grandma said as she picked up the pillowcase from Linda. "I would strongly suggest you get the help you need son. Then the children will be returned to you, but as for EJ. I don't expect much there son. The wounds you caused. I am afraid you both caused!" As she stared at both of them, "go a lot deeper then any physical wounds will ever go I am afraid. I just hope little Danny... I can't even bear to think of it and only hope it's not too late even for those girls of yours.

"We will talk later son, you too Linda... and by the way Linda. I did like you when you married my son and I did trust you with my grandchildren and still do, but not until you seek help. Now then I have said my peace. Your son EJ needs me so I'll be off." Grandma said as she stands and opened the door. "Oh, Jim don't install this window just yet wait a few minutes. Ok, boys, you can come in, be quick. These two have been through a lot today," she said.

"Yes Grandma," they replied.

"Mother!" Jim asked very angrily.

"Yes, Jim? Don't worry... For now, at least, they are just going to look around some that's all, just sit tight. They have their orders not to press charges... for now... and Doc wants to examine the both of you. To find out what kind of parents you are? In fact, we are all wondering that, to tell you the truth. After that, it's up to you what you do my dear. Bye for now. I really need to go." She said as she slings the pillowcase into the sidecar compartment, puts on her gloves and helmet and throws her blue scarf in the back, steps on the peddle of old Harley and with a shattering "roar" that rattles the nearby windows and doors, smoke bellowing out the muffler. She squealed the tires and pops a wheelie and she was off to find Danny. Leaving Jim and Linda behind too standing there with mouths open stunned by the sight.

"Yep, she's a wild one there your mother," Doc Hatfield said scratching his chin.

"What?" Jim asks as he slowly turned to meet the man beside him.

"Oh Doc Hatfield is the name, we should go inside," he said.

"Oh, oh yes," Jim replied not wanting the neighbors to see him.

Chapter 7-2

* * *

"Hello Mr. Jones," Lizy said pulling up a stool for children and her while they look over the flavors. Mr. Jones was an old friend of hers, whom she met in High School science, homeroom of Mr. Davidson long dead now. He's a lot older now, but so is she. His hair gray and wisp flat across the top. His eyes have dulled blue with more white then blue. Liver spots against his hands as she watched him push a towel around the counter. Average height maybe 5'9 if she were to guess and has only met his wife once. Yet he did ask her to the dance once as he stepped on her toes, but now she can tell he's more confident by the way he walks. He doesn't shuffle but walks like a man should with his broad shoulders. It's even surprising to see he has all his teeth. Least she thinks they are real.

"Well now, I'll be a cleaned cat with nowhere to go, if it isn't my dear old friend Mrs. Lizy Dragren," he said as he wiped down the counter in front of him. The store was lit with bright colors of greens and yellows with bluish-green stools long the counter and striped booths in the pattern blue and green along the storefronts open windows. All manner of ice cream flavors featured from glass case behind the counter, with an old fashion mirror that hung on the wall. It hadn't changed in the last thirty years as Lizy gazed around the room remembering days of yesterdays as a spent youth here.

"How have you been Mr. Jones?" She asked as she leaned over the counter to look at the ice cream.

"Can't complain, no sir can't complain and who are these fine looking little ones?" He asked putting the towel to the side.

"These are my niece's and my nephew," she replied.

"Fine looking children I must say. How can I help you today?" He asked.

"Can I get some ice cream for these children please, while we wait for their grandmother to arrive? She should be here momentarily. She had some business to attend too and, while you are added it I think I'll have two scoops myself," she said licking her lips impatiently.

"What, and spoil that girlish figure of yours?" He said as quickly eyes her up and down like most men would see a pretty girl next to his wife. There ain't one prettier.

"Oh please, Mr. Jones. I haven't had that good of figure in ages. You really o't be ashamed of yourself trying to make an old lady like me blush like that," she replied.

"Oh, nonsense."

"What would your wife say, Mr. Jones?" She said as she giggled.

"Aunt Lizy?" Peggy asked.

"Yes, Peggy. "What's Grandma doing at our house, and what business are you referring too?" Peggy asked on a side of caution.

"Humm let's see. That's quite a question now for such a little girl like you to ask. Your Mother and Father; No! Humm, let me see if I can, yes…Peggy; How would like to stay with me for a while?" Lizy asked avoiding the question altogether.

"Why would I want to do that?" Peggy asked feeling very troubled as she eyed her aunts knowing they are not close, not by a long shot. *What has Eric done now?*

"Humm… so, I could get to know you better, I never get to see you girls. It would be just for a little while," she said.

"What about Mama and Daddy?" She asked. *She's not getting off the hook that easily I want answers, and I want them now!*

"Humm, they needed some alone time together to sort something's out, like a vacation just the two of them, a little time off as it were," she replied with caution. *She's not buying it, aunt Lizy,* seeing the evil smirk from the corner of her eye.

"This is because of Eric isn't it, he's been bad again? I knew it." Peggy said feeling trapped and angered about losing the control she had. *"No. I must make them pay."*

"Peggy that's not it at all… Eric's, going somewhere too dear, so… you see in a way you are all getting a vacation. Think of it as a vacation, the only difference is. I get to take care of you and Mary here will be taking care of Dona. We all live close enough that you will see each other once in a while and your parents can come and see you whenever they want to. Now then what kind of ice cream do you want?" She said as she looked over at all Ice cream.

Seeing Mary sigh with relief on which child she was going to get stuck with. She knew Peggy could and would be a handful, but she's had the most experience of the two of them. Dona might not be as bad as her sister Peggy. *"I hope not anyway. Or I am knee-deep in little girl rage and revenge."*

"I am not sure I like this idea Aunt Lizy, but that ice cream sure looks good." Not satisfied but for now it's best to play it cool as she thinks of a plan of attack. *Yes, they will all pay!*

"Aunt Mary?" Danny asked feeling a little concerned that nobody as even mentioned him nor EJ where they are staying takes hold of Mary's hand.

"Yes, Danny?"

"Where I am going to stay if Peggy is staying with Aunt Lizy and Dona is staying with you and EJ. I don't know where he is staying, so where am I staying?" He asked. Dona, Peggy looked up at there aunts as something caught her attention. "Well, guys your Grandma has a surprise for all of you for that answer. I can tell you this Danny," as they take their ice cream and she hands a five-dollar bill over the counter. "Keep the change, Mr. Jones." Finding a seat near the window she said as she turned to Lizy for help. For when came to excuses her sister was the queen by far by avoiding them.

"What do you think Lizy should I tell them?" She asked.

Danny and his sisters are at the edge of their seats. "I don't know? Their Grandma would kill me," she said as she took another bite of her Ice cream.

"Tell us, tell us, Aunt Mary," they begged. Giving the most pleading looks they could possibly muster.

"Alright," she said. Aunt Mary looked carefully around the room, then over her shoulder, bent down close to the table and whispered. "Your brother Eric is staying with another family here in town, now he is hurt really bad so he staying with them for the time being, but…"

She takes a deep breath, "that's not all!" She looked around room making sure the coast is clear. "Your little brother Danny here is on his way to visit him for a few days, then he going to live with his Grandma." Then proud as peacock she slid back into her chair with the biggest grin on her face. Watching the children's eyes pop right out their little heads.

Danny, bouncing around in his seat with excitement, he could barely control himself. "REALLY!" I get go see EJ!" And climbed down from his seat went over to gives his aunt Mary a big hug. Peggy and Dona not sure how to feel at the moment of this new discovery, of finding out they are being broken up or that Eric was still alive and well. Just stared at each other wondering what was going to happen next. At least they won't be fighting with each other that's one good thing at least, or is it? Of course, they didn't have to wait long, hearing the roar of the motorcycle pulling in.

"Look, Aunt Lizy!" Peggy said pointing to grandma as she turned off the motorcycle and removed her gear as she made her way to the door…

"Oh my! It's the wind herself," replied Lizy.

"What do you mean Aunt Lizy?" Dona asked confused by that statement. *The wind who?*

What's Behind the Looking Glass?

Danny turned around. "That's Grandma silly."

"What in tar nations?" Mr. Jones said as he watched from the window ran to the door.

"Well hello to you to Mr. Jones," Grandma replied back fixing her hair as she patted it down making sure everything was still in place.

"Well they said you would be swinging by, but Betty Stuart I never in my wildest?"

"Oh. I see my grandchildren are here," cutting him off. "Enjoying your ice cream my dear sweet children, I hope it didn't spoil your appetites too much before dinner, but your Grandma had some errands to run. Now then come give me a big hug and a kiss and update me on what you been up to..." after she hugged them all and listened to all their little news of childhood adventures. Noticing for any visible bruising or cuts... "Well now I have some news of my own," she said.

"Grandma!" Danny asked impatiently.

"Yes, Danny?"

"When do I get to see EJ?" Danny asked excitedly standing near Aunt Mary away from his sister Peggy as possible as she in turned tightened a fist and eyed him like a piece of meat at him as she swiftly hid the fist behind her back giving grandma a false smile... Mumbled *"watch it you little brat,"* mouthed the words as she gritted her teeth and watched the room around her. *"No, they were all going to pay, starting with him and his brother."*

"Oh, I see somebody has already let my little secret out," as she looked at Mary and Lizy looking little ashamed.

"It was just too juicy and they were asking, we had to think of something," Lizy said quickly looking down at Peggy thinking she heard her and said something as she smiled up at her. *"You got to better than that to fool me,"* seeing her fake smile.

"It's all right, really," Grandma said fixing her hair in the large counter mirror, watched the children excited faces. Grandma looked down at Danny; "real soon Danny. Finishes your ice cream then we will go. So what did you tell them anyway?"

"Lizy and I sort of filled things in for them. Told them they were all going on a vacation except this is for everyone, a private vacation for each of them," Mary replied.

"Oh, I see… Humm…" She said looking over at her grandchildren. "Actually that's not such a bad idea, yes it could work." When it comes to Lizy and Mary they always have a plan of getting themselves out of trouble. But this idea seemed to flourish the more she thought about it and the more she liked it.

"Betty!" Mary said with caution.

"A separate vacation… Okay, that's what we are going to use. They won't know the difference. They're too young. So make it fun for them and keep their minds busy, while their parents work things out. Now EJ, poor boy! I only hope the Downing's can help him there because we have our hands full here!" Especially you Lizy that Peggy, she takes after her mother, watcher her closely, she's got the devil in her. That's why I wanted to separate the kids and bring some peace between them. Hopefully, straighten her out if possible with some motherly love and kindness." She said taking a good look at her grandchildren as tears moistened in her eyes thinking about all the things they have gone through that children shouldn't. *Damn their parents. I should have kept a closer eye on them, nothing to do about spilled milk except watch more carefully as you pour it.*

"Now you can go back to the house to get their things if you like, but don't be too surprised what you find or won't find. In fact, I am pretty sure that these boys don't have much as for as clothing goes. I haven't seen what she put in the pillowcase yet." She said seeing the rags Danny was wearing today. "I shudder to think. So I'll leave that up to you. Just have the girls see Doc Hatfield at his office before you leave town and I'll call you in a day or two. I need to get back to the farm. I've been gone too long already," she said calling Danny over. "Danny?"

What's Behind the Looking Glass?

"Yes, Grandma." He said licking the back of his spoon and hopping down from his seat.

"Are you ready to go?" She asked.

"REALY!" He replied bouncing up and down with excitement.

"Tell your sisters goodbye and stand over here like a good boy," she said.

"Goodbye Peggy," he said being very careful not to get close to her.

Peggy just waved not wanting to say it out loud but whispered behind her teeth so her Grandma couldn't hear her say it. "Good reddens you little brat," but does a fake smile and faked a wave goodbye.

Dona a little more open says. "Goodbye Danny, try not to cause any trouble." Eyeing her sister as she waves with her jaw cinched tight.

"Now girls give me one more hug and kiss from each of you before I go; now that's better." She said as she stands in front of them and lifts their heads up with their chins. Looked squarely into their eye one at a time so they know she means business. "I want you to do three things. One: mind your aunts... Second: have lots of fun... Three: be nice to each other always, and all three of these girls is not an option... got it?" She said then waited for them to reply.

"Yes, Grandma."

"Now then go on your little vacation." With that, she and Danny walked out the door and back towards the Harley.

"Well Danny, are you ready to have some fun," she asked as he looked at the bike almost shaking with excitement. *Yes, its been too long, why have I waited so long to get back on it after all these years...?*

"Do I really get to ride in that?" Danny asked excitedly.

"What else my dear boy, I didn't bring the car, now did I?"

"No Grandma, why didn't you bring the car?" He asked a little scared to get inside the little sidecar.

"It had a flat dear boy, plus I am the wind you know." She said as she pulled out a small leather jacket just little Danny size and Danny's eyes grew rounder then Easter Eggs.

"Grandma!" He turned and puts it on.

While his sisters and aunts inside gasps with their hands to their mouths "Oh My!"

"Oh my Lizy! Look Mary what she is doing?" She said.

Grandma helped him with his little gloves and placed a black helmet on his head with a picture of a cross bone skull. Picked up Danny off the ground, placed him in the little car next to her and pulled out a little white scarf and place it around his neck. Stands up on the bike than with a loud roar brings the old Harley Davidson to life, squeals the tires pop a quick wheelie and she was off down the street.

Peggy, Dona raced out of store turned to their aunts with the biggest surprised look on their faces. Turn and faced their aunts...."Aunt Mary, aunt Lizy is Grandma insane?" They asked.

They stood there and laughed. "No dear. Your Grandma, she is just the wind and she just needed to blow and man can she blow," Lizy replied.

"Aunt Mary?" Dona asked.

"Yes, Dona."

"How can we go on a vacation if we don't have any clothes or suitcases to put any in it?" hoping they might change their mind about this whole idea as she worried about her parents. Or just maybe her father, after all, she was a Daddy's little girl.

What's Behind the Looking Glass?

"Lizy, she does have a point?" Mary said taking Dona's hand as they walk back towards the door where their ice cream was melting.

"Let's go back inside finish our ice cream, while I think on that one." As they were eating there Ice cream Lizy noticed some luggage in the far corner. "Mary watch the girls for a moment; I have an idea," then pointed to the luggage in the corner. Lizy got up from the table went over to the counter and sat at the stool. "Mr. Jones?" She asked.

"Yes, what else can I get you, fine ladies, today?"

"Well, we were wondering about that luggage over there in the corner," Lizy pointed to it in the corner.

"Luggage…? Oh that luggage, yes what about that luggage?" He asked.

"We were wondering if it was for sale."

"For sale?"

"For sale, yes," she replied.

"It was for a display once for a raffle if I recall. I was just getting ready to put it back into storage," he said.

"Would you be willing to sell it to me? You see I need it for my nieces, there getting ready to go on a vacation and they don't have anything put their clothes in and we are kind of in desperate need of some and I would really would appreciate it." Lizy said turning on her womanly charms.

Mr. Jones looked at the girls and rubbed his chin, "oh shucks, you know me. I could never refuse a pretty face. Besides, they would be sitting there, take up space anyhow and they might as well get some use out of them. Tell you what, for a kiss on the cheek and hug from the little ones. It will only cost you 10.00 dollars how's that sound for the lot of them. Just don't tell my wife or she'll skin me alive," he said.

"Mr. Jones you got yourself a deal," Lizy said as she leaned over the counter and gave him big o fats kiss right on the cheek and handed him a ten-dollar bill. Then she went over to the luggage and starts picking it up and hands each a suitcase to the girls.

"Lizy?" Mary asked.

"Yes, Mary."

"You were always were a smooth talker when it comes to men," as she giggled.

"I learned it all from their grandmother," she said as she looked at Peggy and Dona still feeling a little concerned to what she was getting herself into.

"Well, ladies we have the suitcases now we just need to fill them. Tell us what we need to put in them so we can start our vacation." The girls stopped by the house, figured it was best. That way they could at least see their parents off, plus the Doc and the officer haven't left yet so they would be fine.

They knocked on the door to be polite because they didn't want to barge in. Mary went in first to give a break down on the details so as not to upset the girls when they came in. Girls come into the house seeing their parents and ran up to them. "Mama, Mama! Were going on a vacation all of us can you believe it?" Peggy said.

"Yes Peggy, I heard," she said trying to hold back the tears.

"I am going to stay with aunt Lizy while you and Daddy have some fun too, doesn't that sound wonderful?" Peggy said hoping they would put an end to this once and for all.

Her mother trying really hard not too causes a scene. "Yes dear, that sounds great," she said with a tear in her eye.

"You can come and see us whenever you want too. That is if you are not to busy that is." Taking another stab and not gaining any purpose.

What's Behind the Looking Glass?

"Oh we will dear, we will," She said as she wiped an escaped tear. Trying very hard to control her anger as the words echoed. "*Your fault, your fault, we did nothing wrooong*! Shaking her head to silence them as she felt the walls closing in on her and the panic rising almost suffocating her.

"Peggy gives your mother and father a hug then let's go pick out some clothes for you to take dear," Lizy said taking her by the shoulders and steering her towards her bedroom as she carefully eyes Linda and Jim and the state of this house. Lizy wanted to run feeling the cold darkness when she met Jim's eyes of hatred. The house reeked with terror suffocating the room, but it seems she is the only one that felt it.

"Yes, aunt Lizy."

Lizy turned to her mother. "I promise to take real good care of her." Not waiting for a response walked down the hall with Peggy to choose out her clothes. Then after filling the suitcase walked Peggy quickly out to the car leaving whatever is lurking there in the darkness behind. Mary does the same thing and then tells Doc Hatfield that they will be at his office in a few minutes.

Chapter 7-3

Lizy said. "Well, girls we just have to make one more stop before we can start our vacation. Did you know that is required that before you go on any trip you have be checked out by a Doctor?" Watching them shake their heads, "that's right, even us. Your parents were being checked out to before they can go. In fact, they had the Doctor come right to the house so they could leave on their vacation from there. EJ and Danny are being checked out as well, so now it's our turn." Lizy said trying to sound convincing. "Hello, Doc I brought the girls by as their grandmother requested."

"Glad you did after speaking with their parents. Tsk, tsk. And after seeing that poor boy, what a day this has been. One surprise after another, I can tell you... yes sir. Those folks are going too need some serious help. I just hope we have seen the worst of it that's all I can say. I like the idea of the vacation, quick thinking I must say yep. Ok let's start with Peggy is it?"

Doc looked the girls over and does what he can to make them laugh and to keep their minds busy. "Ok Lizy, it's your turn," standing aside from the door as he waited for her to enter.

"See, I have to get checked out too," she says, trying to fake it the best she can. They go in and close the door. "Well, what's the verdict Doc?" She asked taking a seat near the exam table as he closed the door.

"Now Lizy, I may be an old country doctor, but I am not stupid so if you wouldn't mind please put on the gown just like Mary, so I can examine you. After all, I was told to look at all of you, and that's what I am going to do. Or she will skin me cleaner than possum on Tuesday and hang me out too dry." Handing her a gown and stood by the partition screen. "Now that's better," he grinned as he watched her sit on the exam table. "Breathe while I listen to your heart and lungs, that's good girl... Those girls have some mild bruising, but they're old, but they are definitely caused by objects of some kind."

He paused made some notes on a chart placing his pen into his right pocket continues on with the exam.

"I did ask, but they wouldn't tell me or something like they fell, tripped. Or got them from her sister or their brother, but whenever I asked about their parents. They would clam up tighter than clams. Then I asked a question about their brother EJ, they said he was always in trouble. Always in fights at school, but never would say with who. I asked if his parents ever did anything to him or his brother Danny, they would clam up again. We would talk about something else said everything they say or does was just lies." he said waiting for her to dress "Anyway it looks like you have your hands full my dear and you are as healthy as a horse by the way just like your sister," and opened the door.

"Well, I've done my job. So off you go and enjoy your little vacation and try to keep your sister Betty out of trouble, and if you can and off that contraption of hers."

"But Doc, she having such a good time and the grandchildren are loving it?" She said.

"Yes, I know, but she is scaring the dickens out of the rest of us," Doc said as he waved goodbye.

"Ok ladies its time we headed out. Peggy time to say goodbye to your sister Dona for a while, go on now."

Peggy and Donna not sure really how too say goodbye; It's not that they really hated each other, but don't really like each other either so they watched their aunts for some suggestions, just to get through it. Mary seeing this whispered over to Lizy and gave them both a little nudge and whispered in their ears.

"Best way too start dear is to go over give and your sister a hug even if you don't want to," Lizy said.

"Don't worry! It will get easier, trust me! I've been there!" Peggy looked up at her aunt Lizy as she nodded her head, wondering if she could believe her. "Go on now." Peggy grudgingly went over and gave her sister a hug and said goodbye, and then got into Aunt Lizy's car and waited fearing the unknown.

"Mary I'll give you a call in a couple of days when you get settled in." Gets in the car turned the key and pulled away from the curb, headed for home with Peggy looking out the window watching her sister and town fade away.

"Well, Dona ready to go? It's just us now, everyone set out on their vacation except us so, I say its time, what do you say?" She asked.

"Yes, Aunt Mary."

"Ok let's go," she said opening the car door.

Dona takes a big deep breath. "Try to stay out trouble Eric and Danny if you can." Feeling the world she knows disappear behind her as they drove out of Santaquin she sighed with a slight tug in her heart as she thought of her father alone without them.

Chapter 8

Robert heard the loud roar of the motorcycle as it pulled back into the farm. "Look Pa, look, EJ's Grandmother she back. She sure knows how to stir up the chicken and horses that's for sure," Robert said as he and Will went outside to greet her.

"Well, I see you made it back ok and you weren't kidding about an extra package. Don't be afraid son, what's your name?" Wayne chuckled as he welcomed his new guest to the farm.

"Danny sir, I come to see EJ, he's my brother," Danny said a little scared as he looked at man the size of a large tree, but he soon relaxed as he looked into deep blue eyes. The fear melted away he sighed with relief.

"Is that right? Then you best come in." He said as he smiled.

"Wayne any change in my grandson?" Grandma asked knowing it was too soon to expect anything after all it had only been a few hours or so since she has seen him, but she had hoped he would be awake. She needed to find out the truth behind what his parents have done and nip in the butt quickly, and before time ran out before the state could take him away to parts unknown. *"Damn his parents, his grandfather had seen this coming and I should have done something long before now, but he's gone now. It's up to me to solve the mess and make things right, she should have done it long ago... Why did I wait so long too act? Why?"*

"No, but he seems to be resting a little bit more comfortably since Doc came by," he said taking Grandma's arm as they walk back towards the house and opened the door for her.

"That's good," she said trying to shake the dark thoughts from her mind as they echoed. *"Dead... he could be lying in there dead next time...* 'No, not going to let that happen," she said that part aloud enough it startled Wayne.

Wayne cringed as her nails too held tight to his arm leaving marks she seemed far away just for a moment. "Would you like to see him before dinner? So you and Danny here can freshen up," Wayne asked.

"Yes, that would be nice."

"Martha has everything ready and she's in there now. Will, would you mind taking Danny here and his Grandma Stuart," with a quick reminder look, "sorry, take Grandma down to see EJ, please son," he asked releasing her arm as she went through the door. Just for a moment, he thought he saw a shadow of a man and a boy standing in the distance, but when turned to look right at them they were gone. *Humm... that was strange?*

"Ok Pa, come on Danny, let's go see your brother. Now you are going have to be real quiet, or Ma will kill us all and probably your Grandma too," he said.

"Ok Will," Danny replied happily almost skipping into the house and down the hall.

Danny nearly bounced off the walls with excitement. Martha watched Grandma Stuart and Danny walk into the room, "I thought that was you making all that ruckus out in front, and who is this little man you brought with you?" she asked.

"This is his little brother Danny."

"Well Danny, come here let me take a good look at you," she said.

Danny looked at his Grandma unsure, "Its ok Danny." Danny walked cautiously over to her while he noticed EJ sleeping in the bed.

"You know Danny, you are the spitting image of your brother and I would know considering. I had to put him back together a couple of times now. Well then, they tell me that dinner will be ready in about an hour so that should give you plenty of time to freshen up and we can visit, but I think this poor child here," she said as she turned Danny around in circles. "Child, my goodness graces alive, I can't tell if that is dirt or the color of your skin," Martha said. Grandma and Danny laughed with the biggest grins on their faces.

"Will dear?" Grandma calls out into the hall.

"Yes, Grandma?"

"Can you go out to the bike and bring in the pillowcase for me; it has Danny's clothes in it so we can get him changed before dinner?" She asked.

"Yes, ma'am."

"Will?" Ma asked before he leaves.

"Yes, Ma?"

"While you are doing that, send Julie in here please," she said.

"Yes, Ma."

"Julie?" Ma asked watching her enter the room pausing long enough to give Danny a smile.

"Yes, Ma?"

"Would you go into Sam's room, and find that box of Sam's clothes that he grew out of. I think they might fit this poor boy... and run a bath for him," she said.

Danny's eyes popped wide open, "a bath!" Grandma and Martha started laughing.

"Yes, Ma." Julie giggled at little Danny sour expression.

"What Danny, did you think I was going to let you sit at my clean table, and then sleep in my clean bed looking like that? Oh no my boy, heavens no. EJ your brother had a bath and now it's your turn," Martha said with a laugh.

Danny turned and looked at Grandma for help, she just shrugged her shoulders, "Danny, don't sweat the small stuff," and rubbed his hair as Will came back into the room holding a pillowcase that has seen better days.

"Here's that pillowcase Grandma," Will said as he held it out to her.

"Thanks, Will, you mind taking Danny down to the bathroom and helping him into the tub, I will be down in a minute, thanks, dear." Danny takes another look at EJ sleeping and then looked at his Grandma then looked down at the floor and followed Will down to the bathroom as if it was a death sentence.

Will seeing this put his arms around him. "You know your brothers going be ok, my Ma and us got everything under control and you'll feel so much better after a nice hot bath and a hot meal. Then you can spend time with your brother. Look at this way Danny; if you don't take a bath, they won't let you anywhere near him. Then where would you be sleeping, Danny? With the pigs! You can play with them tomorrow if you would like and, the chickens, and the horses. After all Danny boy, we live on a farm."

Danny looked up at Will with his big blue eyes, "You have pigs and horses too?" He asked.

"Yep," he said.

"WOW!" Danny replied.

"Now what do say we get you cleaned up?" Will, asked.

"Ok Will," he said letting Will help him into the tub and giving him one of Sam's sailboats to play with as the bubbles swirled around him.

"Well Martha, I was afraid of that?" Grandma said taking out Danny's clothes from the pillowcase.

"Afraid of what Grandma Stua...? Sorry, Grandma," Martha said.

What's Behind the Looking Glass?

"Yu'll get the hang of it, dear, these clothes that his mother gave me for Danny. They are nothing but worn-out rags if you could call them that even. Well, I am not going back there to see if he's got any better ones, not after blowing off a little steam. I guess we will have to do a little shopping then. Martha, didn't you need fabric to make some kind of apron for EJ? Doc was just telling me about it." Shaking her head at the clothes that held so many holes in them... *"She should be a shame of herself her daughters had the fine dresses, but why theses for her boys?"*

"I'll send Julie in with those clothes. I had a feeling you were going to need them. They might be a little bit big, but I can adjust them later. They may be a little worn. But they still have some life in them," Martha said feeling very sad what these boys had to go through just to be thrown out like wolves. *No, she doesn't know the boy's story. Yet the wounds on this boy in Wills bed frightened her and frightened her husband as well. "How can anyone dare call that a home? And why could a parent hate their children so much to do something like this? No, she may not know the story behind it but she can guess and it tugs at her. The problem is what can she do about it now?"*

"Thanks, Martha."

"Oh they're just collecting dust, and they needed to put to use, I can't see anything better or anyone more deserving than that sweet little boy," she said.

"I think when this boy here wakes up, me and you need to take a trip into town and get some supplies," Grandma said.

"Good idea, now why don't you go down there and give your grandson a bath. I got things covered here, less you think you need me, but after seeing you work. I'm pretty sure you can handle him, you'll be just fine," as they both laughed. Leaving as she frowned at her grandsons EJ and prayed that he would be all right. Then headed on down the hall to the bathroom, which was nearly twice as big as hers at home. Then it would have to be with such a large family.

"Well, Will. Is he minding his peas and cues?" Grandma asked opening the door seeing Danny in the tub as Will played with the sailboats with him.

"Yes Grandma as good as gold, well just good as Sam is when he's in the tub getting water all over the floor," Will said.

"Oh, I see," as they both laughed. "Thanks, Will, I'll take it from here," she said taking the stool and setting it near the tub and watched Will close the door.

"Grandma, Will says I can see horses and pigs because they live on the farm!"

"Yes they do Danny and you can see them, would you like that?" She asked taking the washrag and soap and lathers it.

"Yes, will EJ get to see them too?" He asked sinking a sailboat in the water as if hit a tidal wave of bubbles.

"Yes, when he's well enough. Ok, Danny let's have a look at you and get you cleaned up so we can get you dressed for dinner, I am hungry aren't you?"

"Yes Grandma," he said circling the little boat.

"Are you having lots of fun with your Grandma Danny?" She asked.

"Oh, yes Grandma!" He looked up at her and grinned.

"I am glad, now let's wash those dirty toes of yours," trying to keep her grandson preoccupied and calm not changing her voice or tone. "Can you tell your Grandma where you got these bruises, I promise and I won't be mad, I swear," she said crossing her heart.

"You promise you won't tell Grandma? I could get into trouble." Danny trying very hard to hide them from her.

"I promise," she said crossing her heart again.

What's Behind the Looking Glass?

"I am not sure Grandma," Danny said looking worried.

"Tell you what, you just nod if I say the person ok, that way it's not really telling me anything ok," she said.

Danny grins. "Ok."

She washed his arms and to keep his mind occupied on something else, talks about things on the farm and what he might see and do. "Was it your sisters?" Danny shakes his head no. She washed his other arm, "was it your cat?" she asked.

"Grandma, we don't have a cat." He laughed then frowned think that if they did Peggy would most likely kill it or his father, they both hated animals. Just the mere thought of her and his father tightened their hands around his its neck or his for that matter made him gasp holding his breath in as chest tightened in fright. Grandma shakes him from his thoughts.

"Silly me," she said and rubbed his fingers, "was it the octopus escaping from the zoo?" she asked again being silly to ease his mind.

"Grandma?" He replied thinking the octopus would have a chance against his dad's belt. He almost could hear it whistle in the air as he jumps when Grandma touched him that he almost screamed.

"Was it your mama and daddy?" Danny's eyes quickly open big as saucers and nod his head yes quickly. *Snap goes the belt* .his screams echoed in his mind. "You know, I understand they're having roast beef for dinner with homemade bread and potatoes and fresh vegetables," watching Danny's mouth water, to forget everything they were just talking about. And talked about other things what they might see and do for fun. "Ok Danny, let's get you dried off then you can go see EJ... and your Grandma can change to, ok."

The belt whistled and fade into the shadows that only he could see as well as his brothers scream before he jumped out through the window. He shook with fear as the darkness lessened around him seeing his Grandmas loving face. "Yes, Grandma." He said.

She quickly dried him off seeing the terror in eyes fade she whispered. "My poor boys, what have they done?" As she quickly dressed him in borrowed clothes and sent him back down the hall where his brother was; she grabbed a quick change of clothes, making her look more like her grandmotherly self. Taking control of her anger and putting it away in a box. "Yes, she will deal with it even if their Grandfather wasn't here." They had no one they could count on. "Why did she wait so long, leaving them to live in the darkness so long?"

The words echoed in her mind. "*You left them, you left them alone... Why?*" She shouted. "No. It wasn't me!" As she grasped her chest as the pain shot up her arm her eyes watered from the pain as it soon decreased. Just for a moment, she thought she saw a man in the shadows with red glowing eyes, yet when she turned he was gone.

Danny climbed up on the bed next to his brother, puts his little arms around him. EJ stirred a little but remained asleep. Danny whispered in EJ ear, "Its ok EJ, me and Grandma are here now." Begins to cry not feeling alone at last with his brother beside him, but bothered him seeing him with so many bandages around him.

Martha, with a tear in her eye, seeing the affection of his little brother, just watched for a minute then got up and walked over to little Danny, sitting next to him on the bed patting him on the back as she comforted him while the tears slowly rolled down his cheeks. Telling him, "It's ok my little one, he will be alright, just go ahead and cry if you want to."

After a while grandma returned from freshening up, and headed back down the hall, finding Danny, Martha, and EJ on the bed. Martha turned to her, "well now that looks better, I must say. That's more what I was excepting," she said.

Grandma laughed. "Yes I know, instead of what they met was the wind instead. Hello Wayne," Grandma said seeing him walking in the door.

What's Behind the Looking Glass?

"Well now look what we got here. Is this the same Grandma or this someone else?" Wayne said teasing as he rubbed his chin with a grin on his face.

"You are such a kidder," Grandma replied.

"Are you and little Danny ready for some dinner? You to Martha, he's not going anywhere this time. He can't, I have all the keys; there are no clothes that he can wear in here, and all the doors are locked tight. I posted a guard with a clear sight of the door. He'll be fine. So we are all going to have dinner together, and if you argue my dear, I'll pick up that boy bring him in the kitchen, bed and all, if I have to... so march you two," he said.

"Martha I believe he's serious," Grandma said standing by the door.

"You can count on it," Wayne said as he looked over at Danny. "You two women go on ahead. Why I and Danny boy get ourselves ready; man's business you know." Pa watched the women leave then sat next to Danny, lifted him up and laid his head on his shoulder. "Son I know it hurts seeing your brother like that, but I promise you he will be ok. Now that he knows that you are here and he is safe and if you need to cry son just go right on ahead, I won't stop you. If you want to talk about it we will, but that roast beef sure looks good. So what do you say we wipe those tears and clean your face and go and fill our bellies?" He said then he tweaks his little nose and says "blow." Grabbing a washcloth, he cleaned his face then headed to the kitchen for dinner taking Danny by the hand.

"Pa looks like you have outdone yourself," Ma said as she looked at the spread on the table.

"Actually they wouldn't let me near the kitchen Ma, I had lots of help," Pa said as he smiled at his children. "So all I did was help them instead," Pa laughed. "Now then let's all be seated. I think it's about time we finally get acquainted properly now that things have quieted down for the moment unless there's another storm coming?" He said as he looked over at Grandma.

"Let me check," she said as she put her finger in her mouth then sticks it out test the air as if to test the winds then looked both directions. "Na, looks to me the winds have died down for the moment."

"Pa?" Sam asked.

"Yes, Sam?" taking his seat at front of the table across from Martha.

"What storm? There hasn't been rain or a cloud in the sky all day," he replied feeling confused.

"Me neither Pa!" Anna said. Grandma, Ma, and Pa laughed.

"Children, that's because Grandma here was the storm. The storm has blown itself out for the time being."

"Oh?" with confused looks on their faces.

"Now then where are my manners, we have guests and I haven't properly introduced them. Everyone this is Danny, EJ's little brother and this is well Grandma Stua... Sorry Grandma," he said making the introductions.

"You'll get it dear," she said as he nodded and continued.

"They will be staying with us for a while."

"Pa how long is EJ going to be here?" Robert asked passing the rolls after taking two for his plate and the butter.

Pa, not sure how to answer that question pauses for a moment. "Now let's dig into that roast beef," as he looked over at Danny. "I am sure Danny is starved." Trying to avoid the question, he slices the roast beef putting a large portion on Danny's plate.

"EJ's, going to be here a long time," Grandma said as she looked straight at Wayne and Martha. "I took care of that, he's been left in your care. Nobody will bother him, it's all done and it's all legal," she said as she passed the mash potatoes. "Will, do you mind dear passing me that wonderful looking gravy," and then tastes it. "And who made this?" She asked.

"I did!" Julie replies feeling slightly embarrassed feeling her cheeks redden as she scooped fresh peas on her plate.

"It's delicious," she said and smiled at Julie taking another taste.

Julie glowing, "thank you, Grandma."

Grandma watched to see if it left a shocked look on Wayne and Martha's faces. Instead, she saw only warmth and love and caring in their eyes. As she continued to load her plate and passing down the gravy.

"Pa?" Ma said taking the rolls from Will and the butter.

"Yes, Ma?" Pa cutting the roast beef into smaller bites and taking the peas from Robert.

"Sounds like you and the boys have got some extra work to do then," she said taking a portion of sliced roast beef and passing it on down the table.

"What do you mean Ma?" Pa asked taking a bite of mash potatoes and buttering his rolls.

"Well its time we add a couple more rooms onto the house don't you think? While we're at it, we can enlarge Robert's room," placing a dab of butter on the peas on the plate.

Pa looked over at his boys for a brief moment. "Maybe I should ask them first what do you think? After all, they are the ones that will be doing most of the work," taking another bite of his food.

"Yes, you are right Pa we better ask the kids?" She said. The children were on the edge with anticipation and excitement. Grandma just sat back loving every minute as he winked at her because she already knew what they are going to say.

"Ok children, what do you say, are Downing's up this?" Pa asked eyeing each one in turn.

"Oh Pa, do you even have to ask? We say he's already part of our family he just doesn't know yet." Robert said and the rest nodded in agreement.

Will put his arm around Danny and said. "He is too." Robert and the rest of the family nod their heads with approval that brings tears to their grandmother's eyes.

There was no question in her mind where her grandson EJ needed to be. She knew he would be safe and loved on the Downing Farm. Pa cleared his throat. "Now, how about some of that pie, unless everyone is stuffed?" Clearing his plate with a quick swipe with a roll.

"That sounds good Wayne, Julie dear let me help ya clear the table," Grandma said getting up picking up the plates and combining them with hers.

"But you are our guest Grandma," Julie said trying to stop her and picking up the pile Grandma had in front of her.

"I need to do something or I'll go crazy just sitting watch people doing things." She replied gathering more and following Julie into the kitchen, which was kept clean and sparkled with light yellow paint and brown homespun cabinetry with light blue curtains that set a warm tone. Right away she could tell Martha was a fine housekeeper and more so than EJ's and Danny's mother, not too mention an excellent cook. EJ was not going to go hungry here. It saddens her to see his pale skinny body which sickened her more when she noticed Danny's when she bathed him. *How long has been since either of them had a decent meal? She most likely was feeding them scraps.*

"I know what you mean, sometimes I need a little action to get my day started too," she said. Bring Grandma out of her dark thoughts.

What's Behind the Looking Glass?

"Now then let me help," Grandma says in a sweet, yet commanding voice. Not taking no for an answer.

Ma gets up from the table and started for the bedroom where EJ was, "Martha?" Pa asked.

"Yes, dear?" Stopping her in mid-stride before she reached the hallway.

"Where do think you're going?" he asked he knew where she was going, but he knew they both need a break and it was time to be with the children and their guest.

"I'd thought I go check on EJ," she said.

"I am sure he's fine and he hasn't left the room. You have been in there all day and you need a break. Robert?" he asked.

"Yes, Pa." Robert came around the corner of the kitchen with a white dishtowel with red strips over his shoulder.

"While the table is being cleared, will you go and check on EJ while I and your Ma take a stroll outside?" He asked helping Danny and Sam down from the table.

"Yes, Pa."

"Thanks, son."

"But I?" Martha tries to change his mind.

"Martha I want to show you something," he said. Pa wrapped his arms around her waist. Grandma just turned her head, smiled and gave a quick wink and a nod of her head as they left.

"Now then what was it you wanted to show me, Wayne?" She asked as she looked at the stars as they walked some distance from the house. Barn paint red seemed to throw shadows making it look darker than it actually was and she could hear animals that still seemed like music after all these years living on a farm.

"Oh, just how much I love you that's all my dear." He said as he looked into her eyes glossing in the moonlight as he slowly bends down caressing her back within his arms. He lifted her up and kissed her, knocks her back a couple of seconds.

"Wayne, what has gotten into you? First, you twirl our girls in the kitchen than this. I almost think we were dating." She tried to recover from such a hot passionate kiss that practically curled her toes, checking if there's a full moon out or something. "Wayne, let's try that again. I wasn't sure if that was my husband or if I was just dreaming."

This time he swings her up into his arms and then…"Ahh." They walked back to the house her fingers entwined with his.

"Ma, you are glowing, what on earth happened to you?" Julie asked.

"Oh, your Pa just wanted to show me something that's all Julie," she said patting his check and leaving his side to finish putting the dishes away.

"And what did he show you?" She asked.

"Something you are going to find out in a few years I think," and smiled.

"What's that's suppose to mean?" She said as she looked at Grandma with an amused smile.

"Oh, I think whatever it is dear you are going like it," Grandma said as she winked at Wayne with a smile and girlish giggle.

Robert proceeded to check on EJ, thoughts of him not being there would not be good. His parents would be horrified and might blame him. *This kid has tried once already to leave for some unknown reason. Pa knows something about him, yet he won't talk about it. Questions unanswered. How I am supposed to be a big brother to someone I don't even know? Maybe he doesn't want one? What about all those wounds? Where did he get them? Pa knows, but he won't say.*

What's Behind the Looking Glass?

"What if he's not there?" He stopped and paused Robert walked further down the hall, entered the room with his eyes closed, he opened them and sees EJ still sleeping. He takes a deep breath, "at least he didn't leave." He went over to where EJ was sleeping looked at him for a minute. "He looks like Will and Sam. I can't image what I would do without them." He reached down and put a hand on his bare shoulder. *Feels looks like any other kid on the street.*

EJ stirs a just little Robert looked into his sleeping face. "I trust my Pa, you should too, he says you are safe and you are safe. And if you need a big brother I will be one for you, because I too sometimes wish I had one. If you don't, I'll be glad to be just your friend too." Then tucked him in on the sides to make sure he's not going anywhere then he left the room.

"Now then how about some of that pie?" Ma said seeing Robert walking into the room... "So Robert everything ok with EJ?" She asked.

"Yes Ma, he's sleeping," he replied taking a chair from the dining room and setting it by Will as they both waited for the pie.

"I told you, Martha, he would be fine, stop fussing. He's not going anywhere?" Pa said taking a seat in his favorite stuffed brown chair facing the fireplace and indicating grandma to take a seat on the couch which has seen better days but still was quite comfy.

"I just can't figure it out for the life of me. How he managed to do it in the first place and where would he go and why?" She said taking a seat near the end of the couch and taking a piece of cherry pie from Julie as she passed the plates around the room.

Grandma rested her hand on her shoulder. "Fear most likely, but now that I am here and Danny's here when he wakes up, that will help, but I don't think it will remove it all I am afraid." As they watched the two little ones Danny and Sam drift off to sleep. Martha turned too Wayne "I know two little boys that have had a busy day." As she smiled, seeing pie all over their little faces and halfway down their shirts. "Yes, it has been a long day. I guess we better put them to bed."

Grandma stands to get little Danny. Wayne sits her back down on the couch, "you let me do, it's no trouble," he says.

"Are you sure?" Grandma asked sitting back on the couch.

Without another word, he picked up little Danny carefully on his shoulders and carries him down the hall. Pa carefully without waking him cleans the sleeping child, like he has done it a million times before. With a father's love and gets him ready for bed, then tucked him into the small bed right next to EJ. Then comes back down to the family room then picked up Sam and with the same care, he shown with Danny took him to his room and tucked him into bed and closed the door and returned to the family room.

"Wayne, I have to hand it to you, after seeing you carry these boys all day. You got to be tired; your arms got to be sore too." Grandma said.

Wayne laughed. "Grandma these women around here won't let me do anything else so that's my job and that is what I do around here and I do it well," as he gave his wife another kiss on the forehead, squeezed her shoulders. "Now then, tell us what you have been up to and how we can help. Since everything has quieted down some. I and Martha kinda have an idea, what's been going on and have our suspensions. Now for the children's sake," Pa said as he looked who was still in the room. "Just tell us if we are right or if we are wrong and will go on from there," he said.

"I hate to tell you, nice folks, this, but you are right on the money and it goes deeper than just EJ, little Danny is involved too," she said.

"Oh no, that poor little child," Martha cried.

"But not nearly as severe as, at least not yet. I think we might have caught it in time, thank goodness. There are two others, but I haven't yet heard from them, but I think they might be ok, for now at least. Their aunts are looking after them for a while so nothing further can happen to them," she said.

"Well that's some good news at least," Martha replied.

What's Behind the Looking Glass?

"As I said, everything has been taken care of. Doctor Hatfield and I went saw Judge Parker today, he's an old friend of mine and we have documents signed and legal. That gives you temporary custody of him. So basically meaning I trust you take care of him like he was one of your own and what I have seen here. There's' not a question in my mind or in my heart that I am doing the right thing for him.

"I would leave Danny here too, but I feel he needs his Grandma and it would put too much of a stress on both of you. So what I am going to do for EJ is this. We are going to stay awhile until he wakes up and get him settled in. Then I'll take Danny with me and we'll visit a lot, how does that sound? Then after that well play it out and see how it goes on from there. So in a nutshell, you are his new parents."

Grandma then reached over and gave them each a hug and kiss, looked them straight in the eye so they knew she means it. "Welcome to the family you and all your dear children." Then sat back down...paused long enough for her voice to steady..."Now then as far as his parents are concerned. That's a whole different matter and that Martha, Wayne we might have to go outside were those pigs are. So I can shout real loud if you know what I mean. And the wind better be blowen too," she said trying very hard not to let the anger in her voice control her.

"I think I know just what you mean Grandma," Wayne said.

"Me too," Martha said holding Wayne's hand.

"Well, we don't?" Julie replied.

Pa looked over at his kids and rubbed his chin. "Martha I think it's time we had a talk with the kids," he said.

Ma turned as she looked over at them. "Tell them what dear? Pa, are you sure about this." Realizing how much he hates to talk about things of this nature ever since he came back from the war all those many years ago. She nodded her head as she squeezed his hand with tenderness.

"We can't hide it from them any longer," Pa said.

"You are right Pa, the time has come and they need to know... Anna?" She said.

"Yes, Ma?" Knowing with a sad sigh she was about to leave the room leave the discussion once more as if being dismissed like a child. *Why can't they see I am not a child anymore? I have as much right to be here as Will and Robert and I am two years older than him and yet he gets to stay.* With a heavy sigh, she did what her mother said.

"Would you go ahead and check on EJ and Danny and makes sure they're sleeping and I will come to tuck you in ok dear," she said.

"Ok, Ma," not happy she couldn't stay to hear what they were going to talk about.

Ma saw how disappointed she looked. "Anna you and I will have a private conversation just between us girls later and I'll do my best to explain. So you can understand too ok dear? Now come give me and your father a kiss and hug then off you go," she said.

Anna turned to her new Grandma. "Can I give you one too, even if you are not my real Grandma?" She asked.

"Anna I thought you would never ask. Now get over here give your Grandma a hug, after all, I am now your Grandma too, and that goes for all of you." Then she gave her the biggest squeeze and kissed her on the cheek that lit up that face of hers and she sets off to bed a little lighter on her feet.

Pa waited until everyone settled while he gathered his thoughts, figuring the best way they would understand. "Now I really don't like talking about this children, but we feel that you might be old enough to understand what's going on. Let's see in school do remember what they talk about with slavery?"

"Yes, so what does that have to do with EJ?" Robert asked moving his seat closer closing the gap in the circle of the room.

"Stay with me for a minute," Pa said with his hands resting in Ma's lap as she slips closer to her by sitting on the couch.

"Now what did the white men do to the slave whenever they felt like it?" He asked.

"They beat them?" Will said.

"Yes." He said trying very hard to control his emotions.

"But EJ wasn't a slave," Julie replied confused.

"No, well… some parents today feel they need to do the same thing to get the quality they want out of them. If they didn't like it or if they were bad in some form or no reason at all sometimes." Pa paused for a moment as they make the connection.

"But why?" Robert asked.

"Because they don't like what they see so they want to change it? To them, in their minds, they are smoothing out the rough edges as it were. That's what happened to EJ," Pa said, his emotions getting the best of him.

"Pa?" Julie asked.

"Yes, Julie?" Seeing the tears fall down her cheeks.

Julie gasping in tears, "that's horrible."

"I know dear," Martha said with tears streaming down her cheeks. "Come here, dear." Julie ran too her mother buried her face into her mother's lap. Martha stroked her hair back with her hand to calm her. Wayne stood and took his arms and put them around his two boys with shocked looks on their faces.

Not knowing if it's ok to cry or what to say, but holds them and whispered while holding them tight against him. "Now you understand why I didn't want to tell you, but it looks like keeping the truth from you was hurting you more than facing it now. The question is boys, what are you going to do with it now that you know? Because that boy in there going too wake up and one is already."

"Pa?" Robert asked wiping the tears from his eyes with the back of his left hand and turned his face towards Pa.

"Yes, Robert." He replied as he looked him straight in the eyes with tears streaming down his own cheeks.

"I am going to be his big brother and his friend."

"Me to Pa," Will says wiped his own tears against the sleeve of his shirt.

Pa hugged his boy's shoulders; Grandma looked over at Martha with tears now streaming down her cheeks. She could not believe the love this family had shown for her two grandchildren. All she could do was whisper with a choked voice, "thank you," Then wiped her eyes. Wayne, Martha with tears in their eyes from the compassion their children have shown. All they could do is just nod their heads, for that moment nothing was needed or to be said, for it was pure love that was shown.

Pa clears his voice. "We have a lot to do tomorrow and try to bring back some sanity back if it is possible," he said. "So I suggest we all go to bed. I am sure we are all tired. It has been a big day. So let's head off to bed. Martha has the bed already turned down for you in EJ's room and I am sure Danny is fast asleep so you should be fine."

"Thanks, Martha, you too Wayne, thanks for everything," Grandma said as she wiped the remainder of her tears.

"You are welcome, will see you in the morning," Wayne said.

"If you would like Grandma, I can have Wayne carry you too and tuck you in?" Martha said teasing getting up from the couch.

"Sorry, maybe if I was a little bit younger I'd have a go." She replied as she does a quick wink at him then followed them all down the hall. When they entered the room where EJ was sleeping; they find Danny not sleeping in his bed. Instead, he has curled up next to his brother with his arm over his chest fast asleep.

"Well Martha, it won't do any good to move him and besides that's where they belong right now," Grandma said.

They smiled grabbed a blanket from off the little bed and covered Danny. Martha, with a gentle kiss, kissed them both goodnights as if they were her own children. Then took Wayne by the arm and left down the hall to each of the children's rooms as they gave each child a kiss and tucked them in and turned out the lights then making a full circle to their room. "Wayne?" Martha asked.

"Yes, Martha dear."

"I finally feel my house and my heart is full, thanks for the meal dear you sure know how to cook."

"You are welcome," he said getting into bed.

"But I am sure tired," she said sliding in next to him and turned off the bedside lamp.

"Yes dear, I know what you mean," as she took his hand in hers and fell softly to sleep.

Chapter 9

The sun roses over the mountains as the new day had begun, with new changes in the air. For hope was on the horizon as a rooster cock doodle do's. The Downing Farm springs to life. "Well good morning sleepyhead," Grandma said as she looked down at EJ as she washed his forehead and looked into his face and noticed he was beginning to stir and awake.

"Grrrraaandddmmma isss thaat yyyou?" he asked.

"Yes EJ, it's me. Try not to move around so much yet son. Let's get you a little bit more awake first ok." Grandma shook Danny, "Danny wake up son, wake up Danny, EJ's wakening up," she said.

That did it. Danny opened his eyes with a flash, "EJ! EJ!" Martha and Wayne jumped right out of bed, running as fast as they could, looked at grandma, then at Danny bouncing on the bed. "EJ! EJ! EJ's awake!" he said.

EJ stirred a little bit more and tried to talk, but he was hoarse and the pain had settled in and he felt stiffer than a board. "Grandma?" EJ asked.

"Yes, son?" She sat next to him on the bed as she took her right hand and moved the strands of hair from his eyes so he could see her better.

"Is that really you?" He asked again as if he was dreaming.

"Yes, EJ it is."

EJ tried to look around the room, but everything was still fuzzy and pain complicated things. "Where am I? It hurts really bad?" He said.

"I know son… you are safe. I'll get you something for the pain, just rest now," she said.

What's Behind the Looking Glass?

EJ could not rest yet, he had to know. "Grandma?" he asked again.

"Yes, son?"

"Where's Danny?" He asked thinking he might have heard him but wasn't sure.

"Danny is right here son!" Grandma said as she placed Danny's hand in his. "Can you feel that EJ?" She asked.

EJ nodded yes. "Good now stay here and let me get you something for that pain ok." She said and turned to ask Martha, instead, she finds Wayne, standing in the doorway, and asks. "Where did Martha go?" She asked.

"To go get some pain medicine and I am too guard the door to make sure he doesn't leave, she told me not to move and I am not moving," he said.

Grandma seeing how serious he was, all she could do was laugh. "Then I wouldn't move then," she replied.

"What's all the ruckus about Pa?" Will said seeing Pa standing there in his PJ's in EJ's doorway.

"Oh nothen much," Pa answered back then looked at Will, "EJ's awake that's all." He said in a casual voice.

"What? EJ's awake really?" He asked.

"Yep," Pa said as if wasn't news at all.

"YAH, HOO!" Will started pounding on the bedroom doors. Will, yelling for all he's worth "HE'S AWAKE! HE'S AWAKE!" Everyone started jumping out bed faster than hotcakes on a hot griddle.

Wayne looked over at Grandma. "Well so much for thinking we were going to have a quiet day here at the Farm." Grandma and Wayne started laughing to beat all.

"Did someone call for some pain medicine? I put a little broth in to give it some flavor and cut back on the sleeping aid, but enough to make it comfortable so we can clear his little mind a bit," she said.

"EJ this Martha Downing, she's been taking care of you. Now this is going to hurt so we are going to sit you up a little so you drink this ok. So on the count of three. One two and three now," EJ groans as they set him up. Grandma placed some pillows behind him and tucked the blankets around him.

"I know it hurts, ok go ahead drink it all down; all right that's better. Give it few a minutes to work ok. Now let your Grandma get dressed. I want you to stay put in that bed. Can you do that? Just nod." EJ nodded his head yes. "I mean it stay there. Danny, stay right there," she said grubbing a fresh change of clothing from her saddlebag and a blouse from the closet wishing she had the time to take a hot iron over it. *Well maybe later.* "Well, Martha, I think we can take a deep breath for the moment so let's get dressed while this boy clears his head. Danny will guard him like a hawk won't you son?" Then turned to Danny" You won't let your brother out of your sight, right?" She asked standing next to Wayne as he stands aside to let her through the door...

"No way Grandma." He replied still holding EJ's hand, making it his personal mission to watch him.

Wayne chuckled. "The best guard dog in town is his own little brother."

EJ felt some relief knowing that his grandmother is nearby and his little brother Danny is with him, a feeling of calm falls over him. Still unaware as to where he was, did not seem all that important as long he had reached his main goals. One: Finding his grandmother and Second: He could feel Danny's hand in his. That was all that seemed important at the moment. Now he could he work towards the third goal. Safety... and he knew his Grandma might be able too to help him or give him the solution. EJ waited for the drugs to work and his mind too clear; he could feel some of the fuzziness leaving his body.

What's Behind the Looking Glass?

"EJ, EJ son how are you doing?" Grandma asked. EJ opened his eyes and tried to focus. The brightness in the room hurt his eyes. His grandmother draws the curtains a little bit trying to darken the room so his eyes could adjust. "How's that? Now can you see me?" she asked.

Still hoarse she bends down so she can hear him. "Yes Grandma," he whispered.

"Good son. You've been out for a few days and I don't want you to strain your voice so I brought you a notepad and a pencil, so you can ask us questions ok," EJ nodded yes.

"Good," she said. "Now then I already know pretty much what's been going on." EJ gave her a surprised look, that how do you know look. "By the look on your face, I see you didn't think I would find out did you?" EJ shook his head no. "Well I may not know the story behind it all, which you are going tell me, but I do know who and mostly the how and where it happened and the from and I have seen all the damage for myself?"

"Oh yes EJ. I know the whole thing and done some of the patchwork myself and, so has Mrs. Downing twice now son. So there's nothing you can hide from your Grandma. Now then let me put your mind at ease." Then she put her finger to her lips "Shush now," and then kissed his forehead.

In her calm grandmothers' voice as she sat on the bed next too him taking him all in with a sigh of relief. "You are going nowhere. That's it… you are safe. Danny is safe, you are safe, and everyone is safe. Grandma has taken care of it all EJ. Do understand what I'm saying so far yes or no?" She said as she waited for the answer.

"Yes," he whispered.

"Good. Just wait don't be in such a hurry. Alright, ask your question." as she kissed him on the forehead and rubbed his head.

He writes. "When you mean safe? Where I am Grandma?"

"You are on the Downing Farm. You are going to be in their care and nobody else's."

"What about Danny?" EJ asked as he writes on his tablet.

"Danny's going to be in my care and before you ask about your sisters, they are in my sister's care. Peggy is with aunt Lizy and Dona is with Mary." Seeing his impatient she just waited for him and sat on the bed beside him.

"For how long?" EJ asked in the strongest whisper he could muster.

"That part has not been decided yet. It really depends mostly on your parents, if they can care for them or not depends on them. Now as for you dear boy," she looked him straight in the eye as she lifted his chin. "I'll make you a promise EJ because you got the worst end of the stick. If you decide that you never want to go back. I will understand son and I can live with that and love you just as much. Nothing will ever change that. I will leave that decision up to you to make son and I will not have any regrets if you choose to stay here or return home or go somewhere else. But I think you won't find a better family. So give them a chance. So, for now, just get well. I'll do whatever I can," she said.

Standing up getting ready to leave she gave a quick wink; "as for as the Downing's go they are a good family. You couldn't have tried to steal a pair of better sheets, you silly, stubborn boy. What on earth were you thinking?" Then rubbed his hair, "you could have just called me you know. You scared the living daylights out me. Now give your Grandma a kiss and hug it the least you can do for now." EJ smiled, trying to give her a big hug, but only managed a kiss on the cheek.

"Now get some rest. I need to get your brother dressed and for heaven's sake stay in that bed. But first I want you to write a letter stating… I EJ am not going to get out of this bed and I am going to mind his Grandma…write boy come on, that's better…. mind his Grandma and Mrs. and Mr. Downing I promise." EJ smiled as she examined the little note she made him write. "Ok, that's a good boy. Now she's going to be checking on you in a little while and bring you in some breakfast. Now back to sleep and don't worry, I'm not going anywhere. I will be here for a couple of days at least. Then we will visit often after that.

"Come on Danny, let your brother rest now, we need to get you dressed and down to breakfast, you have a farm to see," she said.

"Yes Grandma," he said.

EJ whispered "bye."

"EJ, stay put!" Danny says turning around. EJ watched his Grandma and his brother leave then closed his eyes and falls back into a soft sleep.

"Martha, I have a present for you and the Downing family. A signed note from EJ, you can frame if you want too," she said as she reads it.

"Well that makes me feel a whole a lot better," Martha said as she laughed then tacks it on the wall, "look Wayne, our first promise," she said.

"Heck, I would have settled for a handshake and called it good," he replied.

"Well, it still not too late," she said as they both laugh.

"No. This will be just fine. You are right. I should frame it right above his door," he said.

Wayne rubbed his chin for a minute as an idea formed in his mind. Then taking down the note he sat down at the breakfast table. Martha and Grandma looked at him with a puzzled look. Martha about to ask and he just raised his hand to hold her off for a minute.

"If everyone would please be seated," Pa asked. "Ok everyone," as Pa clears his voice. "My Martha this looks good. Now then, it has come to my attention," as he smiled at Grandma. "That EJ has written us a promissory note." Pa passed it round the table so they could all read it. I have an idea we should take this promissory note and turn into something else," he said.

"Pa, what do you have in mind?" Julie asked Passing down the eggs and beacon down the table and buttering her toast with homemade apple butter.

"Well Julie, if you would wait just a minute, I'll get to it," he said taking the plate of eggs and beacon adding to his plate.

"I think it is only fair that we Downing's here also give him a promise in return." The breakfast table was all a buzz as they whispered back and forth.

"I think that's a wonderful idea," Martha tried to shout over the noise.

Pa tries to bring the excited children back into order. "A Humm," clicking the orange juice glass with his knife. "So I was thinking that each of us should come up with a simple promise of our own and write it down." Then he looked right at Robert, "Robert?"

"Yes, Pa?"

"Could you make us a wood frame to put the note in? We'll hang it in his room to remind him, and to remind us, how much we care about him," he asked. Martha, Grandma, wiping tears from their eyes, got up from where they were sitting and went over to Pa and gave him and each of the children a hug and kiss then went back to their seats and dried their eyes. Pa looked up at them. "It was just an idea now," he said.

"Yes Wayne, but it was the best idea I have ever heard and we thank you. Now your breakfast is getting cold, I am sure EJ's hungry." Martha replied as she dried her eyes.

"Pa?" Will asked.

"Yes Will?"

What's Behind the Looking Glass?

"I have just the name we should call it," he said buttering his toast and taking a sip of his orange juice.

"And what's that?" He asked chewing between mouthfuls.

"EJ and Downing Declaration of Promise."

"Will, I could not think of a better name. All in favor?" Everyone raised their hands. "Then after breakfast, we will draw one up."

Ma smiling, "that's a great idea Pa, but let's keep it a secret and surprise EJ with it later." Everyone had grins on their faces as they looked over at Danny.

"That includes you Danny boy, you can't tell your brother alright," Pa said.

Danny gives him a little boyish grin. "Ok."

"Pa?" Will asked.

"Yes Will?"

"I'll take Danny out to see the farm so there's no way he can tell his brother, just to be safe," he said chewing with his mouth full.

"Now that's a good idea," Pa laughing. "Danny, would you like to help Will, with his chores today?" Pa asked sipping his orange juice and giving Danny another helping of eggs and bacon.

"Yes, Sir!" Danny said with full of excitement his eyes big as basketballs.

"Then finish your breakfast Danny," as he rubbed his hair, while everyone around the table seeing Danny's excitement and laughed. Finishing their breakfast, they cleared the table while Grandma and Martha put together EJs' breakfast. The children remained at the table with paper and pencil to write their promise for EJ.

"Good morning EJ," EJ slowly opened his eyes "I am Mrs. Downing. You can call me Ma Downing or Mrs. Downing or just plain Ma. Whatever you feel comfortable with son. I am sure you're hungry dear, so I brought you your breakfast," she said as she set it on the nearby table. "Now then let's see if we can sit you up a little bit more in that bed," she said.

Ma grabbed additional pillows, placing them behind his back and helped him scoot up in bed, then placed the tray across his lap… "Well now? That's better," as Grandma comes around to the other side of the bed and looked at EJ then he smiled at her. "Martha, I think looking at some those bandages we should change them," she said.

EJ looked down at where she was looking, seeing that some had come a little unraveled and feeling embarrassed pulled the sheets tightly around him and turning a little red because he realized other than the bandages he doesn't have a stitch on besides the bandages. Martha seeing this understands. "EJ just finish your breakfast son, we'll worry about that later," and tucked the sheets around his waist. "Just so you know EJ. I have three boys of my own now, 4 counting you and a husband. Plus two girls in the family so you can put your mind at rest son. We will figure something out." Then bends down placed a kiss on his forehead and helped him cut up his meat.

EJ was shocked by the affection that she gave him as he watched her and his grandma fuse over him. His nerves where frazzled he felt the walls closing in on him as if the distance he could still see and hear the belt snapping in the air. *"I must get away!"* The voice in his head screamed and then calmed as he looked deep into grandma's eyes. The question is *"can he trust her? And am I truly safe here?"*

His Grandma smiled at him. "Now I want you to eat every last bite EJ," then she wiped his chin. "Now then, we want you to rest awhile after you drink this broth it will help with the pain. Then we will help ease you back down into bed. Ok EJ?" EJ nodded yes they removed the pillows from behind and the tray and lowered him back down and placed the covers back over his shoulders then each gave him a kiss on the cheek and begin to leave the room so he can rest. "We will be back to check in on you in while son," Grandma said walking out the door where the rest of the children are sitting at the table.

What's Behind the Looking Glass?

"Ok children, time to get the morning chores done," Ma said setting down EJ's tray on the counter.

"So Danny, are you ready to go with Will?" Grandma asked.

"Yes Grandma," Danny replied starting to head out the door, bouncing up down with excitement.

"Danny, aren't you forgetting something?" She asked looking down at his bare feet.

"What Grandma?" He asked.

"Your shoes," she said.

"Oh Grandma," he replied he hated wearing shoes they always felt too small for him and slowed him down.

Martha laughed. "Oh he'll be fine; I can't keep them on Sam either half the time," and then looked over at Will. "Come to think of it, Will stills has the same problem, oh let him go, he'll be fine," she said.

Grandma sighed. "Alright, go on then and have a good time, but first come give me a hug."

Danny ran up to her and gave her the biggest bear hug he could give, "thank you, Grandma."

"Now shoo," and pushed him towards Will and Danny waved her goodbye.

"Robert?" Pa asked.

"Yes, Pa?"

"Will you take care of the horses today and put them in the northern pasture." He said asking as he put down his newspaper as he turned the page.

"Yes, Pa."

"Then I'll come out and help you with that frame for EJ," he said.

"Yes, Pa," Robert said putting on his shoes and laced them up outside on the porch steps.

"Anna?" Ma called from down the hall where she was just finishing Sam's bath and brushing her long brown hair in the mirror.

"Yes, Ma?"

"I need you to keep an eye on Sam. You can have him help you with the chickens today," she said.

"Yes, Ma." Bending down placed the dirty towels and clothes into the hamper to be washed.

"Julie dear, we need to make a list of groceries and supplies we are going to need from the store. I think the three of us should be able to take care of that don't you think Grandma? We can leave the menfolk here to hold down the fort." Ma said watching Pa getting ready to leave with Robert.

"That's a good idea, Martha," she said.

"Wayne, do think you can watch EJ while we're gone? After all, he did promise he wouldn't run off," Martha asked hoping she could trust him after all he has been known to run off when he gets scared.

"Yes dear, everything will be fine, if I have to, we'll hog tie him to the bed and lock him in that room, post a guard at the window just in case until you get back dear," as he laughed. Wayne seeing she wasn't laughing. "Dear everything will be fine. In fact, if it makes you feel better. I'll go talk with EJ. He needs to know he can trust me, that he can feel safe here with me. Why you ladies do your thing." Then he grabbed his wife's hands pulled her close to him bends down whispered softly in her ear. "Your blushing dear," and kissed her and walked down the hall where EJ was sleeping.

What's Behind the Looking Glass?

Wayne entered the room and placed his hand on EJ shoulder, EJ shuttered for a moment. "It's ok son. I won't hurt you EJ." EJ turned and sees a man's face standing over the bed. It nearly paralyzed him with fear but remembering the words of his Grandma that he was safe. *Was he?* This man. This huge man was built like a tree, but yet he had a softness in his face and in his voice as he smiled. He had dark brown hair and green eyes that seemed to see everything. He was even dressed like a farmer right down to his boots, which had seen better days. He felt somehow safe, yet strange as if he knew him from somewhere. *But how?* He never even met the man now standing over him.

"Its ok son, I am Mr. Downing EJ. You have nothing to be afraid of son," and then backing away a little. Pa sat in the chair near the bed to give EJ time to calm his fears.

"Now that's better, take it, easy son, put your mind at ease," with a twinkle in his eye. The fear was slowly lifted away from EJ, as he relaxed. Mr. Downing seeing EJ was more relaxed his voice calm. He relaxed a little bit more. "EJ, you mind if I come closer so we can talk a little son." EJ slowly nodded his head yes, but never leaving his eyes off his face, still being very cautious. "Good son, I won't keep you long because you need your rest."

Mr. Downing pulled the chair closer. "Now then, first of all, your grandmother told you that you are safe here, well you are son; you are that and that I can promise you. Nothing and I mean nothing or anyone going to harm you here, you understand that son? Now then, the womenfolk are going to go shopping, so that leaves us men folk except for Anna to keep an eye on your brother, and Sam here on the farm." He said pausing as he smiled.

"Since we live on a farm; everyone on this farm has chores to do every day to make it run right and that includes you son." Then he smiled with a soft chuckle. "And your chore is to stay in this bed and in this room. Do you think you can do that EJ? Or." Leaning back with a big smile and laughing out loud. "Or son do we need to find some rope and strap you to that bed, lock the door and board up the window."

EJ smiled and whispered in a soft horse voice. "My Grandma would skin me alive if I even moved so I am staying right here sir," and smiled.

"EJ, I have no doubt in my mind about that. She'd skins us both son, no doubt about that," as he laughed then stands and rubbed his hair. "Now then get some rest, I'll hold you to your to word son," then walked out the door.

Wayne walked over to his wife. "Is there anything else you need madam?" Then with a quick twirl around the kitchen grabbed hold of his daughter Julie swings her around, Julie squealed with delight.

"Pa," she replied with a giggle.

"And how about you miss?" Taking Grandma by the hand does a quick saw shay.

"Oh Martha, what have you been feeding your husband?" Grandma asked.

"You know Grandma. I was wondering that too, but whatever it is. I wouldn't change the recipe," she said as she laughed.

"Mind if I brow it for a while," she asked as Grandma laughed.

"Well then, if we're going to town we better get this list done. How are you comen, Julie?" Ma asked pushing him towards the door.

"Just about finished Ma." Julie closed the pantry door.

Ma turned to Wayne. "Mind pulling the pickup upfront and please make sure the backs empty this time," she asked.

"Yes dear," he said closing the door behind him.

Wayne, went out to the barn to unload everything from the back and folded the tarp into the box so the back is empty, and pulled the truck up to the porch. "Ok ladies let's go shopping." Julie and Grandma slid into the front seat of the truck while Martha slowly went around the back of the pickup looking into the back of the bed and opened the box-checking to making sure everything is where it is supposed to be.

"Martha, he'll be fine," he said.

"I know, but I can't help it."

Wayne walked down the porch opened the pickup door, helped her in. "Now have a good time. Nothing will happen to him. I'll see to that, now go." With a final sigh, she looked towards the house then started the old pickup and started down the road for Payson. With a cloud of smoke, the farm was in the distance. Wayne walked back onto the steps sat and watched his family farm buzz around him, remembering the days and months that his father helped build it.

"Will, can I can help feed the pigs?" Danny asked as he danced all around him.

"Yes Danny, give them some this feed and try not to fall in as you climb over the fence," he said hefting the feed bucket of grain and scraps from the table.

"Wow! I never have seen real pigs before except on TV," Danny replied as he watched with interest while the pigs squealed when the food went to the trough.

"Will?" Danny asked.

"Yes, Danny?" Emptying the bucket.

"You got baby pigs too?"

"Where did you think big pigs come from Danny? Would you like to hold one?"

"Can I really?"

"Yes Danny," Will laughed at little Danny's amusement, then reached down and grabbed a little pig for him to hold. "Now hold on tight, he's a squirmy little fella." He said closing the pin behind him then handed the pig to Danny, knowing full well what would happen.

The pig squirmed and squealed with all its might against little Danny tiny body. Danny trying hold on to him and the pig won as it runs back to its mother. Danny's arms stretched forward on the ground. Will picked Danny off the ground. Danny had the biggest smile on his face streaked with mud on the base of his chin and the tip of his nose. It didn't matter he was covered in dirt from his head right down to his toes. It was worth it as he brushed the straw out of his hair and all over his now dirty clothes.

"Will?" Danny asked.

"Yes Danny," he said both laughing.

"I think the pig was hungry."

"Me to Danny, let's go wash your face and see what else we can find ok?" Will said taking him by the hand as they headed toward more fun and amusement that little boy like Danny would find.

"There's more?"

"Oh yes, lots more."

"Wow!"

"Robert?" Pa called outside of the barn as he opened the door to the little shop he has set up for the numerous woodworking projects that he and his boys would trade in town for income.

"Yes, Pa." He answered around the corner.

"How's that new colt doing up at north pasture?" Pa asked.

"Just fine Pa, we should be able to start breaking him this fall I think," Robert said measuring the frame he would be working on and setting aside a small coffee table to be stained later on.

What's Behind the Looking Glass?

"Well, the women are off to town so that leaves us men here and Anna to look after things while they're gone so if you want to start working on that frame. I thought I would go take some measurements and draw some plans for the additions to the house. If you need help Robert you know where to find me," Pa said.

"Yes, Pa."

Pa put on his tool belt with his ruler and pencil and pad he headed for the house. Making a list of supplies he was going to need. He stopped into the room where EJ was and checked to make sure he was sleeping. He listened to his soft breathing, whispered to himself. "I knew everything would be just fine, nothing too worry about." EJ turned and saw him standing in the doorway. "Its ok son, it's just me. Go back to sleep." Then he walked back down the hallway towards Roberts's room. Moving some of the things away from the wall to take some measurements, he began to draw up plans for the room…

Chapter 9-1

* * *

"Jim?" Linda asked as she paced back and forth in the small unkept living room scattered with boxes of unused storage and dust and old cobwebs hanging from the pictures on the wall. She hated being trapped in this house that seemed so small. Now quiet as the children are gone. She was not sure what was worse the quietness or their constant noise. Is this what she wanted? The words echoed in her mind. "*They're gone and it's your fault, your fault!*"

"Yes, Linda?" Jim said standing in the doorway as he was getting ready to work on the window. His son's eyes haunted him still. "*No, not boys' eyes at all, but whose were they?*"

"I am not going to sit here and take this, not from her, not from anyone. Who does she think she is, the Queen of England? Those nosey neighbors need to stay out of our business. What right do they think they have to tell us how to raise our children? Everything was just fine. Until they came into the picture… if you ask me their ones that need help… them not us. There is nothing wrong with us. It's them. We were just trying to smooth out the rough spots. That's all… if they would only just leave us alone." She said as she paced with the court document in her hands. The anger boiled over in her thoughts. "*We did nothing, nothing wrong.… Or did we? No.*"

"The girls were just becoming angels. And I am sure Eric would sooner or later step in line and Danny too. She always hated the name EJ, it was like an insult to her and to her husband. His grandmother had no right in thinking to change it, just so she and he could disregard the name she personally picked out for me. "We were making progress I thought. If wasn't for those bad genes always popping up. Now, look Jim. She has taken all our children away, stolen them right from under our very noses. You said. 'Oh she's mellowed out, not too worry dear; you have nothing to fear from her.'" Throwing the paper right in his face, "WHERE ARE THEY NOW JIM! Not here I can tell that!" She said angrily.

"So what do want me to do about it? Linda, she has a court order." Jims said angrily as his voice begins to raise his fist tighten into a hardball wanting to punch a second hole through the wall. He winced remembering where EJ stood once long ago before he was taken away the last time. *"NO! These are family matters. No one has the right to tell me how to raise my own children! Not even his mother. Why couldn't she have left things alone? Why now get herself involved after all these years? No she in the wrong!"*

"So you are going to let a little piece of paper stop you? After you let me down trying to find him when we could have avoided this whole mess and her breathing down our necks after all these years. Well, we know where he is now don't we?" Linda pointed at the address below on the form.

"Yes, I know that," he said with a low growl.

"I WANT HIM BACK!" I want them all back," she screamed.

"But, Linda he's hurt, what makes you think you can care for him when we both know neither of us really want him. How many times have we tried to get rid of him and his brother only to have his grandmother and child services being him back; if it was me I wouldn't even want to come back and let you near me. Your cooking stinks and you have no bedside manner. You are the worst mother when it comes to caring for sick children, and we both know it." he replied trying to change the subject not wanting him or his brother Danny back if only she could see that.

"Yes, I know that I am the one that should be taking care of him, maybe now that he is older I can learn how to care for him, besides I am not the one that nearly killed him if you remember. I wasn't the one holding or swing the belt so hard that nearly ripped off the skin off him. NOW GET IN THE CAR!"

"Yes dear," he said not happy.

***

"Let's see now we need some butter, 6 bags of flour, Oh Julie!" Ma said stopping down the street on Payson Main Street; which was somewhat bigger than Santaquin which had some clothing stores and small barbershop and home bakery around the corner, plus the new fabric store with new prints displayed in the window, but right now that's not what caught her eye as she stops in front of the Grayson Hat shop.

"Yes, Ma?"

"Look at that bonnet over there in the window, isn't that pretty?" She asked.

"Yes Ma, It would look really good on you," Julie said admiring the bluebonnet hat with painted daisies circled around the hat.

"Actually, I was thinking of you dear."

Grandma grabbed the ladies by the arms. "Girls, I was thinking it would look good on both of you," she said pushing them through the door.

"But, you shouldn't," they replied.

"You know better by now not to argue with me, dear. Martha, come on." As she gave her a wink and smile, "let's go try it on," Grandma said opening the door letting the door ring as it closed behind her.

Girls posed in the mirror with different hats. "If that won't drive your husband crazy and those fella's Julie," Grandma said admiring a new bonnet herself. A pretty but simple pink one with little rose's buds tucked in the corner.

"But, we can't," Martha said.

What's Behind the Looking Glass?

"You can and you will. Now help me find something for Anna and the rest of my new grandchildren," she said not taking no for answer, picked up a nice yellow one with tulips for Anna.

"Oh thank you Grandma." they each said.

"Now come give me a hug and will go, we got lots of shopping to do." They gave her hug with packages in hand picking up items as they went. "Martha, we need to find some fabric. Oh, look, theirs the store. Now then tell me about this apron that you want to make EJ. Can you draw it for me and make a pattern?" She asked walking in the store after leaving their items in the back of the pickup placing the tarp over them.

"Yes Grandma," she said. Martha drew the pattern. "It sort of looks like butchers apron except it folds in the back and you can tie in the front instead of the back. That way it covers everything that needs to be covered. Then, later on, we can get him a long nightshirt to wear. After that, the wounds on his back will have healed enough. Then he should be fine," she said.

"I have to admit, you've got talent dear; now than what kind of cloth where you thinking of?" She asked finding some prints and cloth at caught her eye.

"Well, that I wasn't sure about that part. I wanted something durable, yet something that was going to comfortable too. I figured I was going have to make at least two or three. That way I can have spare. Plus always have a clean one," she said.

"Martha, you are smart all give you that. I would suggest cotton is the best way to go. Now sheets are fine for now, but they do get hot and messy and make the wounds sweat. I would add a little color to them to make them more like their cotton underwear or shorts. That way they have little more comforts of home to them; nothing girlish either you know how boy's get," as Julie rolled her eyes thinking of Will and Robert. "Something more like this. Now I can see my grandson wearing this Martha. This will be just fine I think," Grandma said picking up a pattern of sailboats.

***

Pa scratched his head and rubbed his chin as he looked at the ceiling and the floorboards of the room of Robert's room. Making some notes on the pad then got off the bed and put the furniture back in place and went back down the hall towards EJ room. EJ turned in his sleep seeing Mr. Downing in the doorway. "It's just me son. Just rest, I just need to make some measurements. We have plans to build you a room son since you are going to be with us for a while. So I'll just be a few minutes then you can go back to sleep." EJ nods his head and Pa moved the future so he can make the plans. "Than I am going to sit here for awhile son if you don't mind. So just go back to sleep," he said.

"Danny, look! Can you see clear over there?" Will asked standing on the rail fence pointing the trees nearby.

"Where Will?"

"Over by that tree."

"A pony!" Danny shouts. Seeing a real horse that not on TV and one that looked a lot like his little toy horses when he plays cowboys and Indian's in his room and sometimes with his bother EJ when his home.

"Yes Danny, that's a colt and his mother," he said.

Will turned around and saw a cloud of dust coming down the road, it looked like a car. He watched the car pull into the farm. He could see a man and woman in the car. Grabbing Danny he started to shout for Robert "ROBERT! Anna!" With little Danny tucked under his arms as he ran as fast as he could. Robert came busting out of the barn seeing the car and the woman and man in the car. The woman and the man opened the car getting ready to bust into the house.

Robert yelled back at Will. "Take Danny too Anna, she's with the chickens!" Robert ran towards the house shouting for Pa. "Pa! Pa!"

What's Behind the Looking Glass?

Will ran with Danny under his arms while Robert ran towards the house. Danny scared and crying, Will shouted, "ANNA! ANNA!" Anna came running out of the chicken cop with Sam, Will out of breath pointed to the car near the porch "EJ's...in trouble." Will said panting, "Anna take Danny please." Anna took Danny and they both went into the chicken coop to watch him and Sam. Will ran towards the house, the man and woman ran toward the hallway, Robert and Will at their heels.

Pa seeing, hearing them yell from the outside and the slamming of the front door leaped across the room. The man and woman entered the room seeing EJ in the bed. EJ's eyes lit up with fear. His face turned ghostly white with terror. Pa stepped in front of the bed.

The woman screamed. "GET OUT, OF MY WAY, WE'VE COME FOR THE BOY!"

Pa stood right in front of her shielding EJ reaching his full height of the room, his body tense as a tree trunk, his eyes hard as steel. Looked at them... With a loud booming and a calm stern voice. "Woman, I don't know who you think you are, but you are not coming any closer and you are not going to lay one finger on him. Now get out of my house and off my farm. You are not welcome here, now git both of you!" Pa said turning towards Robert and Will standing in the doorway. "Boys I believe we have some un-welcomed guests. Can you be so kind as to show them the way out?" He said.

"Yes Pa," they both answered sternly.

Pa walked them every inch to the door, then turned to EJ. "Don't worry son, I've got it," and closed his door behind him then ushered them down the hall. With Will and Robert in the lead and with them in the middle, they reached the front porch. Pa pointed to the car "Now git back in that car and git off my farm!" Then watched them hang their heads and drive off empty-handed.

The three of them headed down the hall toward EJ's room; when they opened the door they find him shaking in bed. Will and Robert put the room back together while Pa sits on the bed next to EJ. Pa turned to EJ and looked him straight in the eye. "Son, you can always count on me. I promised I would keep you safe and that's what I am going to do. Nobody will ever lay one finger on you son that I promise, now rest. Your Grandma will be back soon to make sure. I am not leaving this room until they get back. Will, go get Danny." Pa said.

"Yes, Pa."

But that wasn't necessary because Anna seeing the car leaving was bring Danny and Sam into the house. Danny ran down the hallway into EJ's bedroom and jumped right onto the bed. Danny seeing EJ was still there and puts his arms around his brother's neck. "I thought they'd stolen you again," and buried his face against his chest in tears.

EJ whispered. "And what, leave you? No way! Grandma would skin us all," he said.

Pa, Will, and Robert laughed, Pa said. "They still might if we don't get you cleaned up before they get back."

Will, looked at Danny. "I don't have to tell you what that means do I?" he said.

Danny looked down at his dirty clothes, his hands, and feet. He watched Mr. Downing pulling the straw, chicken feathers and dirt out of his hair. Danny put his two lips together said "bath time."

Robert watched Sam heading out the door trying to escape as he picked him up. "Going somewhere? I think that included you to Sam," he replied.

Pa laughed. "Anna you've got your hands full today dear," he said.

"Oh, it's no trouble once they're in the tub, getting them in there is half the fun," she said.

"Well, today you have help. Will, give her hand with these two rascals," he said.

What's Behind the Looking Glass?

"Yes, Pa. Come on boys, EJ needs his rest now." Will said marching them both down the hall with Anna in the lead.

"Robert wasn't there something in the barn?" Pa asked.

"Oh yes, barn. It's working just fine. I'll have you look at it in a while."

"That will be fine son."

* * *

"Julie dear?" Ma asked.

"Yes, Ma?"

"I'll just be a moment. I am going to give the boys a call and check on EJ. I forgot to tell your Pa that I fixed them a lunch and it's in the fridge and to heat up the broth for EJ?" she said.

"Ok, Ma."

"Julie?" Grandma asked.

"Yes, Grandma?"

"Where's your Ma going?" She asked.

"She thought she'd check on EJ," as she smiles "that's Ma."

"Oh, I am sure everything's fine dear, your Pa's got a good head on his shoulders."

"I know Grandma, but Ma?" She said.

"Dear, when you have children of your own, you'll understand. Now let's see what else we can find," she said.

* * *

Wayne, hearing the phone ringing in the kitchen, "EJ I'll be back son...Hello... Hi Martha, no everything's fine, just like I said it would be. Why I do I sound out of breath, well...I was outside when the phone rang. How's EJ? Well, last time I checked a few minutes ago and he seemed fine. Yes dear, still in the bed resting, where he should be. How are you girls coming with your shopping? Are you having fun? Seeing any nice things? No, I am not trying to change the subject dear," as Wayne wiped the sweat off his brow.

"Hiding something from you? I told you everything is fine, EJ and Danny are fine, a little dirty perhaps. Yes dirty, he's in the tub with Sam now and they're both fine. We're all fine. Now then stop worrying. Have I fed them yet? I... I was just about to start some lunch dear when you called. Oh, check-in the fridge you say, already prepared our lunch. Thanks, dear and heat up the broth for EJ, add the medicine two, 3 tablespoons got it and mix it really good and make sure he drinks it all, will do dear. Now then you ladies have a good time, please don't worry about a thing. All right dear, I love you too. Goodbye dear, see you soon." Pa hangs up the phone sweat poured down his face.

"Pa?" Will asked.

"Yes Will," Pa replied turning around and wiped his brow one more time.

"Who was that on the phone?" Will asked.

"It was your mother, she was just checking in to see if everything was fine."

"Pa?" Will asked.

"Yes Will?"

"Everything is fine, isn't it?" He asked.

"Yes Will, now it is," Pa said wiping his brow one more time, realizing how hot it was inside the house with even with every fan on and very window open, and the swamp cooler going full blast. "Will?"

"Yes, Pa?"

"If Ma ever asks, just say some people were lost and we gave them directions and sent them on their way."

Will smiles, "Actually that's the truth really, but ok," he said.

"Tell everyone else too. I want your mother worrying over nothing. You know how she'll fuss."

"Yes, Pa."

"Are the boys almost done with their bath?" he asked.

"They're being dressed now Pa."

"Good, help me with lunch then," he said.

Chapter 9-2

* * *

"Well is everything ok back on the farm Martha?" Grandma asked.

"Yes Grandma," she said with a puzzled look on her face, "I just get this funny feeling he's hiding something from me," she said.

"Martha, that husband of yours has got a good heart and good head on that shoulder of his, you have nothing to worry about. I am sure everything is just fine," she said.

"I suppose so," Martha sighs.

"Now then, I say there's a little café just around the corner. How about us three ladies get a bite to eat," she said.

"Well, that sounds marvelous Grandma… Hello Mrs. Collins." Mrs. Gertrude Collins a lady of high society at the age of 65 she may be short and stubby with spindly arms and legs, but she could move down a street faster than a bug on a windshield. Gertrude was a woman of means and knows more about people and their secrets then most people would like her to know.

Considering she was born and raised in her home town of Payson Utah. Her husband died in the war leaving her well provided for in real-estate and stocks and bonds. But it was her highfalutin ways that seemed to be her downfall when comes to people not made of money or high status. She walked tall and seemed to rub people the wrong way, but never stopped her from gossiping about others less fortunate than herself. She was always nicely dressed and always stayed in the current fashion. Silver hair and round beady eyes that matched her pointed nose and angle chin. Yet nobody knew she wore a gray powder wig, ever since she began to lose her hair within the last year or two.

What's Behind the Looking Glass?

Mrs. Collins said. "Well hello, Mrs. Downing and how are you this fine day?" She asked.

"Just fine, this is."

Grandma introduced herself, "I am Mrs. Stuart." She said to keep it formal, "but my friends just call me Grandma."

"Glad to meet you, Mrs. Stuart," giving Martha a puzzled look.

"And who's this fine young strapping lad, Mrs. Collins?" Grandma asked noticed Julie couldn't take her eyes off nor him glancing at her.

"This is Bill," she said introducing him.

"Well, what a fine-looking boy," Martha replied.

"What brings you too town Mrs. Downing?" She asked.

"I needed to do some shopping."

"Are you planning on coming to the annual picnic this year? After all, you have such a large family and life on a farm must be hard on you dear. We never see you anymore." Mrs. Collins replies adding to the gossip she has already heard from in town. (*Something about a missing Scarecrow.*)

"Wouldn't miss it for the world, of course, I might need an extra table thou," as she looked over at Grandma. "Considering how my little family has grown a bit over the summer." With a big smile on her face, "I'll need three extra places this year." Watching Mrs. Collins swoon a little, "Oh that's right, you haven't heard, I have four boys now actually make that four 1/2 boys," she said giggling "and the two girls of course then their new Grandma."

Seeing the startled look on Mrs. Collin's face, "You poor child, how do you handle the strain? It must be hard?" As Mrs. Collins replies patting her hand, in a form of sympathy, of not understanding that Martha really likes having a big family, besides she had come from one herself.

"Oh, it's no strain at all, it's a joy really," Martha said.

Mrs. Collins gave her a look of insanity. "Well I must be on my way, you take care now," and quickly walked away shaking her head.

"Martha?" Grandma asked.

"Yes, Grandma."

"You sure know how to make the phone lines sizzle." She laughed as she watched Mrs. Collins go down the street gossiping as she went.

"I never did care what the neighbors thought about me, so… if they want something to talk about, let them, I don't care. It doesn't bother me one way or the other," she said.

Grandma started laughing. "Are you sure there's no Stuart blood in you dear?" Then looks at Julie watching the young lad leaving "handsome boy," she said.

"What was that Grandma?" Julie asked blushing.

"Oh, nothing." Grandma and Martha laughed

"Well let's finish up and start heading back," Martha said.

* * *

"Heat up the broth for ten minutes," Pa says to himself.

"Pa?" Anna said seeing Pa messing around with the stove.

"Yes, Anna?"

"What are you doing?" She asked.

"Fixing lunch," he said.

"You are doing it all wrong. Here let me do it," she said.

What's Behind the Looking Glass?

"Now wait just a minute. I was just getting the hang of it to until you came in." Pa smiled at Anna, then rubbed his chin then turned to Will. "See what I mean, just like her mother," he said.

"Yes Pa," he said.

"What can we do to help?" He asked.

"You Pa, Humm. Think you and Will can set the table and bring the boys in here so I can keep an eye on them," she asked.

"Yes Ma'am," they replied.

Anna smiled at Pa for letting her be the lady of the house. She brought the boys into the living room to play while lunch was being prepared. "Alright Pa, I've setup EJ's tray. If you and Will want to go in and give it to him. I'll ring the bell for Robert so he knows lunch is ready and I'll feed the boys and then put them down for their afternoon nap," she said.

Pa and Will take EJ's tray into him. EJ stirs and opened his eyes. "How are you feeling son?" His voice starting to come back a little stronger, but still rough said "ok."

"Sounds like you swallowed the whole frog son," Pa said and EJ smiled a little embarrassed. "It will come. Do feel like eating?" EJ nodded his head yes…"Alright then, we're going to sit you back up." Pa grabbed the pillows and placed them behind his head. "Ok ready one, two, and three." EJ groans.

"Yes, I know it hurts, it will get easier," Pa said after he tucked the sheets back around his waist. "Drink this broth first it will help with the pain." EJ nods, Pa sat in the nearby chair and Will sat on the bed next to EJ while he ate his lunch. EJ looked over at Will then looks over at Mr. Downing, him seeing this. "Oh that's right, you haven't been introduced yet, kind of," as Pa smiles. "We may know you fairly well, but you know nothing about us."

"This is Will, he's just a little bit older than you and boy earlier was my other son Robert is his older brother and the little one about

Danny's age is Sam. I also have two girls, Julie being the oldest and Anna our youngest daughter. She helped prepare your lunch while your Grandma and they are in town. That's our family. I'll sit in here until they come back, I just want you to rest son."

EJ, still feeling nervousness keeps looking towards the door. Expecting any moment for his parents to return, Pa seeing this felt he needed to set his mind at ease, "EJ I made you a promise that I would keep you safe son and that's what I intend to do. They are not coming back son." He said looking at the door. "I won't let them lay a finger on you or anybody else son. You have my word on it," he said.

EJ looked into Mr. Downing's face and looked into his eyes then looked at Will. Will said. "When my Pa makes a promise, he keeps it and so does." Will got off the bed and goes over next to EJ, Will put his hand on his shoulder. "And we won't let anything happen to you. You're my brother now and brothers protect their brothers so listen to Pa." EJ not knowing what to say looked at Mr. Downing sitting in the chair he just nods his head.

"Now if that's settled, let's see if we can set you back down so you can rest." Will takes the tray and they lower him back into bed and Will leaves the room leaving Pa with EJ.

"Everything ok Will?" Anna asked.

"Yes, Anna."

"I just got the boys down for their nap," she said laughing while clearing the table. "They tried to tell me they weren't tired, but after five minutes they were out like a light. It never fails. A hot bath and meal and two little boys playing all morning, humm never gets old does it?" She said as she looked over at Sam and Danny sleeping on a quilt side by side. "So, Will?" she asked.

"Yes, Anna?"

"Who was that earlier? I am not stupid you know. Someone tried to take EJ didn't they?" she asked.

"Anna, what do mean?" He replied.

"Humm," Anna tapped her foot waiting for him to answer, starts to stare right at him to make him sweat.

"Let's just say, they were lost and Pa had to give them new directions and sent them on their way." He replied wiping the sweat from his face.

Anna gave him a puzzled look. "Will, for now, I'll accept that since there is some truth behind that, but Will?" She said.

"Yes, Anna?"

"You owe me a favor." Knowing it's always good to hold a few extra secrets for something better later on and much more juicer, Ma says hold on to those and guard them well.

"A favor? What kind of favor?" He asked.

"Oh you'll see, but not right now, just remember it for now," she said.

Looking out the window they see the pickup pulling up into the farm. Will walked down the hall to EJ's room. "Pa it looks like they're back," he said.

"Thanks, Will, go find Robert and let's bring in the supplies."

"Yes, Pa."

Pa looked down at EJ. EJ hears Mr. Downing moving around, "Its ok EJ, they're back from town. I told you we are going to be fine son, now didn't I?" EJ nods his head yes. "Are you going to be ok if I leave? I need you to rest son," then pats him on the end of his foot. EJ nods yes. "Alright, then we'll check on you later son, now rest. Ma and your Grandma will be in here soon son, I am sure," he said as he smiled then left the room. "What you did do buy the whole town, Martha?" Wayne asked walking outside to greet them.

"Oh Wayne, just a few things, that's all really." Wayne laughs looking at the pickup packed to the gills and scratches his head.

"Ok boys," with a big sigh, "let's get it inside."

Martha asked. "Now then how was your day? Anything happens while we were away?"

"No, not a thing dear, really; Oh just a couple visitors got lost and asked for directions that's all," as he looked at Will and Robert. "Other than that, been fairly quiet all day, really, did you have a good time in town?" He asked.

"Yes Wayne." Ma said still trying to find something, but can't. "How's EJ?" She finally asked.

"He's resting, just gave him his lunch a while ago. Anna put Sam and Danny down for a nap about an hour ago so everything's fine dear. So go put your things away," and then shoved her towards the house.

"Grandma?" Wayne asked.

"Yes, Wayne?"

"I wanted to show you something out in the barn if you got a minute? I want to show you the little present we are working on for EJ," he said.

"Oh, I would love to see it," she replied.

Wayne and Grandma walked a bit, getting some distance away from the house. "Grandma this is a good place to test some of that wind you were talking about," Wayne said as he looked back at the house, making sure Martha was in the house.

"Wayne, what's on your mind?" She asked, noticing he was looking to see if the coast was clear.

What's Behind the Looking Glass?

"You heard me mention a couple of visitors that were looking for directions. Well, I don't want Martha to worry about it, but I felt you should know those weren't ordinary visitors," he said.

Grandma's eyes started blazing, "You mean they tried to?" Wayne nodded his head.

"They didn't get very far, weren't here long enough and they didn't get more than 5 feet in front of him and were quickly ushered off the farm. I don't think they'll be back though. I thought you should know. That way if they try it again and get to the others," he said.

Grandma tries to remain calm. "Thanks, Wayne. I knew I was right about you. I will not have to worry about EJ. He is in good hands. Now then I see you have some firewood, you mind if I chop some?" She asked.

"But?".... Grandma never minds, I've chopped at lot myself." After Grandma chopped for a few minutes and cooling off and deciding what to do.

"Wayne?" She asked.

"Yes, Grandma?"

"I think its best not to tell Martha. It would just worry her, just keep the story about the visitors, you didn't get their names did you?" She asked.

"I didn't ask," he said.

"Did they see Danny?"

"No, Will stuck him in the chicken cop with Anna and Sam," he said.

"Smart thinking, good, that means, they'll still think he's with me," Grandma said and started laughing and slapping her knee. "It must have been a sight to see though?" Wayne looked at her puzzled and if she'd gone off her rocker. "Finally somebody standing up to that windbag and knocking the wind right out of her sails. I thought I could have felt a breeze," she said as she looked at Wayne. "You were busy creating your own storm," she said and punched him right in the arm. "Now let's head back or Martha will think I was keeping you for myself," she said.

"And what have you two been up to out in the barn?" Martha asked as she turned around as they walked through the front door.

"What do you mean Martha? I was just showing Grandma here some of the things that Robert has made and the project we're working on for EJ." He said as he then leaned over and gave her a kiss.

"If you say so dear," and sighs; "*there's something funny going on around here... humm,*" as she looked at both them with a mischievous grin.

"Martha let's go check on EJ," Grandma said to take her mind off Wayne for a minute. Plus she a little concerned herself. Grabbing fresh medical supplies clean bandages she placed them on the tray while grandma mixed the broth with his pain medicine they headed back down the hall towards Wills room…

Chapter 10

"That's right, I was going to change those bandages now wasn't I now is as good a time as any. Grandma, you grab that soap and water over there and I'll take these." With arms loaded they head down the hall.

Pa shook his head. "Poor EJ, I bet he's going to wish he was sleeping by the time they get through with him," he said seating in a comfortable chair in the living room worked on the figures for the new additions of the home.

Entering the room EJ turned and opened his eyes and sees his Grandma and smiled. "Miss me, son?" She said coming around to the other side of the bed.

EJ nodded and answered with his frog voice. "Yes, Grandma."

"Oh my, that's better," as she laughed. "But did you have to swallow the whole frog. Now we need to open up the curtains too let some light in so we can get a better look at you. We will do it slowly to give you a chance to adjust to the light." She turned drawing the curtains open. Now then, that's better, feeling any better?" She asked.

EJ croaked. "Yes, but it hurts too move my legs, arms and my back itches and its sore."

"I understand EJ. How about your ribs, do they hurt?" She asked taking the tray from Martha and placing it on the little table by his bed, noticing it too must have been homemade like most of the furniture in the house either that Martha and Wayne had fine tastes, but after seeing some the work he has done in the barn she felt a little jealous of Martha, perhaps she could get him to make something for her as she ran her hand over the fine enteric patterns of the table.

EJ nods and croaked, "very tight and hard to breathe."

"Alright now, we need to clean the wounds and change the bandages that will help." EJ nods his head. "And we also need to change the bed."

EJ eyes went as big as saucers, croaked. "I can't get out of the bed Grandma. I don't have anything on."

"EJ child, who do think put you in this bed? We already know that you silly boy." She said.

EJ grabbed the blankets and wrapped them close around his body croaked. "No Grandma, no way!" He might trust his grandma to a certain extent, but there was no way he was going to let Mrs. Downing see him naked, she not even his mother beside it had been years since... *No, it wasn't going to happen. Not now, not ever...*

Seeing how frightened he was they compromised. "Ok EJ, we have to change some of the bandages, but we still have to change the bedding. Will you let us start with the ones on your legs and feet?" She asked.

EJ thought for a moment then croaked out. "No further than my knees Grandma."

Grandma sighed and agreed. "All right EJ, Martha is going to pull up the blankets and the sheets." EJ held them down making sure they don't go any further.

Martha just shook her head. Picking up one leg and a foot while washing it and looked at EJ then turned to his grandmother. "And I thought my boys were stubborn," she said and they both laughed. Then doing the same to the other one then lowered the sheet and the blanket back over them. Ma turned to EJ. "Now that wasn't so hard now was it?"

"Let's remove these," Grandma said and pulled down the blankets thinking she was going to trick him but he grabbed hold of the blanket and started to pull them back.

"That's far enough, Grandma!" He said.

What's Behind the Looking Glass?

"But EJ, the wounds go a lot further," she said.

"I don't care! That is far enough," he said with fear in his voice.

"All right, but we're going have to set you up to remove the bandages," Grandma said.

"I am not going any further," EJ said and placed his arms across the sheets holding down the bedding.

Grandma sighed. "Just to the waist, silly boy; EJ, I have changed your diaper many times. Bathed you countless times boy... Why are you being so stubborn? Martha, it's always the same when they reach a certain age. They forget I think until after there married until they have kids of their own then it doesn't matter anymore."

"Alright EJ, you win for now," Grandma said and rubbed his head. "What am I going to do with you son?" She said. They sat him up and tucked the sheets around him and start removing the pins around his waist. "Ok now, this going to hurt, so hold your breath." No sooner did they unwrapped the bandage from around his chest. EJ gasped, his eyes watered. It was like the air was sucked right out of his lungs. "Martha looks like we have a little bit of infection here too. Some of the glass is still in there." Grandma said seeing the puss forming around the sides.

Martha looked over at EJ. "This is really going to hurt son. It can't be helped." Grandma took the tweezers from off the table and pulled out the stitches and carefully pulled out a small piece of glass and set it on the tray and squeezed the puss and blood out and cleaned the wound.

EJ screamed and nearly passed out due to the pain as she wrapped his chest back up. "EJ are you still with us?" Grandma asked. EJ slowly nodded. "Sorry son, it had to be done. EJ drink this broth and we will give it a few minutes to work. Martha, while we're waiting. See if you can get Wayne to come in to move EJ so we can change the bed." Grandma said wanting to be alone with EJ for a minute. Martha left the room as she left she shook her head giving them some privacy.

"You stubborn, silly boy… EJ I understand that your parents came by and tried to do something foolish," grandma said. EJ nodded his head. "And Mr. Downing stopped them didn't he son?" EJ nods. "Well EJ, Grandma trusts them and so should you or she would not leave you here, now would she?" She asked.

EJ thinks about it. "No Grandma, I trust you." *Well not in entirely, but we will wait and see. Since is obvious I am not going anywhere in this condition. I can treat it just like just another foster home. What does it make it…? Number eighteen?* He grimaced remember the last home as the gunfire still echoed through his mind and those dead cold eyes staring back him, it still shook him to the very core of his soul.

"Good son, now you know I'll be leaving in a day or so with Danny, but I want you to feel safe and you know I love you right EJ?" EJ nods his head yes. "Good. So you have nothing to fear from Martha, she is a good person. Wonderful mother and Wayne's a good father, remember that. I want you to mind them both. You hear me son?"

"Yes, Grandma," EJ croaked.

Grandma gave him a gentle kiss on the head, "that's a good boy."

"Did somebody call for arms?" Wayne said as walked into the room.

"Why Wayne, if you are not too busy that is?" Grandma asked.

"That's what I am here for."

"Well have a seat, we just need to finish cleaning this stubborn boy up. It was easier when he was asleep. He didn't care so much what he was not wearing at the time," Martha said and shook her head.

"I thought as much." He said smiling at EJ as he understood completely.

What's Behind the Looking Glass?

"Alright EJ, let's finish cleaning the wounds on your chest," Grandma said. EJ nearly screamed when they applied the disinfection to some of the tender spots on his back.

"EJ we need to scoot you forward a little… alright, we are just about done. I know it hurts. Ok. Hold your breath while we wrap this back around. Little tuck here and there. Now then that was pretty bad. I wish you'd allow us to do the rest of you," Martha said.

"OH NO!" EJ croaked. "That's it. I am done. You promised." Tightening the blankets close around him. Martha and Grandma sighed.

Wayne laughed. "Just like the rest of our boys Martha, he knows."

"Alright Wayne, I guess we don't have any choice. EJ we will give you some privacy. We will leave the room and close the door. Wayne just set EJ over on the other bed for the moment we'll be outside the door."

"Alright dear," he said. They looked at EJ and shook their heads and closed the door. "Well son, are you ready?" He asked.

EJ nods his head and croaked. "I guess so sir." But deep down he was shaking, he did not want this man or any man touching him ever again. *Maybe I can crawl way after grandma leaves knowing Danny is safe. But where would I go? Grandma trusts him or she would have never leave me here alone. Is she wrong? Could they be hiding something from her?* EJ sighed as if his thought conflicted with him as if there were two people inside his mind. Something the way Mr. Downing made him feel safe and as if he could feel… *Strange it's gone…*

Wayne removed the blankets leaving the sheet that covered him tucked in, then gently picked him up and sat him on the other bed and opened the door. "Come on in ladies the bed awaits." They changed the bed, turned down the covers and closed the door. EJ's face felt a little green seeing all the blood he had left behind on the sheets they had just removed. He felt bad that he was the source of more work for Mrs. Downing. He knew if he was home, his mother would whip the tar out of him for causing more work for her. Mrs. Downing acted like it was no big deal, and that bothered him, knowing very few people would be this nice to him. In fact, most people he had lived with would be angry because he was such a burden and they didn't get paid enough to put up with it.

Wayne nods too EJ. He picked EJ up, placed him back in bed. He pulled the fresh sheets over him, removing the old ones, opens the door, and bowed. "My arms are at your service madam." And gave them each twist and a turn in the room and his wife a kiss on the cheek, then handed her the old sheet. He too didn't care about that sheet would never get the blood out. Yet it was nice to see that he did, in fact, care about him and that bothered him because most people he knew didn't. Again the voice in his head yelled run, don't trust him, don't trust anyone. All they want to do is hurt you. EJ pressed his hand to his head trying to shake the voices inside head.

"Hi EJ, my name is Julie," she said as she entered the room. EJ was dumbfounded at first as he looked upon her features. She had long brown auburn hair almost shoulder length. Deep blue-greenish eyes wearing a blue dress with little flowers and a dark blue apron tied around her waist. She was the most beautiful girl he had ever seen. EJ hurried and checked to make sure everything is covered as she entered.

Julie laughed and rolled her eyes. "Oh come now, you don't need to be shy around me. Remember, I do have a house full of brothers and I have bathed them changed them too. Just as many times as Ma has," she said as she giggled. "You silly, silly boy," and then sighed as she watched him blush.

Ma and Grandma laughed even harder as they watched EJ turn red with embracement, Mrs. Downing went over to him. "Its ok son, we'll work something out," rubbing his head and kissed him on the cheek. "I don't know how or what? But there's got to be away and we'll find it EJ," she said.

EJ looked up at Julie standing in the room. "I thought you would like some pie. I made it myself, it is from last night." She said then sat it on the tray across his lap. She cut the pie and feed

What's Behind the Looking Glass?

it to him. One bite at a time and gave him a glass of milk to drink, wiped his mouth and smiled. Then looked into his big blue eyes, "EJ I am glad you are here, you are just what this family of ours needs, another brother. Welcome home little brother," she said with a peck on the cheek, EJ eyes flashed wide open and his face blushes red. Julie giggled, "Now get some rest," and left the room taking the tray and the empty plate with her.

Ma and Grandma looked over at EJ with a wide grin. "Like she said rest dear," Grandma said trying not too laugh and walked out the door. "Martha?" Grandma asked.

"Yes, Grandma?" As they walked towards the kitchen together.

"Julie's got spunk that's for sure," she said.

"She takes after her father."

"Making my grandson blush like that, it was a sight to see. All I can say is, fella's watch out! Julies in town. Leave her alone in the room with him for an hour with some of that pie, and she'd have those bandages changed before he could blink an eye." She said as they laughed down the hall into the kitchen.

"Well we better get dinner started," Martha said setting down the tray of old bandages and supplies on the counter.

"Mind if I use your phone, Martha? I need to check in with the rest of my brew." Grandma asked. Thinking about the news she had heard. It worried her to no end on what his parents have been up to. Instead of getting the help they were causing trouble as if they haven't done enough already.

"No Grandma, go right on ahead," she said, pointing towards the phone.

"Thanks." Picking up the phone and dialing home listening to it ring a couple of times before her son Richard answered.

"Hello, Richard.

"Hi, Ma... How's EJ?" He asked. Richard had his fathers build and was considered tall compared to his mother reaching five-feet five inches and lengthy, for some reason he was able to keep his dark brown hair from balding unlike his father and two bothers. Now partly bald in the center and began losing their hair before age of twenty; blue-eyed and hard straight nose with high cheekbones like his mother. Richard could be considered man-made by hard-living, not by education or status, but neither are his brothers. He did not leave home like his older brothers, remained at home to stay close so he could care for his mother after his father died, yet he had regrets that he would never have a life like his older brother Steve.

Instead tied himself to the house very seldom did go out like most boys his age and date young girls or go to spring or summer dances. Instead, he stayed at home either reading a book on cold nights or took care of the house and the yard while his mother was away visiting old friends. Sometimes his felt he was wasting away as others were out enjoying life as he tinkers around the home and still feels him with grief every time he sees pictures of his father staring back at him, wondering if he was proud of the choices he has made.

"Everything's fine, he's awake and recovering. How's everything down at home?" She asked. Looked around the kitchen and seeing Wayne playing with Sam and Danny on the living room floor. She wonders in her mind if Jim ever took the time to ever spend time with his boys. Somehow she doubted it.

"Well, you certainly caused a disturbance that for sure. If you wanted the phone lines to buzz you did that alright"

"Richard, you know I never cared what neighbors think," she said to bring her mind back to the conversation pulling up a chair to rest her sore old bones from a very long day.

"I know Ma but?"

"But nothing! Have any un-welcomed guests been looking for Danny?"

What's Behind the Looking Glass?

"They came by yesterday, but I told them that he wasn't here, but they didn't believe me, she searched the whole place Ma. It was a good thing he was with you. She was in a rage, they both were. After they left, I called your sisters too give them a heads up."

"Thanks, Richard. I knew I didn't raise an idiot," she said giving a heavy sigh and trying very hard to keep the anger out of her voice.

"Thanks, Ma, anyway your sisters took them out, they took them both out of town somewhere overnight camping. I think for the weekend and was just getting ready to leave when I called. They said to tell you they all went to the Doctor as you asked. They were fine accepted for a few minor bumps and old bruises and they are adjusting well and having the time of their lives."

"Well, that is good news. Richard, do you have everything ready for me and Danny when we come home? We're leaving for home in the morning," she said.

"Yes Ma, everything is ready."

"I believe EJ is going to be just fine here and he needs to have time to bond with them without me and Danny. It's going to hurt taking Danny away from him, but I can't leave him here. I feel it would be too much of a stress on this family. Even though they don't think so, so, for now, we will visit often and give him some time to grow, both of them." She said as she wiped a tear from her eye. "It breaks my heart knowing how much these two love each other. Alright, see soon son, love ya."

"Love ya too Ma." Grandma hearing the line go dead sets the phone down back in the cradle her thoughts going out to Jim and Linda and her two grandchildren staying with their aunts. How long can she keep them from harm? The answer made her angry as she watched Wayne tickle Danny and Sam as he rolled on the floor with them. *No, they can't have them back!*

Martha said watching her hang up the phone. "I didn't mean to eavesdrop Grandma, but did you say you are leaving us in the morning?" bring grandma out of her dark thoughts.

"It's alright Martha; yes. I need to get back home. EJ is doing better and you and your family have everything under control. You have completely set my mind at ease. Plus I do have two other grandchildren that need their Grandma as well and I have two naughty parents to contend with," as she looked at Wayne not saying anything else. In hopes, he could help change the subject.

"Well then," as he cleared his voice. "Grandma, I need some help here to finish this project before you go. I understand you have a fine hand?" Taking the slips of paper the children have written for their promise. From his pocket gets up from the floor patted Danny on the head. "What I need is someone to put the promise on a fine sheet of paper like this parchment paper," he said. Walking over to a shelf and pulling it out trying hard not to wrinkle it. "I want you to scribe down these promises. Do you think you can do that?" He asked as he leaned over her shoulder.

Grandma looked up at Wayne with a gentle smile on her face. "I would be glad to help. Are we really going to do this?" Taking a seat at the kitchen table as Wayne laid out the promises and the parchment.

"We Downing's always keep our promise Grandma, and EJ needs to trust in that more than ever," he said.

Martha walked up to her husband and placed her arms around his waist, stood on her tiptoes while she reached up to give him a kiss on the cheek. "Yes, we do Grandma. You do this and I'll start dinner," she said.

Wayne seeing Martha busy in the kitchen leaned down and whispered in Grandma's ear. "Those naughty parents, were they successful?"

Grandma whispered back. "No Wayne, I too have a smart son at home and I have two very smart sisters, they got nothing, but the wind."

Wayne smiled. "I am glad."

What's Behind the Looking Glass?

"But I need to go home in case they try it again. They can meet the tornado in person. But you won't have anything to fear son with those trees on your arms and your boys. They won't come within five miles of this place," she said.

Wayne laughed. "Yes, I did scare them pretty good. I could have sworn they almost made water in the hallway. Yet my wife and my children know I am as gentle as the morning sun."

Grandma giggled; "yes, and as smooth as a baby's bottom," as she rubbed his arms and watched Wayne blush.

"Grandma, are you making my husband blush?" Martha asked as she turned to look at Wayne.

"Why would you say that Martha?" Turning her head towards the kitchen.

"Because that's the nicest shade of red his wearing," she said as they both laughed.

After a few minutes of copying down the children's and Wayne's promises she asked.

"Well, what do you think?" She said finishing the parchment.

"Well, that looks good so far. I just need to add the women folk then fit it to the frame. Then we should be set. Martha, what do you think?" He asked as she came to look over the document. As she reads it, it brought tears to her eyes and looked down at Grandma.

"It's just beautiful. I think after it's written we need to embroider it so it will last forever." Then wiped her eyes, "but it's not finished yet. The girls and I haven't given our promises yet." Ma turned to Julie in the kitchen. "Julie dear can you watch over things for a few minutes? She asked taking a seat next to grandma.

"Yes, Ma," Julie said putting the rolls into the oven and wiped down the counter.

Chapter 10-1

* * * *

Ma sat down at the table grabbing a pad and pencil and began to think of EJ and the promise she could make. Taping the end of the pencil to her lip's, she smiled at her husband and looked over at Sam and Danny playing in the corner nearby.

"I promise to be the best, caring, understanding mother. I also promise to treat you with compassion, love, and dignity as if you were my own child. To me, you already are my son."

She reads it over a couple of times and hands it over to his grandmother and Wayne to read and waits with tears in both their eyes. Wayne bends down and whispered in her ear "My thoughts exactly my dear." He said and kissed her on the cheek and wiped her eyes with his fingers. Grandma nods her head in agreement.

Martha quickly composed herself and called Julie over. "Julie dear?"

"Yes, Ma?"

"Can you come here for a second…?"

"Sure Ma," she said washing her hands and walked over to the table.

Julie came over to the table Pa handed her a pencil and a pad. "We need you to write down your promise for EJ," he said.

Julie looked over what has been done and what her mother has written. Julie reads and looked over at her Pa and she smiles. "You would think this would be so hard, but after watching EJ eating my pie and looking into those big blue eyes of his," she smiled and wrote.

What's Behind the Looking Glass?

"I promise to be the best sister, to love you, to care for you as my brother because you are my brother. To tease you, make you blush and squeeze the stuffing out of you because I already love you."

Then smiled and handed the paper to her father and gave him a hug and kiss and went into the kitchen to help her mother. Grandma looked up at Wayne. "Wayne. She's a spitfire that's for sure, I almost feel sorry for EJ." She said as he looked toward his room and they both laughed.

"I only hope she waits to squeezes him after the bandaged come off," he said.

"Yes, I am worried about that too. He won't let us near them and I am afraid the infection has gotten into his thigh and lower half below the waist, and he won't let us look at it. You men are sure stubborn I give you that," as Grandma sighed. "I don't want that fever coming back and we need to get him out of that bed and soon to prevent bedsores and get those muscles and joints moving again. Well, that's another problem for another day. Let's finish this maybe a solution will turn up," and sighed.

Wayne looked around the room for Anna. "Grandma we just need one more than we can fit this into the frame. "Anna, Anna dear? Can you come here for a minute?" He asked.

"Yes, Pa." Letting Danny and Sam to play on their own.

"Do you remember what we're talking about this morning at breakfast about the promise that EJ made us and how we thought we should each make a promise of our own?"

"Yes," she said. Pa then hands her a pad and pencil then has a seat.

"I want you to think of a simple a promise dear you can make," he said and lets her read what has already been written. Anna looked at her father and looked at her mother and sister working together in the kitchen then looked into her father's eyes and smiled.

"I promise to work beside you brother with a sisters love as a sister should, to help when you need it, to be there when you need me, for that's what sisters do. For you will always be my brother and I love you too."

Then handed it to her Pa with a hug and gave a hug to her new Grandma and a kiss then went back to watching Danny and Sam. Grandma and Wayne read what she had written.

"Wayne just like your other daughter. I would have never of thought this from such a young child such as her. Your family is just full of surprises," she said as she wiped her eyes. "Now then let's add to the paper," she said after it was finished. "Well, Wayne. There it is, what do you think?" She asked.

"Its fine piece of work I must say. At dinner I'll have everyone sign it then we'll all go into his room and put it up, Martha how's dinner coming?" He asked.

"It should be done in about 20 minutes," she replied.

"Alright then, all go head and find Robert and see about getting this into the frame while you ladies set the table." As he rolled up the parchment and leaned over to his wife to test the gravy.

"Slapped his hand away with the spoon, "it's not ready yet," and dropped the spoon.

"Alright," trying to look hurt, "but?" The ladies all laugh.

"Boy's, they never seem to learn, but you got to love them all just the same."

"Robert?" Pa calls.

"Yes, Pa," making his presence known and where he was asking if dinner was ready.

"How's that frame coming?" He asked.

"Oh it's nearly finished," he said putting on the last coat of varnish and dabbing it dry with his rag.

What's Behind the Looking Glass?

"Well let's take look at it. I have the parchment right here so we can finish it. Ma tells me dinner should be done in about 20 minutes. It's should be done by then I think," he said.

"Yes, Pa."

Pa placed the parchment in the frame. "That looks really good Robert. Nice craftsmanship on the frame. I think he's going to like it," Pa said holding the finished work to admire it.

"You think so Pa?" He asked cleaning up his mess as he turned to face his Pa and looked deep into his eyes.

"I know so," Pa said as he looked straight into Robert's eyes. "His grandmother is leaving us tomorrow Robert. That means he's going to need us more than ever. And Danny will be going with her too, so he will feel all alone. So now it's going to be up too you boy's to make him feel at home."

"Yes Pa, I understand," he said as Pa placed his arm around his shoulder.

"There's a problem son. He won't let anyone near him and the infection is spreading and we have to find a way to help him. The problem is he as stubborn as you boys are," then smiles." If you know what I mean son," he asked.

"Yes Pa, were not as young as Sam or his little brother Danny anymore. It seems to matter more."

Pa laughed and slapped him on the back. "When you have kids of your own son and you will someday, you will say to yourself. How silly I was back then," he said laughing.

"Pa, you got to be kidding, Pa. I'll never say that," he replied.

Pa chuckled harder. "Then let's take this inside the house or Ma be wondering where we are."

Everyone gathered around the table Pa cleared his throat. "I have an announcement to make. I would like to wish our new members of our family and her grandson Danny a safe journey home tomorrow and let them both know," said with a tear in his eye and a choked voice. "How much we love them and hope they come back real soon to the Downing Farm. For they will always be in our hearts and in our thoughts so they never really say goodbye." With that, he sat down and turned to Martha as she too wiped her eyes.

Martha stood up with a shake in her voice. "Well now. Dinner is getting cold." Trying to composer herself the best she can and started to pass down the rolls.

After a few minutes of silence at the table, Pa, start's up the conversation at the table. "So Danny, what did you do today?" He asked.

"Will let me hold a baby pig," he said feeling the hunger gnaw on him as he listened to his stomach growl. He only wished his mother could cook this good and cared more about him and his brother then his two sisters who were always mean to him. His father, on the other hand, was nothing like Mr. Downing, and he didn't understand why.

"He did now!" Pa said with a smile across his face towards Will. And taking a heaping spoon of mashed potatoes and three rolls and watch Will pile large pieces of Turkey on Danny's plate. Knowing very well that Danny could easily put it away and still have room for seconds...

"Ya, but it got way sir, I tried to hold it and hold it tight, but it got to lose," he said putting his two lips together trying to pout. "We guessed it was hungry so it went back to its mother," he said. That started everyone laughing at the table.

"Danny?" Grandma asked helping him cut up his meat into smaller bites.

"Yes, Grandma?"

"Did you see anything else?" She asked.

What's Behind the Looking Glass?

"Oh yes. I got to see a pony than a bunch of chickens with Sam?" He said with his mouth full.

"Did you have fun?" She asked buttering his roll.

"Yes, Grandma until I had to take another bath."

"Were you dirty?" She asked attending to her plate holding back a grin.

Danny grinned. "Yes, Grandma."

"Well then," she said.

"I know, don't sweat the small stuff," he said.

Wayne rubbed his hair, "and they were too." He said and they all laughed. "From head to toe if I remember right," leaned over and picked a piece of straw out of Danny's hair.

Danny eyes in wonderment. "How did that get in there?" Grandma just rubbed his head and kissed his cheek, putting the grin back on Danny's face.

"Now if I could just get that other grandson of mine in a tub, without a fight." She shook her head, sighed and looked toward Wayne. "Did you keep that stick EJ was biting on at the creek?" She asked.

"Yes, Grandma. I did," he said.

"Will?" Pa asked turning his attention to him.

"Yes, Pa." Will swallowed hard nearly choking on his food from stuffing his mouth so full.

"Would you bring it over, please? I put it over there on the mantle." Will got up from the table and picked it up and brought it over to Pa and retaking his seat next to Robert.

"Why this stick?" Will asked placing another spoonful of mash potatoes on his plate and started in on his second helpings.

"Oh no reason really, just a thought. Grandma got a story boys and I want you to listen. It may help and may not, but that's what Grandmas do." She said holding the stick and placed it down on the table in front of them.

"In the old west, they didn't have modern medicine to kill the pain. In fact, most of the time when someone was hurt and the Doctor was miles away, a lot of the healing took place on its own. Now if they were lucky, they would be found by a tribe of Indians for shelter, where they'd find a squaw or medicine woman to help them. After a time they would become brothers of that tribe and would provide trade and live among them for showing and giving thanks. It never mattered to them who they were. For he was their true brother to them, but they all believed in the old west." She paused as she allows it to sink in.

"To prove their courage and bravery on their own, they would strip down a bark of a tree branch like this one and put it between their teeth. This way they would not scream out in pain or break their teeth and ministered this to themselves. It showed courage and bravery against the odds to do this to survive.

"This stick represents that for EJ. Wayne, I'm glad you kept it. The only problem is he in need of a different kind of courage and bravery." With a slight turn of her head, she looked over at Wayne. "I only hope he can get past it without traumatizing him to death or there won't be any other choice," she said.

Will was in deep thought playing with his mash potatoes. Building little tepees then smashing them down. He would look at Robert with a silly grin then kicked him underneath the table. Robert did not understand what he wanted. Will grabbed his fork, knife, and spoon and built another tepee. Robert still did not understand, whispered, "Will stop playing with your food."

Will grinned back at Robert. "I got an idea, but I don't think you are not going to like it. But I'm going to need your help," he said. Robert shrugged his shoulders as it was nothing new. His brother always had crazy ideas and sometimes got them into trouble from time to time. But Pa nor Ma ever laid a hand on them compared to what EJ and Danny been through, but they have been grounded enough times to know better and extra hard labor to match the punishment. Robert's body still ached from their last one. Repainting the entire barn with the smallest brush Pa could find. After putting honey and Julies' hair using her hairbrush.

"Pa?" Will asked.

"Yes Will?" Chewing his food slowly and adding some more too his plate.

"You know that timber out back by the barn that we're going to make posts for rail fencing?" He asked as the idea formed in his mind.

"Yes Will what about it?"

"I was thinking I might have an idea how to solve a problem," he said taking a sip of his milk.

"What problem Will?" Pa asked curious to hear what mischief he had in a plan on now.

: "Oh, it's complicated. Can the three of us go outside?" Will blushed.

Wayne looked over at Will to see him turning red. "Oh that problem, I see. Martha, ladies if you would be so kind as to excuse us," he said.

Robert whispered over to Will. "What this all about?" Not wanting to leave the table or get involved in another scheme of Wills.

"I'll explain it in a minute once we're outside." The men left the table and headed outside for some privacy.

"I wonder what that was all about Martha," Grandma asked feeling almost guilty planting ideas into such young minds.

"I haven't the slight idea?" She said and watched the three men leave the house and head towards the barn through the window.

"Julie, you were sitting next to Will did he mention anything to you?" Ma asked.

"No Ma. He just kept looking at that stick, made weird shapes with his food and had a funny grin on his face," she said.

"Well, they'll be back in a moment," Ma replied cleaning her plate with a roll dabbing the last bits of food.

"Alright Will, what's this all about?" Pa asked leaning against the outside of the barn noticing a spot of paint that Robert must have missed.

"I was thinking about EJ," he said standing firm in front of Pa and followed Robert with his eyes he joined Pa as tried to cover up the missing paint. *She so deserved it after leaving pudding under my pillow. After all, it was Wills idea.*

"Yes, we all are," Pa said wondering what his son was planning now.

"And that stick, then Grandma said something about courage and bravery," he said

"Yes," Pa replied.

"Pa you were telling us about something about it down at the creek and Ma was nagging me about it when we first brought him in," Will said.

"Yes," Pa replied trying to figure out where he was going with this.

"And how I had a hard time with her letting her... you know?" He said.

"Yes, I know," as he smiled nearly blushing himself.

"Well EJ's awake and now, he is having the same problem. But he won't let her help him and it's going to get worse, right Pa?" He asked driving right straight into the hornet's nest.

What's Behind the Looking Glass?

"Yes Will, it is getting a lot worse." Will looked at Robert then looked back at Pa. wondering if this was such a good idea, but nothing else came to his mind so he continued on.

"Then we have no choice," he said and kicked a rock with his foot. "If he is my brother then he needs me and I am going to do it," he said.

"Do what Will?" Robert asked looking at Will like he just lost his marbles.

"Spit it out son," Pa said almost fearing what he has come up with now and how much trouble he would be in if Martha found out he didn't stop him after the last time; which was why he went easy on them, besides it was only honey all she had to do was wash it out. Good grief he had done a lot worse growing up with a house full of girls.

"Alright, I want to build a tepee," he said.

"A what?" Pa said looking stunned.

"A tepee," Will says again.

"What on earth for?" Pa asked.

"To sleep in just the four of us, me Robert, EJ and Sam until he has recovered enough," he said.

"Ok, and how is that going to help him?" Pa asked. Will kicked the dirt some more and swallowed.

"It going to sound crazy," Will said.

Robert looked over at Will; "crazier than building a tepee?" Now standing up straight with shock.

Will swallowed. "I want us to be Indian brothers?"

"Have you lost your mind; you want us to dress up like Indians?" Robert asked.

Will nodded yes... Robert slapped his forehead. "Do all our chores dressed as Indians too"...Then swallowed harder. "That way Ma can change all of EJ's bandages and clean all his wounds every day," Will said as Pa looked at Will and Robert tried to recover from the initial shock.

"She is still going to need to bathe him. You do know this Will?" He asked.

Will paced for minute swallowed really hard...Swallowed a couple more times...Then looked at Robert, then looked Pa straight in the eye..."If Robert will agree," as the sweat poured from his face. "I'll let Ma bathe us all in the tepee in front EJ every day." He said swallowing hard then looked at Robert then looked at the ground and kicked the rocks in the dirt.

Robert turned to Pa then looked at Will. Paced for a couple of minutes thinking about what Pa said earlier. Puts his hands in the back of his head looked toward the sky... Then he looked back at Will then shrugged his shoulders. Walked back over to Will and put his arm around Will's shoulders then looked straight at Pa. "Pa … I agree." Robert turned to, Will. "I should say, brother, if that's not the craziest thing I have ever heard. Indians! You want us to become Indians!" He replied in disbelief.

Then with a big squeeze that nearly knocks the breath right out of his lungs. "I can see it now. "I can see it now. Farmers running around in loincloths; people will think we're out of our minds... Heck, I say let's do it Pa," and slapped his brother on the back. "Ma will get a kick out this one, besides she'll have less wash to do." Pa started to laugh as the three go back into the house.

"Everything ok Pa?" Ma asked as the boys and her husband retake their seats.

"Oh yes, Ma. I believe the problem is solved." She watched as the boys returned to their seats at the table to finish their dinner with the biggest grin on their faces.

"Wayne, you mind filling the rest of us in on what's going on?"

What's Behind the Looking Glass?

She asked gathering the plates and the empty dishes on the table.

"Sorry Martha, this is between the four brothers for now. I'll fill you in on the details later," he said with a big silly grin on his face.

Ma looked down upon her boys with a critical motherly look. "You boys are up to something aren't you?" She asked.

Robert and Will blushed and nod their head. "Yes Ma, but I think you are going to like it," Will replied blushing red.

Wayne turned to Grandma and whispered in her ear. "EJ's problem has been solved. He just doesn't know about it," he replied.

She whispered back, "how?"

"Something to do with Indians," Grandma gave Wayne a puzzled look,

"Indians?" And sees the blushes on the two boys her eyes open wide with a silent, "OH!" And smiled back at Wayne.

"Julie and I picked up a nice chocolate cake while we were in town, so lets clear the table and have a piece," Ma said.

They cleared the table Martha joined Wayne. "Wayne, what's this all about dear, you mind filling me in? I don't like being kept in the dark, not like this. The suspense is killing me," she whispered in his ear.

"I know dear." He said then leaned over and plants a kiss, "buts it will have to wait. It's between them. They have to be the ones to work it out. I can tell you this dear you are in for quite a show and I mean literality dear," and with that, gave her another kiss.

Martha gave him a puzzled look and turned to Grandma in the kitchen. All she would tell her was one word, "Indians" laughed then winked at Wayne. Martha looked at them as if they had lost their minds. She heated the broth then loaded it onto his tray and headed down the hall.

Chapter 10-2

* * * *

"EJ, EJ," turning on the light, EJ opened his eyes.

"How are you feeling son?" Martha asked.

"Sore, it hurts all over," he croaked.

"Well, I have some more broth that should help that. I think we'll try moving you around a bit tomorrow get those muscles moving again to work some that stiffness out." EJ nods his head. "Alright, I have your dinner. So let's see if we can sit you up. Do think you can help me." EJ nods his head. "Good, let's place these pillows behind you. Ok one, two, three-push."

EJ groaned. "I can't, it hurts too much, my legs won't budge," he said.

"I need to take a look at those bandages EJ. I think your legs are infected," as she starts to pull back the blankets and the sheets.

EJ gripped them tightly and yelled with a loud croak "NO!"

Seeing the frightened look on his face she let go. "EJ it's getting worse," she said.

"NO! No WAY!" He screamed.

"Alright then, I'll get someone to help sit you up," shaking her head, "silly boy."

"Wayne?" Martha called from down the hall.

"Yes, Martha?"

"Can you help me please with EJ, he needs help to sit-up," she said."

What's Behind the Looking Glass?

Grandma came over. "What's the matter?" She asked.

"I think its getting worse, but he won't let me look, he says he can't move those legs. It hurts too much," she said.

"I was afraid of that; come on Wayne, we are going to need your arms again," she said stepping aside to let him in the room.

"Yes, ma'am."

"EJ will you let Grandma see your feet and just below your knees?" She asked coming around the other side of the bed.

"No higher Grandma!" They pull back the blankets and the sheets up to his knees. His legs and feet were swollen.

"EJ, Grandma needs to look just a little bit higher," EJ's eyes go wide.

"How high?" He asked as she draws a line across EJ, EJ shakes his head, shouts "NO!" And re-drew the line, she sighed and they roll up to that line. EJ held the blanket down. "That's it! No more! I am not budging!"

Grandma turned to Martha. "I don't think we have a choice." She said and tried to comfort her scarred grandson. "Alright EJ, we are not going any further." And lowered the sheets and blankets back over his legs, turns to Wayne. "Ok, go ahead set him up in the bed so Martha can give him his dinner." Wayne picked him up as gently as he could and Grandma gave him a kiss on the forehead and Wayne rubbed his head and they walked down the hall. "Wayne?" She asked.

"Yes, Grandma?" Stopped and whispered standing across from Wayne wondering maybe she should force EJ to let her look. *No, he's been traumatized enough.*

"How soon do you think your boys will be ready to work on that problem?"

"Why?" He asked standing on the side of the hallway.

"I would say that boy in there needs it like yesterday looking at those legs," she said.

"I'll have them start tonight then."

"Thanks, Wayne," walking back down the hall to see if she can do anything more.

"That bad?" He said stopping her in her tracks.

"Yes," she said turning back with a worried grin.

"Robert, Will?" Pa called.

"Yes, Pa?"

"Can you come outside for a minute?" as he opened the door and stood to hold the door as they walked out on the porch.

"Sure Pa."

Pa looked them straight in the eye. "Did you mean what you said about becoming Indians for EJ? You weren't joking because it's really bad? His legs are swollen and he won't let anybody touch him and Ma needs to change and clean those wounds every day? That means you have to sacrifice that little pride of yours sooner than you like."

They looked at each other and swallow hard, Robert said "We know Pa, it's not like Ma hasn't done it before," Will agreed as they looked down at the ground.

Will said "But if we don't. EJ could get very sick and could… So what's a little embarrassment vs. that? You said we're brothers right, well brothers help each other," Will said.

"Robert, what do you say? You are older than Will. So would it be harder," he said.

"Not really Pa, because all four of us would be in the same room together, going through the same thing. So we would be there for each other. Brother for our brothers," he said.

What's Behind the Looking Glass?

Pa put his arm around his two boys. "For the first time, I do not know what to say. Except the Indians are coming to the Downing Farm; so after dessert and we deliver our little surprise to EJ. I need you two to come out to the barn and I'll help you make that tepee and those loincloths you boys are going to be wearing. I think I have enough dear skin and leather in the shop. Your Ma and sisters will think we've gone mad," as he laughed. "Indians on the Downing Farm."

"And where have you boys been?" Ma asked putting her hands on her hips standing in the doorway on the porch.

"Just working on something for EJ," Pa said with grins on their faces.

"Martha it looks like it's going to be a long night for me and the boys. So after we have our dessert and give our little present to EJ the boys and I need to go out to the barn. We have some work to do, and it can't wait," he said as he gave a wink to Grandma as she came out to join them.

"Wayne, are you going to tell me?" She asked standing aside to let them in the house.

"Sorry Martha, it would spoil the surprise and it's going to be a whopper. In fact, it might even take your breath away. If I were you, I would prepare lots of soap and water. That much I can tell you."

Ma still looked puzzled as she shrugged her shoulders. "Anyone for some cake?" She said. Not knowing what else say or do.

They quickly ate their cake. They could barely wait to give EJ his surprise. Pa grabbed the frame, which he had wrapped, tucked it carefully under his arm. They all headed to EJ's room. EJ, still sitting up seeing the entire family together, croaked, "Hi, what's going on?"

Danny jumped on the bed with EJ, put his arm around his neck and whispered. "They brought you something, but I am not supposed to tell you." Pa came around the other side of the bed and rubbed little Danny's hair.

"That's right EJ, we did bring you something. We figured since you made us a promise that it was only fair that we would all make you one." They placed the frame in EJ's hands. He unwrapped it and began to read it.

EJ and Downing Declaration of Promise

I EJ am not going to get out of this bed and I am going to mind his Grandma and Mrs. and Mr. Downing I promise.

The Downing Family Promise

Pa Promise
I promise that I would keep you safe son and that's what I intend to do. I won't let anyone lay one finger on you or anybody and will give you love, guidance and fathers caring heart son.

Ma Promise
I Promise to be the best, caring, understanding mother, I also promise to treat you with compassion, love, dignity as if you were my own child to me you already are my son.

Four Brothers promise
I Robert, Will, and Sam and Danny Promise that we four brothers are going to be your brother and your brother Danny's bother and friend You are our brother now and forever, brothers protect their brothers and love their brothers no matter what, we love you too as our brother.

Julies Promise
I Promise to be the best sister, to love, to care for you as my brother because you are my brother. To tease you, make you blush and squeeze the stuffing out of you because I already love you.

Anna Promise

I promise to work beside you brother with a sister love, as a sister should, to help you when you need it to be there when you need me, for that's what sisters do.
For you will always be my brother and we love you.

What's Behind the Looking Glass?

EJ looked up from the frame bewildered. Tears formed in his eyes, he looked over at his grandmother. Tears welled in her eyes, she ran to his bedside and hugged him and whispered in his ear. "Yes son, they mean every word." Then kissed his tear, drenched cheek, "it's ok to cry son, just let it all go." As he buried his face against her shoulder, she gently patted him on the back. Martha gave him a hug and a kiss on his head and Pa laid his hand on his shoulder as they left the room one by one.

Will and Robert each put a hand on his shoulder and whispered." You are our brother now, it's going to be ok," and walked out of the room. Julie and Anna stroked his hair one at a time then bent down gave him a kiss, one on each cheek. Danny and Sam gave him a hug as well. Martha wiped the tears from her eyes with the back of her right hand. She took the boys by their hands and lead them away so he could be lone with his Grandma.

"Alright girls," Ma said trying to regain her composure. "Let's see if we can get things put away." Noticing the boys were already heading towards the barn she mumbled "Indians. What's that's so supposed to mean?"

"What was that Ma?" Julie asked coming on the other side of her placing the last dish into the cabinet.

"Oh, just something your Pa said to me, something about Indians." Then she shrugged her shoulders as she watched them go out to the barn and sighed.

"Well Martha, EJ settled back down again," she said walking back into the kitchen to help as she wiped the remaining tears from her eyes. "I sure hate leaving him like this, but I know I am leaving him in good hands. If I don't, it will only get harder for him and me and for little Danny. They both need to grow, and I do have other grandchildren that need me too. It's just so hard seeing him like this. It breaks my heart but knowing he's here with you and this family. I can rest a little easier.

"I won't have to worry so much, I just hope this plan your boys are working on works for EJ's sake. Or you won't have a choice dear, but to drug him enough to *sleep* which is dangerous in itself." Grandma added. "Hopefully he will allow you to remove those bandages every day so you can check for infection. Lord knows that child is frightened enough already."

"Grandma, do you have any idea what they're planning?" Martha asked drying her hands on the kitchen towel.

"No... not really, I think it's going take a lot of courage for all your boys and EJ and that's what he needs, so let them do it. What harm could it do? I have a sneaky inkling that your little farm is about to go a little bit native," she said and turned in for the night.

The boys worked through most of the night. Pa and the boys set up a tepee in the middle of the yard. Martha couldn't sleep so she went outside on the porch. Seeing the tepee being erected, she walked over to where Pa was standing. "Wayne, what in tarnation are you doing?" She asked.

"What does is it look like I am doing? I told you about the Indians," He said tying ropes and tethers.

"Yes Wayne you did, and who are these Indians you keep referring to?"

"Oh, just our four boys that's all. They'll need a place to sleep and this is their tepee," he said.

"Wayne our boys have bedrooms, they don't need a tepee," she replied.

"I know that dear, but they'll be Indians come morning and need a place to sleep." He said smiling seeing her confused face.

"Hi Ma, I thought you were in bed," Will said dressed in one of the loincloths. He looked over at his Ma then turned to Pa as if nothing was wrong, "Pa how's the tepee coming?" Pa smiled at Martha. She had a shocked look on her face seeing her son Will dressed in an Indian loincloth.

What's Behind the Looking Glass?

"Just about got it; just need to cinch the last rope up here and we'll have a nice looking tepee," he said.

"Well, Roberts almost done and I have EJ's and Danny's finished. Roberts is almost done and I have a start on Sam's Then we can start building one those stretcher thinger a bobber's to load him on and we can put a mattress in for EJ and sleeping bags for us. Then tomorrow we'll set up camp. See ya Ma, still, have lots to do," Will said and turned around headed back to the barn.

"Wayne?" She said watching her son Will and eying him up and down with disbelief.

"Yes dear," he replied as she watched her Indian son Will walk away.

"Please tell me that was not what I think I saw?"

"And what was that dear?" He asked grinning from ear to ear. "Hey, they thought about it all on their own. I had nothing to do with it. I would suggest dear lots and lots of hot soapy water. Now go back to bed," he said as he pushed his wife towards the door of the house.

Martha took one more look back then shook her head and mumbled. "Indians" and walked back into the house and down the hall. She walked down the hall to EJ's room and checked to make sure he was okay.

Grandma turned. "What's wrong Martha?"

"Oh my little farm has gone a little native that's all," she said.

Grandma laughed. "Indians a' well you'll be ok, see ya in the morning," she said.

Chapter 10-3

* * * *

That night EJ screamed as the cold sweat glistened on his body. He found himself running through a forest of evergreens. Large yellow eyes and creatures with long scaly necks like a dragon and part wolf with sharp claws and sharp long teeth chased him through the woods trying to kill him. His father angered voice yelling behind him with a burning torch in one hand and a long butcher knife in the other yelled. "Come back here you brat, it is time for your punishment. How dare you run from me and your mother? I am going too whip you to the inch of your life this time and peel the flesh from your bones."

EJ ran faster as he leaped large logs nearly tripping over his feet and the broken chain tied around his ankles dragged behind him getting caught in the underbrush as he ran. It slowed him down having to pull it to get it loose as it snagged around the debris as he tried to run and hide.

He screamed. "Grandma where are you? Save me," only seeing darkness through the endless forest. He turned his head seeing Mr. Downing joining the pursuing party of monsters as he transformed into a huge beast. Part bear and part man as it ran on two legs beside his father. His teeth gleamed white with strips of human flesh hanging limp in his mouth as he tossed Danny's half-eaten leg over his large shoulders like it was a finished chicken bone.

He knew he was next if they caught him. Crimson blood smeared against his chest as the beast took the torch from his father not breaking stride as he chased after him. The beast and monsters behind them howled when they came closer to its prey. Their eyes glowed with hunger and larger teeth snapped with anticipation of raw flesh, his flesh that they soon would be dining on.

Deeper and deeper he ran into the forest as they seemed to be gaining on him getting, closer with every step he takes. Their large grotesque bodies leaped bondless as the wind as the howls got closer. EJ stumbled

What's Behind the Looking Glass?

and fell and tries to get up before they reached him, but it was too late. The beast and his father's hands reach out as he scrambles back just barely racking their nails down his back as he tries to crawl way further into the underbrush.

The pain was burning as warm blood slid painfully down his back the poison in it clawed hands numbing his body making it harder to move and stay awake. The beast's teeth snapped wildly with a low hungry growl trying to gain purpose. EJ screamed as his father's knife plunges into his left side burning as more blood spills upon the ground. The beast hissed. "You will never be safe boy, not here or anywhere. As I strip your flesh and grind your bones as I have done with your brother. We will use your head as a candle and a reminder to those that dare run or upset the balance of the light."

His father's hand pulling on the chain dragging him closer to his doom… "Your grandmother can not help you now. And why would she help a worthless whelp like you?" The words echoed in his mind. "Worthless, bad seed, garbage." EJ crawls dragging his limp body further trying to get away as they and the monsters dig after him pulling on the chain wrapped around his ankle. The ground shook around him as there feet and claws grew closer…

* * *

Grandma tries shaking EJ awake as he screamed crying out her name. "Why Grandma did you leave me? Why…?" EJ eyes flashed open seeing grandma's face as he buried his face against her begging her not to leave him. "Please don't leave me." He sobbed, his voice cracking into gaps as she tries to comfort him. "They are going to kill me, Grandma please don't leave me."

"Shhh, it's alright I am here now," She said hugging him tight against her as she looked up seeing Martha coming into the room.

EJ griped her tight not letting go, yelled. "Grandma, don't let the monster touch me," Seeing Mrs. Downing eyes glow bright yellow and her hands long like bone like claws stained with fresh blood as they reached out for him; hearing her growl with sharp white teeth. He shutters against grandmas chest. The darkness lessens as his thoughts bring him to wake as sees the light in the room.

He shook in his grandma's arms as his brother Danny took his hand, pleading with him. "EJ it's me and Grandma. The monsters are not here. Mr. Downing killed them all."

EJ looked up over grandma's shoulder as the room comes more into focuses and the nightmare leaves him. He hears sing almost angelic as a soft warm voice sung to him EJ relaxes against her.

"On the wings of doves, you glide my son. Softly you slumber beneath them. May the angels guide you safely home and protect you on their wings. Rest my son and let them calm you…"

EJ's eyes closed as the words echoed in his mind.

Martha kept humming as she helped put Danny beside him and grandma turned off the light with a tired yawn. She placed a kiss on both their cheeks watching Martha close the door. And watched the sun from the windows as the rooster crowed with the coming of the dawn and the shadows receded once more.

Pa walked in the front door yelled at the top of his lungs. "We are surrounded by Indians come quick! They are taking over the Downing Farm." Everyone leaped out of bed as fast they could saw smoke rising outside around an erected tepee with two Indian boys running around it. Hooping and hollering for all their worth as they danced around the teepee. Ma and the girls ran outside. They could not believe what their eyes were seeing. Will and Robert dressed in their Indian loincloths, Grandma laughing nearly busting a gut. Sam ran up to Will to join in the fun with little Danny right behind him.

Will and Robert grabbed the two boys as to kidnap them and took them inside the tepee. Martha ran to the edge of the porch, Pa stopped her. "No Martha, this is between them," he said.

She looked over at Grandma and she nodded her approval. "It's ok, I think I know what's he's doing, I think," as she looked over at

What's Behind the Looking Glass?

Wayne. After a few minutes, all four boys came out. Now four little Indian boys are running around the tepee hooping and hollering. They make a couple of circles.

Robert and Will grabbed the stretcher and started to head for the house. "Ma if I were you and the ladies, I would stand clear of the doorway. I think they mean business. They mean to take prisoners," he said.

Martha turned to Wayne. "You wouldn't dare?" She said. Thinking her husband has gone insane.

"Actually Martha, I mean to help them. You wanted a problem fixed. Well, there's your solution." Pa said as he opened the door and led the way for the Indians down the hallway and closed the door. The boys entered the room alone with EJ while he remained outside waiting to be called.

Will and Robert went over to EJ. "Good morning EJ." EJ opened his eyes taken back as he looked at Will, Robert, Sam and his own little brother Danny all dressed as Indians.

"What are you guys doing dressed like that?" He croaked.

"What do you mean? We were wondering why you are not dressed like us. You are our brother aren't you?" Will asked.

"EJ croaked. "I'm not really sure."

"Well then I guess we better fix that," Robert said.

"But I am hurt," EJ replied.

"We know that stupid, we'll be careful. Pa locked all the girls outside so we can get you dressed and bust you out of here," Will said.

"And go where?" EJ asked.

"To our tepee silly, where else?" Robert asked.

"But I'm supposed to stay in this bed. I promised?" EJ said.

"Oh we took care of that, didn't we boys," Robert replied as they all nod their heads.

"We're all in the same room now," Will said.

Robert went over to EJ's bed. "Ok boys, let's get these blankets off and start peeling this banana. Be careful we don't want to take off those bandages. Ma will have our hide. EJ hold still. Man, you are a mess," he said.

"Robert glad you made this a little bigger," Will said as they lift it over his waist.

"Ouch, that hurts," EJ replied.

"Sorry," Robert said.

Will said. "EJ, say goodbye to those sheets," EJ eyes go wide. "You are an Indian brother just like the rest of us."

"But." EJ tries to get a word in.

"No buts," and they cover his mouth with a clean bandage strip of a sheet so he couldn't say anything else and held down his head. All he could do was feel himself turn blushing red. "Ok Pa, were ready," as Robert yelled through the room.

Pa came into the room and looked at his five little Indian boys and smiled, turned to EJ. "I hear you are bustin out son?" All EJ could do was nod with his mouth being covered "well it's about time," he laughed with a slight chuckle. "That bed was getting tired of you being it so let's say we give it a rest."

Then they picked him up and put him down on the stretcher. "Alright boys, I'll go check to make sure the coast is clear." Pa ran down the hall and yelled. "Stand back, they are on the warpath, the natives, are not too friendly, they have got they're prisoner…! Alright boys, bring him through and watches his head now." Pa said helping on the sides as they carried EJ to their tepee.

What's Behind the Looking Glass?

Grandma slapping her knee busting a gut with a tear in her eye as she watched fives little Indian boys ran by. The look on Martha's face not sure what to think, wondering if everyone on the farm has lost their minds. The girls glanced at their Pa and their new grandma, and then their new Indian brothers and burst out laughing.

After a few minutes, the shock wore off, Martha grinned and put a hand to her mouth trying to hide her giggling, but it was too much, she burst out laughing. The flap closed and the boys set him down on the mattress and cover him back up. "Ok boys, it's up to you now," Pa said.

"Yes, Pa we know. We will start slow so he can adjust; besides we need to set up camp and Ma needs to clean him up, what she can for now. Then we need to rest after chores of course," Robert said.

Pa left through the flap of the tent as he wiped his brow and walked over to Martha.

"Martha," he said as he kissed her on the forehead. "Don't push him, our sons will help you. It looks like you got your wish; go clean him up a little at a time. After all, you now have five Indian boys for sons.

Martha looked over at Grandma slapping her knee then looked at Wayne "I would never have believed it with my own eyes," Grandma said.

"Oh, that's nothing. The hard part yet to come, Grandma for them and for EJ too," he said.

Martha turned to Wayne. "Wayne, what do you mean the hard part is yet to come?"

"Martha they struck a deal between them. An honor code it was," he said.

"Go on," she implied.

Wayne swallowed. "It was not my idea Martha. They came up

with it on their own and they mean it." Wayne said as he started to turn red.

"Wayne you are blushing," Martha said.

"Your boys, say you can't touch EJ without them being present and they have to be first that includes bathing them all before him. They'll never leave his side or the tepee without him. He goes wherever they go, they promised him. And they intend to honor that promise every day and they mean it. You could say it's their honor code for their brother."

Martha gasped then looked at Wayne straight in the eye. "They would do that, Will and Robert?" She asked as she shook her head in bewilderment. "I can't see them doing this, but Sam and Danny they're too young understand... But Wayne? Robert and Will?" She asked.

"Yes dear, they're not joking, but for right now I would clean up what you can so they can set up their camp. It's been a long night and they are tired and they have a long day ahead of them."

"Wayne?"

"Yes dear."

"How long?"

"They say until he recovers enough, most likely two weeks," he replied.

"Two weeks?" Martha gasped.

"Look at this way dear, you will have the best tan boys around and less wash to do." He replied laughing.

Grandma laughed to beat all. "And to think I' am going to miss it all, poor Danny he looked so cute in his little loincloth," she said wiped the tears from her eyes. "Wayne you were right. That was quite a show; do you ever have a dull moment here on the farm?" Then stands up and slapped him on his back.

What's Behind the Looking Glass?

Wayne turned to her and rubbed his chin. "You know Grandma. I always hated the dull moments," he said.

"Whys that?"

"Too much time waiting for the excitement to happen," he said as they all laughed.

"Well Martha, let's go see what's with those Indians in there want and I would like to take a good look at EJ's legs while I can," she said. Martha and Grandma headed into the tepee seeing EJ lying on the mattress in the loincloth surrounded by the boy's tribe trying to ignore the old musty smell of canvas, sweating in the morning Sun...

Chapter 10-4

* * * *

Will looked up at Ma and stepped in front of her. "EJ is wounded and needs help, we're here to help," he said.

She nods, "I am glad son. Now we just need to look at his legs."

The brothers nod and stand by his side, putting a hand on his shoulder. "EJ we're here." EJ nodded his head. Grandma and Martha bent down on the ground next to EJ. They could see the swelling in his legs. They moved the loincloth a little, being careful to not expose anything that would embarrass him and removed the bandage ever so slightly. The smell is rank and puss formed around the wound and the skin was hot to the touch. When EJ screamed with the pain they stopped immediately.

"Martha I was afraid of this," Grandma turned to Will. "Go get your Pa and bring that stick," she said.

"Yes Grandma," he said.

"Robert you call Doc Hatfield to tell him to get here double time you hear," Grandma said.

"Yes ma'am," he said.

Pa rushed into the tepee as fast as he could. "Wayne we need that kitchen table outside of this tent and then we need to put this boy on it," Grandma said taking charge. Will and Pa rushed in the house and grabbed the kitchen table issuing orders to the girls to heat water and grab the sheets and bandages.

Robert quickly looks up Doc's number and picks up the phone as he paced waiting for Doc to answer. "Doc this Robert Downing... Ma says for you to double-time it quick. EJ's legs are infected," he said.

What's Behind the Looking Glass?

"Ok son. I'll be right there. Tell them to put some ice on the wound until I get there. I'll be there in five minutes," he said.

Robert hung up the phone and quickly relaying the message to Pa as he grabbed the ice from the freezer. Girls ran down the hall with sheets and bandages ran outside. Pa sets down the table by the tepee. Anna and Julie covered it with a sheet and pillow and a quilt. Pa rushed back inside the tepee. "Alright, we're ready. Let's get him moved out there. Robert says Doc will be here in five minutes and to put ice around the wound until he gets here. EJ this going to hurt son, but it has to be done." EJ nods his head, "put this stick in your mouth and bit hard as you can when I pick you up, one, two three."

Wayne picked him and swiftly carried him out of the tepee and laid him out on the table and propped his head up. The boys surround EJ and put their hands on his shoulder not leaving his side for an instant. Martha laid the ice and towel around the wound to help numb the pain. Grandma stroked his hair to calm him. "Everything's going to be alright son," she said.

Martha went over to Julie, "Julie I need you to go into the house and take Anna with you and the two boys, heat some broth for EJ to help with the pain. Then after that, I want you girls and the two small boys to grab a light breakfast and put it into the basket when the Doc gets here, take them clear down by the horses and let them play for a while," she said.

"Yes Ma, I understand," she said. Julie went into the house with Anna and prepared the broth and a picnic basket for them and boys. Julie brought out the broth to Ma.

"Thanks, Julie," she said taking the broth mixture from her.

"Your welcome, the basket is made and I believe I see the Doc coming in the yard," she said as his car pulled in to the farm.

"Sam?" Ma called.

"Yes, Ma?"

"Take Danny and go with Julie and Anna for while, they're going to see the pony," she said.

"The Pony!" Danny replied. "Do we still get to be Indians?"

"Yes you can still be Indians; they even packed you some food to take with you." Ma said. "Don't worry Danny," she said seeing the hurt in his eyes. EJ will be here when you get back," she said.

"Ok," he said. Sam takes Danny by the hand, Julie leads them into the house with Anna and Ma watched the four of them head to north pasture from the backdoor.

"EJ lift up your head son. I need you to drink this; this will help with the pain." EJ lifted his head trying not to spit it out then laid his head back down.

Doctor Hatfield pulled into the farm and gazed around. "For a minute there I thought I was at the wrong farm." Seeing Wayne then eyed the tepee in the middle of the yard; then turning seeing EJ lying on the table surrounded by two Indians boys that looked a lot like Will and Robert.

Wayne chuckled. "No Doc, you are at the right farm. We just decide to go native that's all," he said.

"Got tired of farm life I see, needed to try something different? Yep, I see… Well boy, let's see what we got here. Oh, that is bad. EJ we are going have to remove that. What's that called boys?" He asked.

"It's a loincloth sir and you can't. We have a code, a brother's code," Will said stepping in front of the table blocking Doc.

"Boys I am Doctor. And I outrank that code and so does your Ma and his Grandma," he said puffing out his mustache.

"Sorry sir, we made him a promise and we intend to keep it," Robert said stepping in. Will and Robert stepped in front of the table not taking no for answer. Doc looked over at Wayne, for help.

What's Behind the Looking Glass?

Wayne looked at his boys then back at the Doc. "Sorry Doc, we take our promises seriously around here," he said.

"Well, what did they promise him?"

"Well Doc, they promise that they had to go through anything EJ does first before anyone lays a finger on him, with them in his presence," he said.

"They what?" Doc replied dumbfounded. Wayne nods his head.

"Well, I'll be… and your misses, she knows?"

Wayne nods his head. Then Wayne explained it to Doctor Hatfield. "Martha, what are ya standing around here fer?" Doc said looking at Wayne and the three Indian boys. "Martha git the soap and water and Wayne find some rope and a sheet to make a curtain I know some boys that are going to get a bath and bring lots of towels. While you are doing that I'll grab my bag," he replied.

"Yes, Doc," Wayne said.

Doc watched and shook his head as he walked towards his car mumbled. "All mull headed stubborn…"

Pa put up the rope across, to create some privacy for the boys, while Ma and Grandma filled the metal basin with water for the boys. Robert and Will try to comfort EJ by one holding his hand and the other placing a hand on his shoulder, letting him know that they're not going to leave his side.

Each time the water pitcher filled the basin the boys swallowed, it was if time had slowed down. The boy's knees were shaking even though it was far from cold, for summer had just begun. Ma and Grandma placed towels and washcloths for the boys on the table and just nod their heads. Robert and Will swallowed as they looked at each other. Will whispered. "I guess I should go first since it was my plan after all," he said.

Robert swallowed hard… "No Will, I'm the oldest. Let me do it." And walked over to his Ma and nods and plant's his feet into the water and turned around and closed his eyes.

Will whispered to Robert, "pssssssst" then pointed towards his waist. Robert just calmly pulled the string and tossed it to Will and tightly closed his eyes. Ma dried him off and handed him a towel to put around his waist and joined his brothers around the table. Replaced his hand on EJ's shoulder turned too Will. Will swallowed and looked at his brother Robert then looked down at EJ lying on the table then he looked straight ahead. He copied his older brother Robert. He too planted his feet into the water unties his loincloth and tossed to him, closed his eyes and waited for his towel then joined his brothers behind the table.

Ma shook her head, "what silly, silly boys." Disappeared behind the curtain, "Ok Doc, I believe we are ready now," went over to where EJ was and bent down and whispered. "See my son, there's nothing to be embarrassed about," Ma said in a calming voice.

EJ looked up at Will and Robert as they whispered in his ear. "If we can do it EJ you can, and we won't leave your side, not for a minute."

EJ slowly nodded his head still with a frightened look on his face, croaked. "Alright, I guess it's my turn then. If it's ok, can I close my eyes too?"

They just smile, "if it helps, go right on ahead, we promise not to look," Robert said.

"Now then since we have that all settled boys," Doc said looking at EJ and boys all wrapped in towels. "Let's see if we can get this boy fixed up Martha," he said.

Doc lifted the towel and started to remove the bandages from EJ. EJ's hand gripped tighter. Will and Robert tried to calm EJ, "EJ it's ok, we're here," he relaxed a bit. Doc pulled back some of the bandages. EJ screamed in pain and nearly flew off the table. Wayne grabbed EJ's stick for him to bite on, seeing the puss and blood coming from the wound leaving a rancid smell.

Doc turned to face Martha. "It's bad I am afraid, we are going to have reopened those stitches," he said. Sweat poured down from

What's Behind the Looking Glass?

EJ's face and his grandmother wiped his forehead. Doctor Hatfield pulled out the needle to numb EJ's leg and waited for him to calm down a little. Robert and Will looked worried but refused to leave his side.

Doc just nods his head. "Alright boys, we'll continue." Then, he placed the stick back into his mouth, with Will holding EJ hand and Robert hand on his shoulder; Pa does what he can to keep EJ's legs and feet down. Doc pulled the bandage off then snipping the stitches, around the wound. He could see bits of small pieces of fine glass and debris from the creek bed and what was left of Mr. Scarecrow's pants.

Taking the twisters and forceps he carefully removes them as he flushed out the wound. Then he stitched him back up and shook his head. "What a stubborn grandson you have Betty," he said.

She smiles and kissed EJ's head. "I know, silly boy."

Doc removed the towel so he could look at the wound joined from hip to thigh and shook his head, "Martha, not nearly as bad, but it is infected too." Turning EJ towards his right side, EJ nearly fainted.

Grandma whispered to EJ "are you still with us EJ?" And waited for him to respond, EJ slowly nodded his head and opened his eyes and looked up at Will and Robert to make sure they were still there.

Will squeezed his hand as Robert bent down to whisper. "You are doing fine EJ," he said.

Doctor Hatfield administered a shot for pain. Then they waited for a minute for EJ to catch his breath before proceeding. They replaced the stick in his mouth. "Ok EJ, bite hard, this going to sting a bit." As Doc pulled off the rest of the bandage the pain strikes like a fire and he lets the puss and blood drain, allowing the numbness to settle in then cuts the stitches and finding the source of the infection. He removed more glass shards, small debris of cloth and then cleans the wound before sewing him back up.

They lay him back down on the table and mopped his face. Then replaced the towel back over EJ waist and turned to Martha as he shook his head, "I assume the rest of him is ok or do I need me to check Martha?"

"Well while you are here Doc," Martha said, Grandma just nods her head. "We did change his chest bandage last night and was about to do it again," she said. "EJ will you let us change the rest of your bandages now?" Martha asked.

EJ looked over at Will and Robert and slowly nodded his head. With a towel over his waist, they undo the pins around his chest and unwrapped the bandage, helping EJ sit up Robert and Will supported his back and EJ gasped as the wind is knocked out of his lungs. Doc Hatfield continues to exam EJ. "Yes, yes there's an infection, but not much, too many bandages, we need to expose these wounds to allow more air I think. These sheets are too hot for him Martha." He said unwrapping them. "Wayne there is some cotton cloth out in the car; can you run and get it for me?"

Wayne ran out to the car grabbed the cloth and handed it to the Doc. "Take this and rip it into strips like so then warp it here and here... Hold in your breath EJ. That's a good boy. Tie it like this with the pins. He won't sweat as much, less infection. Alright now you can lay him back down boys, Will, Robert if you want to help put that watch-ma call it back on him?" Doc said.

"Its Indian loincloth Doc," Robert corrected him.

"Yes boys put the loincloth back on him," he said. Grandma, Martha, and Wayne followed Doc Hatfield back towards the house. "Now then Martha how about a nice hot cup of tea," he said.

"This way Doc," she said.

"Now that wasn't so bad?" Robert said still trying to calm his nerves.

EJ shook his head. "It was horrible, what do you mean? I don't think I could have done it alone," he croaked.

What's Behind the Looking Glass?

"EJ, that's what brothers are for, now let's get you dressed. I for one prefer wearing at least this," Will said as he handed Roberts his Indians loincloth and removed the towel and three of them laughed. "And since you still don't have any other option, let's put this back on you before they come back." As he looked towards the house and EJ quickly nodded his head in agreement.

"Well, Martha this is excellent," Doc said as they all sat in the living room drinking their tea.

"Thanks, Doc," Martha said not really paying much attention to him, just stared out the window watching her boys setting up camp around EJ. With a tap on Wayne's shoulder, she whispered. "What are they building now?" She asked.

"It's a little lean-to for EJ," he said. "Martha they're fine. I'll it explain later, you need to listen to the Doc now."

Doc seeing Martha had not heard a word he had said and clears the air. "A humm Martha?"

"Yes Doctor Hatfield," she said with a start. He looked out the window where she was looking and takes a look for himself and closed the curtains. "Martha the boys are fine." Then sits back down, "Now that I have your attention again, do you remember that apron you were going to make EJ?" He asked.

"Yes, I remember. I have the material and everything it's over there in the corner," she said.

Doc twisted the corners of his mustache seeing the cloth then turned back to Martha. "I think you can pretty much scratch that idea." He said slapping his knee." Your boys, your Indian farmer boys had a better one." He replied, Doc busting a gut and then Grandma and Wayne joined in.

Martha shocked and dismayed, did not find it all that funny, thinking her little farm had just gone mad. She stood up from her chair went over and picked up the cloth and handed it to him.

"Doctor Hatfield then what I am supposes to make this into then?" With a fiery voice.

"Doc turned the cloth over in his hand seeing the seriousness in her face, stopped laughing and cleared his throat. "Humm... Martha when EJ is healed enough he's going to need some underwear now isn't he?"

With a surprised look on her face and then a grin "I never thought of that." Martha said reached down to old Doc's cheek and planted a kiss on it and watched him turn two shades of red. "Oh my Doc, you are blushing, if you want I'll get my husband Wayne to make you a loincloth too and that will take the blush right out of you. I am sure of it." She said as she laughed, then sat down sipping her tea, watching him trying to compose himself.

Doc wiped his forehead and turned to Betty. "There's one more boy I came to see today if I remember right?"

"Oh that's right, Danny; just in time to Doc, we were planning on leaving sometime today for home." Grandma turned to Wayne. "Wayne, you mind bringing everyone back so Doc can look at him," and tries to hold back the tears.

Wayne nods his head "I'll be right back," he said.

Martha turned to Wayne "and you can just lay EJ on the couch for now, while I prepare his lunch." She was already hoping that they all would change their minds. "*EJ was going to go back to his room and things would return to normal at least "something's would."* She thought as she looked outside at her Indian boy farmers and shook her head. "I am sure they're hungry since they all missed breakfast," she said. With another quick nod, Wayne leaves the house to gather everyone in, leaving Grandma, Martha and Doc alone.

"Now Martha I am going to write you some prescriptions for some strong skin oils for EJ and for your sons. You will need to apply them twice a day to keep the sunburn down. Plus I want those muscles of his to be loosened. Arm, legs, and feet, oh yes, check their feet for blisters and sores and any slivers. All of them. Well, you know what I mean? Work the oil in his muscles just to get him moving again. He will be stronger in no time a ta'l and don't push him before his time, you'll know. This is very important to make sure he stays clean as possible and the wounds get as much air to them as possible, but I don't want them drying out either, that's what the oils and lotions are for," he said.

Chapter 11

Doc drew the curtains and watched the boys work. "Yes, sir. Martha, you are going to have the tannest boys in Santaquin County," He laughed. "And probably the strongest after carrying that boy all around the farm. Now, where's that boy she wants me to look at?" Doc asked.

Wayne walked out to the field where Julie and Anna are watching Sam and Danny play with the horses spread out on a quilt. They waved their arms and he walked over to them and sat on the ground with them. "How are my two angels doing?" He asked.

"Ok Pa, how's EJ, is he going to be ok?" They asked.

"Well there was a lot of infection and Doc had to reopen some of the wounds, but he thinks he got all this time. Thing is, we would have known about it sooner if he wasn't so stubborn like your brothers; if he would have let your mother or his grandmother look?"

"Pa that's just silly, we bathe Sam and Danny and they don't seem to have that kind of a problem and they are only six," Anna said.

Pa laughed. "It's different when you get older girls. We guys seem to forget until after we are married and have kids of our own or mature enough that it seems it doesn't matter anymore," he said.

Julie and Anna just shook their heads. "Plain stubbornness if you ask me," Julie said as Pa sighed at his two girls for their lack of understanding.

"Looks like the two Indian boys are having fun chasing the horses," he said.

"Yes Pa, it has been a real scream that's for sure, we never laughed so hard in our lives," Julie said.

What's Behind the Looking Glass?

"Well, one of those Indian boys has to go back today, sad really. I am going to miss him and so is EJ and I am afraid you girls will have to be there for him. It's going to break his heart to let him go," he said.

"Yes Pa, we know that," Anna replied. Pa gave them each a hug and a kiss and helped them gather their things.

He waved his arms for his two Indian boys to come in. They see him and come running with the biggest smiles as they leaped into his arms. "Did my Indian boys have a good time playing with the pony and the other horses?" He asked.

"Yes, Pa. "Yes, Sir."

"I am glad," he said.

"How's EJ?" Danny asked.

"Oh he's fine and resting with your Indian brothers," he said.

"Can we go see him?" Sam asked.

"In a minute, your Ma is waiting in the house with some lunch and the Doc wants to see this Indian boy," as he touched him on the nose. "Before he leaves," he said.

"He does? But why?" Danny asked.

"Because he heard he was special that's why Danny."

Then Danny grinned. "Ok, sir." Pa sets the boys back down on the ground and watched them run with all their might towards the house. They all stand laughing as they watched the two Indian boys take off in flight kicking up the dirt with their little bare feet as they ran towards the house and around the corner. Anna and Julie headed towards the house while Pa walked towards EJ.

EJ's, eyes are open as his watched Will and Robert set up camp around the tepee.

"Robert, Will" Pa called.

"Yes, Pa?" They came when he called them.

"Grab the stretcher we're going to put him on the couch for now. Then after lunch will bring him back out here under the lean-to where it's nice and cool to rest while you two do your chores. I have asked your sisters to watch him this one time if you don't mind. He'll be ok because you all need to rest as well," he said.

"Yes Pa, but we're bringing out our sleeping bags right next to him. We're not leaving his side." Pa just nods his head.

They picked up the stretcher and put EJ on it and brought him back into the house and laid him on the couch for lunch. Martha biting her tongue as she looked toward the hallway, knowing that there are four good beds down there. Shrugged her shoulders and prepared their lunch mumbled. "Silly, silly, stubborn boys… Robert, Will I have prepared sandwiches for you," she said.

"Thanks, Ma."

"Julie, will you help me with EJ's tray? I have some more broth and it's just about heated so we can bring it over to the couch," she said. "Anna?" Ma called.

"Yes, Ma?"

"Run into the room and grab some pillows and a sheet off the bed for EJ," she said.

"Yes, Ma." Anna returns from the room with the pillows and a sheet.

"Here you go Ma," she said handing them to her.

"Thanks, Anna." She then returns to the kitchen and sets Danny's and Sam's lunch on the kitchen table. Taking a seat next to Sam as she waited for Danny to return from visiting Doc down the hall. "Wayne if you can help me prop EJ up so I can put these pillows behind him… Alright EJ this going to hurt." As she waited by his side as Wayne help scoot him up.

"Sorry son." She placed the pillows behind his head then unfolds the sheet and covered him up and placed the tray over him.

"Alright EJ, I'll go get the broth it will help with the pain. Then I'll give you some lunch," she said.

EJ looked down at Will and Robert next to him and waited for Mrs. Downing to leave the room… whispered. "Do I have to wear this stupid sheet? It already makes me sweat," he said.

Will looked towards the kitchen where their Ma is busy and whispered back to Robert. Robert pulled the corner of the sheet so it fell onto the floor. Then Robert quickly stuffed it behinds his back. Will grabbed it from behind him to hide it completely so their Ma won't find it. Pa watched what his boys have just done quietly laughed and grabbed the sheet from behind their side's stepped out of the room. Will and Robert turned to see Pa. Pa placed his fingers to his lips, "SHHHH," whispers. "I got it," and tossed it down the hall where it belonged then hurry's back to stand in place as if nothing was wrong or out of place.

Martha turned around with the broth and plate of sandwiches for EJ and sets it down on his tray. "Drink this EJ," she said and hands him the broth. Then looked down at his bare legs and feet turned to Will and Robert. "Where is his sheet?" She asked.

"Ma, Indians don't have sheets. Ma you know that, besides he was hot," Robert said.

Then she glared right at Wayne as he shrugged his shoulders. "Martha I told you they were Indians now." He said watching the fire in her eyes.

"Yes Wayne you did," she said.

"And did I not tell you I would explain it to you later?" He asked.

Martha sighed. "Yes, Wayne…But"

"Martha let it be, just trust me it will be ok," he replied.

Martha looked down at EJ and her four Indian boy farmers gathered in the living room and shrugged her shoulders. "Alright Wayne, I'll trust you for now. But you better have a good reason," shaking her finger in the air at him. Then turned back to EJ and smiled and rubbed his hair, "I do know one Indian boy, one silly, stubborn boy who has been really stubborn lately. Are you feeling any better EJ?" She asked.

"Yes ma'am," he croaked. She bends down and kissed his forehead, then removed his tray.

"Alright, I want you to rest awhile… Ok EJ?" EJ nods his head. Pa picked EJ up and put him on the stretcher then watched Will and Robert carry him out to the lean-to.

"Wayne?" She said with fire in her voice.

"Yes, Martha?"

"What do think you are doing? That boy needs to be put back into bed so he can rest not out there," she said pointing her finger outside of the house.

"Martha his bed is out there with his brothers. You heard the Doc, he needs fresh air and sunshine so his wounds can breathe. Your boys will watch him, now let them do their thing while they finish setting up camp and do their chores and his sisters are going to watch over him so the boys can rest."

Martha turned to Wayne. "Out there? Outside? In that tepee?" She gasped still not believing it.

"Yes Martha, all four boys." Martha swoons a little then looked out the window in disbelief. Wayne takes her hand and held her tight, and tried to comfort her. "Look at it this way, think of it as if their camping underneath the stars except they are just in the yard," he said.

What's Behind the Looking Glass?

"That's really funny Wayne. Except they are not camping out are they? Instead, they running around dressed as little Indian boys," then giggled. "They do look rather cute though. I do have to admit. I was trying so hard not to laugh when giving Will and Robert their bath. When they closed their eyes so tight, Grandma and I had to turn our faces just not to laugh. It was so hard just keeping a straight face. Those poor stubborn silly, silly boys," she said.

"Doctor Hatfield this is my other grandson Danny," Grandma said as she introduces him.

"Hello, Danny so you are an Indian too?" Doc said as he picked him up and set him on a stool

"Yes, sir. We are all Indians," Danny said.

"I can see that. Did you know it's my job out here to exam all Indian tribes and they must all get a checkup by me personally?" He said watching Danny shake his little head. "Yep it's true, ask your Grandma?" Grandma nods her head yes. "EJ your Indian brother just got his checkup and so did the rest of the Indian brothers," he said.

"Really!" Danny asked.

Doc smiles. "Yep" then with a quick glance over and sets him down. "Danny, do Indians like suckers?" He asked.

Danny's eyes got big as saucers "WOW! That's for me?"

Doc pulled two suckers out of his bag. "Ones for you and the other is for the other Indian boy Sam." And opened the door and watched him run down the hall. "Well Betty that's all of them, what a shame. It looks like EJ's got the worst of it as I can tell. Danny just like his sisters still have some bruising, but they're healing. EJ poor kid, his wounds will heal too, but some wounds go much deeper," he said. "Time will tell for the rest. I would strongly suggest his parents seek physiological help before the children return home, except for EJ," he said closing his bag.

"I doubt he will ever, I don't know Betty. Too hard to tell, too soon really, for now, leave him be. I think you made the right choice. Well, I'll be going. I'll check in on him in a few days. I am sure Martha will have that boy fussed over more than he can probably even bear. Yep," then shakes his head. "Indians here on Downing Farm." Doc waved goodbye to everyone with another gaze at the tepee in the yard. He shook his head, got in the car and headed back down the road.

Walking down the hallway towards the bathroom, grandma saw visions of her sewing EJ up. Then further down the hallway turned towards the bedroom where EJ has slept, she stared at the now-empty bed, with a tear in her eye knowing it was time for her to leave. She knew she might not have the strength to leave EJ if she stayed much longer. EJ was where he needed to be.

She sat in the chair for a minute to compose herself not seeing Martha and Wayne standing in the doorway. They came over, put their arms around her and told her how much they loved her and understood that she must leave. They helped her gather her things and Wayne loaded them on his back and took them through the backdoor out to the barn as so not to disturb the children. Martha and Grandma composed themselves as they walked out towards the tepee. Martha instructs the girls to take Sam and wait for them in the barn. With a tear in her eye, Julie nods okay.

Grandma took EJ's hand and looked him in the eye. "I have to leave now and you are going to be ok." She said and knelt down on her knees, kissed his head and whispered. "I love you so much, my grandson." Not letting go of his hand with a choked voice, "Danny its time to go. Give your brother a hug," she said. Shaking a little she stands up and hugs each of the boys, Will then Robert with a pat on the back and whispered, "thank you."

With one last big hug and kiss on EJ's tearful cheek, she says goodbye and let go of his hand trying not to hear the agonizing cries of. "NO! Don't go! Don't go!" As her heart breaks.

Grandma looked to Wayne for help, Wayne picked up Danny, Danny clings to EJ with his tiny little hands crying as he carried him to the barn. His head buried against his shoulders, trying to comfort this small boy. Grandma put his jacket over his shoulders and placed his helmet over his tear-drenched face. Strapped him in the bike then hugged everyone one more time. Thanking them all before putting the helmet on her head.

Climbing on the bike she brought it to life. Wayne opened up the doors. Popping a wheelie for the grandkids she sped down the road allowing the wind to wipe her tears dry. Patting Danny's head she assured him they would return in a few days. Danny smiled "Really Grandma?" He asked.

"Yes Danny, I promise. Let's see how fast we can go shall we," she said.

Wayne, Martha and the rest of the family headed toward EJ and put their arms around him allowing him to cry himself to sleep. Wayne gently laid him down under the lean-to. "Ok boys go do your chores and your sisters will watch him now. Then I want you two to get some rest before supper," he said.

"Yes Pa," they replied.

Martha looked at EJ under the lean-to. "You're not going to leave him out here like this?" She asked.

"I am Martha, he'll be fine. Let's go into the house and I'll help you start dinner and you can ask me anything you want, but for now, leave him be." He said as she gazed back at EJ now sleeping under the lean-to next to Julie and Anna. While watching their little Indian brother Sam tagging along after two other Indian brothers. Just yesterday they were plain old farm sons.

Martha took Wayne by the hand as they entered the house and shook her head then smiled. "You know it wasn't a bad idea really, it just needs a little work that's all," she said.

Wayne turned then looked her straight in the eye, "a little work?" He replied dumbfounded.

On her toes, Martha wrapped her arms around his waist and kissed him. "That's what I said dear, a little work. Now help me fix supper since all my help is elsewhere these days playing Indian," she said.

Chapter 12

"Anna?" Julie asked as the two girls sat on the ground next to the boys doing some embroidery for a new pillowcase killing time before supper.

"Yes, Julie?"

"What are you thinking about?" She asked.

"Oh nothing really," as she giggled softly watched her brothers head toward the barn.

"Tell me anyway," Anna asked.

"Oh all right," Julie said turning around to face her. "I was just thinking about something you told me yesterday after I got back from town. How hard it is sometimes to get them into the tub that's all. But once you get them in that tub, they're not a problem at all." They giggled as they looked down at EJ sound asleep between them.

"Yes I remember," she said as Anna giggled."

"Well, that must have been a pretty big tub, because look what we now have for brothers," Julie said as she looked towards the barn and at EJ. "Four Indian brothers;" they laughed with a sigh. "What are we going to do with you silly, silly brothers of ours?" They looked down upon EJ's face and blocked the sun out of his eyes.

"Robert?" Will asked taking the feed and placing it into a bucket as he stood on the rail to feed the horses.

"Yes Will?" Robert said handing him and another bucket and taking the empty one from him.

"Thanks," Will said.

"Thanks for what?" Robert asked.

"You know. I don't know if I could of…. You…. You know pulled it off without your help," Will said climbing down and moving on to the next one.

"Will, that's what brothers are for, you know that."

"I know." Taking another feed bucket and doing the same.

"Will, if you really want to know the truth. I was scared to death. If it makes you feel any better," Robert said. "I was too if you weren't there," Robert said rubbing his fingers through his hair. "My knees were shaking."

"Mine too," Will said as they laughed at each other while feeding the pigs.

"Will?" Robert asked.

"Yes, Robert?" Dumping the scraps into the trough as the pigs squealed noisily to the food that awaits them.

"It's still a crazy idea brother, but I like it," Robert said twisting around in his loincloth. "Did you see the look on Ma's face? I thought she was going to have a cow when we kidnapped everyone. Pa nearly had to hold her from fainting when we took EJ as our prisoner," Robert said.

"Yeah, that nearly done her in for sure, but how else was she going to look at his legs?" Will said. Robert slapped Will hard on the back "Ooooh that smarts."

"Sorry," Robert said. "I think you are getting a little sunburned."

Will slapped Roberts back "Ooooh."

"Sorry," he replied.

"Hey now," Robert said.

"Looks like I am not the only one with a little sunburn brother," Will said smiling at the red mark.

What's Behind the Looking Glass?

"Eh, it will be worth it for EJ's sake anyway. I just hope we have lots of... Ooooh, lots of lotion."

Slap "Ooooh. Hey now," Will said.

"Sorry that hurts," he laughed. "Robert?"

"Yes Will."

"Do you think he's going to be ok?" He asked.

Robert picked up Sam and put him on his shoulders. "Will with the three of us as his brothers, he's going to be just fine. Let's say we finish our chores because "slap.""

"Ouch... quit it now." Will replied

"Sorry."

"That stings," Will said.

"I am tired," said Robert and smiled as he wrapped his arm around Will and grabs Sam's hand with one more good, slap "ouch Ooooh."

"Sorry."

"You'll think sorry," Will said as he laughed with another slap across each other back. "Slap,"

"Ooooh, uncle. You win."

They rolled in the hay laughing as brothers do. "Robert?"

"Yes Will."

"Let's go find that lotion," Robert said lying next to him in the hay.

"Good idea and don't tell our sisters," Will said.

"Now that's a better idea," Still laying in the hay as they waited for the sting to wear down a bit laughing at themselves.

"Wayne?" Martha asked.

"Yes, dear?" Wayne said coming over to stand by her side wrapping his arms around her as she leaned against him.

"You do realize that my kitchen table is still outside?" She said feeling quite safe in his arms as she slowly turned and faced him placing his arms around her firmly.

"Yes dear, I know that," he said.

"I suppose you want us to eat out there as well?" She asked looking deeply into his eyes as she loses her self in them.

"Actually dear, I never gave it any thought really," letting her go as he rubbed his chin pretending to leave. "I could bring it back in if you want, but that would mean you would have to haul food out to the boys since they won't be coming inside."

"Why would I be hauling food clear out there dear?" Martha asked with fire in her eyes.

"Remember dear, they won't leave EJ's side. I told you they promised him that," he said.

Retuning and placing arms back around her as he slid his hand against her back and stroked the back of her long brown hair.

"Alright Wayne dear, for now, I'll let them keep their promise, but I am going to set some guidelines of my own," she said.

"Martha, this is between them," Wayne said trying to calm his loving wife. "Martha dear I know you want to help EJ, but they did get you this far in somewhat of a corky manner didn't they?" Wayne said as he softly stroked her hair and gently brushed the worry lines off her forehead then with a twinkle in his eye. With his right hand, he brushed her cheek and kissed her softly... The muscles in her body relaxed and the fire in her eyes turned back to soft blue crystals of mothers love...

"Yes, dear." She smiled and laughed. "They did, my silly boys did get me this far. Alright let them play Indians for a while," she said.

"Martha I hear it's going be a nice night out tonight. Let's eat underneath the stars with the boys," holding her in his arms as they sway back and forth.

Martha looked into his soft green eyes and warping his strong arms around her body whispered. "Wayne I also heard there will be a full moon out tonight."

"Yes dear, I heard that too." He whispered leaning forward with a lover's embrace; time slowed down just for them.

Pa placed chairs around the table outside for dinner with Julie and Anna's help. The four boys were fast asleep next to EJ on top of their sleeping bags under the lean-to. At times EJ would stir and moan due to the pain, Julie stroked his hair to calm him and settle him back to sleep.

"Pa?" Julie asked.

"Yes, Julie?"

"How did you ever get Ma to agree to let us eat outside like this?" She asked placing the plates around the table as Anna set down the silverware next to them.

"Yes, Pa tells us both," as they turned to watch the four boys sleeping under the lean-to.

"Alright, you might as well know what's going on. You see your two brothers Will and Robert made EJ a promise. That they would endure anything he would go through even if that meant going before him. They wanted to show him there was nothing to be afraid of and that they would stand by his side every step of the way. And watch over him every day like a brotherhood because to them brothers protect their brothers doing whatever it takes. They were going to do it together and face it together as brothers do. They thought that in the Old West Indian tribes formed brotherhoods. That's why they became Indians," he said.

"Pa?" Julies asked as she giggled at her brother's foolishness.

"Yes, Julie?" pouring milk into the glasses on the table.

"That's silly, that just proves how stubborn they truly are," and they both laugh. "But I do have to admit, they do look kinda cute." As they looked over at their sleeping brothers then giggled. The girls whispered in each other ear. "This is going to be fun," and nodded their heads

Pa looked over at his two girls and saw little devilish smiles on their faces. "What are two thinking about doing?" He asked.

With a smile, they learned from their mother. "Nothing, just a little harmless sisterly fun that's all Pa."

Pa rubbed his chin knowing they were up to no good, "just like your mother," he said.

The girls laughed. "We're not going to hurt them too much. Oh no Pa we never harm them. Tease them to death maybe. Make them blush a little, then squeeze the stuffing out them." They said as they hugged their Pa and gave him a kiss on the cheek.

"Yes girls I know, just like your mother. You got that little devil in you that I love so much." And they laughed as he rolled his eyes and shook his head then gave them each kiss on the cheek. "Now go help your mother in the kitchen," as he laughed watching them go. "I'll finish up out here."

"Yes, Pa."

Pa turned to his four sleeping boys. "If only you knew what your sisters have planned for you my poor boys," and laughed.

Chapter 13

"Well, Danny we're home," Grandma said as she pulled the bike into the driveway and saw Richard running to greet them.

Richard looked at Danny in his matching leather jacket like his mothers with a worried look on his face then looked over at Ma. "Looks like you two have had quite the trip?"

Danny not sure how to answer waited for his Grandma. "He's had a rough day today Richard, let's get him inside." She said as she picked him up and handed him over to Richard and his pillowcase. While Ma carried in her saddlebags into the house.

"I think he'll feel better after he's had a warm bath and full tummy," she replied as she rubbed his stomach, that made Danny laugh. "That's better, I knew I could make him smile," she said as she pushed little Danny's nose.

Richard watched his Ma hang up his little jacket in the closest.

"Ma what on earth is he wearing?" He said as he laughed.

"Oh, this?" Danny said as he looked up at Richard with his big blue eyes. "Haven't you ever seen an Indian before?" And started to dance around the kitchen and around the house whooping and hollering… Danny stopped in front of him. "Will and Robert made it for me, neat ha. We are all Indians now, EJ is too," and danced some more.

Richard turned to his Ma with a puzzled look, she just busted out laughing. "Well, Richard what can I say?" Then hung up her jacket as well, headed into the bathroom to run him a bath. After she bathed him and gave him a hot meal. Grandma was right, as she watched him doze off in the middle of the floor. She carefully picked up the tired little boy and put him to bed and gently kissed him on the cheek as she wished him goodnight.

"Ok Richard, sit with me awhile and I'll fill you in on the details of the farm," she said as she set a pot tea on the table. "First of all, EJ's fine." She said after a quick sigh and dabbed a tear from her eye. Richard took a deep breath.

"Now what's this about him becoming an Indian and Danny?" He asked.

"I'll get to that in a moment." She said as she sipped her tea and smiled and laughed thinking about the earlier events of the day. They talked about what happened on the Downing farm and Richard talked about the events that happened while she was gone. She sat there for a minute pondering. "Richard?" She asked.

"Yes, Ma?"

"Are my sisters back yet?"

"I believe so. Why?"

"I think its time we had a little get together." Richard almost turned white right on the spot. Ma smiled and laughed. "No son, not that kind of get together." Richard took another deep breath. "I think its time the girls came over and see their little brother and we sisters can chat awhile," as she patted his hand. Richard feeling relieved wiped the sweat from his forehead with his sleeve, for just a moment thoughts of old Harley coming to life. "I think I'll give my sister Lizy call right now. You said they are back?" As she got up from the table and went to the phone.

"Now Ma?" He asked sitting there stunned.

"Why not Richard? You said they were back, and you know how I hate waiting around for the other shoe to drop," she said.

"Yes, Ma." As he shrugged his shoulders, "I think I'll go check on Danny." Then got up from the table, afraid to hear what might happen and shook his head as he left the room muttering. "Indians of all things, and I was worried about the neighbors."

What's Behind the Looking Glass?

"Hello, Lizy," Betty said as Lizy picked up the phone.

"Why Betty you are home already?" She replied.

"Yes, and I understand just in time too," she said.

"Yes, Richard has filled me in on everything that's been going on down here. I've got some news of my own and I think it would be a good time if we brought the girls down for a while. So they can see their little brother Danny while we chat awhile."

"When?" Lizy asked.

"Oh I was thinking about tomorrow, would that be ok, say for lunch?"

"Good idea," Lizy said.

"You call Mary and arrange it."

"Yes I can do that," Lizy said.

"And give her the details ok. Thanks, Lizy alright now, will see all tomorrow. I am sure Danny will be glad to see them too. Thanks, Lizy and be sure to thank Mary for me, bye now."

"Oh, that will be such a nice surprise for Danny to see his sisters again. What a day. I sure hope EJ is alright, poor boy. I really didn't want to leave him like that, but if I didn't. I would never have found the strength." She said as she wiped the tear from her eye and headed down the hall towards Danny's room. She glanced over at the sleeping child in the bed and brushed his soft hair, he stirs only a moment and mumbles "EJ" in his sleep, she bends down and kissed his forehead, knowing how it still broke her heart and wondered how?... why? Then walked to her bed and she cried softly to sleep.

* * *

"Linda, I was thinking maybe it is time we consider the possibility that we need some help," Jim said as he turned to his wife across the room, who was staring out the window. "Did you hear what I said?" He asked as he walked closer to her.

"Sorry, I wasn't listening. Did you say something important?" She asked.

Jim took a deep breath, as he stood right next to her. "I was thinking we might need some help dear?" He said again.

"Help with what Jim?" She asked not looking at him. "You are the one who screwed up. I'm fine. It is your family that has all those bad genes. We were perfectly fine until your mother and everyone else got involved. Now you think we need help, do you?"YOU ARE THE ONE THAT NEEDS HELP JIM…DEAR!" She screamed. "I never wanted them in the first place; always whining all hours of the day and night, feeding, changing them and tying me down all the time. You said it would get easier when they got older.

"You said the first one would always be the problem child. Three kids later, sure it got easier. Only because we knew what we did wrong and what was wrong? I ask you, Jim. What was wrong? I'll tell you what was wrong. BAD GENES! You said he'll grow out of it, they all will. Jim, where are they now? You want help. Fine, you go get help. It's your fault anyway. Maybe you can ask those nosey neighbors of yours. Since they seem to know more than you do." She said as she slammed the bedroom door. "I am going to bed."

* * *

"Pa?" Sam said tugged on his pant leg, "Pa what are you doing?" He asked.

Pa bent down and picked Sam up off the ground and watched him rub the sleep out of his eyes. "Sam I'm setting the table for dinner," Pa said.

"But Pa, we're outside," he said.

What's Behind the Looking Glass?

Pa laughed. "Yes Sam, we are and where do little Indian boys like yourselves eat?" He asked.

Sam thinks a minute, "OH! Outside Pa."

Pa laughed and rubbed his hair. "Now go wake your brothers, I need their help," Pa replied with a soft nudge.

"Yes Pa," and set little Sam back down on the ground. Sam ran over to Will and gave him a nudge, but he was sound asleep. Sam not willing to give up, he nudged Robert, still no response.

Anna nearby watched Sam trying to wake his brothers smiled and whispered to Sam, "tickle Wills big toe," Sam smiled. Pa watched around the corner as he sat on a nearby log next to Anna. "Shush, Pa." She said and waited to see what Sam was going to do. Sam went over to Will crotched down like a tiger in the weeds reached and snatched Will's foot and grabbed his big toe like a snake. Will with a startled yell, Will came to life as he grabbed his foot with his little brother Sam attached to it then tickled him to death.

They rolled in the dirt as they laughed so hard it woke Robert and EJ with a start. Seeing the fun, Robert started tickling Will and Sam and EJ started laughing then they started tickling him. Pa and Anna laughed so hard they fell off the log. Ma and Julie came out of the house to see what the matter was.

Ma looked around the farm. "What is going on?" She asked. The boys rolled in the dirt laughing to death. She ran over to EJ. "Son, are you hurt?" She asked.

EJ laughed. "Yes ma'am it hurts," he said as he laughed holding his sides in before they burst.

Ma ran over to Pa. "What's the meaning of this?" She asked.

Wayne picked himself up off the ground and laughed. "Martha it just sorts of a hit," he said.

"What did?" She asked as he came closer to her husband.

"The boys caught the tickling bug and it spread like this," and he started to tickle his wife as she started to run for the house.

You could hear him chasing her in the house. "Wayne? You wouldn't dare?" She said as she laughed. Then all you could hear was her laughing. Julie got bit too as Anna caught her as they fell off the log again.

"Pa, Sam said you wanted to see us!" Will and Robert now covered from head to toe in dust and dirt.

Pa tried not to laugh. "Yes boys, I thought it would be nice if we all sat at the table tonight," he said as he brushed the dust out the boy's hair and grinned.

"What did you have in mind Pa?" Robert asked as Pa looked over at EJ under the lean-to as he rubbed his chin.

"As you know it would be hard to get EJ to sit at the table because his legs are still too swollen to bend. So I was thinking of taking some platforms and put them across under the table for his legs and feet to rest on. Then we can set a pillow behind his back. I have an extra leaf for the table in the barn. That way he won't feel so crowded," he said.

"Alright Pa," Robert said.

"Then you better find some water and get yourselves cleaned up, you know how your Ma gets," he said.

"Yes Pa," Robert and Will said as they shook the dust out of their hair and laughed.

Will and Robert helped clean EJ up the best they could as Pa came over to the lean-to. "EJ, I think its time you started to eat with us as part of the family son. What do say?" He asked.

EJ still a little horse croaked. "I like that sir. But I don't see how, not like this," he said.

What's Behind the Looking Glass?

"Why not? How about you boys?" Pa asked.

Will and Robert shook their heads. "EJ you are our brother now," Robert said.

EJ nods head yes, "ok," knowing they really do mean it. "Alright sir, I'm ready." Having no idea how he was going to sit at the table. Pa picked up EJ brought him over to the table with some adjustments for his legs and back made sure he was comfortable. Robert and Will sat on each side of him keeping him in the middle so he wouldn't fall out.

"Martha, we're just about ready, is there anything you need from the kitchen?" Pa asked.

"Yes Wayne, can you grab EJ's tray for me. That way I can give it to him while we're out there without leaving the table," she said.

"Oh, that won't be necessary. They have already set him at the table for you." He replied with a grin on his face.

"You did what? How?" She asked surprised.

Wayne smiled at his wife. "I thought you would like to have nice family dinner under the stars dear," and kissed his wife. "Now come on, the foods getting cold and knowing our Indian boys they can be savages at times," he said.

Downing family sat around the family table under the stars, with lanterns and fire pit in the background for light; the tepee throwing off shadows of the family as they gathered around the table. Pa sat at one end and the Ma at the other. The girls and Sam sat on the opposite side of the three Indian brothers.

Ma looked at her four boys then at Pa then at girls. Ma gave Pa a slight grin. In her mind, she tried to picture a family dinner. Somehow this was not what she had pictured in her mind, but was willing to make the best of it for now. She looked at her four boys and tried to image them all in clean farmer shirts and smiles, not as four Indians boys, "Now that's better. Pa mind cutting the ham and Julie pass down the peas," she said.

They talked about the events of the day and what went on in town and plans they had for the farm and how the crops are doing and when they needed to think about harvesting putting in the planting of the corn and wheat and bringing in the summer hay.

"Will, Robert?" Pa asked.

"Yes, Pa?" Passing down the rolls.

"I was thinking of a better way for you boys to carry EJ around the farm while he heals?" he said placing a large portion of ham on his plate.

"Yes Pa," they said. Robert chewing half with his mouth opened.

"When the swelling goes down in his legs he should be able to bend them, but he won't be strong enough to walk yet. I was thinking you could build him something like a chair and put sides and handles on it," he replied.

"Pa?" Julie asked as she set down the butter and sipped her milk giving her milk mustache as she wipes it off with her cloth napkin.

"Yes, Julie?" Cutting up his meat into smaller bites.

"I have seen pictures like that in Rome and Paris," and giggles. "Oh what fun," she said.

"Will?" Robert asked placing some more vegetables on his plate.

"Yes, Robert?" He asked cutting up his meat into more manageable bits as he chewed and swallowed the food already in his mouth.

"I think I saw an old wicker chair in the barn loft that should work and should be sturdy enough with a little work for this little guy." Then he gabbed his head under his arm and rubs his head with his knuckles.

"Ouch that hurts," replied EJ.

"Sorry," Robert said.

Ma smiling as she tried to sound cross with the boys. "Not at the table please," she said.

"Yes, Ma." Pa chuckled while he looked at his boys.

Ma looked at Pa from across the table then looked at her family then looked at stars, "Pa you couldn't have picked a better spot I think," she said as she yawns.

"Ma?" Julie asked.

"Yes, Julie?" Tearing up her roll and putting small pieces into her mouth as she chewed.

"I think me and Anna and can clear the table, why don't you and the boys go sit by the fire and toast some those marshmallows and I'll bring some these rolls over and some chocolates out for dessert." Pa winked at Julie and Anna as they winked back with a mischievous smile.

"Wayne you are up to something," Ma said as he rubbed his chin trying to hide a mischievous plan.

"Did you hear dear, there might be a full-moon out tonight?" Wayne asked as he went around the table and slides the chair out from behind her, stands her up and brought her chair around to the fire. Then comes back for EJ and helped him by putting him back on the stretcher and Will, Robert carried him then sat next to him around the fire. Julie and Anna cleared the table to bring the treats and joined the family around the fire.

"Will, Robert? I think it's time we start building on to the house and EJ can help too when he can. Since one of the rooms is going to be his." Pa said as he rubbed his chin. "And he can help with your chores too when he gets stronger."

Ma nearly fell off her chair. "Pa he can barely move," she said.

"Yes I know that, but he will in a few days or so, we need to get those muscles moving again. So a little hard labor and some fresher air will be good for him; I think you boys got the right idea, crazy or not, but a solid one at that. So I'll let you keep your promise." He said as he rubbed his chin then fires a marshmallow into the fire. Pa looked at his startled wife thinking he just lost his mind than seeing little Sam starting to doze off, he smiled, placed the marshmallow into his mouth whispered to his startled wife. As he leaned down placing a kiss on her forehead, "don't go anywhere, I'll be back," he said.

Pa walked over and picked up Sam and carried him into the tepee and put him to bed, while his wife watched with a startled look and shook her head. Will and Robert picked up EJ and followed Pa and sat him gently on the bed inside the tepee then closed the flap and turned out the lantern and laid on top of their sleeping bags and fell asleep.

Julie and Anna turned to Ma then kissed her on the cheek and headed into the house to their nice soft beds down the hall giggling too themselves.

"Wayne you mind telling me what that was all about? I was hoping you were going to put a stop to all this foolishness. Alright, they were Indians for a whole day. I even let them dress that way for dinner," she said.

"Well, at least Martha you had the entire family there, including EJ. I thought that it would make you happy," he replied as she stood placing her hands on her hips.

With a tear in her eye, she softly pounded on his chest. "It did Wayne, it did? It was beautiful, the stars, the firelight, everything. Then you had to remind me of their stupid promise, that stubborn boyish promise. What were you thinking?" She replied.

"Let's go sit on the swing for a while." He said with a twinkle in his eye, knowing that only he could melt that stubborn heart of hers... They sat in the swing and he pulled her tight into his arms she leaned close to his chest as they rocked back and forth. "Martha

What's Behind the Looking Glass?

dear," he said as she looked into his eyes. "Do you remember that full moon?" Not taking his eyes off hers. Martha listened to his heart as it beat in his chest and the warmth and comfort of his arms she sighed and melts. The Indians, the tepee and farm in the distance, all that remained are stars and the man in her arms... He leaned down and looked into her eyes.

"Wayne?" She says.

"Yes, dear?"

"I love my Indian boy farmers."

"I know dear."

She sighed then looked at the tepee and put her arms around his neck for another kiss. "They just need a little work that's all." And fell asleep in his arms and he carried her off to bed.

Pa put his wife to bed placed the covers over her shoulder walked down to the girl's room and whispered. "Goodnight my sweet angels," and placed a kiss on each of their cheeks. Instead of going to the boy's room he went out to the tepee and carefully walked around to each of his sons Will, Robert, Sam, and EJ brushed their hair from their forehead gave them each a kiss as well. "Sleep my Indian sons, sleep well my farmer sons," and walked out of their tepee.

Then climbed into bed next to his wife and put his arm around her, she nuzzled close to him and whispered. "Everything ok dear?" She asked.

"Yes dear, thank you for the meal and my house is full so is my heart," he replied.

Chapter 13-1

* * *

The morning sunrise rose over the mountains as the rooster greeted the morning. It could be missing a few feathers though. I wonder why? And what are those sounds? Julie and Anna sneaked into the boy's tepee for a little mischief of their own. With a couple of feathers, they have plucked from Mr. Rooster. Quietly they patrolled the hall nearing Ma and Pa's room cracking their door slightly making sure they were still fast asleep.

Covering their mouths they giggled and closed the door then on their tiptoes they went out the front door. Being careful not too let the door make the slightest noise when it closes. They took a breath not daring too move then tiptoe to the tepee. The problem was Ma and Pa was already up and were watching their two mischievous little girls. For every time the girls looked back, Ma and Pa would quickly duck behind the curtains covering their mouths as not give themselves away.

Ma turned to Pa. "I really should put a stop this." She whispered back to Pa, "but I can't. It's too much fun and they do have it coming," she said. Pa grinned and covered his mouth as they peeped through the curtains. Girls reached the tepee as they looked to the sides putting their ear to the tepee making sure they were still all sound asleep. They could hear the boys snoring inside. Julie slips in then Anna, it began slowly... Pa and Ma quietly go outside to the tepee not making any sound and waited for the explosion.

Julie finds Robert's foot and Anna finds Will's. They pull out their feathers and starting slowly at the bottom of the boy's feet working up to the top and down around the side of their legs up to their chest and back to their feet slowly... It didn't take long before one of them turned over on their side.

What's Behind the Looking Glass?

Taking the feather once again they went down his back and under his arm. That did it, they burst into a laugh then threw a pillow at them and the war was on. When Ma and Pa came into the tepee all they could see was four boys and two girls laughing with feathers falling from the sky. Ma glanced at Pa; he was on his knees hunched over from laughing so hard. Because poor EJ had the biggest pile of feathers on his head with a pillow in his hand. All Ma could do was laugh. Her laughter grew seeing Sam throwing feathers at Anna while she was tickling him with the feather.

She was laughing so hard she was crying and had to wipe the tears from her eyes. Trying to clear her voice. "Alright, girls we need to get breakfast started," and wiped more tears from her eyes.

"Yes Ma," Julie said with one last tickle for EJ on the foot with the feather, Julie followed Ma out of the tepee with Anna right behind her.

Will and Robert were still laughing. "Pa?"

"Yes Will?"

"They started it," he said.

Pa still chuckling rubbed his chin and placed his hand on his shoulder. "Yes they did son," smiles, and chuckles a bit more. "I would clean this up," he said.

"Yes, Pa."

Pa sets the chairs back around the table for breakfast and went back inside the house.

"Wayne I was thinking what you said last night," Martha said heating water for the boys and more broth for EJ.

"What's that dear?" He asked.

"Oh all that work that needs to be done," she replied. Wayne rubbed his chin with puzzlement on his face. "The girls gave me an idea and they're going to help me," she said.

"With what dear?" He asked.

"Oh, I decided there are a lot of muscles that needed to be rubbed and feet that need to be looked at and lotion and oil twice a day. I am just one woman and this is a big farm. You said it yourself; they'll be working hard. So I was thinking I would recruit some help of my own dear that's all. Now then you mind taking this out to the table and have the boys wash up since their morning chores are done. We have lots to do. Then after I take care of them I want my kitchen table put back where it belongs dear. We'll be eating inside. By the way dear I have a surprise for them at breakfast," she said as she walked over and leaned up to kiss his cheek. "Thanks, dear," then continued down the hall.

Pa looked shocked and puzzled and shook his head, picked up the platter of eggs and bacon and walked out to the table." Will, Robert?" he called.

"Yes Pa?" they answered coming from inside the tepee.

"Do you have your morning chores done?" He asked.

"Yes, Pa." They answered coming outside to greet him.

"Good. Ma wants you to wash up for breakfast then you can help me get EJ up to the table," he said.

Ma strolled out of the house with shirts under each arm and placed one behind each of her boy's chairs, one for Will, one for Robert, one for Sam. Something more like a vest than a shirt that could be tied around the waist and neck with only a front for EJ.

She stood and waited for the boys. "Before you say anything boys shush not one word," as she pulled out the chair for EJ calmly in a motherly fashion. "Will, Robert I am going to honor your promises, but this table… Shush," Before they can open their mouths, they nod and put EJ in his chair…"Now then as I said, this my table so…" Ma looked down at EJ, "How are you, my son?" She asked.

"Fine ma'am," he replied.

What's Behind the Looking Glass?

"That's a good boy; go ahead drink your broth." Then looked over at Will, Robert, and Pa, "Shush... Now as I was saying," as she unfolded the little vest. "EJ dear can you lean back a bit?" Thanks, dear." Then slips the vest around his chest and ties it loosely around his neck and waist. "EJ that's not too tight is it dear?" She asked admiring it from the front. EJ shook his head no. "This is my table and while you are at my table you will wear those." As she handed each boy a shirt to wear then helped them button the front, then sits them in their chairs as she scooted them in and stood back to have a look at her four boys. "Now then we can eat," she replied.

Will and Robert just looked at Pa. He just shrugged his shoulders and sat down then turned to them. "Sometimes you just have to learn it is best to give a little boy's. Remember the pillow fight? Ma this is a fine breakfast," he said trying to remain on her good side. Then he rubbed his chin and looked over at his boys. "Your Ma does bring up a very good point," he said.

"Pa, she does, how Pa?" Will asked devastated.

"Well, how can I take you and Robert and EJ into town dressed as Indians? You'll scare all the people. It's fine out here on the farm and the wounds he has needs the fresh air and sun and you boys are white as a ghost. We need to deliver supplies and pick up wood to build all those rooms. You mind your Ma and keep your promise, I think you can do both, my sons," he said.

Will and Robert looked at Pa. "Yes Pa you are right, we never thought of that. We never thought about going into town like this," Robert laughed. "Mr. Stringum would have a cow, not to mention everyone else. "Also there's the town picnic and our friends in school too."

"Now that would be hoot four Indian brothers dressed as Indians 'EXTRA, EXTRA READ ALL ABOUT IT!' Downing Farm gone to the Indians. Ok, we see what you mean." Will said finishing his breakfast.

Ma watched Julie place the washing tub inside the tepee. "Ma?" Julie asked.

"Yes, Julie?"

"The clean bandages and towels and washcloths are in there too as you asked." She looked over at the four boys in their shirts. "If you need any help Ma, just give me a call." Then watched them all blush as the four boys swallowed hard and dropped their forks on the plate.

"No Julie, I think me and your Pa can handle it," as she smiled at the boys seeing the blush forming in their cheeks.

"Pa?" Julie asked.

"Yes, Julie?"

"The water ready too." She said as she leaned over and kissed his cheek and made sure she winked at her brothers.

"Thanks, Julie, you and Anna can start clearing the table." Ma said as she stood up from the table and started to untie EJ's little dinner vest. "Ok boys. I don't want you to dirty those shirts." She said as she waited for each one to give them back to her one by one, and then she placed them in Julie's arms. "Julie, hang these up for them for dinner," she said.

"Yes Ma," she replied with a quick smile.

"Ok my four boys." Will and Robert take another hard swallow and looked at Pa than each other while they loaded EJ on the stretcher and headed for their tepee with Ma right behind them.

Pa filled the tub and brought in three stools. One for Ma, one for him and one for the boy too sit on except for EJ who is not lucky enough just yet sit on one. "Alright, boys, who's first?" As Ma crossed her arms.

Sam, of course, couldn't wait and looked at his brothers Will and Robert, "Its just Ma?" and shook his head at his brothers.

They whispered back. "We know that." Standing scared as their knees begin to shake from embarrassment.

What's Behind the Looking Glass?

Pa chuckled. "Come on Sam." And helped him climb in the tub and gave him his bath and shook his head at their silliness. Pa whispered over to Ma, "I thought you said it was easier yesterday?" He asked.

"Well give them a minute. Go get some more water, I'll be fine, take Sam with you when you are done," she said.

Pa dried Sam and dressed him back up and left the tepee… Ma went over and pretended to re-arrange the bandages and heard a splash of water. Will sat on the stool, she didn't say a word just picked up the soap and water and dried him off and handed him a towel walked over and checked on the bandages. Splash Roberts on the stool she does the same thing. After the two boys are back standing over by EJ she calmly walked over to EJ. "Ok EJ, you are the last, I know you are still frightened," she said.

"Yes ma'am," he said with a horse voice.

"Well there's no need to be is there you silly boy?" And shook her head. "I'll start slow and it will be over before you know it," she replied.

EJ nodded his head slowly. Will and Robert stood there with one hand on his shoulder and one in each hand. Ma leaned over and whispered. "If you want too, it's ok to close your eyes. I'll understand," she said.

EJ just shook his head. "No, I'll be all right." He said as he looked up at Will and Robert. "They had theirs. I know it's my turn. Besides, there is nobody left," he said.

Ma grinned as she washed his feet and legs. "Ok Boys set him up so I can remove those pins around his chest and waist." EJ took a deep breath as the air left his chest as she unwrapped the bandages.

"Ouch that hurts," he said.

"I know. Lay him back down for a minute so I clean those wounds. This is going to sting EJ." Will, Robert try not to look way.

"Ouch that stings," he said.

Will said. "Eh, oh those are nasty."

Ma placed the towel around his waist as she cleaned the rest and dressed his wounds. "Oh good Pa, you are just in time, EJ here needs some more broth and then the boys can dress him. Tell Julie and Anna they are ready for the lotion and oil while I clean up these bandages and then the boys are ready to go outside," she said.

Pa hands Ma the broth then walked backs to EJ. "EJ go ahead drink this, it will help with the pain," she said.

"Ma?" Will asked.

"Yes Will?"

"Why are Julie and Anna coming to put lotion on us instead of you?" He asked.

"Why not Will? I do have other things to do and they can do it just as well as I can, can't they?"

"Yes Ma," Will said taking a big swallow.

"I know if I were you, I would get EJ dressed unless you want, they could do that too?"

EJ looked over at them and drank the broth quickly and threw the towel to the side quickly while Will and Robert helped with his loincloth just in time before Julie and Anna walked into the tepee and giggled. Ma just smiled as she watched EJ blush and whispered to him. "She used to bathe Robert and Will all time son. You have nothing to be embarrassed about." As he looked at Robert and Will, pats EJ on the leg and picked up the discarded towel turned to her boys "I have work to do and so do you." And picked up the old bandages and dirty towels and put them back on the tray and left the tepee.

"Alright who's first? Because you are not stepping outside until we've checked your feet clipped your nails and put this lotion on to loosen those sore muscles and that will be twice a day brothers, Doctor's orders." Julie said as they guarded the door.

Will and Robert fall on the mattress next to EJ. "EJ we are in trouble," they moan. EJ nodded his head in agreement.

"Well Anna, it looks like we have to pick a brother, lucky for us Sam is already done."

You take left, I'll take the right and we'll work our way to the middle, but who will guard the door?" As they giggled.

Pa poked his head in through the door. "Hi girls, are they causing you any problems?" He asked. "Ma said you might need a hand."

"Pa, these boys are just being a little stubborn that's all, but you mind watching the door," Julie replied.

Pa seeing the three boys lying on the bed. "I heard the news. Well just remember what I said earlier boys, give a little," he said.

"Yes Pa," they said as he pulled up a stool.

"I swear you two girls get more like your mother every day, I almost feel sorry for that poor fella you marry someday," Pa said.

"Pa?" Robert asked as he was being manhandled by his sister Julie.

"Yes, Robert?" He replied as Julie rubbed him down with the lotion and oil.

"I already do." He said as he looked at Julie as she put the cold lotion on his chest, "OH that's COLD!" He shouts.

Pa laughed. "That's my boys."

After the girls finished with the boys they were as clean and smooth as a baby bottom and pink as a newborn baby with little extra rose in their cheeks. They gave each of them a kiss and squeeze including EJ, not too hard due to his ribs and watched him blush pure red as they left.

Pa nearly fell off his stool from laughing so hard, the only one laughing in the room beside the girl giggling as they left with a shake of his head. "Alright you two, you teased them enough for a while, go help your mother," then kissed them on their head as they left out the door.

"Yes, Pa."

"Yes, Pa."

Pa turned to his boys. "Robert, Will? Go ahead and take EJ out to the lean-to for a while. Robert you can go get that chair from the hayloft and Will you can help me bring Ma's table back inside," he said.

"Yes, Pa."

"EJ, you think you'll be fine out there watching them work from there?" He asked.

"Yes sir, I'll be fine," he said as the boys helped him to the homemade stretcher.

The boys carried him out then set to their task while EJ watched with interest. He'd never seen a farm work before and wondered what it was all about as he saw Sam playing in the corner. "Looks like Mrs. Downing won," EJ said seeing him back wearing his little boy's clothes, smiles as he watched his brothers run past him. "Well, that didn't last long," and grins. There go his shoes and socks and after few minutes he ran out of the barn just wearing his bib overalls with one strap trailing in the wind and one over a bare shoulder tailing after his brother Will with a grin on his face.

Now looking over at the porch he could see his sister Anna shaking her head as she picked up his clothes and carried them back into the house. "Well, some battles you just can't win." He reminded him of Danny, but knowing he was with his grandma made him feel a little better, but he missed him something awful, but least he was safe.

EJ turned his head towards the road then looked back at the house seeing Mr. Downing, Will, Robert and thinks of what they promised him. Then the day his parents tried to take him away and how he stepped in. He leaned back on the pillow. "I wonder maybe I am safe too; nothing has proven that I am not. I'll do what Grandma says for now at least and stay here for a while. Besides, it would be nice to have a family who actually cares." EJ said to himself as he drifted off to sleep.

Robert set the wicker chair down next to the lean-to then gathered some polls and laid them down along the sides. Pa brought some strong rope from the barn so Robert could strap them together to the sides. The chair begins to take form.

"Well EJ what do think?" Pa asked as he rubbed his chin as he watched Martha come out of the house.

"Looks pretty cool sir," EJ said as he looked at the wicker monstrosity with interest.

Martha looked at it, "Oh no you don't! Wayne, you are not just going put him in that without first trying it out. I am not going to have him dropped all over the farm just so I can sew him up again," she said with a stern look at her boys.

"Ma what do you suggest?" He asked.

Ma walked around it a couple of times. "I think a few trial runs are needed," she said.

Pa nodded his head, "ok," then looked around the farm. "Who wants to go first?" As he looked at his wife as she calmly, but quickly backed away as if he was suggesting she would be first.

Sam hurries and jumps into the chair. "I will Pa, me first, me first," they all start to laugh. Ma's eyes grow big as Will and Robert grab the handles and watched her little boy squeal with delight. "Faster, faster," he yells.

Ma yelled. "You be careful with him boys, you hear me?"

"Yes Ma," as boys ran around the farm with Sam in the chair. Pa and EJ laughing as the girls come rushing out of the house to see what was going on. Everyone got a turn including Pa before Ma would even consider being placed in the chair herself with some coxing. After a few minutes of her backing away, Pa just picked her up and sat her in the chair and Robert and him carried her up and down the farm.

Chapter 13-2

* * * *

Oh, how she squealed. "Slow down Wayne, you're going to fast, watch those corners," after a few minutes she too was laughing with her head back like a schoolgirl with a grin a mile wide. Setting the chair back down next to EJ she calmly tucked her hair back into place and walked around the chair. "It just needs a little something more," she said as shook her head then smiled at Pa. "It still needs just a little work," nodding her head taping her finger on her chin. Pa and the boys had a puzzled look on their faces.

"What do you mean Ma?" Robert asked. Ma puts her fingers to her lips to shush the boys.

"Julie on the bed, grab a quilt a couple of those pillows and bring them here dear." Then she turned to the boys, "it just needs a woman's touch boys, that's all," and smiled.

"Here you go Ma," Julie said as she handed a quilt and two pillows to her.

"Thanks, Julie."

Ma put one in the back and one on the seat and took the quilt and tucked it around the pillows and stood back to admire her handy work and smiled, nodded a couple of times then turned to the boys. "If you drop him and tear just one of those stitches I will... " Not finishing the sentence.

"Yes Ma," they replied standing up straight knowing she meant every word.

Ma then turned to EJ and bent down and placed a kiss on his forehead. "You be careful."

"Yes ma'am," he said then she rubbed his hair.

"Ok, go see our farm and try not to get into any mischief boys," and laughs. "Lunch will be ready in about an hour."

"Yes Ma," they replied.

Will and Robert picked EJ up and sat him in the chair, Pa put on a little platform so he could rest his feet on it. "EJ looks like some of the swellings has gone, can you bend your legs a little?" he asked.

"I'll try sir," he said.

"That's good son. You don't need to go all the way just yet, practice that far today they're stiff and sore," Pa said adjusting the platform so he could sit more with his legs up as of in an easy chair.

"Yes sir," EJ said.

"Ok boys go do your chores; I plan to go into town tomorrow to get lumber and seed for the field." Then turned EJ, "would you like to come with us this time not as a stowaway, but as one of us?" He asked.

EJ smiles, "Really! I can come?" He asked.

"I don't see why not." Then EJ looked down at himself," but sir I don't have anything to wear."

Robert, Will started to laugh. "Oh I wouldn't worry about that, we'll think of something. After all, you are our brother aren't you?" They asked.

EJ looked at Will and Robert, "I guess I am," he said.

Will and Robert put their hand on his shoulder then knelt down close to him. "To us EJ, you are our brother."

Pa nodded his head in agreement with his boys. For he could not be any more prouder with a tear in his eye as he looked at EJ then knelt down close to him, "I would and will do my best if would like son for me to be your Pa," as he gave him hug.

For the first time, EJ let go and buried his head into this man chest. Softly whispered, "Sir I would like you to be my Pa," cried softly in his arms. Danny is right he killed all the monsters hiding in the shadows and wouldn't let his father nor his mother come near him. He felt safe and loved for the first time in his life as he cried on his shoulder letting the darkness fade away. The old man inside him felt at peace as his reality begins to change. It was the unknown that he still was afraid of; perhaps the man called Death really does have a plan?

The two boys gathered their arms around EJ and round their Pa in the barn until the tears were all dry from their eyes. For them, on that day they emerged from the barn as three brothers, and a father with one heart and one mind.

Chapter 14
A Hidden Past

The wind was cold as the rain fell against the stone rock mountain known as Blood Cliff. Its sheer height would astound any climber whoever dared to climb the mountain. Some would say when the sun reached twilight its rocks looked crimson red. Some would say it earned its name Blood Cliff for the simple fact people would spill the blood of slaves upon the altar of black stone, hidden deep beneath the very mountain its self. Morgan knew better of the rumors that spread across the lands. His lands, the lands of his father Glen a guardian of the masters of light, but no longer. As he remembered the day his Master Hess aka Shadow King killed his father almost two centuries ago this very day.

Some say Morgan looked more like his mother with raven black hair and her firm jawline. But he had the nose of his father. A sturdy nose pointed just at the tip some would say aristocratic, but he had his height. 7 feet 9 inches, broad shoulders; he used to have the same color of eyes green like his father. Even that has changed over the years, now red crimson, as well as his strength and his hunger for more power, had increased.

"Power… that's what makes the man." His Master Hess would say, now locked away deep inside the **Cross Bone Gate Prison** by the Guardians of Light themselves. "Worthless Bustards," he mumbled remembering his friend and onetime college Derrick and the day he refused his offer to join his cause. Instead, he walked away from having power and glory that he himself could have given him. More so than those fools he severs now. If only he would have stayed the course. Now he is a member of the light among the keepers of Death. According to his most recent spies, he himself angrily watched his interference numerous times. Now he has gone too far helping Jeff hide the boy from him. "I tire of these games of cat and mouse," his voice grated against the wind. As he watched the boy EJ slip away

What's Behind the Looking Glass?

from him soon after Jeff died. Ever since then he has been trying to locate him and now his spies have located the boy once more.

Morgan rubbed his hands together for warmth as he blew hot air into them, thinking of EJ's father and the contract that he now holds. Locked away in a safe place, giving the boy too him. Just so he might live longer unharmed when he reached the age of 13, ripe with the power hidden deep inside him. In fact, he was the one who caused his mishap just so he would give anything for the chance to live. Morgan grinned wickedly remembering that day and how easy it was to trick him. "They never do read the fine print of a contract," he mumbled. After all, he would have lived only with a slight limp and lived a very happy life. "Happy." What a disgusting word for such mere mortals," he said into the wind. "But now I have him and the boy will soon be mine forever."

Morgan walked alone. His black hooded cape covered his face, keeping the hard rain and wind out as he moved swiftly along the hidden pass. Ever so often he would have to stop and gaze down at the compass and map locating the hidden doors to the cave deep inside. For the time had come, after waiting so very long when the boy would be ready to take his place by his side as the Dark Prince. "His Prince." The one the prophecies have foretold of. That the Dark Prince would hold the key to unlock the power hidden away upon the outskirts of his homeworld known as early Earth in some distant city. The township of Goshen, "yes, at last, the power will be mine." He growled his hand clenched into a tight fist. Blood dripped down between his fingers splashed against the cold wet ground.

Morgan noted the place on the map and reread the notes seeing the figure of a naked woman made of rock to his left and a man at least he thought was a man knelt beside her. A slave no doubt or perhaps her lover, as the stories are told among the men in taverns below the city of Kandorhash. The centuries have not been kind as he wiped away the fragments of broken rubble to read the inscription. 'Beneath this mountain lies the temple of the Goddess Athenian, servant to the house of Kandor.'

Morgan's eyes glowed red feeling the rich dark power so very near. He knelt at the base of Goddess Athenian finding the silver chalice. Morgan reached inside and pulled out his dagger and pulled it against the palm of his right hand. He squeezed his hand letting the blood drip into the chalice, saying the words. "Athenian I kneel before thee. 'Astone'a sovern turn'a floness de'set.' Hear my payer and guide me unto the stone of blood. Stay my hand as I seek the shadow which holds the power and the glory. 'Ner'noss terna' Hess' not'to.'

Morgan raised his bloody hand and placed it upon the man's shoulder and raised his left hand and drew the rune for the beast of Kandor with his two middle fingers watching the silver light connect the lines in the air before him. A loud grinding noise was heard as two shelves of rock lowered, reveling the hidden cave. Morgan took a strip of black cloth and wrapped it around his wounded hand. Sprinkled some healing dust, knowing it would be healed before he even left the mountain. Gone are the days of true wizard healers that could heal worlds and its people from any injury or curse. Thanks to him and his master Hess four centuries ago. "What pleasure it was to end their pathetic lives as we grew strong drinking their blood and grinding their bones into dust. They too tried to stop our reign. Now our glory to rule will be unstoppable as I release my Master to stand by my side once again as it should be."

Morgan released the power and watched the silver chalice burn with green fire. He always had loved the smell of blood burning as he licked the metallic taste of the recalled memory from his lips. Morgan lifted his small pack on to his shoulders and waved his staff creating a ball of light to hover above him. The doors closed once he made it past the threshold. The mountain seemed hushed against the storm raging outside as he made his way down the corridors. Many bones of old skeletons lay crumbling against the walls. Many of them slaves of old when they were minions of the Shadow Guardians who sacrificed these weak souls of man and their children upon the altar many centuries ago.

Now their dead haunt this very mountain. The memory warmed him as he recalled his first sacrifice, his mother strapped down. The knife cold against her bare skin as her warm blood dripped down the altar. Her dying screams echoed the chamber, "what a glorious sound it was." His eyes glowed with power as he remembered that day. "So many good memories," his voice echoed in the dark tunnel ahead.

What's Behind the Looking Glass?

A wisp of smoke filled the tunnel as green yellowish eyes seemed drawn to the center of the smoke. A gremlin beast from the early days of Kandor blocked his path. It hissed. "Who dares disturbs the Goddess rest?" Its eyes bore down upon him. Morgan not answering shot a blue fireball from his staff. He listened as it whistled as he twirled it and struck the ground in front him, causing the ground to shake around him. Watching the fragments of blue lightning spider towards the beast, dust and debris swept around him. The monster growled as he struck out with it claws raking the air. Missing Morgan by inches, the monster roared in anger. "You do not belong here, wizard!"

Morgan only growled. "Kneel slave or I end you here," his teeth clenched.

The monster laughed as he beat his wings of smoke as to challenge him. It has been so long since he had devoured a wizard and one that reeked with such raw energy. He slowly licked the front of his teeth remembering the flavor, so tantalizing as his stomach growled with anticipation. Just the mere thought of the marrow of his bones, so hungry, so very hungry. "It is you that will die here like so many of your kind."

Morgan was prepared, knowing that he needed this beast that stood in front of him. For it is one of the sacrifices he needed to release his master spirit form. Plus he loved the challenge itself. Morgan took his left hand and pushed with an energy barrier. Closing his hand into a tight fist says " Ta'na, De'kin." He could hear the monster bones crunch and snap as it shrank to 3-inch height, frozen in placed as it howled in pain. Morgan took his staff waved it over the monster and created a harden glass globe. With his left hand, he motioned the ball to float towards him. "Now you are mine to do with as I please. Challenge indeed, ha."

Morgan fought his way through the corridors collecting the various species he needed for the ritual. At last, he made it to the altar, its white marble base stained with blood. A statue of the goddess stood behind the altar while her servants cast in stone circled the altar. Their stone hands held torches of light that lit instantaneously with a single word "flare'a'nos" Their cold black eyes shimmered in the torchlight as they seemed to follow his every movement. If he listened closely, he could hear their voices echoed in the soundless wind. Morgan reached inside his pack for the book titled **The Way of the Shadow** written by Narasome Gilding 15th century of Knox. He turned to the marked page and reread the instructions. Placed the twelve candles around the altar. Six red, three white and three black made with Delanar Spider Venom and melted wax of Hindorm tree, and crushed bone of a gray griffin now extinct in the wilds. Ashes of Eldon a God among wizards whom people worshiped at the beginning of Time itself, some say he might have been the first king of the shadow. The spell was simple.

Black Cauldron
Written By author Eric Shepherd

Cauldron of black, fires of amber red, I speak to thee this very night.
Wart toads of green and venom from a snake, thine eye from a ogres wife.
O spin of darkness, O spin thee this on hallow night.
A kraken of blood, a mothers tear of fright.

Cauldron of black, fires of green. I speak to thee this very night.
Bat wings, gosen tail and flower of dread off a brides maids bed.
O spin of shadow, O spin thee night shade a blood moon of night.
Death baited breath in hands I speak, I call upon you this very night.

Cauldron of black, fires of blue. I speak to thee this very night.
Cemetery moss from a hangman's tree. The bone from single man.
O spin of sorrow, O spin thee of pain. Sparrow of darkness this hallow night.

A groom of Darkness I call upon the night of flight. A mistress of mourning. I seek this very night. Blood from thine veins of pure red and cold heart of pain.
Awake from the fires, I call upon thee. Awake into the night.
Screams of children this hallows eves. Spread thine wings O darkness upon the night. We ride the skies upon the moon lit skies.

What's Behind the Looking Glass?

Cauldron of black, fires of black I speak to thee this very night.
Dragon bones of old and a warrior's dead heart.
O spin of Death of victory this Hallow eve.
A Bride and Groom shall never be.
But a heart of stone upon my thrown.
O Spin me this night a gift of true delight on the blood moon of the night.

Morgan's voice echoed throughout the chamber as he watched the spirit form of his Master Hess hung in the air above the altar. Morgan took the blood of each creature he had gathered and grinded their bones add a little of his own blood to complete the spell. Poured them into the metal bowl he placed on the altar. "Master," Morgan said. "The prophecies that you have foretold is at hand. I have come as you have instructed. What must I do to release you from your prison?"

"Where is the boy I have spoken of? For I do not see him, "he answered angrily. "For without him, there is no hope to gain the prize we seek, for he holds the key."

"Master he has eluded me these past years for the Guardians of Light watch over him. But my spies tell me he has returned once more alone to his father's house. I have the contracts signed by him and soon I will have his mothers as well if the future holds true. He will be ours and his destiny changed forever. Jeff is dead so the White Solan can not be nor will he be able to rise from the ashes."

"Good. You will find what you need among the books **Shards of Life** written by Hasting of Stronghold. You will also find the list of the needed ingredients and the spell to release me. It must be done on the blood moon of Eacnor. Do not be late and prepare your soul Morgan if you truly intend to release me. For the glory and the power will be yours as all will bow down too you as king and their god, then we shall watch the heavens fall together. No more will the light take what is rightly ours. Now go, my son. Go, and fulfill your destiny."

Morgan knew the first thing he had to do was stop Mike Cotwellar and his wife Margaret, EJ's Aunt from interfering in his plans. He was smart up until now not to even mention his problems with Mike whom now holds the leader seat for nearly 300 hundred years, as he and the other Guardians of Light kept getting in his way. "Soon my prince, soon you will be mine," he laughed wickedly.

Chapter 15

"Peggy, are you excited to see your sister Donna and your little brother Danny again?" Aunt Lizy asked. "You haven't seen them for almost a week," she said.

Peggy tried to smile for her aunt's sake, "I guess I am," and gave a little bored sigh. Actually what she was really hoping they had dropped off the planet and got lost somewhere. "Aunt Lizy. I haven't seen my parents yet. And I was hoping by now they would of least have stopped by and said hello, or something," she said.

Aunt Lizy knowing the answer to that question just shook her head at Peggy. "I am sure they are fine dear," she said to keep the conversation going. "I hear your brother EJ is doing well too and on the mend."

Peggy just rolled her eyes and looked out the window. "Can this day get any worst, ugh." Thinking *he was probably causing more trouble and I don't want to hear about it, will this day ever end.*

"Oh look, there's Mary and your sister Donna, looks like we arrived right on time," Lizy said.

Getting out of the car, Danny flew down the porch steps right into his aunt's arms. "You made it. I've been waiting all day." He said then grabbed his sister's hands, tugged them unwilling into the house to play and share his adventures of the farm and EJ.

Mary and Lizy shook their heads then looked at each other.

"I swear sister, it was like pulling teeth just getting her in the car to get here," Lizy said.

"I know what you mean, well let's go in before they kill each other," Mary replied.

"Hi Betty, we made it," Lizy said as they looked at the three children sitting in the living room where Danny was trying his hardest to get them to play with him.

"Looks like they've been through a rough ride," Grandma said.

"Oh, you don't know the half of it," Lizy said.

"Well let's have some tea and I'll fill you in." She said as they watched the children play and mingle a bit and gave them some sandwiches.

"You mean they tried to...?" Mary asked sitting back comfortably on the couch as Lizy takes the chair from across the room; setting the small teacup on the arm of the chair after taking a long sip that warmed her from the inside out.

"Oh yes Mary, but Mr. Downing stopped them." Taking another sip and wiped the corner so of her mouth trying very hard not to smear her lipstick.

"Poor EJ," Mary said as she reached over and poured her another cup while stirring with her spoon as setting along the side of the plate.

"But he's going to be alright I think, as long they leave him alone," Grandma said as she filled them in about the Indians, they laughed their heads off.

"My goodness that must have been a sight," Mary said as she wiped the tears from her eyes with the corner of her napkin. In return, they told them of the events down here.

"Betty you were right to leave him there," Lizy said as they reached over and patted her hand then looked over at Danny.

Mary said. "Yes it will be hard for him too, but I think for the time being we need to get some help for those parents so least these children can be return to them, but you still have to watch over them. With a little time, she'll come around."

What's Behind the Looking Glass?

"Alright we need to head back for home, Peggy," Lizy said.

"Yes aunt Lizy," Peggy said, at last, it was time to go back and have fun without having to deal with her sister or the whinnying of her little brother. With some hope, EJ will die due to some illness caused by all those wounds he surely deserved and she will be at last the oldest without any more doubt. She sighed as a smile touched her lips remembering the screams before the sound of breaking glass.

"Time to go, come give your Grandma a kiss and hug." Peggy ran up to her Grandma and planted a great big wet one on Grandma's cheek and Grandma nearly hugged her to death.

Grandma whispered."You be good now," she said.

"I am Grandma," Peggy said with a mischievous smile.

"Now give your brother and your sister one," Lizy said.

"Do I have too?" She asked as stood by the door waiting to go.

"Yes Peggy, we talked about this remember."

Peggy sighed. "Yes, Aunt Lizy I remember," as if she was walking a death march. She slowly gave each one with no heart in it a hug and headed for the car.

Lizy shrugged her shoulders. "I wonder sometimes if that child even knows what love is? Because she despises it so much or least tries to," she said.

"It's got to be in there somewhere, you just got to keep on digging. Her mother buried it deep, very deep," Betty said standing to give her sister a hug.

"See you in a week or so," Lizy said then headed for the car.

Mary gave her sister a hug before leaving. Dona gave her brother a hug and told him to stay out of trouble and gave her Grandma a kiss and hug they both walked to the car as Danny waved goodbye.

"Well Danny, was it nice seeing your sisters again?" She asked as they waved goodbye from the porch.

"Sort of," he said.

Why's that Danny?" Grandma asked opening the door as Danny went back inside.'

"They are not as fun as Will, Robert, and Sam. Plus I really miss EJ more Grandma at least they'll play with me. Peggy and Dona are boring and mean to me most of the time," he said.

"I see," and shook her head. "Well don't worry; we'll visit EJ and them in a few days. I promise, now it's time for your nap," as Danny yawns.

"But I'm not tired," he said going back to his toys on the couch.

Grandma smiled. "I know," then watched him doze off on the couch as she removed his shoes and put away his toys.

* * *

"Pa?" Julie called out towards the barn.

"Yes, Julie?"

"Ma says lunch is ready and to come into the house when you are ready," she said.

"Thanks, Julie, will be right in," Pa said putting his work away for the moment.

Boys finished feeding the rest of the livestock with EJ as he watched them pick up the handles and carry him into the house, Ma at the door with a basin of water. "Ok boys wash up for lunch, please. I've placed your shirts over there on hooks," she said as she pointed to each one of them.

"Yes Ma," they replied and cleaned up EJ and tied on his little vest.

What's Behind the Looking Glass?

"Alright, you can sit him down at the table now. Be careful, I just ironed those shirts and I don't want them to get dirty," she said.

"Yes Ma," they replied taking their seats at the table.

Everyone seated around the kitchen table Ma smiled. "Now that's better, I must say." And took a deep breath as she looked over at Pa at the end of the table and her four boys at the right and the two girls on the left other than that not looking under the table she was happy, satisfied and calm. With a twinkle in her eye, she got up from the table giving each of her boys a warm kiss and a thank you on the cheek including Pa than sat back down in her seat. Ma turned to EJ. "How's the chair working out so far?" She asked as she helped him cut up his food and placed the sandwich on his plate.

EJ whispered in a low voice, but she could hear it. "If you don't mind, I rather just call you Ma if that's ok," as he whispered softly.

Ma bent down close to his ear. She shook, but only a moment as she gave him a hug with a tear in her eye. "Yes son, you can." She said then looked over at Pa with puzzlement and wonderment of what happened in the barn today.

Pa cleared his voice. "A hum... Ma." and waited for her to settle and compose a little bit more.

The girls not quite yet realizing what just had happened. Knew something, but waited for the air to clear. Sat silently as they watched their parents as they wiped their tears from their eyes and then looked across from their brothers for hints, but the boys just bowed their heads to hide their eyes from them. They knew what had transpired between them and tears were still in their eyes.

"Martha it's time we go to town, the boys and I. We need seed, supplies, and lumber. I was also thinking of taking EJ along too if you don't mind?" He asked.

Now that brought her head up with a start. "You what?" Ma said as it brought her head up so fast the girls thought it was going snap off like a chicken and her eyes popped out of her sockets. The air changed in the room in an instant, as Ma looked straight at Pa. "Did I hear you right? You want to take EJ with you into town?" But he didn't get a chance to answer.

Instead, she heard a soft voice on the right side coming from EJ. "Yes Ma, I'll be fine, my brothers will watch me and Pa won't leave my side," he said. Ma stopped and melted back down into the chair with the wind taken right out of her. The girl's hands reach for their mouths with eyes tearing up. It now dawned on them as they looked at their brothers then at Pa then at their mother. It hits them hard right between the eyes. Something did happen today. They got up from their chairs and walked over to EJ gave him a hug and kiss then gave each of their brothers one as well and just to let it sink in they kissed EJ one more time on each of his cheeks and rubbed his hair before sitting down.

Robert cleared his voice and tried to recover from the blushing of his sisters. "Ma he's going to need something to wear, something temporary of course, something we can put on him, and take off again, yet be comfortable too," Robert said.

Pa waited for Ma to respond, but she was still speechless for the first time and smiled. "Martha it's not like we are hiding him," he said and then everyone laughed.

That got her to smile and brought her around. "I know Pa," she said, then turned to EJ "do really want to go with them son?" She asked.

With a more assertive voice. "Yes Ma, I do." He said as he realized that this was not as hard for him for the first time in his life. To call someone else Ma or Pa like it was before in all the homes he had been in. This time this home seemed normal. Like this is where he was meant to be and these are the parents he wanted and the family he could love and feel loved. Yes, Ma and Pa sound right in his mind and in his heart.

"But if your parents see you and try…" She said.

Pa and boys stood up, EJ looked up at them. "Ma I trust them,

Pa and my brothers won't let them touch me and I'll be right back I promise." He said wiped the tears of love from his eyes.

She sighed as she looked straight at her boys then at her husband and shook a finger at them. "If you let so much as a hair or stitch of this boy...!" She said as she pointed to EJ. "Come loose. Me and his grandmother will...!" They all swallowed hard just at the mere thought. Ma watched their heads snap back a little. Then calmed herself down and gently kissed EJ on the head. "Now drink your broth and finish your lunch. It sounds like I have some more work to do," she said.

"Yes Ma," EJ replies.

As they were eating lunch Ma looked out the window then looked over at her four boys and smiled. "Pa?" She said from across the table.

"Yes, Ma?" finishing his lunch.

"Do remember what I said about just making few of those minor changes to that promise of yours, but still honoring it?" The boys swallowed hard and looked at their mother as they waited for the shoe to drop.

"Yes Martha I do, you said it just needed a little work," he said.

"That's right. So after these boys finish lunch you can take down that tepee," she said.

"But?"

"Shush," putting her fingers to her lips. "You can still be Indian brothers and keep your promise. I think if you move all the furniture out of Wills room except for the mattress for EJ move your sleeping bags in there, you boys can all sleep in there. Plus I won't have to carry water to bathe you, boys. We can just walk down the hall, which would be much easier. Now that is settled, girls these Indians have work to do." As she stood and started untying EJ's little vest. "Boys please leave those shirts on the hooks so they don't get dirty and wrinkled and I'll be out in a few minutes to measure EJ for those clothes for town," she said then rubbed his hair on his head.

"Yes Ma," they all replied.

They got up from the table with their heads hung low, removed their clean shirts, hung them on the pegs by the door, then came back to the table to load EJ back into the chair and headed back to the tepee.

Martha quickly took hold of Pa's arm before he went out the door and asked. "What happened out in the barn today?" She asked.

"It was all between his brothers and him and then he just knew," he said.

"Wayne?" She asked.

"Yes, Martha?"

He wanted me, me to be his Ma." She said with tears running down her cheek. Wayne wrapped his arms around her tight.

"Yes I know dear because you will be and I can't think of anyone better and I get to be his Pa," he said holding her tight.

Chapter 15-1

* * * *

It was a sad day when the tepee came down, but it wasn't really needed anymore. It served its purpose as it brought brothers closer together as one. Everyone under one roof like it should be shared as one family. Ma, Pa, two sisters and four brothers in the room eating at one table; what brings it together now? Now the healing can start as they build a home and put it back together as we tear the tepee down.

Timber with a loud bang, the tepee fell to the ground with a loud crash, dust flew under its eves with some lost feathers from the morning pillow fight.

"Alright Robert, Will let's gather up the polls and stack them near the house for now. We might be able to make them into ladders or platform while we build the rooms," Pa said. gathering the ropes and the pegs from the ground.

"Yes Pa," they said heads bowed and discouraged.

Pa seeing the disappointment on their faces as they watched tepee fall. "Will, Robert?"

"Yes, Pa?"

"It was still a good idea," as they all looked at EJ sitting in the chair. "Look what you have accomplished so far?" Pa pointed to EJ as he sat as he watched them work.

Will and Robert looked at him then looked back at Pa. "Yes your right Pa, it was a good idea, we just need to give a little that's all and Ma's right it did need a little work," replied Robert.

"Pa?" Will asked rolling up the canvas as Robert gathered the polls.

"Yes Will?" setting the items aside for the moment.

"She never did say how much work did she?" He asked.

Pa rubbed his chin then smiled. "Come to think of it, she never did say, boys," as they all laugh.

"Well that's Ma for ya, and that's why we love her so," Robert said watching Ma come out of the house with her sewing basket over her arm.

"EJ holds still, I'll just be a minute," Ma said.

"But that tickles Ma," EJ laughed as she tried to measure his legs and waist around his hips

"Now I'm going to try to make these overalls as lose as possible," she said taking the measuring tape writing down his measurements as she has done with all her boys from time to time.

"Yes, Ma." EJ said trying to hold still while he sat in the chair watching his new Pa and his brother's work.

"Now they may look funny to you, but nobody will know the difference as long you don't move around too much." Will and Robert came over to see what Ma has made. "Alright since you two boys want to take him into town, let's see how these fit. So I can make the adjustment."

She had taken a pair of Robert's old pair of overalls and split them down the sides so they were in two pieces, measured EJ legs and put snaps on the inside along the sides so they would come apart and be made to put them together again.

"Pa you are going have to stand him up. EJ this may hurt a little, you haven't been on your feet for quite some time and those wounds on your legs and chest may feel the strain so brace yourself. Pa, Will. You hold him up," she said.

Hop, hop. "Oh, that hurts," EJ replied.

What's Behind the Looking Glass?

"I got you," Pa said, everyone watched his face turn white.

"Wayne, are you sure about this?" As they ease EJ back into the chair.

EJ out of breath and sweat-drenched from his little body from the short work out. Whispered," I'll be fine, really Ma, I want to go." While wrapping his arms around his chest and rubbed because it hurt like hell. Clamped his teeth smiled back hoping she wouldn't notice.

Ma shook her head. "You stubborn silly boy… You should stay here and rest," and sighs, "Alright drink this broth son. You can't fool me."

"Yes Ma," taking the biter cup from her and quickly swallowed it without gagging too much.

Ma stood back so she could admire the work. With a little tuck here with a pin or two there, "EJ are you sure son?" She asked one more time.

"Yes, Ma," EJ replies again with confidence.

She looked at the cuts on his feet. "Well I'm not putting shoes on those," She said as she lifted his feet and rubbed her hands down the sides of them and turned them over.

"Tell you the truth Ma, I always hated shoes anyway." Will, Robert, and Pa busted out laughing.

Ma shook her head and turned to Pa. "For some reason that does not surprise me, just like your brothers I see," and rubbed EJ hair.

EJ smiles. "Yes Ma."

"Well those wounds on your back and chest, I can't do anything about them for now, but least you'll be decent anyway. I don't want you getting too hot or risk infection so this will have to do," she said.

"Thanks, Ma," EJ replies.

She bent down and placed a kiss on his cheek. "You are welcome son; now then I need to finish sewing and get these washed and put supper on. Pa stands him up again so I can have those back." Getting them off was much easier than putting them on since all they had to do while he was sitting was unsnap them along the sides and pull the back part from behind.

Just in time too. "Hello, brothers." The boys swallowed hard seeing the lotion and oil in their hands. "We cleaned out the room so just bring EJ into the house so we can change his bandages; Ma says just change the ones on his leg for now and one around his chest she'll change the others later," Julie said as they watched him blush.

Will and Robert looked over at Pa. Even EJ looked at him. "Its alight boys they promised me and your Ma they would be gentle and I won't leave your side for a minute," he said.

"Yes, Pa." They still swallowed hard blushing all the way down the hall.

Pa whispered in the girl's ears, "not too rough now." Pa opened the door so the boys could get by and followed them down the hallway.

"Pa we are only teasing them. They have nothing to fear from us, Ma says your arms could use a little soften too you know," Julie said as she put his arm around her.

"She did huh?" As they entered the room Pa placed EJ gently down on the mattress. The next thing you could hear coming out of the room was. "Oh, that's cold… easy now…hey that tickles."

"Alright, boys that's it for now. Pa's your turn to roll up your sleeves."

Pa looked over at his pink boys. "Alright my girls, my arms are yours, if my sons can take it then I will. OH MAN! That's cold." EJ, Will and Robert bust out laughing. "Oh, that tickles," that made the boys laugh even harder.

What's Behind the Looking Glass?

Ma walked in the room as the girls were cleaning up and announced dinner would be ready in about an hour. She turned seeing Pa rolling down his shirt sleeves and whispered in his ear. "Tonight dear I'll do the rest myself," Ma replied.

Pa's eyes opened wide. "There's no full moon out tonight dear," he whispered back, but all she did was a giggle and smiled back then left the room. Pa stunned once again turned to his boys and rubbed his chin. "Boys we are in trouble," as he shook his head.

Will and Robert fell back on the mattress next to EJ, "now he notices," they all laughed. EJ holding his sides because it hurts too much to laugh, EJ turned to Robert. "Didn't Danny say something about horses and a pony?"

"Would you like to see one?" Robert asked.

"Sure," he replied.

"Well then let's go finish our chores. We still have chickens that need to be fed and pigs to feed for the night. I'd let you hold one, but Ma would probably kill us." Robert said.

"Oh so that's how Danny got so dirty," EJ said as they helped him out the door with one arm over each shoulder and placed him into the chair.

"Yea it was great. He loved every minute of it, except for the bath part. I don't think the pig enjoyed it nearly as much as he did though," Will, Robert, and EJ laughed as they carried him back forth all over the farm.

"EJ see that old brown painted horse with spots?" they asked setting down the chair as they rubbed their sore and tired arms. Even thou he didn't weigh much it was still a workout.

"Yes, I see him, so that's the little colt that Danny was talking about." EJ pointed to the horses and the pony standing out the field as the chewed the soft green grass and whipped their tails back and forth. He wondered what it would be like to ride one. Just to feel the wind through his hair as he galloped through the open field.

"We plan to start training him in the fall. Would you like to help?" Robert asked to bring him back as he envisioned the new possibility of life on the farm.

"Would I? I've never even ridden a horse before," he said sitting back in the chair as each of his brothers picked him up to carry him. He grimaced as the chair jolted his sides and wounds rubbed against him. The thoughts of the dream still echoed in his mind as father's face and handheld the knife to his throat. *No. Mr. Downing killed all the monsters.*

Will and Robert laughed. "EJ, believe me, that's not all you haven't done brother," as they heard Ma ring the dinner bell.

"Robert?" EJ asked letting the vision go as he smelled the sweet grass of the field and far away from his parent's touch.

"Yes EJ?"

"What else do you do on the farm besides feed the animals?" He asked trying hard not to bounce around in the chair as they carried him back towards the house.

Will and Robert laughed, "EJ remember all that work Pa said about harvesting and planting crops?"

"Yes," he replied.

"Who do you think does all that?" Robert asked.

"You mean."

"Yep, you are a farmer son now, EJ welcome home."

EJ looked around the fields from his chair; he would take a deep breath if it didn't hurt so much. Then he looked back at Robert then at Will and turned towards the house. "Having you as my brothers, I think I can live with that, but those sisters." Will and Robert laughed so hard they nearly drop him.

"Hey now," EJ said clenching the arm of the chair.

What's Behind the Looking Glass?

"Sorry. They sometimes get be a little bit much, but after a while, you'll see they are not so bad," said Will.

"Don't worry EJ, Will and I have got a plan," as they laughed.

Reaching the house they open the door and the water basin was waiting for them to clean themselves up before stepping inside. Pa and Robert helped EJ to his seat while Ma tied on his vest for dinner and the boys dawned on their shirts and sat at the table sliding next to EJ. Everyone seated around the dinner table, Ma is humming to herself as she brought the last dish to the table. Ma placed a kiss on each of the boy's heads and then went over to Pa whispered in his ear to remind him she had a surprise just for him later on.

As she watched him drop the butter knife on the plate, she softly giggled back to her seat. Ma started the conversation by turning to EJ. "EJ, so how do you like our little farm so far?"

"Oh there's lots to see Ma, that's for sure. Will and Robert let me help feed some of the animals," he said as he waited as she cut his food for him and looked at all the food on the table that seemed a feast compared to the scraps he got at home.

She quickly stared at them. "Oh, they did huh? How nice… I hope they were on their best behavior? I hope they didn't let you get too close?" She said as she stared them down.

"No Ma, I was safe the whole time. I wanted to hold a baby pig, but they…" She waited with fingernails drumming the table… The boys swallowed hard. "They wouldn't let me," he said.

She let out a sigh of relief… with a motherly calm back into her eyes and picked out the straw out of his hair and with her fingers wiped the smudge of dirt off his cheek. "Well, I am glad you had a good time. EJ drink your broth," as she spooned the peas onto his plate and cuts his meat for him.

After a while Will and Robert's eyes and heads started to drop slowly, they were so tired from carrying and running EJ all over the farm. Pa noticed Robert gave him a slight nudge and grin. "Boys I think you need to go to bed after dinner," as he began to watch Will start to snore, his sisters began to laugh. Pa just rubbed his chin then looked out the window at the chair and pulled out a pencil rubbed his chin. Ma and girls cleared the table leaving them there as Ma shook her head.

Pa nudged Robert seeing Will half asleep and EJ too started to doze off. Pa brought them all awake.

Robert stretched and yawns. "You are right Pa we better get to bed," he said.

"Before you go, Robert, Will lets make a few adjustments, it might make it little easier on you boys and won't tire you out so much," he said.

"Pa we can handle it. It's just been a long day that's all." Robert said starting to scoot back the chair

"Just listen for a minute, what could it hurt?" He said.

"Alright Pa," regain his seat.

Pa took the pencil and drew a little bucket seat of a wagon with a small floorboard to put his feet then instead of polls on the side like the chair for carrying, places two small wheels on each of handles in front.

Robert and Will scratched their heads, "Pa this is crazy," then looked over at EJ. "Do think we could build it?"

"I don't see why not, there is that old broken down seat in the barn we could add some boards and some bicycle tires from the store in town," Pa said.

Robert rubbed his hands and arms from caring EJ all day. "Alright Pa we'll do it," he said as he looked at the sketch. "It could work. EJ want to go for a spin?" He asked.

EJ looked over at the drawing a little puzzled then looked over at his two new brothers and his new Pa, "I trust you, sure why not," then yawns.

What's Behind the Looking Glass?

Ma comes over to the table with some pie…"You boys ready for dessert?" She asked and watched them all yawn, "Oh my, you boys are tired," she said.

"Yes Ma," the boys said yawning.

"Pa you have worn my boy's cleanout. We better just put them straight to bed before they fall down." She said as Pa laughed.

"Yes Ma," he replied.

Ma unties EJ's vest and they climbed into their sleeping bags. Ma turned off the light then closed the door. Ma turned to the girls warning them. "No funny business, let them sleep," she said.

"Yes, Ma." They knew there's always tomorrow to tease them with love, for that's what sisters do best as they too head to bed.

Martha whispered in Wayne's ear "dear are you ready?" She asked as she hums down the hall.

"Ready for what dear?" He asked.

"You'll see, you go check on the children, and then come to bed," Martha said as she walked humming softly on down the hall with a water basin in her hand entered the bedroom and closed the bedroom door behind her. Wayne enters the boy's room steps carefully around to each of his sons on the floor brushing their soft hair, bending down then placed a gentle fathers kiss on each of their heads, whispered in their ears before rising to his feet, "sleep my Indian brave sons, sleep," to each one. Tiptoes out the room and closed the door. Walking down the hall he enters each of his daughter's rooms gently strokes their cheeks with the back of his hand then lends forward, placed a warm kiss and whispered in their ear "sleep my little angels, sleep. You may have your mother's wit and charm, but you are my pride and joy."

Walking down the hall he took a hard swallow as he hears his wife humming in the bedroom and wonders what she has in store for him in there, rubbed his chin and grins "I don't remember the moon being full tonight, but I could be wrong," he said to himself.

He opens the door, "Hello dear." His eyes go wide seeing the candles lit in the corners of the room and basin of water and oils near the bed. She shuts the door behind them "I heard you need some softening too, so I figured." She said as she smiled and giggled like a schoolgirl. While she undid the buttons on his shirt and sits him on the bed, humming to herself…"Oh, that's cold," he said.

The girls giggled down the hall and boys laughed across the hall…" hearing Pa laughing, "That tickles Martha," then … "ahhhhhhhhhhh."

"Now that's a good husband… "Goodnight children," hearing their Pa snoring.

Chapter 15-2

* * * *

Ma must have softened those arms of his a little too much. For the rooster was late the next morning when he crowed as the sun reached high above over the mountains the next morning. Ma was in the kitchen preparing breakfast. Julie seeing Ma humming over the stove with a glow on her face, Ma turned to Julie "Shush they are all still asleep." Then still humming turning to Julie "mind helping me set the table?" She asked with a smile on her face.

"Ma where's Pa?" Julie asked as she looked out the window?

"Shush Julie, I told you they are still all asleep," Ma said.

"All them Ma?" Ma calmly nodded her head.

Julie giggled softly. "When you soften, you really soften." Then shook her head and they both giggled softly as they set the table.

Anna walked into the kitchen seeing Julie and Ma setting the table they turn to her "Shush they are still asleep. Help us set the table."

Anna with a puzzled look went over to her and whispered, "Where's Pa and Robert?" She asked.

Julie turned to her "Shush, told ya, they are still all asleep." Anna looked at Ma face then looked at Julie and softly giggled.

Ma turned to the girls. "Now hurry set the table we're all going to town on our own girls as soon as I finish with the boys, we're going to town after they leave for some shopping of our own, so no funny business. Go finish your chores after you eat your breakfast," she said.

"Yes Ma," as they giggle taking their seats.

The girls and Ma quickly ate their breakfast and cleaned their plates while Ma went down the hall to wake the boys. Stepping into her room where her husband is still sound asleep she brushed his hair gently then slowly pulled the curtains to let the sun in and quietly sat on the bed next to him, whispered in his ear. "Dear breakfast is ready," she said.

His eyes pop open with a start. Turning his head towards the window he could see the sun had already come up. He jumped out of the bed, "Martha I am sorry, I think I overslept. I'll kill that rooster and buy another," he said.

"Oh no, dear. It wasn't his fault. I bribed him to last night," she said grinning.

"You what?" He said as she got off the bed.

"I left him with the other chickens. They needed him," as she giggled softly in his ear. "Now go wake the boys, like I said breakfast is on the table the girls are out doing the chores. You have a lot to do today," and then left him standing in the room.

Pa threw on his clothes, walked across the hall with a puzzled look on his face as he watched his wife head for the kitchen. He scratched his head and wondered what was she up to? Pa opened the boy's room seeing the boys are waking up, "Boys. They have done it again," he said.

"What Pa?" they asked as they turned their heads climbing out of their sleeping bags.

"Not sure yet, but breakfast is ready and we do have a lot of things too do today."

"Yes Pa," they said.

"EJ how you feeling son?" He asked

What's Behind the Looking Glass?

"Sore and stiff," he said as he moved his legs.

"Well you sound better anyway," Pa replied looking him over as and helping him to sit up.

"Thanks, Pa," he said.

"Still want to go to town with us EJ?" Pa asked sitting down beside him.

"Yes Pa, I do."

"Then we better get a move on it." Putting his hand on his shoulder and stood up and placed his arms around his neck as he carried him towards the door.

Will and Robert noticed Sam was already gone with the girls. "Sneaky little devils," Robert said as he shook his head.

Pa laughed. "I just bet boys they have something planned. So we won't spoil their fun."

"Pa?" Robert asked.

"Yes, Robert?"

"That's what worries me the most, what do they have planned? And how does it involve us?" As he looked at Will and EJ swallowed hard.

Pa chuckled. "I guess we will find out soon enough son, we better get down to breakfast you know how Ma gets if we keep her waiting," he said with EJ in his arms he started down the hall.

"You boy's coming? These hotcakes are getting cold." She yelled down the hall.

"YES MA!" Robert replied.

Pa helped EJ to the table while Ma made sure breakfast was down their tummies as she cleared the table. "Alright boys the waters ready," she said.

EJ whispered in Robert's ear. "Just set me in the tub this time. I'll go first, its just Ma."

Will and Robert looked at EJ. "Are you sure?"

He nodded his head. "You'll still be there, I think I'll be fine," as he swallowed hard.

Robert and Will carried EJ down the hall sat him in the tub, not leaving his side for a minute as Ma came in. EJ turned his head. "I'm ready now Ma." Ma closed the door and pulled up the stool. Looked at her three boys with a tear in her eye she wiped them away with her apron, gently gave EJ his bath.

With a kiss on the cheek of each of the boys, she thanked them. "I knew you could do it, there was nothing for you to be ashamed of boys, after all, I am just your mother," she said.

"Yes Ma, we know that." Handing them each a towel she dried them off and wrapped the towel around EJ. "Now let's get him back to the room so I can change all the bandages and get him ready for town."

"Yes Ma," they replied and carried him back to the room. Ma put the oils and lotions on herself while the boys dressed. When the boys returned for EJ she smiled seeing three brothers together, just as it should be three farmer sons then Sam came running in with Pa right behind him. Sam leaped into Robert's arms, The picture was now complete. Her face glowed with radiance as she smiled seeing her four farmer sons, she nearly wept.

Ma turned to Pa as she shook a finger at him. "Remember what I said, not one hair. I want him back Pa!" She went over to each of her boys and gave them one more kiss on the head. "This is all I really wanted, thanks boys you did your Ma proud, my little Indian farmer sons." She wiped the tear from her eye, "now go. I have work too do and so do you." And watched them walk out the door as they carried EJ with them, while Sam stayed with her and his sisters.

"Well, Robert?" Pa asked parking the pickup near the porch.

What's Behind the Looking Glass?

"Yes, Pa?" sitting next to EJ with Robert on the other side.

"Looks like we're ready to go," he said as he looked over at EJ as he sat on the porch swing.

"Now then how are we going to do this son?" Pa asked.

"Pa?" Will asked.

"Yes Will?"

"I was thinking I could ride in the back with EJ and we could lean him up against the back of the truck to support his back. Plus I could prop something in the back to make it a smoother ride," he said.

Pa rubbed his chin for a minute, "what do think EJ, do you think, could hold still? Ma would kill us if anything would happen to you," as he laughed with a serious tone.

"Yes Pa, I'll be fine I won't move a muscle I promise."

Pa picked him up tossing his legs gently over the truck. Robert helped set him down on the spread-out quilt while Will grabbed a pillow for his back.

Pa turned to EJ, "not a muscle right?"

"Yes Pa," as Will sat next to him.

"Robert?" Pa asked.

"Yes, Pa?"

"I think I'll drive, and you watch for the ruts, it seems last time we must have hit a few," he said.

"Yes, Pa."

Pa and the boys turned out of the farm and headed into town. "Alright, girls I've left a note so if your Pa gets back before we do there's lunch for him and the boys in the fridge. EJ's broth is there too. All they have to do is put in the medicine and stir."

"Ma?" Julie asked.

"Yes, Julie?"

"How are we going to get to town, Pa took the truck the wagons not hooked up?"

"Oh, I didn't tell you did I?" Martha seeing Grandma's car as she pulled up into the driveway of the farm. "EJ's grandmother, she wanted to do some shopping for EJ and Danny for school clothes and I had his measurements taken yesterday and she wanted it to be a surprise," Ma replies.

"Hello, Grandma." Everyone said opening the door.

"Hello my dears, was that EJ in the back of the pickup next to Will?" She asked climbing the stairs and enters the house with Danny beside her.

"Yes," Martha said giving Danny a quick hug and a kiss on the head and an extra squeeze.

"Grace's mercy alive if one hair on…"

"Grandma I have already warned them twice. Besides he really did want to go and I didn't have the heart to say no," she said.

"Those boys must have pulled off a miracle seeing the happiness in that boys face back there," she said walking back down the stairs towards the car. Grandma opened the car door so Danny and Sam could get inside, giving Sam a big bear hug and kiss on the cheek.

"I guess we are ready Grandma let's go to town and I'll explain on the way," Martha said as she brought Grandma up to the current advents of the farm. She wiped a tear from her eye.

"Martha I've got to hand it to you and your boys, yes sir EJ's doing just fine I know a few folks that could use a few of those lessons of yours. Now Danny here he can't wait to see his brother, isn't that right Danny?" She asked.

"Yes Grandma, do I still get play Indian?" He asked.

Martha laughed. "Well, I don't see why not, when we get back on the farm you and Sam can play Indian all day if you like."

"YEA!" as they watched two boys jump up down on the backseat. Grandma gave the girls little wink and a little nod as she closed the trunk of the car.

* * *

Pa pulled into Stringum Hardware Store on Main. Pa getting out of the pickup turned to EJ, "remember?"

"I know Pa, not a muscle." He made himself comfortable as he sat against the truck bed.

"Pa?" Will asked.

"Yes Will?"

"I'll stay here if you don't mind, just to make sure," as he smiled and winked at EJ.

"I would like that, thanks Will," EJ said.

"Hey, that's what brothers are for," then socks him in the arm.

"Ouch that hurts," he replied.

"Sorry," Will grinned from ear to ear.

EJ looked up at Pa, "I'll be fine."

Robert and Pa headed on into the store. "Well hello, Mr. Downing. I didn't expect you back so soon." Mr. Stringum said as he looked out into the back of the truck and rubbed his head. "I was wondering what happened to EJ." As Wayne, Robert and they glanced through the window. EJ and Will waved back to them.

"Yes, Humm, EJ's been…" Pa looked at Robert as he gathered his thoughts. "EJ has been working on my farm and is going to be there for some time," Wayne said.

Mr. Stringum taking another glance through the window noticed few chests bandages, but doesn't say anything, thinking of the rumors of what he heard from Doc from down the street, just rubbed his chin."Yes, I see, well then how can I help you?" He asked standing behind the counter with a note pad and pen.

Mr. Dave Stringum a man that always stood what was right and one of the few men in today's world that understood farmers in how to judge a man by his deeds and how he treats his family. Even thou he prides himself of being the one to put Santaquin on the map, selling the best-traded goods he can find homegrown and bought. He loved to gossip according to his wife who been dead two years gone from lung cancer.

He was a man everyone counted on when they needed something done or built. He had just turned sixty-five this past spring, his dark brown hair starting to gray and he still seemed nimble with an average height of six feet. Brown eyes and a handsome square jaw that still made a woman quiver when he whispers in their ears. Despite most of his teeth were man-made as his white teeth glistened as gave each person a wink when he did something on the sly.

"Just need some supplies for the farm and some seed to plant. Oh and we are adding on to the house this time too. The wife wants to add a few extra bedrooms to make some larger ones for the boys," Wayne said.

"Oh!" Mr. Stringum replies as he glanced at the window at EJ and Will. "Extra rooms you say," as he rubbed his chin. "Well then got some figures to start with?" Wayne handed him the paper and the plans.

"Dave?" Stringum calls.

What's Behind the Looking Glass?

"Yes, Mr. Stringum?" He answered around the corner. Dave was a young kid fresh out of college in his early twenties. With a solid build from carrying heavy items and used to hard work hauling supplies all over town. He stood at the average height of five feet nine inches, Blue eyes, and yellow curly hair. Dressed in a nice pair of workman overalls and a white tee shirt that showed of his strong muscular arms; the girls that noticed him would all lick their lips moaning with deep satisfying pleasure as he carried out their order. With apron that said Stringum Hardware and Goods painted on the front.

"Can you start loading some these supplies into the pickup?" He asked.

"Yes, sir." Dave grabbed the list and picked the items off the shelves putting them in a box and carried them out to the pickup.

"Hi, Dave, how ya been?" Dave looked up seeing Will and EJ sitting in the back of the pickup. Will gets up to help him with the supplies, Dave flabbergasted as he took a step back.

EJ said. "I'd shake your hand Dave, but I promised not to move."

"EJ how... are you? Where have you been?" Dave stutters back.

Will steps in. "He's staying with us, he's my new brother... cool ha?"

"Well, I better get those supplies, nice seeing you," as he backed into the store scratching his head.

"Well Mr. Downing, your wife's sheets have arrived and the quilts you order have arrived too. Dave, can you go in the back get them?" He turned to ask.

"Yes Mr. Stringum, did you know that EJ's out there?" Dave replied stunned as he turned around lifting another box as he hands it to Robert.

"Yes, please go get the order son," turning back to Mr. Downing.

Robert pointed down the street "Pa?" When he came back into the store as the door clanged shut behind him.

"Yes, Robert?"

"We have a problem," Robert said.

"What is it, Robert?" Then saw where he was pointing, seeing EJ's father walking towards the store. "Robert you and Will stand next to EJ so he doesn't see him coming and I'll finish up here," Pa said.

"Yes, Pa."

"Robert dashed out of the store, "Will quickly jumped out of the pickup stand right next to me," he said as he pointed then whistled in the air. Tried not to be noticed and whispered back to EJ. "EJ don't move." EJ freezes seeing his father crossing the street near the Post Office.

Mr. Stringum not as dumb as he looks and sees what's about to happen, "Mr. Downing I'll have that lumber delivered to you by Friday." Dave seeing it too ran the remaining goods to the pickup around the back and ran back into the store. While Mr. Stringum walked right behind Mr. Stuart, blocking his view from the back of the boys.

"Hello Jim, how are you?" Walking right next to him and at the same time, he pushed Mr. Downing out the door with a wink then turning just right to knock over a few cans so that they would spill over blocking the door into the path. "Oh dear, that always seems to happen," as he shook his head..."I knew I put those out too close to the door," he replied.

Mr. Stuart watched Mr. Downing quickly jump into the pickup with EJ in the back taking off, "was that my son Eric Mr. Stringum?" He asked. He hated the name EJ as much as his wife did. He hated everything that stated that he was his son, and everyone reminding him. Oh god how he wished people would leave him and his family

What's Behind the Looking Glass?

alone, and now he had one more person to add to the list of who would like to see dead.

"Now Jim, didn't you just tell me he was at Scout Camp just a few days ago and he's not due back for few more days yet?" He replied.

"Yea, that's right," Jim said nervously.

"Then how could that be him? Now how can I help you? Dave, I seemed to have knocked those cans over again," he called out.

"Yes Mr. Stringum, I'll grab a mop."

After they watched Mr. Stuart leave with his purchases they both walk out of the store. "Mr. Stringum?" Dave asked.

"Yes, Dave?"

"That was EJ I saw wasn't it?" He asked.

"Yes and No," as he winks at Dave, "and he was never here," he said.

"Pa that was close," Robert said looking back over the seat at the store quickly fading in the distance.

"Yes, Robert it was," Pa said as he wiped the sweat off his head, turning around to face EJ.

"EJ how you holding up son?" He asked.

EJ looked over at Will then turned around to face Pa, his face almost white. "I am still here Pa, that's all that counts, Pa?" EJ said after swallowing hard, "I didn't move a muscle, I was too scared too, but next time we go too town, do you mind moving the pickup around back?" As they all laugh.

"You know son, for you, that's not such a bad idea," as he wiped his face one more time.

As they pulled into the farm, Pa said opening the door of the house, "let's get you into the house into something more comfortable." Pa said as he and Robert lifted him back out of the pickup and carried him back into the house and laid him on the couch. Will helped him off with Ma's town clothes and hung them back on the hook. Pa sees the note on the table. "Boys your Ma and your sisters have gone to Provo," he said.

"How they get to Provo Pa?" Robert asked.

"They say it's a surprise and lunch is in the fridge and to make sure EJ drinks his broth love Ma."

"I knew she was up to something," as Pa rubbed his chin and grins. "You boys are right, we are in trouble," he said.

"And now he notices," the boys laughed.

"You boys better get change so can get the chores done, be sure to hang up those shirts or your Ma will skin ya live." Will and Robert walked down the hallway to their bedroom to change their clothes.

Chapter 16

"Well, girls are you ready to paint the town?" Grandma asked when she got in the car and turned the key and right arm hung over the long front seat of light blue 1969 Buick her husband bought her for their twentieth wedding anniversary. She and Richard always kept in good repair.., mostly Richard did. She slowly backed out of the farm and headed up the road smelling the apple blossoms and sweet grass of hay along the side of the road.

"Yes Grandma," the girls replied seating the boys down on the seat between them.

"Martha, I thought while we were here we would get some clothes for all the boys and something nice they could wear to the summer picnic," she said glancing out the window enjoying the summer breeze missing her Harley as she remembers the days her and husband would travel the roads on the weekends during good days like these, she sighed heavily with regret.

"Oh you don't have to do that," Martha said turning round to face her.

"Nonsense, it's my job to spoil my grandkids especially after what they just did for EJ," Grandma said glancing back at her and children in the back.

"But I don't have their shoe sizes with me or anything just EJ's" Ma replied.

The girls started giggling in the back of the car, "Ma yes we do," they said.

"What do mean you have their sizes?" She asked turning completely around to face them.

"Well not their sizes, but everything else you would need to get them," as they giggled some more.

"Alright what have you two done?"

The girls looked at each other. "Let's just say we know the man in the moon and he called in a favor," Julie said.

Ma thinks about that breakfast morning outside the tepee for a minute. "Why that sneaky ... So that's why he just let me..."

"What Martha did I miss something?" Grandma asked as she looked over at her.

"Grandma you are right, we need to do a little extra shopping today." Then turned back around to the girls, and smiled at them. "So what did you bring with you girls?"

"Just some of their clothes that they are not going to be wearing anytime soon," Julie held up their work shoes, "and we have some of their shirts and pants too. Pa has everything else in a box except what we consider good town clothes," as they all laugh.

"And when did you do this?" Ma said thinking about the previous night out on the swing. "Never mind girls," and smiles. Ma turning around "Yes Grandma we have some extra shopping to do. I too know the man and the moon and he's has been very naughty," and smiles. Grandma looked at Martha with sort of a puzzled look, but kinda has an idea that Wayne is behind this somehow. After all she the one that told him to come up with the idea in the first place, noticing the redness in her cheeks just thinking how he must have done it.

* * *

Will opened the bedroom walked in and set his clean shirt on the bed, opened the closet to hang it. He rummages through his shirts can't find any of his work shirts or pants except the loincloth that they made hanging on the hanger, with a note and craftsman tool belt from Pa. "With love and thanks. I am proud of you son," on it. Robert walked in the room where Will was and showed him the same thing. They sat on the bed together and stared at each other for a minute.

Pa walked in the room. "Lunch is almost done boys," knowing they must have found their belts. Walked in and placed his hand on their shoulder. "I thought you would like it and I am so proud of you, theirs one for EJ too. I would like you boys to give it to him, thanks," and walked out of the room... "Oh before I forget the lotion and oil are on the table, so make sure you put it on. I have already taken care of EJ."

"Yes, Pa."

"Now change your clothes we have lots to do. Over lunch I'll tell you what I have planed while the girls are away, I think you have a score to settle," he said as he rubbed his chin.

"Yes Pa," as they grin, "we do."

"Pa here can teach ya a trick or two of his own. So hurry now and change your clothes."

"Yes Pa," and left his boys alone as he walked back down to the kitchen whistling a merry old tune.

The boys changed back into their Indian clothes and putting their lotion and oil on and walked down into the kitchen where Pa was. Robert with EJ's belt in his hand they walked over to him. "We have a present for you," Robert said.

EJ not sure what was has a puzzled look on his face. "What is it? It looks like a belt of some kind, but I don't know what kind." He says.

Pa came over to EJ. "It is a craftsman tool belt to hold tools in while you work around the farm for woodworking. Do you know that frame in your room? Robert built that. We are going to teach you how to build things like that too. Now let's see how this fits so when those wounds heal on your waist you can wear it," he said.

EJ nodded his head because he did not know what to say whispered, "thanks."

Will, Robert, and Pa just put their hands on his shoulder and nod, Robert said. "EJ that's what families are for, now ready for some lunch, so we can build you something else today because are arms are tired of carrying you all over the farm?" As they all laugh. They sit and have some lunch as they go over the plans.

"Now Pa, you said something about showing us a couple of tricks?" Robert said.

Pa smiled. "Yes." As he looked over at EJ and rubbed his hands together than taking a notepad and pencil outlined out the plan. "Robert, do you remember me telling you about how I could cook besides making cold sandwiches?" Robert nodded his head. "Well EJ's, grandmother has taken your Ma and your sisters out. I was thinking we would surprise them with a home-cooked dinner from us. They would never in their wildest dream expect that I am talking flowers, fire in the fireplace the works," he replied.

"Pa?" Robert asked pushing his plate aside on top of Wills and EJ's, taking small sips of his milk as he wiped his mouth with the back of his left hand.

"Yes, Robert?"

"How is that going to help us?" He asked.

"Believe me, son, if you want to watch a girl melt and put out a fire before you get burned. Kill them with kindness and they are all yours; you might see them blush for a change," setting his plate with the rest and pours himself another glass and one for EJ.

Will, Robert even EJ laughed…" Blush Pa they can blush too?"

"Oh yes, but you have to set the mood." He whispered, way down, "this is what we're going to do?" And they smile and hatching plans whispering smiled some more,

"Really?"

"A huh," he whispered some more. Pa looked up at the clock. "I'm expecting Grandma to call me soon so you better go start on your chores and build that cart and then come help me in here," Pa said.

"Yes Pa," they said.

Chapter 17

"Girls, I just need to make a quick phone call home for a minute to check on Richard, I'll be back," Grandma said setting down her shopping bags on the floor next to Martha's as the girls gather the rest and take them out to the car.

"Ok Grandma," Martha replied.

Grandma finds a payphone around the corner near the restrooms in the back where she can keep a good eye on the girls and dials the Downing Farm letting it ring until Wayne picks it up. "Hello, Wayne," Grandma said as she looked over her shoulder making sure they were not watching and couldn't hear her. "Yes, we're fine. No, she doesn't suspect a thing. Yes, Anna and Julie managed to put the clothes in the car. How did you get them without her knowing? Oh, I see... You sly dog, so that's what she was talking about... No, I haven't figured that out yet...? Still working on it, how long do you need? I see, all right we will be back by then."

"Well now isn't that a pretty dress Julie?" Grandma said as she walked back into the store.

"You think so, Grandma?" Julie asked.

"I do," as she whispered in her ear. "We need to stall," as her mother approaches... "Yes, it matches the color of your eyes," Grandma said trying not to give away what's going on.

"Everything ok?" Martha asked seeing grandma back.

"Just fine Martha," Grandma said as she winked at Julie.

"Anna?" Julie asked.

"Yes, Julie?"

What's Behind the Looking Glass?

"Can you help me try this on?" Julie asked as she pointed to the dressing room.

"Sure," Julie and Anna headed for the changing room to try the dress on. "What's going on?" Anna asked closing the door behind her in the dressing room.

"Grandma says we need to stall Ma, but won't say why?"

Anna gave her a puzzled look. "You don't think she's up to something?" She asked helping her sister try on the dress.

"Who, Grandma? No!" Julie said not sure herself.

"So Martha?" Grandma asked riffling through the clothing studying one nice blouse after another and putting it back as she looked out the corners of her eye.

"Yes, Grandma?" Doing the same, finding some more nice shirts for Sam and Danny that would make good play clothes.

"What did you have in mind for Wayne? You said something about him being sneaky." Martha laughed than smiled. "Yes," her cheeks redden.

"Oh my Martha, he has been sneaky," and laughs. Then whispers in her ear; "You did what?" Then grabbed Martha by the shoulders pointed towards the dresses. "Martha I think you need to try this on for size. If this doesn't turn his head and make it spin. Yes dear now, scoot. Oh my! What I am going to do with these two," as Grandma shook her head, "The man and moon he needs to play or leave his calling card at," ...O my." Grandma said as she looked outside towards the car and the clock.

Taping her finger to her chin, seeing Anna coming out of the changing room. "Anna Grandmas stumped. How do I stall for time?" As they watched a man and boy change a tire cross the street. They shrugged their shoulders.

"Grandma, how much time do you need?" Anna said looking at the clock.

"4 hours maybe 5 hours," she replied.

"It's to bad Grandma we couldn't have a flat," Anna said.

"Whys that Anna?" She asked as they watched behind the glass of the shop they were in.

"That boy out there is kinda cute and strong, he could change my tire any day," she said as she blushed a little.

"What did you say, Anna?" Grandma asked. Not sure she heard it right.

"The flat tire…The boy over there." Anna pointed.

Grandma gave Anna a big squeeze, "that's a wonderful idea." Leaving Anna puzzled.

"Grandma, what's that for?" She asked.

"Never mind," Grandma said walking back to the boys while they lay on the floor with their coloring books and crayons.

Anna just shrugged her shoulders, thinking Grandma has lost her marbles. "Julie you look beautiful in that dress now we need find one for Anna," she said.

Martha comes out of the changing room wearing a simple yellow dress with white ruffles along the sleeves and low neckline as it barely hung from her shoulders. "Well now."

"Ma you like you an angel," the girls replied.

"You think so?" As she twirls around in the dress seeing it hug at her curves in the right spot feeling like a girl again going to her first prom.

What's Behind the Looking Glass?

"Aha yes," nodded their heads.

Grandma stalling said, "I think we need a couple more," and hands a blue one with a different style to her, then one more then scoots her back to the dressing room. "Julie, can you watch things and the boys for a minute?" She asked.

"Sure Grandma," Julie said as she watched Grandma walk outside to the car let some air out of one of the tires, comes back into the store. "Thanks, Julie," she said.

"Grandma?" She asked confused by what she just saw.

"Yes, Julie?"

"What did you do that for?" She asked.

"Do what dear?" And winked back. "So you girls ready to do some more shopping?" She asked picking up the dresses seeing, Martha coming out of the dressing room.

"Grandma, don't you think we should start heading back?" Martha asked looking at the clock and all the items they have already bought.

"Oh Martha it's early yet, we still have three more stores to go to still and there's a little bistro I want to take you, girls, too, the boys will be fine," she said.

"Alright Grandma, if you say so," Martha said gathering their things and the two little ones.

Julie whispered in Anna's ear. "Grandma's nuts, she just let the air out of the tires and we're going shopping," and shook her head.

Anna shrugs whispered back; "I know, she got excited over a guy about a flat tire."

* * *

"Robert, help me with this seat if we can just loosen it from these old floorboards. That should do it. EJ what do think nice and comfy," as they jump up and down on it, listening too it squeak when Robert sat on it.

EJ laughed. "Yea, ride'em cowboy, just missing the horse," he said.

"Hey wait minute Will?" Robert laughed. "Aren't you the horse, giddy yup?" EJ grabbed his sides of his ribs because they hurt so much to laugh.

"How's it common boy's?" Pa asked seeing the cart and Robert and Will trying it out.

"Works like a charm Pa," Robert laughed. "Sure beats carrying that chair all over the farm," he said.

Pa walked around it to test the sturdiness of the box and checks the tires. "EJ what do think son?" He asked.

"Will and Robert make a good horse Pa," he said.

Pa chuckled. "Yes, they do. Boys," Pa said as he looked at the clock. "The roast is in the oven. So we need to get started with execution blush," as they smile in unison.

"Yes, Pa."

"EJ you peel the potatoes," as he leaned him up against the porch outside the door.

"Yes, Pa."

"Robert, go get some firewood the apple and pine wood for the sweet scent.

"Yes, Pa."

"Will, you go out to find some daisy for the door and the table?"

What's Behind the Looking Glass?

"Yes, Pa."

"And I'll start on the gravy and the rolls," Pa said issuing the orders and watched them run off to do the errands.

* * *

Martha began to watch the clock as Grandma kept trying to stall as they shop while she carefully distracts Martha and the girls long enough as they go to buy a few more things.

"Martha, can you put these in the front seat for me?" Grandma said as she bent down-dropped the keys on the ground and let more air out of the tire. "Now let's stop and get a bite to eat, Julie mind watching my purse from me while I'm in the ladies room?" Making sure she had enough change for a phone call. "I'll be back in a few minutes you just wait here for me dear." She said setting her purse down on the table as they ate a nice crisp salad and sandwiches and some chicken fingers for the boys with orange soda.

Grandma making sure the coast is clear picking up the phone, "Wayne how are you and the boys coming? .... Oh good glad to hear... Yes it was touch and go I must say...but I need a favor...Yes, can you call Richard? In about say ten minutes, I want him to be a stranger... To come help me... Yes... That's right... A stranger...I am...I am about to have a flat... Let's say somewhere between Provo and Springville... You wanted time dear... that's best I can do dear... Make the best of it... see ya when we get there."

"Oh, Anna? I didn't see ya, dear." Grandma said hanging up the phone.

"Grandma, what are you up to?" She asked eyeing grandmas hand as she replaced the phone back on the hook.

"I had to go to the ladies' room you know that dear," she said.

"Grandma?" As she stepped in front of her and smiled then looked back at the car. "You know... that tire seems a little bit low to me Grandma," she said.

Grandma looked at the tire and Anna. "It does?"

"I have been watching you," Anna replies back standing in her way.

"Come on child, are you saying Grandma here is up to something?" Anna nodded her head yes. "Oh my! What on earth gave you that idea?" Then turned Anna around, "let's head back before your Ma thinks we're both up to something," not explain anything.

* * *

Wayne hanged up the phone smiled as he rubbed his chin and chuckled." How in the heck did she manage to pull off getting a flat on purpose? Poor Martha she going kill me, but it will be worth it and boys will learn a lesson besides," and chuckles to himself.

Picking up the phone dials Richard. "Richard this Wayne... Yes ... Wayne Downing ... Yes EJ's... Fine... Your mother... Wanted me to relay a message to you... Now, this may sound strange... Oh, I see... I'm starting to see that and understand that too... Anyway, she wants you to play a stranger... Yes, a stranger...Why? Well... She's going to have a flat tire...Yes," Pa laughed, "Yes a flat tire...She'll explain later... Where? Somewhere between Provo and Springville... in about 10 minutes... No, I don't know how she managed it, but knowing her, she's the one to pull it off... Well... I better... Let you go... were both on a deadline. Thanks, Richard."

"Who was that Pa?" Robert asked coming through the door with the wood in his arms as Pa hung up the phone.

What's Behind the Looking Glass?

"Just some extra help Robert from EJ's grandmother. She needed a favor so I helped her out," he said taking the wood and placed it near the fireplace.

"Smells good Pa," as Will walked in the door with the daisies.

"EJ how're those spuds coming son?" He asked turning back around.

"I've just peeled the last one Pa," EJ replies letting it splash in the tall kettle.

"Alright, Will grab the kettle and some water and put them on too boil." Robert set the rest of the wood over there and wash your hands and face, you too Will. Now put on the apron like this," and they all laugh. EJ nearly falls off his perch.

"If the girls see us they'll kill us, but they won't, will they Pa?" Robert asked.

"No," as Pa chuckles and they all laugh out loud.

They dressed the table in the finest tablecloth, plates, and napkins that Pa has been hidden way to surprise Ma with. Flowers in the middle as they made individual ones for each of the girls including Grandma and placed them across the plate… EJ starts mashing the spuds while Will finishes the gravy, Roberts making the fresh apple cobbler and Pa cooled the rolls.

* * *

"Well girls let's start heading back," Grandma said as she looked at the time at the last final store. Are you boy's tired of shopping?" Grandma asked as she watched them fall asleep, girls giggling in the back seat.

"Yes Grandma," they yawn.

"Well, Danny, you can play all day on the farm tomorrow," Grandma replies.

"Really?" He asked with a tired yawn.

"Yes," she replies.

When Grandma thinks she has gone far enough as she looked for a spot on the side of the road away from all the traffic, she slows down the car. "Oh, dear!"

"What's wrong Grandma?" Turning to Martha. Grandma seeing Richard about a mile or so down the road.

"Martha I can't believe it. I told Richard to check those tires before I left, we have a flat tire," she said.

"Clear out here? Now?" She asked.

"Yes, dear can you believe it? It just my luck too and not to have a man around when you need one," she said trying to sound frustrated.

Anna looked at Grandma then at Julie then whispered in her ear, "I just bet she had something to do with this?" Then gave Grandma a hard stare, Grandma just winked back.

Martha turned to her girls in the back seat and the boys falling asleep. "Looks like we are going too have late supper tonight," and sighs.

"Oh Martha, the boys will be fine. I am sure Wayne can manage things until we get back," she said turning around to face her and patted her hand.

"It's not them I worried about, it's us at the moment," Martha said very worried as she watches the sun lower in the sky. Who knows how long it would before they got home being stuck out in the middle of nowhere.

"Martha I do know how too change a tire dear, I am not helpless as some may think. I just prefer good strong young lad to

What's Behind the Looking Glass?

do it. Right girls?" Then they all laughed. "Oh look here comes one now," she said.

"Hi, ma'am can I help ya?" As Grandma winked at Richard as she rolled down the window to greet him.

"Looks like I got myself into a pickle and needs some help," she said acting all innocent and playing the part of a damsel in distress.

"Looks to me you have flat tire miss. I'll have that fixed for ya in a jiffy," he said playing along as he winked to the pretty girls in the back.

"Oh thank you, kind sir," Grandma replied placing a hand over her heart as to swoon a bit with joy.

"No problem ma'am," Richard said.

Richard put on the spare and gave his Ma another wink whispered. "See ya a couple of days." And hands him a bill for his trouble and the girls give him a kiss on the cheek.

Danny waved bye start to yell..."BYE Ric," as Grandma quickly covers his mouth with a piece of candy. Anna looked down at Danny then looked at Grandma. Grandma just winked.

Anna whispered in her ear, "You owe me a favor Grandma, you are up to something," and Grandma just winks back.

Chapter 17-1

* * *

"Ok boys everything's ready, what are we missing? Pa said as he looked at the table. "Food is done, fire, flowers. He checked each item off with his fingers. "Oh boys look at the clock we need to change," he said.

"Pa what are you talking about, change into to what?" The boys replied.

"Oh didn't I tell you, your suits are in the bedrooms complete with bow ties."

"Pa you got to be kidding?" Robert replied.

"Son, trust me. You want to see your sisters faint on the floor and quake at the knees, hurry bathroom, bathe quickly. All take care of EJ; I think I have something that just might work for him." Picking him up as they rush down the hall, water running fast as the boys quickly spot polished themselves. Pa dressed EJ in one of his shirts being careful with his bandages.

Oh, how they looked smart and dashing. Will, Robert, EJ, and Pa right down to bow tie. He slicks their hair and smarts the bow tie. Lights the fireplace to all a soft glow, turns down the lights as the car pulled into the driveway seating EJ on the couch. "Wait, boys. Let them come in on their own. He walked down the bedroom grabbed a rose for each of the girls then waits for Grandma to bring them in the house.

"That's strange?" Martha said seeing the lights turned off in the house as they pulled back into the driveway. Everything was too quiet as she wondered where husband and boys were, hoping nothing is wrong.

What's Behind the Looking Glass?

"What's strange Martha?" Grandma asked acting like it was no big deal not letting the cat out of the bag.

"Wayne usually comes out to greet us," she replied.

"Maybe they didn't hear us pull in?"

They get out of the car and headed towards the house, Danny and Sam started to run towards the house. Grandma was too late to catch them and shrugged her shoulders; Sam opens the door with Danny right behind him. Pa grabbed Sam and Danny. Then quickly pass them to Robert sets them on the couch next to EJ. "Shush" their eyes open wide "OH!" as they looked around the room.

Ma the girls walked into the house seeing Pa, Will, Robert and EJ all decked out. Then looked around the room, Pa bows to Ma with a rose. "Dinner is served," he said.

Robert stepped forward and bows handing a rose to Julie. "Dinner is served this way madam," taking her hand. Will, copied Robert taking Anna's hand.

Grandma went into the house seeing EJ. "Grandma I would bow, but I can't, but I have roses for you too and Pa will have to help me too the table," he said.

With a tear in her eye, it did not matter she walked over and kissed his cheek. "I'd be so honored young man." Ma and the girls were blushing red as could be, as they looked around the room again and quaked at the knees and looked at Pa and the boys with new wonder. They were speechless, shaking like a leaf, with tears in their eyes as they looked at the kitchen table. "Wayne, we can not eat like this, please let us girls freshen up a bit," Martha said nearly falling on the floor.

"If you ask your boys first, after all, they are ones that prepared the meal," Pa replies with a smile.

Their sisters were speechless. That finished them off right there and then. The brothers they had won that day and had even the score. They nodded their heads as girls left the room to freshen up.

Grandma went out to the car grabbed some of the packages with nice dresses for each of the girls so they could look their best too after all. She was not going to give them a win that easily, but still she gave Wayne and the boys a kiss and a hug. Then whispered in Wayne's ear; "you have been a very naughty boy I see, teaching these boys. I am so proud." With her hand, she brushed his cheek to make him blush just a little and smiles and then walked on down the hall with the clothes.

While they waited for the ladies to change; Will and Robert helped with clothes for Sam and Danny and got them ready for dinner and sat them at the table. Pa and Robert put EJ in his spot at the table. As the ladies entered the room the boys all stand and pulled out chairs for them and slide them in behind them. Ma and their sister are all amazed and dazzled, watching. Will, Robert, and Pa severing them as if they were all at a fancy place with waiters with linen napkins. "Pa, where on earth did you?" Ma replies stunned as she looked at her new tableware china.

"Oh, that?" Pa said as he just smiled then bends down close to her ear. "Theirs a full-moon out tonight dear, and I bought the stars too for later." And hums in her ear then watched her drop her knife on the plate. Then went back and sat down in his chair and winked at Grandma, while the boys served themselves and Pa cleared his throat.

"We would like to welcome back to our humble home, our most loved guests Grandma Stuart and EJ's little brother Danny. Welcome back to our farm, my you have as much fun and love as possible," and then looked at EJ. "Well as much or less mischief as possible," as he chuckles and they all laugh. Knowing trouble is always around the next bend unavoidable. You just deal with it when it gets here and hope for the best.

Ma looked at her boys all decked out at the table. She was as proud as a peacock when she looked at Pa across the way. She was truly happy. *But the question is how he managed to pull this off, how did he? And what did he have in store for her later?*

The night was not over yet, for Pa and the boys still had Ace's up their sleeves and rabbits under the hat, for there was magic in the air. Pa turned to Will and whispered, "Queen's boys."

Will nudged Robert whispered, "Queens." Pa stands, the boys stand, Robert went over to the record player and turned on the music. Then Pa walked over to, Ma and bows, "madam, May I have this dance?" And gently pulled out the chair for her so she can step out; Robert went over to Julie and followed suit and Will copied with Anna. Again their sister faces blushed red and quaked at the knees.

Grandma's eyes tear up and watched them dance as she thought of her husband and missed him very much. Danny and Sam looked at each other, "what's going on EJ? They have all gone mad." Pa comes over and gave Grandma a dance while each of them with their sister and Ma. Danny and Sam looked at each other again then turn to EJ. "They made them cry, they must be mad at them."

EJ whispered back almost laughing. "No Danny, Sam that's the point they are so happy they can't stand it."

"Really! You got to be kidding?" As they watched them.

Pa went over and picked up EJ and sat him on the couch so he could be a little more comfortable sees him sweating helped him off with the jacket and hangs up Ma Dinner vest leaving on his town pants she made him. He was fine as he whispered back. "Thanks, Pa I was getting hot."

Grandma went over sat next to him to admire Martha's handy work. EJ whispered, "Ma made them for me so I can have something to wear to go places," he said and smiled.

"I'm glad EJ," she said with a tear in her eye noticing how happy he is. EJ told her about Will, Robert, and Pa about the craftsmen's belt, how they going to teach him how to build things and work on a farm. Grandma could see the happiness in his face when he looked at Will and Robert when they smile back at him.

The music stopped as the next signal is given; "The Kings are coming." Pa whispered to Robert. Meaning let them down easy boys it's time for dessert. Pa brings the chairs into the living room as Robert ushers the ladies by the arm to their seats. Will, Pa brought out the apple cobbler with plates and passed them to the ladies. Will unfolded the napkins in their laps with a quick snap at the side then lying it gently in their lap. Then bowing, "dessert for madam." To each of the ladies then the gents each served themselves then returned for light conversation.

"Oh my Pa, when did you boys have time to do all this and how?" Ma asked as they just smile.

Robert nodded. "Pa helped me mostly, but I made the cobbler, EJ peeled the apples." The girls again tasting were flabbergasted.

"Pa, I didn't even know you could cook?" Julie said.

The boys laughed, Pa said. "So what did you think I did before I met your mother? Starved to death?" Pa said as he looked at girls and chuckled and boys laughed again.

Grandma wiped her mouth with her napkin. "All my boys know how to cook and are quite good in the kitchen. I consider it an important skill for them to learn because you never know when it comes in handy," she said smiling back at Wayne and winks.

"Grandma?" Anna asked setting down her fork for a moment

"Yes, Anna?" She replied taking another bite of this heavenly cobbler knowing she must get the recipe.

"How many boys do you have?" She asked lifted her fork to take another bite as she licked her lips almost moaning as she rolled her eyes because it tasted so good.

Grandma knowing where this was leading answered the question. "Three, Anna why?"

What's Behind the Looking Glass?

"Oh just curious that's all," giving Grandma a wink." Anna whispered to Julie "I think I know who that stranger was."

"No, she wouldn't?" But inside thought *he did resemble her and Danny.*"

Pa noticed that Danny and Sam are all tuckered out from shopping and tonight's festivities. "If you ladies will excuse me, I need to put these two young princes to bed. Please talk among yourselves why these other fine gentlemen clean and clear the table and finish the dishes." Their sister nearly swooned right off their seats onto the floor. As the boys got up and bowed themselves out and began clearing the table.

Grandma slapped her knee giving Martha a whisper and nudge, "I wouldn't get too used to it, but enjoy it while it last," she said.

"Yes Grandma," Ma giggled. "I am, every minute, my poor daughters just look at them."

"I know, I think that was the idea," Grandma replies as Robert came back and gathered the plates and napkins from them.

After everything was cleared and put away the adults in the room talked about the events of the day, Pa noticed the boys yawn and girl's eyes starting to drift, eyelids starting to drop. He nudged for the last card for the boys, "The Ace of Hearts."

Will, whispered to Robert, "Aces of Hearts." Pa and the boy all stand and bow in the front. "May I take your ladies' hand?" Robert too Julie and Will to Anna.

Pa too bows to Ma whispered in her ear. "You dear you get wait right here," he said.

Then Pa bow's again to Grandma. "I have prepared our bedroom for you Grandma so may I take your hand?" He asked.

"You may," Grandma replied almost giddy as she gets up and takes his arm and says goodnight as she walked towards the bedroom.

Robert and Will lead their sisters to their bedrooms doors, opening their door then bow. "Thank you for a pleasant evening and we wish you goodnight," and closed the door behind them. Walking down the hall to where the boys all share the same room and got ready for bed.

When Julie closed the door and sat on her bed she shook her head. "What has gotten into my brother's head? They have all gone mad today." Then turning around on the bed placed near her pillow, a token was placed; finding a small bottle of perfume and little wooden heart necklace with a note from her brothers.

"Dear sister Julie; I just wanted to tell you to thank you and how much we all love you, and how much you mean to each one of us.

Signed by Robert, Will, EJ, Sam."

That mere thought was too much for them to bear alone; she had to run into Anna's room find her and sit together on the bed wrapped her arms around each other and cried. They were so happy they could not stand it. Their brothers have given them the most wonderful night of their lives. Then returned to their rooms tired and emotionally exhausted from tonight's advents after placing a warm kiss on each of their brother's cheeks while they slept. Wayne returned to the living room where he left Martha still in a daze. He crossed the room." Wayne, what on earth are you up too?" She asked

"Did I ever tell you how pretty you look tonight dear?" As he walked across the room humming, then takes her by the hand then quickly twirls her into his arms. He then picked her up in his arms and whispered. "I promised you the moon and the stars dear and I brought them." All she could do was throw her arms around his neck as they go out the back door. "Madam your carriage waits." He said and gently sets her up on the wagon with a quick guide of the wrist they were off too excluded spot behind the barn.

Martha looked around seeing what he had done; shaking her head as it brought tears to her eyes. There was a private room just for them, a honeymoon suite for two. He had built it in his spare time a new four-posted bed draped with flowers. "It's beautiful Wayne," as she ran her fingers across the headboard.

"Martha I just wanted to show you how much I love you, dear," he said.

Martha was speechless for the first time that night, just stood there gazing at him then falls into his arms whispered. "Just hold me close to you," and cries into his arms. "Wayne I love you so much. Thanks, dear for tonight, for the meal, you filled my house. And stuffed my heart and I might need an extra one, I don't know if I'll ever have room for more." They retired for a lover's night encounter under the stars behind the barn. (*Sorry, the chickens were too busy to give details with Mr. Rooster.*)

With morning sun pecking over the mountains the rooster again was late for some reason. Grandma and the girls were busy in the kitchen. "Julie?" Grandma asked.

"Yes Grandma," she replied whipping up the pancake batter while Julie tended the sausage as Anne set the table.

"Will you go wake up your brothers and tell them breakfast is almost ready," she said.

Julie walked down the hall and opened the door to the boy's room and kindly said. "Good morning my dear brother's, breakfast will be ready in about 20 minutes." As she enters the room with gentle care with and soft nudge on the shoulder and kiss on the cheek. Her heart was not into teasing them this morning. Not after what they did to them last night. Instead, she wanted to wrap them all in her arms and hug them tight but would do that later when they were all awake. Will, Robert yawned seeing the morning sun already up over the mountain.

"Julie, did you say 20 minutes?" He asked.

"Yes Robert," she said.

"But we still have our chores to do," he replied.

"We already did them. Now hurry Grandmas waiting." Then she hurries and closed the door behind her.

"Will, did hear that? They must have gone bonkers," Robert said looking around the room.

"Danny and Sam already up again. "Those sneak sisters of ours when they knew darn well it was our turn to feed the animals."

"Well EJ looks like we better get down to breakfast. How you are feeling today? Your legs look a lot better," Robert said noticing the swelling had completely gone and the bruises were beginning to fade.

"Robert?" EJ asked setting up grimacing as his chest hurt and moved slowly as he laid on his other side.

"Yes EJ?" Robert said rolling up his sleeping bag and setting it next to Wills in the corner of the room.

"I want to try standing on my own." Will and Robert picked him up one on each side and he put his arms around their neck," ready one, two, three."

The door opened Grandma walked in. See EJ standing by himself and about to fall. "What do you think you are doing child? You are going tare those stitches!"

"But...Grandma, I wanted to see if I could do it?" He said.

"Put him down boys, he's not ready yet," shaking her head. "You silly, silly boy! Wayne just in time," she said watching them come through the back door and looked at Martha with a warm glow on her face. "This boy here was just trying to stand on his own," she said.

"EJ, what we're you thinking?" Ma said rushing over to him.

"Ma, I just wanted to see if I could that's all. Will, Robert would have supported me," he said.

What's Behind the Looking Glass?

Martha ran over to check his legs to makes sure he didn't tare anything then kissed his cheek then rubbed his hair, "I know EJ, just don't be in such hurry, it will take some time," she said helping back on to the bed and sits down beside him.

"Yes, Ma," EJ sounding disappointed.

"But your legs do look a lot better. Let's get you down to breakfast," she said. Wayne picked up EJ as EJ put his arms around Pa and carried him down to breakfast.

"Martha?" Grandma asked standing quietly beside her.

"Yes, Grandma?"

"Did you and Wayne have a good time last night?" She asked letting the curiosity get to her. Martha grinned as she blushed as she tells grandma what Wayne had done by building them a new four pollster bed out behind the barn as they slept in it under the stars. Her face flushed as she reconstructed the night in his arms as they made hot passionate love under the stars. Her knees quivered as she thought of his well-muscled body as he took her into his arms. She sighed heavily as she remembered it.

Chapter 17-2

* * * *

"Danny, hold still!" Anna said trying to hold Danny down long enough to put lotion on him as he tried to squirm away from her.

"But that tickles," he replies.

"Well if you are going be an Indian like your brothers, we need to put lotion on you so you don't sunburn."

"Grandma, Grandma! Help!" Grandma saw Anna chasing him with the bottle of lotion in her hand when she walked onto the porch and taking a seat in the swing on the side with her needlepoint that she was working on as she takes in the country air around the farm.

"What's the matter, Danny?" She asked setting to work as she placed the hoop on her knee as she picks the color of thread from her bag she stored the work in.

"They want me to put this on me before I be Indian," he replied trying to get away as Anna clamped down on his arm.

Grandma laughed as Anna came up to the porch where Danny is with Sam right behind her. "It's all right Danny. All Indians around here wear it. Sam's got his on, EJ, Will, and Robert does too. So if you want to be an Indian like the rest of them, you have to put it on too." Anna hands Grandma the lotion and she rubbed it on him. "Alright go on, go play," she said picking the hoop back up.

"Thanks, Grandma," Anna replied taking a seat next to her on the swing as she pushed her legs back and forth slowly barely touching the ground with her toes.

"Oh that was nothing, it was least I can do," as they watched

What's Behind the Looking Glass?

Sam and Danny play in the yard together and worked the needle through the pattern.

"Grandma?" She asked turning to face her as the swing stopped moving.

"Yes, Anna?"

"Do you remember that favor you owe me from yesterday?" She asked.

"Yes," Grandma said letting her legs swing underneath bring her hand up as she pulled the colored thread through the cloth and design and worked it back through in time as they swung on the swing.

"You really don't owe me it anymore, I figured that you were just trying to make it so we would all be surprised and we were. Thank you. But tell me one thing. Who was that stranger? Because it is bugging the heck out me, he looked a lot like Danny and resemble a lot like you and EJ," she said.

Grandma laughed. "Yes he did, didn't he? That was EJ's and Danny's Uncle Richard and yes one my three boys. But I still owe you that favor," as she winked. "After all you are the one that gave me the idea." She said, seeing EJ, Will, and Robert coming out on to the porch. Nodded to the boys as Pa carried a large potato sack tide with little blocks of wood inside.

"Ok Pa I am ready," EJ said.

"Alright, boys just sit him down over there in the shade next to the house." Pa brought over a pile of wooden blocks and some sandpaper and small carving knife with wooden handle and then sets it on the small table. "Will, Robert go ahead and get started with the move while I show EJ his task," he said.

"Yes, Pa."

Pa picked up a completed block. "EJ? Your job is to turn these into wooden blocks," Pa said pointing to the massive pile around him." into this." EJ looked all the different rough, sizes shapes, with nothing on them except the letters drawn in ink and the huge pile. His eyes nearly fell right out of his head. Then Pa picked up a piece of sandpaper and showed him how to sand each of the blocks. Taking a block and showed him how too measure it so its same size as one of the completed ones. Pa picked up the small chisel and showed him how to handle it and then to indent the letters into the blocks and how to use the carving knife.

Pa took the sandpaper and re-sanded the edges of the letters, "ok EJ, now you try it." And Pa watched him do a block and then examined all four sides. "Humm not bad, not bad at all. EJ it looks like you are going to make a fine helper." and rubbed his hair. "I'll be back to check on your progress in a while, that should keep you busy." As he smiles at the pile blocks all around him and rubbed his head again.

"Yes Pa, but Pa who are or what are these blocks for?" EJ asked.

"EJ that's a surprise son, and I think you're going to like, now get to work."

"Yes Pa," EJ began his work by picking up a block and starts sanding the edges.

Pa laid his hand on EJ shoulder to instill confidence before walking back into the house. "See you in a while EJ," and walked away.

EJ busy examined the unfinished blocks piled around him lets out a puff of air, whispered, to himself. "What have I got myself into?" Looking towards the barn he could see Will and Robert dismantling the new bed as they loaded it onto the wagon to bring into the house. "Strange I would put it on the pickup," he said and shook his head "I'll have to ask why they did that."

EJ picked up a block and studies it, getting engrossed in his work with his mind busy thinking and watching his work and what's going on the farm. His grandmother sat beside him on the porch, watching him for a couple of minutes. She smiles then slowly, says. "EJ." EJ jumps with a start

"Grandma, I… I didn't see you," he said.

"I know dear," then they both laugh." I used to do that to your grandpa all the time when he got busy, he would tune everything else out too. Anyway I thought," she said as she pulled out her needled point. "This would be a good time for me and you to have that talk. Since Danny's over there playing with Sam and everyone else is busy doing their thing and it's just us out here, unless of course, you have something else you rather do," she asked.

Grandma picked up the needle and thread and starts to thread through the design that she is working on again; EJ thinking about it for a minute. "All right… so what do want to talk about Grandma?" EJ placed the wooden block next to the completed one checking the size to see if it was the same then determining it was and picked up the little wood chisel and started to indent the letters on the block.

"EJ I want to hear your side of the story, what's been going on and how you received all those wounds?" Without looking up from her needlepoint and kept her task at hand. EJ dropped the block and his mouth goes dry, his lips begin to tremble. Grandma could see EJ hands shake just a little, but the fear was evident in his eyes. She squeezed in a little closer next to EJ and put her arms around him and laid his head against her shoulder as she brushed his hair. "EJ, it's alright son, it's alright," Wayne and Martha seeing EJ with Grandma just quietly sat closely by.

EJ slowly looked up with tears in his eyes and nods and whispered. "Grandma they hurt me real bad this time." He said as he looked around the farm. "I've decided for now I never want to go back… I can't go back," EJ cries into her shoulders and she wiped her eyes.

She whispered. "I know they did, but what did they do? You need to tell me. Can you lest try for Danny?" EJ looked over where Danny and Sam are playing then whispered in a choked voice.

"I'll try Grandma," he said.

Grandma brushed his hair to calm him and whispers to him. "Your Ma and your Pa are just over there, can they hear it too?"

EJ lifted his head and gave a little nod. Feelings of safety with Pa and loving care of Ma being nearby he whispered. "Yes Grandma," he said.

Pa and Ma came closer and Pa moved the pile of blocks so they all could fit in around him. And Ma takes EJ's hand with other wiped the tears from his eyes. "We are here for you son," Pa said and puts his hand on his shoulder. EJ nodded his head then slowly he tells them all that has happened to him that he could remember, all the fights that weren't fights, being tied up with chains and beaten, everything including things that happened in last foster homes and before, and being caged outside alone in the cold.

How they even put him somewhere like a prison but wasn't. It was for kids his age, with rooms that you could not get out of at night. It was cold and dark and smelled bad, felt horrible. After he got it all out he just buried his face into his Grandma's shoulder and cried, "That's why Grandma I'm never going back, I can't, I won't live through that again. I was hoping you would help me and save Danny from going through that too before its too late. I tried to get him out, but I couldn't," EJ said gasping with tears.

Martha, Grandma with tears streaming down their cheeks sat silently next to EJ; trying to calm him and compose themselves. At the same time, anger was building inside Grandma and Wayne for what they have done to this little boy. But this, not the time to deal with it, Grandma looked up and whispered, "Wayne sounds like me and you a have problem we need to deal with," she said.

Wayne rubbed his chin, "what did you have in mind Grandma?" He asked.

"Not sure yet," she replied. EJ calmed down a little bit more as he got himself together getting it all out in the open actually made him feel a lot better. "Now then does that feel better to get that off your chest?" She asked.

"Yes Grandma," he replied.

"Good let's get you cleaned up and I believe lunch is almost ready so let's get you inside." She said as she kissed his cheek and let Wayne pick him up and bring him back into the house for lunch as she thought what she needs to do.

Chapter 17-3

* * * *

Pa picked up EJ and sat him on the couch and Martha placed some pillows behind his back and brings him his tray with some sandwiches and some more broth to drink and rubbed his hair and bends down kisses his forehead.

"Wayne?" Grandma called from down the hall as she watched the boys moving furniture from the bedroom to the next as they make room for her and Danny on more permanent bases, for whenever she decided to stay. She tried to tell them there was no need to fuss, but Martha insisted on it and Wayne refused to argue the point any further.

"Yes, Grandma?" He said leaning against the wall as she and he watched the boys and their daughters work together as they helped make the beds with fresh clean sheets and light quilts for the beds.

Grandma said as they both looked at EJ from around the corner. "I think it time you and I paid a visit of our own to his parent's house, you too Martha." Seeing her come around the corner and join them as they watched them work. "I would like you to come too. I want them to see what good parents you are for EJ and so you can set their minds at ease. Plus at the same time, I want to make it clear that they are treading on very thin ice and not too step within fifty-feet of him without your permission. That way… when he is able to get around he can without having to worry about them or Danny, because soon Danny and his sisters will be returning home to them," she replied.

They looked at her with fear in their eyes. "I know, I know, I don't like it either, but the law is the law according to the State child services. Don't worry, EJ still safe, they won't touch him. Doc and I have taken care of it so far." Martha, Wayne let out a sigh of relief as they looked at EJ on the couch eating his lunch.

What's Behind the Looking Glass?

"Grandma?" Martha asked.

"Yes, Martha?"

"How long do we have before we have to be concerned?" She asked.

"Oh at least," she said as she looked at EJ. "Maybe 1 maybe 2 years if we are lucky," hating the very thought of these children being returned to them because of some useless laws and guidelines. She mumbled. "*They are more on the parent's side not having the children's best interest. Why can't they see that?*" As she gritted her teeth in anger.

"Then what?" Martha asked just the mere thought of any child living in those conditions scared her senseless.

Grandma shrugged her shoulders. "I don't know," they wouldn't give me a time frame. It depends, when they feel that he's ready to go home, we don't have a choice," she said.

"Pa?" Robert asked walking towards them in the hall.

"Yes, Robert?" Pa turned his head towards him keeping the anger out of his voice.

"The wagons loaded we are ready to bring in the bed."

"Good, have you boys moved the other one down the hall yet?" He asked

"Yes Pa, everything's done except for this one and our sisters are just finishing up making up the beds and last of the touch-ups."

"Alright then, let's bring it in then and set it up, and then you boys can have some lunch and rest for a while."

"Yes Pa." and walked away leaving to do what his Pa told him to do, after all, it none of his business on what they are talking about. But he caught snippets of Danny having to returning home, which made his blood boil all the same…

Grandma watched the boys set up the new bed in the bedroom and admired Wayne's craftsmanship. "Wayne, this is a beautiful bed, I must say," she said.

"Thanks, Grandma. So Grandma, when did you want to pay them this little visit?" Wayne asked as she admired his hard work.

"Oh I was thinking about today would be fine. Since I am already here and it is fresh on my mind and I don't think I'll be able to sleep until I had my say. Other than sit and stew looking at Danny and EJ all day now knowing what has taken place, apparently I have been left in the dark far too long. Some of it I knew because I had to rescue him several times over the years, but apparently not everything and still think there is more he is not telling us. Plus thinking what in tarnation are those no-good parents doing right now? Because so far they haven't done one thing that courts and Doctor Hatfield have asked them to do."

Pa and rubbed his hands. "Then we have to come home and chop some more firewood out by the barn. Because I'm also steaming as well, just thinking about it," he said.

Martha then said well, "I hope you guys are going to be hungry tonight because I'll be cooking up a storm, after we get back," as they turned and watched EJ finish his lunch.

"Julie, Robert?" Ma called.

"Yes, Ma?" They replied.

"You two mind watching the farm for a while. Why Pa and Grandma and I go somewhere? We will be back in a few minutes. Just keep on eye on Danny and Sam for us will be back soon as we can," she said.

"Oh, Robert?" Pa called before he left.

"Yes, Pa?"

"I am expecting the shipment of lumber today if it comes while

What's Behind the Looking Glass?

I am gone just start unloading it by the back of the house," he said.

"Yes Pa," he said as he watched the three adults go out the door.

"Robert?" EJ asked.

"Yes EJ?"

"Where are they going?" Turned to see Pa and Ma leave with Grandma.

"They said they had to take care of something and would back in a few minutes."

"Did they say where?" EJ asked, but he could guess that it was mostly like they were going to confront his parents. He cringed knowing that all that was going to do was make them even angrier at him and Danny.

"No, but don't worry EJ, we won't let anything happen to you, I am here Will's over there. Julie and Anna, Danny and Sam are too."

"I know Robert, Thanks."

"Good because they skin us all alive if you decided to just to leave." Not that he could get far even if he tried too.

* * *

Grandma pulled up to the driveway of EJ's house and they knocked on the door. His Dad opened the door and growled as he eyed Mr. and Mrs. Downing the very two people he wanted to kill for making his life a living hell, and then there was his mother, who refuses to stay out of his business. "Hello Jim," she said ignoring the hateful stares and the angry growl. "I thought it was time we talked. May we please come in?" His mother said. Jim sighs knowing it was best not stir the pot anymore than necessary, but something had to be done and he wasn't going to take any more crap from them or anyone when they did nothing wrong in the first place, he opened the door lets them in. "Where's your wife Jim?" She asked.

"In the bedroom, I'll get her," he said as Grandma grabbed some chairs for Wayne and Martha to sit down. Jim went down the hall where his wife is and knocked on the door.

"What do you want now Jim?" She asked from the other side of the door.

"We have company at the door."

"Who is it?" She asked.

"It's my mother and she brought "those people" from that farm," he said snarling the word those people. His fist tightened as he wanted to do more than just punch Mr. Downing in the face, he wanted revenge, he wanted him to pay for embarrassing him for the lies circulating around town about him and his wife.

"She what? Here? Now? She brought them here?"

"Yes, dear."

"What do they want?" She asked.

"I didn't ask. Most likely because of that brat of yours spreading more lies about us."

"Jim I swear, do I have to do everything myself? Alright, I am coming," she said. Jim walked back up to the living room and sat on the couch and waited for his wife to join him.

Wayne and Martha trying very hard not too stare at him and let the anger inside them burn, knowing what they have done to EJ and Danny. It breaks their hearts at the same time thinking of them and their kids and what would happen if their kids were missing. How could they live with themselves? It was if a giant vacuum could suck out the life in a room for them. Yet here you couldn't feel it in this home or when they looked at EJ's father across from them, it was if nothing was even missing.

Slowly EJ's mothers entered the room and gave them at least a courtesy nod before sitting down, but not to their grandmother, she got a cold hard stare. Grandma understood and paid it no mind. "We won't keep you long Jim and you too Linda, I thought it was time you should meet and get acquainted, and we needed too set some ground rules," Grandma said.

"Ground rules? I have just about had enough of this from you!" Linda replied letting the anger boil over into her voice as she growled angrily. Jim reached for his belt, by instinct before realizing it. Knowing if he did so in front of his mother, she'd have the cops here in a matter of minutes. Who's to say they are not outside waiting for him to do it; like last time, he quickly removed his hand and clenched them into a fist.

"Linda hush...! I am trying very hard to be polite, we all are. I want you to know we have heard everything.... seen, all we need to see from EJ regarding this." Linda', Jim's face nearly turned white. "That's right, he has told us the whole story to last detail he can remember. Now then least you can do is listen too what we have to say and then will leave you alone." Grandma said as she looked down the hall, "Jim I see you got that window replaced, that's nice." Jim nodded his head. "That's good because I wouldn't want my grandson Danny too freeze this winter when he comes home."

Linda slowly composes herself. "Did you say they are coming home?" She asked.

"Yes dear," Danny, Peggy, and Dona will be coming home before school starts this fall," she replied not happy about it.

"What about Eric?" She asked. She refused to use that horrid name his Grandmother and them uses.

"No dear, he's not coming back. That's what we want to talk to you about." Linda stopped smiling and glared at Grandma then at Wayne and Martha sitting across from her.

"Why not?" She asks with anger in her voice nearly coming off the couch to strangle her. The very thought of her hands squeezing the life out of her filled her with joy as she imagined her limp dead body falling to the floor. But there would be witnesses and this man across from her scared her to death as she tried to control her fear when she looked into his burning cold eyes.

She knew she would lose the fight, but perhaps she could get Jim's mother alone. *Yes, she thought alone... long enough to kill her and stop the words echoing in her head. It was her fault; she took them away from her.* The blood pounded hard in her chest just with the thought of death and revenge that would be so sweet. *Nobody would miss a little old lady like her*, as a growl left her throat.

Grandma Stuart continued as she set calmly back into the chair as she looked into Linda's cold dead eyes that burned with anger as she heard the low growl when she looked at her. Jim, on the other hand, seemed bored and cared less to what she had to say. "For several reasons, one: he still badly hurt, but he is mending quite well. He did give us quite a scare a few days ago, but he is doing much better now."

"The second reason is," she said as she looked at EJ's father; "I think you know what that is so we won't bring it up. The third reason is he is happy where he is and I am not or anyone else going to take that away from him," as she glares back at both them. "So to keep him happy, there are going be some ground rules and you are going to follow them or it's going to get very messy and you know I can do it. Right?" She waited for them to answer.

"Yes, mother," Jim replied with a growl of his own. As she looked at her son then looked at Linda and waited for her to answer.

"All right Grandma," she said as each word sounded punctuated and angered.

"You can call me Grandma Stuart," she replied with a growl of her own as she glared back just as hard. She knew it was time to leave before this woman decided to come unglued and cause a scene, that would make her regret the other choices she would make and they would never see their children again regardless of the law. She would move them so far they'd never find them. Most likely send her to prison for it, but it would be worth it. "*My late husband would do no less,*" standing her ground.

What's Behind the Looking Glass?

"Yes, Grandma Stuart." She said with a frown as the anger inside her burns.

"That's better," Grandma said. "This is Wayne Downing and his wife Martha Downing. They are the ones taking care of EJ. You will treat them with respect and common curtsy when you see them. Because one of the requirements will be for you to drop off Danny at their home or I should say farm. At least every other weekend so Danny and EJ can spend time together. And if EJ wants to see you, which he may not, that's his choice," she replied.

"Other than that, we don't want you to come anywhere near him, just leave him alone. You've done enough to him, not just to him either. I will have my eye on him and the other children for now on. A very close eye… and if I see one mark on them or hint of anything wrong," as Grandma shook her fingers "I'll. Do more then remove them temporally from your care."… Grandma looked at Wayne and Martha sits back down, tried to calm her self.

Martha looked at Linda trying very hard to keep the anger out of her voice said as polite as she could. "I promise to take real good care of him," as Martha looked at Wayne. "And already do love him like he was our own son. So you have nothing to worry about and little Danny too."

Wayne looked at EJ's father he controlled his anger which was not easy after seeing and hearing all the things they have put him through. "You have quite the boy, I am very proud of him like he was my own son and Danny too." Jim doesn't say anything just looked away like it didn't matter what he thought. Wayne could feel the coldness in his eyes and almost felt sorry for him, but he could tell by the look and feel of Jim's presence alone that he just did not care what he said about his boys.

It frightens him that this man in front of him could be so cold, showing no compassion. He was more than ready to leave and go where he could feel the love of his own family around him. Now realizing this person had no regrets of the things he had done to his boys, it brought tears to his eyes how a man who was supposed to be father could be like this. "Well Martha we need to get back Will,

Robert, EJ and I, we got lumber to get unload for their rooms." As they stood up getting ready to leave with one hand on the doorknob he turned before opening the door. "Nice meeting you folks," and three walked out of the room and headed back to the farm.

* * *

Jim followed them and watched them leave making sure they didn't stay around too spy on them and his wife or even poke their noses into their business, then walked back into the house after making sure there were no cops around like last time. Linda screeches, "oh that woman... Jim your mother has really made a mess of things. First, she dangles a carrot in front of your nose then pulls it away. Oh, I hate her, if she could have just left things alone. We wouldn't be in this mess.

"Yes dear, I know! Least you get something out of it." Closing the door behind him as her voice came up another octave that made his ears cringe and put shivers down his spine.

"What Jim? What do I get out of it?" She asked.

"Your daughters will be home and Danny," he replied turning around to face her letting the anger boil inside as he clenched his fist wanting very much to strangle her and his mother for putting him in this situation in the first place and those damn neighbors. *He did nothing wrong, nothing. In fact, he should have done more* fingering the belt on his waist.

"Oh yes, that will be nice, except you are forgetting something. Everyone will be watching every move we make. We will be living in a glass house with her eyes bearing down on us all the time. I ask you, Jim, how are we going to smooth out those bad genes with her watching and everyone else? And who knows what else they have been added on since they been away.

"That's not the worst part. Oh no! Not by a long shot! She expects me to let those people raise Eric as if he were their own son already, by leaving him alone. By setting ground rules like the State

What's Behind the Looking Glass?

Foster Care System for such a worthless child and their damn rules that govern them. The only difference is she and Eric chose the family he would be placed in and the rest of us is supposed to go along with it, right under our nose. Because you couldn't find him and let him get away with it." She takes a deep breath and stumps her feet as she walked back down the hall to her room pushing the door open with a hard push putting a doorknob dent in the wall and screams.

"Then she expects me to deliver Danny to them as well. Oh, that burns me to the core, Jim. You tell me at least we get something out of it; you are as crazy as she is. Let me know when that something gets here." Linda slams the bedroom door yells. "Leave me alone."

Chapter 18

"Well Wayne, that went fairly well," Grandma said glancing in the mirror as Wayne stretches out in the back seat of her car where his long legs wouldn't feel so cramped as Martha sits up front.

Martha looked at Grandma little puzzled "Grandma?" She asked.

"Yes, Martha?"

"How do you figure that? I've never seen two people in my life that had more warmth than a snow pea. As if I was to build a snowman in that house I very much doubt it could ever melt," she said.

"Yes Martha I know, I am a little worried about that too and for Danny and his sisters. But the state law says they have to be returned to their parents since they can't find anything wrong with the other children according to their cases file on hand. And the girls won't say anything about it. Danny is too young to understand what's going on. EJ is the only one who's bad enough and traumatized the worst and has been in out of the system so much he becoming a yoyo or to them a troubled teen and this isn't the first time he has runaway do to his father's temper or his mother's neglect. We can keep him safe from that for a while at least, but there's a limit."

Wayne turned to look at Martha who is very close to tears reaching over and taking her hand as he leans against the seat. "Grandma?" he asked.

"Yes, Wayne?"

"Can we ask you something? Suppose," taking Martha's hand in his. "If we decided we... after awhile we want to... How do we do this? Say this?" Wayne said stumbling to find the right words.

What's Behind the Looking Glass?

"Say what Wayne?"

"You know we... already love EJ like he is our own son... Suppose," He took another look at Martha as their eyes meet, squeezing her hand. "We want to make it so he is our son, so nobody could take him away," he asked.

Martha looked at Wayne with tears in her eyes whispers..."Yes Grandma, how do we?" She replied.

Grandma pulled over the car for a minute to the side of the road. They could see the farm just up ahead. She turned to face Wayne and Martha. "Do you really want to do this?" she asked.

Martha and Wayne turned to one another and nodded yes..."Yes Grandma we do," they replied.

"It could take a while and it may be difficult getting him away from them, after all. I doubt they would be willing to put him up for adoption easily after this. And there could be lots of red tape and a lot of hoops to go through. I can't promise you anything, but there might be a chance, a small one if you are really willing," Grandma replied.

"Grandma, if we don't at least try, will lose him then where will he be?" Martha said.

"I know that's why you can't tell him. You don't want you to get his hopes up or it will. I'm afraid, I don't want to think about what would happen," she said.

"Can we least give him some hope?" She asked.

Grandma thinks about it for a moment, "I did make EJ a promise that he could make his own decision what he wanted to do. So if you ask him, if he wants to do it and he knows what the stakes are. Maybe it will be easier maybe it won't. I can't promise you anything, but I'll do my best...Wayne looks like your lumber has arrived, guess I better get you back. I'll drop you guys off and stop at the Courthouse and pick up the paperwork so you can at least start and have a talk with Judge Parker, he's a close friend of mine and we go back a ways. Maybe he will do me another solid for old time's sake… Then when I get back I'll call Richard to stop by with his birth certificate, I have a copy of it at home and some of his pictures you might like to see. By the way, I would keep it to yourselves and don't tell his parents, they might try to ruin everything. Sometimes they don't know when to leave things well enough alone as you already know."

"Thanks, Grandma, we'll keep that in mind," they said.

"No thank you." She said and wiped the tears out of her eyes with the back of her sleeve as she dropped them off at the farm and headed back up the road.

"Pa, your back, where is Grandma going now?" Robert asked as he watched her drive up the road in a hurry.

"She had a last-minute errand to run that's all, she'll be back," Pa said.

"Is everything ok?" Robert asked watching his Ma wiping tears from her eyes.

"Yes she's fine, we had some thing's we need to discuss that's all," Pa replied.

Robert looked puzzled wondered if this had to do with EJ and Danny returning home, but didn't say anything. He needed to put his thoughts together before he addressed it. After all, he was eases dropping on private matters but concerned him never the less. "Well we are just about finished with unloading the lumber and EJ's over by the side of the house and the boys are down for their nap," he said.

"Thanks, Robert go ahead and finish up," Pa said.

Wayne and Martha walked over to where EJ was. "Hi Ma, hi Pa, I am still here, I didn't go anywhere," he said.

What's Behind the Looking Glass?

Pa rubbed his hair and chuckled. "I am glad son because we would have torn this county apart looking for yea then skin yea live when we found you," he said

Ma bent down and kissed his forehead. "That's because you know this where you belong, isn't it EJ?" She asked. She wasn't sure what name to use now after his mother called him Eric, but for now, that wasn't important.

"Yes Ma, plus Will and Robert made sure I didn't move a muscle and Julie and Anna checked on me every five minutes just to make sure," as he laughs. "Where's Grandma?" He asked.

"Oh she had to go to town for something and will be back in a minute," Ma said.

Pa sat next to him on the ground as Ma took a seat on the other side taking EJ's hand and nodded to Pa to go ahead and ask him as she dried her eyes with the back of her other hand. "EJ can we talk to you about something for minute… Now we want you to know we love you like you were our own son, even thou you haven't been here more than few weeks, but that doesn't matter to us or to the rest of the family. This is your decision and a hard one and I can't promise you anything and we will support whatever choice you make. And so will your Grandma. In fact, that's where she has gone so if you decide to." Pa said as they put their arms around him. "We'd like this be your home son so you never have to worry about not being safe again. Do you know what that means EJ?"

EJ looked up at Pa and Ma with tears in his eyes. "Yes, Pa I do. What about Danny?" He asked.

Ma turned his chin so she could look in his eyes so he knew they meant what they said. "That's one thing we can't do anything about. The law won't let us touch him. He has to go home soon, but your Grandma is going to watch him closely and so are we," Ma replied.

"How Ma?" EJ asked feeling nervous and a little bit scared of Danny going back home. The home he has tried so hard not to go back to.

Ma looked deep into his tearful eyes and took her fingers and wiped his tears away and the fear that held them. She only hoped he wouldn't run away and take Danny with him as soon as he was healed enough to do so. "We paid a visit to your parents today and set some ground rules they have to follow. When Danny is returned to them, he will visit; and spend weekends here on the farm with us. That's best we can do, your Grandmas done everything in her power to keep you and Danny safe." Ma said with as much love as she can to alleviate his fears.

"It's your decision you'll be with us for a long time, they say at least 1 maybe 2 years before we have anything too worry about and most like take that long for the paperwork. There's a lot of red tape and hoop's to go through providing if that's what you want to do. So think about it, don't give us your answer until you are really, really sure son, but for right now we will start it ok?" Ma said.

EJ nodded his head and gave them a big hug and whispered." Thanks, Pa, thanks, Ma," with tears in his eyes and a choked voice.

"Your welcome son," Pa said as rubbed his hair and Ma kissed him on the head.

Ma and Pa leaving EJ alone walked into the house hand in hand seeing Danny and Sam laying side by asleep on the quilt in the living room. It brings tears to her eyes knowing theirs nothing she could do for him, but least there might be hope for EJ and she would keep a close eye on his brother while he was here and provide as much love as she could to both the boys while they were here no matter how long. "*If she had to they would pick up and move to her father's milk farm in Canada if it would keep these boys safe and Damn the law?*" Julie asked coming from inside the kitchen as she sets the yeast aside for the rolls for dinner.

"Yes, Julie."

What's Behind the Looking Glass?

"Where's Grandma?"

"She had to run up to town for something. Oh, here she comes now," as she watched her pull into the farm.

"Did you have any problems?" Wayne asked as he opened the door for her and stepped aside to let her in.

"No, I have them right here Wayne, Martha. Got some good news and some bad news… All right let's sit down. Julie dear, Grandmas going need a strong cup of tea and think your Ma might and would like one too," she said taking a seat at the table as she set down the papers she'd gotten from the courthouse from Santaquin in town.

"Yes, Grandma." Removing the kettle from the stove and poured two hot cups of tea for them as she tried to listen in on the conversation after speaking with Robert her mind could not sit still without knowing the outcome of her two new brothers.

"Grandma we already talked to EJ about it," Martha said taking a seat across from Wayne.

Grandma looks at both like they lost their marbles, "you did what?"

"You said it was his decision and we also told him about Danny and about visiting his parents," Martha said. Grandma's eyes nearly fell right out of her head.

"Grandma here's your tea." Julie handed her a cup, placing the other on the table towards her Ma.

"Thanks, Julie," Grandma said nearly gulping it down. "How did he take the news?" She asked after a couple more gulps.

"He was disappointed, especially about what's going to happen to Danny, but he felt a little better after we told him he will be visiting Danny," as they both looked at them sleeping. "He understood and was willing, said we could start the paperwork for now," Martha said.

"I just hope we're not setting him up for a big storm because you are in for quite a rough ride. I kinda of wished you would have waited to tell him when I got back." Grandma sighed, "Well, the damage has been done. Nothing to do but hope for the best," she said taking another sip.

"Now as I was saying there is some good news and some bad news. The bad news it's going to take longer than I would have liked and more time for them to process the paperwork than I would hope due too… First, you have to become foster parents. Meaning you two must qualify in front of state board and a judge and found worthy of becoming good parents.

"That's the easy part since Judge Park is a friend of mine and was willing to put a rush on the procedures himself and get Doc Hatfield to agree and sign the documents needed. The problem is just time-consuming and the State Government who is the wildcard have to like you that's all. Second, after they find you can handle the job as foster parents for a period of time then you can process the paperwork for adoption. So, yes it can be done," she said.

"So what's the bad news Grandma?" Martha asked taking a sip of tea and taking Wayne's hand from across the table.

"This is the part you are going to hate, so is EJ. He has to make or at least to try visitation with his parents, both parents. Its how the state foster care system works they have visitation rights too. You control the guardianship of him, but they have the right to visit him, supervised of course until no longer deemed necessary, she said. "You and I may not like the law, but we must abide by it." *"Worse comes to worst, she'd send them out of this forsaken state altogether and the law be damned.*

"You have got to be kidding? After what they just did too him… They expect us to just let them visit him so they can frighten him some more or give them a chance to beat up on him again, while we are not watching. What kind of government do we have? If they could see what he has already gone through already, I bet they would leave him alone. I just don't understand it!" Martha said sounding angry.

What's Behind the Looking Glass?

"I know Martha, but it is his only chance, It's up to you both and EJ of course. Either way, he'll have two years with you unless you want him to go now. It's that or State will place him somewhere else to make it easier on you," she said.

"No Grandma! He's not leaving this house, how could you even think that?" Martha said in tears as she replied.

Grandma smiles, "I didn't dear, that's why the Doc and I filed the papers for you because we knew what your answer would be." Grandma looked at Martha and Wayne straight in the eye. "You see Grandma was right, now come give me a hug and wipe those tears dears." Martha and Wayne reached over gave her a hug, she patted them both on the back and Martha wiped her tears. "Alright, I need to call Richard, Martha mind if he stays for dinner?" She asked.

"No, not at all," Martha said as she wiped the tears with the back of her hand.

Wayne laughed. "Looks like we are going to need a bigger table at the rate our little family is growing and maybe a bigger house," he said as they all laughed. Getting up from the table as everyone slides their chairs in. Julie calmly wiped her tears as grandma came up beside her and kissed her on the cheek.

"Will?" Pa calls outside.

"Yes, Pa?" He said coming around the corner of the house as he finished speaking or rather argued with Will on what's happening, neither of them liked the idea of Danny or EJ leaving and contemplated their own plans to stop it as Pa came round the corner of the house hoping to hear some news regarding this.

"Can you go out to the barn and bring in the second and third leaf in for the table?"

"Yes Pa, why Pa?" He asked.

"Looks like we got more family coming to dinner," he said and went to help EJ put his things away.

Martha was true to her word and was baking up a storm in the kitchen to release some of that frustration of the day. Pa went out to where EJ was and to check on his work. Pa picked up a few of the blocks and examined a few of them and stacked them in a pile of completed work. "EJ looks real good son."

"Thanks, Pa… Pa did you mean what you said earlier about me staying here and not having to worry about ever going back?" He asked.

"Yes EJ, we meant every word. We would never lie to you son and I want you to know upfront EJ." Pa said as he looked him straight in the eye. "They tell me it's going to be hard and going to take a long time and going be very difficult for all of us, especially for you. But for right now the most important thing is. I want you to know is that we love you. This is your home and you are not going anywhere and you are safe. Whether if you choose to be a Downing or Stuart makes no deference son, I'll love you just the same." He said putting his arm around him.

"So does your Ma and your brothers Robert, Will, Sam and your little brother Danny. And I'm pretty sure your Grandma in there loves you too because of she's the one that helped us do all of this. Then, of course, you have your two sisters Julie and Anna that just want to hug stuffing out you, because think your so cute when you blush," he said.

"I know Pa that's what makes me worried," he said.

"But they love you too. So let's put this work away and get you back inside and get you cleaned up because I understand we have company coming," he said placing the unfinished blocks back into the sack and the unfinished ones in a wooden box with his tools for later.

"Who Pa?"

"Just your Uncle Richard, that's all."

"Pa at this rate you are going to need a bigger house."

What's Behind the Looking Glass?

"I know son!" Pa said as he picked up EJ and brought him inside and sets him on the couch.

Ma turned to Will and Robert. "Will, Robert take EJ and get him cleaned up and you boys get cleaned up as well. The girls and I have some nice clothes for you in your room that we brought in from town for school. EJ well just have to wear the one I made for him for right now but is better then what he got on."

"Yes Ma," the boys said.

"Julie is Anna just about done with Sam and Danny. I want them to look nice when he gets here?" She asked.

"I'll go check," Julie replied.

"Well, Grandma is he on his way?" Martha asked seeing her hang up the phone as she worked on dinner in the kitchen.

"Yes dear, his on his way and bring everything." As she walked over to the sink and washed her hands to lend Martha and Julie a hand fixing dinner, she hated it when she couldn't help and sit and watch. Even though they tried to tell her to sit and relax and remind her she is there guest. But grandma would never hear of it.

"Good. I was thinking he might as well just stay the night instead of driving all the way back after dinner," she said.

Grandma looked at her as if she has got bees for brains. "Martha dear, where on earth are you going too put him? On the roof?" She asked.

"Don't be silly Grandma, we have plenty of room," she said. Checking the turkey and cooling the rolls and the fresh apple pies on the counter.

Grandma shook her head then turned to Wayne. "Wayne your wife is as stubborn as you are I believe?" She said as she helped set the table.

"Why's that Grandma?" He asked placing the table extra leaf as he extends the table nearly bumping into the wall as his dining room gets smaller.

"Your house is busting at the seams and she still thinks there's plenty of room for one more," she said shaking her head.

Pa looked around the room. "Grandma she right," and laughed. "And that's why we love her so. The more the merrier, after all, we still have the barn to fill and I can always set up the tepee."

"I don't think Richard would like the barn or the tepee, he wouldn't make very good Indian." She said as she laughed at the mere thought of her son Richard wearing a loincloth and running around the farm with the rest of them. Made her chuckle inside, but it did give her time to pause wondering if that's not such a bad idea. He could use a little fun in his life and that would free her to spend time with her granddaughters before they returned home.

Martha turned to Grandma. "He won't be sleeping in the barn either, not as long as I have a nice comfortable couch or a cot or a spare mattress in the house. Don't worry Grandma, we'll make do after all he's family now," she said as she looked straight at Wayne with an icy cold stare.

Wayne could see she was serious and rubbed his chin. "Grandma, if she says he staying don't argue, just plan on him staying, I'll go find the mattress or the cot." Then walked over to his wife and whispered in her ear. "Yes dear, you are always right. There is always room for one more," he said and kissed her and headed on down the hall.

Richard arrived at the Downing Farm. First thoughts go through his mind. Indians and farmers, "This family has gone nuts." He said to himself expecting to find the tepee in the middle of the yard and find all the boys running around dressed as Indians. At least according to what his mother has told him the last time and what Danny came home wearing.

Richard looked for the tepee as he pulled into the farm. "So far looks like a normal farm," he breathes softly to himself. He sees his mother's car in the yard. "Must be the right place?" He said as he scratched his head.

Wayne came out of the house to greet him with his mother at his side. "Richard this is Wayne Downing." His mother said as she introduces him as they shake hands. Richard noticing how tall and big he was, perhaps the size of Paul and his blue mule. He could envision this man swing a huge Axe and felling a tree with one strike. Yet he did not fear him as his eyes held something that reminded him of his father when he looked at him.

Richard had his fathers build and was considered tall compared to his mother reaching five-feet five inches and lengthy, for some reason he was able to keep his dark brown hair from balding unlike his father and two bothers. Who are now partly bald in the center and began losing their hair before age of twenty. Blue-eyed and hard straight nose with high cheekbones like his mother, Richard could be considered man-made by hard-living, not by education or status, but neither are his brothers. He did not leave home like his older brothers, remained at home to stay close so he could care for his mother after his father died, yet he had regrets that he would never have a life like his older brother Steve.

Instead tied himself to the house very seldom did go out like most boys his age and date young girls or go to spring or summer dances. Instead, he stayed at home either reading a book on cold nights or took care of the house and the yard while his mother was away visiting old friends. Sometimes he felt he was wasting away as others were out enjoying life as he tinkers around the home and still feels him with grief every time he sees pictures of his father staring back him wondering if he was proud of the choices he has made but that was before he became a young farmer boy and liked it. Life will never be the same for him.

"Finally we meet, at last, welcome to our farm, here let me help you with this," Wayne said grabbing a couple of books and a package from the back seat of his car.

"Don't you think I need to lock the car first before we go inside?" Richard asked.

"What for Richard? Oh, that's right. You are from the city. If it makes you feel comfortable go ahead, but out here there's not a house or another farm for 10 maybe 20 miles and you are out further than that from the city," Wayne said laughing.

Wayne and Grandma waited for him as they shook their heads, she whispered. "He doesn't get out much," as her mind hit on a plan and had a silly grin on her face when she thought of Richard wearing a homemade loincloth and the possibilities of getting out of the house and out of her hair.

Danny seeing Uncle Richard runs out of the house to greet him "Richard you made it," he said as he danced around him in his little farmer clothes." Richard sighs with relief. "So far no Indians, maybe they haven't lost their minds after all?" Walking into the house he smiled seeing EJ sitting on the couch dressed in little farmer clothes as well, mostly anyway except for his feet, which he could see that he can't handle shoes. Due to all the cuts and sores on them or a shirt with all the bandages around his back and waist, other than that he was at least EJ not some Indian.

"Hi Richard," EJ said as he waved "I'd come over, but I still can't walk yet," he replied, "without tearing the stitches."

Richard went over to him. "That's ok EJ, I understand, glad your ok," he said.

"Richard this is my wife Martha Downing," Wayne said making the introductions.

Martha looked at Richard and laughed. "I believe we have already met stranger," as they all laugh. "Julie, Anna you are not going believes this," as they come into the living room. "This is EJ's, Uncle Richard," Ma said.

Julie turned to Grandma shaking her finger at her."You tricked us," and smiles. "How are you Richard," and laughed. "You make a pretty good stranger," she said.

What's Behind the Looking Glass?

Anna wasn't at all that surprised since she already figured it out. "I knew I was right all along, he does look a lot like the three of them," she said as Grandma winked back at her.

"Richard these are my three boys Robert, Will, and Sam. Other than the chickens and horses and the other animals on the farm that's everyone," Wayne replied.

Richard just a little shocked and overwhelmed looked at his mother. "What's wrong Richard were you expecting to find Indians?" She asked as she laughed.

"Yes mother, I was." He said feeling a bit guilty and shy as he looked around the room excepting them to jump out at any moment.

"Oh they're still around, we just put them to bed for the night, they'll be back in the morning son," she said as she looked at the four boys and smiled.

Martha turned to Richard; "dinner will be ready in about half an hour if you like to freshen up and Robert show him where the bathroom is. Richard make yourself at home dear, all have one the boys show you to where you'll be spending the night, welcome to our family." Martha said gave him a hug. "Here let me take that jacket," knowing he placed his car keys in it and handed to his mother. Went back into the kitchen and the girls gave him each kiss on the cheek and poor Richard turned the nicest shade of red.

Richard turned to his mother to argue; she squared his shoulders and points him down the hall whispered in his ear. "It's best not to argue with her, she already won, now go on son," she said.

"But?" He tries to say something.

Wayne and Robert walked Richard down the hall towards the bathroom. "Mr. Downing sir… is your wife always like this?" He asked.

"Let's just say its best to do what she says," Wayne replied with a chuckle.

Richard shrugged his shoulder, "but I am not becoming no Indian," he said.

"That's ok we have enough of those," Robert said as they laughed. Richard went into the bathroom to wash up for dinner with a slight pause as he watched Wayne and Robert walk back up the hall. He puts his lips to together and sighs under his breath. "Mother, what are you up too?" Turned on the water and washed his face hands and looked in the mirror, "I will not be no Indian and I will leave first thing in the morning and that's, that," he said too himself.

Drying his and hands, thoughts of seeing EJ again, "well just dinner and I would like to visit for just a while with him," as he smiled. "And it is good to see him again. I guess one night couldn't hurt and it is a long way back, but first thing in the morning I'll start back."

All gathered around the table for dinner was a full out feast. There was turkey and mash potatoes and corn on the cob, string beans, hot rolls and sweetbreads of all sorts with gravy. Martha went all out. The girls on one side of the table boys on the other with EJ in the middle of Robert and Will to make sure he didn't fall out.

Ma and Grandma were happy as pie seeing everyone together it brought a tear to their eyes. Grandma whispered over in her ear, "everyone here except for two, my other two grandchildren, but at least I know where they are and I miss them too," she said.

Pa brings the table to order by standing and clearing his throat. "We would like to welcome Richard to our farm and to our home and also we want to welcome him to as part of our family." Then Pa looked at Martha across the table and a nod from Grandma. "Speaking of family, I have an announcement to make as of today we are in the process of…" Pa with choked voice looked at EJ… Then stands behind him placed his hands on his shoulders… "Adopting EJ into our family on a permanent basis, but it's going to take a while, so, for now, were going to be his foster parents… and we made arrangements for his little brother Danny to visit us on the weekends twice month," he replied.

What's Behind the Looking Glass?

Pa smiled at EJ. "Son, welcome home, this where you belong," he said.

EJ is speechless and nods his head then in a whisper, "Thanks Pa."

Pa patted him on the shoulder then returned to his chair, but not before rubbing little Danny's hair and whispered. "We'd keep you too if they'd let us son, but we will keep both our eyes on you."

Danny nodded his head; "can I still be Indian?" He replied.

Pa and Grandma laugh. "Yes Danny, you can still be Indian," and Danny faces lit up.

Richard shook his head and rolled his eyes, whispered under his breath, "Indians." Then if that wasn't bad enough, Julie and Anna got up from the table and went over to EJ and each gave him a kiss on the cheek and welcomed him again to the family, but before sitting down they stopped at Richard and gave him a hug each. That knocked the wind right out of him and two kisses each on the cheek, then sat back down in their seats and giggled.

Julie said. "Your right Anna, he does look a lot like Danny and he blushes just like them too."

Ma and Grandma looking at Richard and laughed as he turned the nicest shade of red, "Richard welcome to our family," Martha said as she smiled.

"Thanks, I think, but I am not any Indian!" He replied in a stern voice.

"But Richard... You would look so cute," his mother replies.

"Mother I said no!" Richard said with an assertive voice.

Martha turned Richard. "It's ok, we have plenty of those in the family already." Then sighs and laughs.

Richard, of course, didn't find it at all funny as he looked at the boys down the table. *"Yes, sir… first thing tomorrow morning, I getting out of here, this family is crazy, just like my mother."*

"Robert please set up the cot in the boy's room for the night after dinner for Richard. I think he'll feel more comfortable in there then on the couch," Pa asked.

"Yes, Pa." Robert and Will feeling like a weight had been lifted off their shoulders knowing EJ was going nowhere but was still very concerned for Danny mumbled a soft prayer into the havens for a solution for him unaware of who was listening in our watched over them as Derrick stood in the shadows of the home. As the old man of EJ stood with him and nodded his approval.

Derrick remained hush, hush regarding on how he planned to change both their destinies and the family sitting around the table. But some secrets are best kept for now as he returned back behind the looking glass, for time is short as the darkness gathers all around them. If he plans on saving his world and others like this one he needs to gather his force and soon. Providing **the Council of Light** will accept his plan that will save their world from damnation under Morgan's rule…

Chapter 18-1

* * * *

"Now that we are all settled, pass those rolls and some of that turkey. I am starved and Danny here is thin as a rail," he said placing some more meat on his plate.

After dinner, they all gathered in the living room for some light conversation. Robert sets up the cot in the bedroom. "Will why don't you take Richard with you boys and go finish your chores for the night, I am sure he would like to see some of the farm," Pa said.

Robert came back from setting up Richard's cot to help Will pick up EJ and put him in the cart that they made him. EJ turned back to look at Richard and laughed seeing his puzzled face. "What do think, that I stay in the house all day?" He replied.

"Actually I did EJ, what in the heck are you doing in that?" Richard asked.

EJ laughed. "I'm doing my chores silly, come on, it will be fun."

Richard shook his head. *"Crazy, maybe they have lost it, but I do want to see this farm."*

Martha, Wayne, and Grandma sat on the couch looking out the window, watching the boys' head out to the farm, Grandma said. "Martha thanks for making him feel so welcomed, it's nice to get him out of the house once in a while," she said.

"Glad to have him and EJ would have like to see him too."

Grandma sat on the couch pondering about her granddaughters. "Wayne, could you use some extra help on the farm for a while?" She asked.

"Yes I could, what do have in mind?" Wayne asked.

"I would like to spend some time with my granddaughters before they go back home. I was thinking about leaving in the morning anyway, but Martha gave me an idea. I really hate to impose, but could I leave Danny here for a few more days?" She asked.

Martha, Wayne smiled Martha said. "Grandma you can always leave him here, you know that," Martha said squeezing Wayne's hand.

"Thanks, Martha thanks, Wayne." Then she turned looking out the window, "I also want to leave Richard here as well. I think it would be good for him to get out and get some fresh air and out of the house," She replied. "Plus he never really got along with two granddaughters and could never see eye to eye as they argued constantly, driving him and everyone around them crazy.

Wayne, Martha laughed. "You want to take the city out of him, get him to relax?" Wayne asked.

"Yes it will do him good, he's wound up so tight and he worries about everything. Doesn't know what's like just have a good time anymore. Need to loose him up. I believe this is the place and get a little sun, put laughter back in that boy. Give him a couple of weeks here with EJ and Danny and he'll be a new person."

Wayne turned to Martha with her hand in his. "Grandma, of course, he can stay, but how are you going to get him to stay where you want him? He's a lot older then EJ," Wayne asked.

Grandma smiled. "He may be stubborn, but he won't have a choice. I have the keys to his car and I'll remove the sparkplugs. Car won't be an option. He might need a change of clothes in the morning to Martha, but I think you can find something, your good with a needle and thread," she replied as she laughed to herself.

Wayne looked at Grandma and slapped his knee then chuckled. "We could turn him into an Indian," he said as he laughed.

What's Behind the Looking Glass?

Martha gives him a hard stare. "We have enough of those dear, besides his a little old to be playing Indian. No, he'll make a fine young farmer boy and that's, that," she said.

"Yes dear," Wayne said. Knowing better not to cross her when she not in the mood.

Seeing the boys back from doing the chores, Wayne asked. "So Richard what do think of our little farm?"

"I wouldn't call it little sir, not by a long shot. Sir a person could get lost out there very easily if they didn't know where he was going," he replied.

"Glad you liked it, son, now go wash up and we will have some dessert and take a look at some of those pictures you brought."

"Yes sir," followed the boys back down the hall to wash up.

Will and Robert sit EJ back on the couch next to Danny and Grandma. Grandma turned to Danny. "Danny, how would like to stay here for a few more days?" She asked.

"Really! Can I Grandma?" He asked.

"Yes Danny," she said.

"EJ did you hear that?" Danny said then puts his arms around his brother and gives Grandma a hug as well. "Alright go play with Sam," she said.

"Yes Grandma," he said climbing down from the couch and grabbed a toy truck out of the box of toys in the corner and joined Sam on the hard wooden floor.

"Martha he really likes it here, at least he has someone to play with. The sad thing is when he goes home, his sisters; they won't play with him there," Grandma said.

Wayne watched Danny play with Sam. "Yes, and to think he has two girls here that think he is so adorable, they just can't get enough of him and spoil him all day long."

Julie and Anna brought in the dessert as Richard and the boys come back into the living room. Richard hands EJ a package. "This from me and your grandmother, it's a get well present," he said.

EJ opened the package. His eyes nearly fall out of his head. "Grandma, it's a leather jacket just like yours and Danny's," he replied. Wayne and Martha shook their heads, but then again they were not all that surprised.

"I thought you would like it EJ, that should make your parents mad," she said.

"What else is new Grandma? They are always mad about something, doesn't matter if me or Danny did it or not."

Grandma sighed "I know son, I know," as she gives him a little hug. "Ouch Grandma!"

"Oh you'll be fine," she said.

"Now then Martha, Wayne." Passing them the photos albums, "you're going to like these, you too Julie and Anna. These are pictures of EJ and Danny," she said.

"Grandma, you didn't?" As EJ looks at them and Grandma and starts to blush.

"I thought they would like to see what you two looked like when were just babies." Julie and Anne giggled as they turned the pages.

"Oh he's so cute," they said, EJ blushes more and more as they giggle.

"Oh look there are even some pictures of Richard," Grandma said.

Richard dropping his fork and blushes red then under his breath. "Mmoother!"

Wayne and Martha showed Grandma some pictures of Robert,

What's Behind the Looking Glass?

Will and the rest of the family. The boys blush as well. After they looked at all the pictures Grandma gave them a copy of EJ's birth certificate. "You're going to need this for all his paperwork and his social Martha so don't lose it, guard it with your life," she said.

"Yes, Grandma. I was wondering when his birthday was. I tried asking him about it, but he wouldn't tell me that silly boy. Said they, never celebrate it," she said. "So it's true his real name is Eric. So how did he get the name EJ if I might ask?"

"Most likely they don't, but Grandma does and Danny's too," and writes down Danny birthday for them to. "As for the name, I gave it to him as a joke at first, but the thing is. The name EJ made more sense because we both hated it because it named his mother used for one of her dolls. No grandson of mine was going to be named after a girl's doll. So we took his first name and shortened it and did the same to his mild name as well since most people really never use their full middle name and only write their initials. Personally, I like it and could care less about how his parents feel about it.

"His grandfather and I tried to suggest it to them, but his Mother refused and you can guess how his father felt since he never calls him by the name his mother picked out unless he has too. So that's why everyone calls him EJ because once they meet his parents and learn how he got his name in the first place they simply agree that No boy child should be called after some girls doll."

Grandma looked over at the two little boys. "Looks like they have played themselves out," seeing them with cake all over their faces and chocolate in their hands spread eagle on the floor.

Wayne went over and picked up little Danny in his arms and laid him against his shoulder then carried him down the hall. After cleaning him up, he put him to bed and returned down the hall for little Sam with the same care then tucked them both into bed before turning out the light. "Well, we have a big day tomorrow boys. I want to get started building onto those rooms; plus almost time to harvest the hay again so we need to get an early start tomorrow," Pa said.

"Yes Pa." they yawned getting up put the chairs around the table and headed to their room saying goodnight as they left. Richard checked out the window to make sure everything was ok and then walked outside to check the doors on the car and then walked back into the house.

"Everything ok Richard?" Wayne asked watching come back through the door as he closed it behind him.

"Yes sir, just checking that's all, habit," he replied.

"Richard I set a pair of PJs on the cot for ya son," Martha said.

"Thanks, ma'am."

Grandma watched Richard follow the boys down the hall. "Wayne, can I borrow a light for a minute?" Grandma asked as they all go out on the porch to enjoy the cool night air before turning in.

Pa went to the barn and brought back a lantern. Watching Grandma pull Richard's keys from out of her purse, she opened the car door and popped the hood and removed the spark plugs wires from the engine. Putting them in the trunk of her car and then taking the spark plug wrench from the toolbox, removed the sparks plugs and puts them into the trunk with the wires. Wayne shook his head, "Grandma you are just full surprises," he said.

"Wayne, who do you think works on the bike when it breaks down? I like to tinker now then." She said as she laughed closing the hood of the car and locked it and placed the keys back into her purse. "Martha did do you what I asked about those PJs?" She asked as she giggled.

Wayne gazes over at her then at Grandma with a questionable look. "Oh he'll be fine Wayne," Grandma said and pats him on the knee. "We just gave him the wrong size that's all. Yours were too big so we gave him a pair of Will's instead because Robert doesn't have any."

Chapter 18-2

* * * *

Down the hall in the boy's room, Richard and the boys are getting ready for bed, Will and Robert helped EJ off with Ma's town clothes and hung them up in the closet and then they change back into their Indian clothes, while Richard was in the bathroom changing into the PJs. Richard puts his arm through the shirt. "What in the heck? They are too small. If my mother thinks I'll take this." He put back on his shirt and walked down the hall, seeing his mother in the bedroom sitting on the bed, "Mother?" Richard asked.

"Yes Richard, something wrong dear?" She asked as he held the PJs in his hand.

"They are too small and I can't wear them," he replies.

"Is that all dear? It's late; just go on to bed dear, you'll be fine. We just didn't want you to sleep in your clothes so just put them on the dresser and go to bed. I'll see you in the morning," she said.

Richard shrugged his shoulders and walked back down the hall. "This place is crazy; I need to get out of here before I go mad." Richard turned into the room and gets ready for bed, climbs into the cot. Punched the pillow a couple of times, blows puffs of air, turning his head whispered. "Indians… No sir… they are not making me into no Indian," then drifted off to sleep.

Ma, Pa made the rounds down the hall, stopping into the boy's room first, being careful not to wake Richard. They almost felt sorry for this poor boy, but Grandma was right, he still quite young. He still in his early twenties, just a kid wound up so tight. Pa and Ma each tuck in the boys and wished them goodnight. Then headed on down the hall to Grandma's room and gave her hug, telling her not to leave without first saying goodbye. She agreed then closed the door and turned out the light.

Ma and Pa turned to Danny and Sam's room and bent down and brushed their hair and tucked them in and whispered goodnight. Making full circle they enter each of their daughter's room, tucking their angels in. When they stopped at their bedroom door and enter the room. Wayne kissed his wife and said. "Martha it has been quite a day and a night."

"Yes dear it has," as she wrapped him in her arms, "and you have given me the best present of all." She said as they climbed into bed.

Very early the next morning before Mr. Rooster crowed or the sun peeked over the mountains. Martha, Wayne, and Grandma are up and down in the kitchen. Martha is preparing Grandma a light breakfast before she leaves, Wayne loaded up her car, while Grandma makes her rounds to say goodbye to the sleeping children. Quiet as a mouse Grandma walked into each of the children's rooms and gave each kiss on the cheek with a tear in her eye and closes the door.

When she went into the boy's room she carefully nudged EJ whispering in his ear. "EJ" its Grandma," and waits for him to wake. "I just wanted to say goodbye and give you one more hug before I leave, I'll be back in a couple of weeks. I'm leaving Richard here and Danny too, so I can visit your sisters before they go home... EJ will you be ok?" She asked.

"I'll be fine Grandma," and then gave her a hug. Then he watched her pick up Richard's clothing including his shoes. Grandma put her finger to her lips "shush" then smiled and whispered back," he doesn't know yet!" And closed the door.

EJ turned towards Richard who is still sound asleep. "*Come morning, man is he going to be mad*," and laughed softly at what his Grandma has just done.

Grandma loaded his clothes into the back seat of her car and walked back into the house giving them each one more hug and kiss on the cheek and waves farewell. They watched her leave the farm and drive up the road. Thinking what is going to happen in a few hours when the sun comes up. Wayne smiles and Martha shook her head then giggled to herself. "Might as well get breakfast started and you might need some cotton for your eardrums when that lad finds out what his mother just done," Wayne said.

They didn't have to wait long either because as soon as Mr. Rooster crowded Richard jumped off the cot with a start. "What was that?" He replied.

Will, Robert, and EJ started laughing. "Oh that's our alarm clock, he's early today," EJ said.

Ma entered the room." Breakfast is almost ready boys," as she sets down her sewing basket taking out the measuring tape and notepad and sat on EJ's bed. "Good morning Richard, I just need some measurements so I can fit you for some work clothes," she said.

"Work clothes? What for?" Richard asked surprised and bewildered as he looked around the room for his clothes.

"Oh, didn't your mother tell you?" She asked then sighs grabbing the measuring tape from her basket.

"Tell me what?"

"That you'll be staying here on the farm for the next couple of weeks, while she's away," Martha said.

"She what?" Richard stammered out dumbfounded.

"Yes, she left this morning to go see her granddaughters. Now I have a lot to do so stand up so I can measure you," she replied, as Will, Robert, and EJ start laughing.

"I will not be an Indian," he replied.

"Don't be silly dear. I told you we have enough of those. You are just making it hard on yourself. I'll come back in a few minutes let you get adjusted. I swear you boys are all the same," she said and shook her head and closed the door.

Will and Robert looked at EJ then at Richard. "Well you might as well figure you already lost Richard because sounds like you're staying to us," they all replied.

"She can't do this to me, she can't," he replied.

"You don't have a choice, Grandma took all your clothes," EJ said as Richard looked around the room for them.

Ma shouted down the hall. "Boys you coming?"

"Yes, Ma!"

Will and Robert pickup EJ and head down the hall leaving Richard in the room alone. He watched them leave dressed as Indian boys and rolled his eyes. "I knew it, crazy. They are all crazy." Wayne entered the room, sits on the bed across from Richard. Richard looked at him, "is it, true sir?" He asked.

"I am afraid so son, no use stewing about it. She said for you to have some fun, get some sun and unwind a bit," he replied.

"I'm not an Indian sir," he said.

"No, you are not, just a young lad that's all. Now let's find yea something to wear," he said. Mr. Downing brought him a pair of overalls. "These will work just fine, for now, hurry now breakfast is waiting and Ma still wants to get you fitted," he said and closed the door.

Richard steamed as he blows puffs of air seething. "Mother, what you have done to me now? There is no way you can keep me here, my car is just outside. When I get home you'll be sorry," he said to himself.

Richard put on the overalls. "Now where are my shoes?" Nearly tearing the room apart as he looked for them, "just great!" He said as stormed down the hall, tripping over the pant legs, having to stop to roll them up steaming mad.

Martha seeing Richard coming down the hall said. "Breakfast is on the table Richard, after breakfast I'll take those in for you."

Richard seeing his car still sitting out in the yard in a fit of rage gritted his teeth. "No thanks, ma'am. I need to be leaving for home."

What's Behind the Looking Glass?

Richard not waiting for a response walked out the door. Martha and Wayne went out to the porch and waited; Richard getting out the spare key from the hidden compartment under the wheel well. Unlocked the door of the car, the car doesn't start. Richard hits the steering wheel with his fists. Now he's really mad, he pops the hood of the car to see what the matter is. Richard finding the missing spark plugs and wires missing, he slammed the hood of the car, yelled down the road. "MOTHER!"

Wayne, Martha walked over to him. "I guess it wouldn't do any good to call home either I suppose?" He replied.

"No son, she's not there and if she was it wouldn't do you any good. Now your breakfast is getting cold so let's go back inside." Pa said as Richard looked down the road and hangs his head then follows them back into the house. Danny seeing Richard coming through door climbed down from the breakfast table running, "Richard! You're still here!" and gives him a big hug. "Where's Grandma?" Richard doesn't answer.

Wayne picked up little Danny. "She went to visit your sisters for a while, now finish your breakfast." And sets him back on the floor, points him back to the table. Martha gave Richard a little nudge and they all sat down for breakfast.

The girls looked at Pa then at Richard with his head hang low. Pa just casually as if nothing was wrong, or has changed, looked at the boys, "Boys," Pa said and looked over at Richard. "We have a lot to do today. Soon as your Ma gets done with ya and the chores are done this morning. I want to start building on to those rooms. Richard your mother has left the room down the hall for you so after breakfast get yourself cleaned up and Martha will measure those clothes for you," he replied.

The girls looked puzzled as they looked over at Richard wearing Pa's overalls, but not wanting to ask they just sit eating their breakfast and whispered. "He is kinda cute."

Richard blushes a little trying not to stare back at them. Ma leans over squeezes his hand. "Eat your breakfast Richard, you'll be alright," she said.

After breakfast was over, it was the same old routine except for poor Richard. Thinking they have all lost their minds, as he watched Mrs. Downing and three boys leave the table. Ma unties EJ's dinner vest and the other boys hung up their shirts on the pegs by the door, then picking up EJ and head on down the hall, leaving Sam and Danny with Julie and Anna to play and rubbed lotion on them for the day.

"Mr. Downing sir, where are they going?" He asked.

Wayne turned to Richard from his morning paper and towards the hall. "It's time to change EJ's bandages and give him his bath." He said as if nothing was wrong without so much as a pause. Wayne went back to reading his morning paper and planning the day.

Richard blows more air between his lips. "*These people are crazy,*" as he shook his head. "*Mother, what have you done to me?*" Running his fingers through his hair.

After a few minutes, Julie comes back. "Pa, Ma's ready for you to take EJ so she can change the bandages. "Richard, Ma left you a clean pair of shorts and some towels in the bathroom so you get cleaned up and then she will measure you," Julie said as Pa walked down the hall.

Richard just sat there at the table. "*I am not moving one inch from this spot,*" he said seeing the phone Richard thought that his brother Steve would help "*maybe my older brother or my mother's sisters will get me out this mess*". Picking up the phone he calls his older brother Steve.

Steve married young right after he served an LDS mission to a gal named Loraine. Had made his money designing and building houses and was a brick mason on the side when things were slow. He looked a lot like his father, dark brown hair or what's left of it and brown eyes which seemed to turn gold when the sun hit him just right. Steve worked out a lot from carrying lumber and bricks and large wheelbarrows of cement, which in turn gave him the broad shoulders. And stood tall like his father, reaching the height of five feet nine inches, his face and skin hardened by the long hours in the sun, he had hard jawline like the rest of the family.

What's Behind the Looking Glass?

"Hello, Steve this is Richard... Yes, I am fine, well sort of," Richard said looking down at himself... "The reason I called...Oh... What? What do you mean she already called you?"... He can hear his brother laughing over the phone. "Yes, she left me in the middle of nowhere... EJ's fine... So are you going to come and get me? What do you mean your not? This is not funny... Listen here, Steve. I am stranded in middle nowhere with no clothes, with crazy people and you want me to relax and have fun... Oh, you'll call me in a few days. Thanks a lot." Richard said slamming the phone down. "Ooooh" Richard really mad stamps his foot on the floor. "Ouch" garbing his foot, not used to running around barefoot, haven't done that since he was least Will's and Robert's age.

Mr. Downing overhearing Richard on the phone just walked over to him. "Richard you might as well accept it that you are stuck here. She knew you would call him so she called him last night and most likely has already talked to her sisters by now, so son, go get yourself cleaned up, we have work to do." He said. Richard looked at Mr. Downing and hangs his head walked down the hallway.

Richard passing Will, Roberts and EJ's room where Mrs. Downing was; "Richard there you are. I put a clean pair of shorts in the bathroom and some fresh towels for you and ran a nice hot bath. Get yourself cleaned up and I'll be into measure you for those clothes. Just set those clothes outside the door please," she said.

"Ma'am, I am not going to be no Indian," he replied.

"Richard, I told you, son, we already have enough of those," Comes over and squares his shoulders and points him on down the hall, "you silly boy," she replied.

Richard stared at the ground heading to the bathroom slowly, murmuring under his breath "mother why have you done this to me? How could you?" He enters the bathroom and gets cleaned up seeing he has no other choice. Martha knocked on the bathroom door. "Richard, can you hand me those overalls and your shorts so I take them in and wash them or do I need to come in there and get them?" She asked as she waited a couple of minutes then knocked again.

"You wouldn't dare?" He replied she started to open the door. "Alright, alright!" And a hand pops out behind the door with one pair of shorts and one pair of overalls.

"That's better; I'll be in your room waiting so hurry now if you are worried about the girls, don't. Wayne is keeping the girls in the living room just wrap a towel around you if you want to." She replied then walked down to his room with her sewing basket in her a hand and waited for him on the bed.

Richard looked in the mirror; "they are mad, absolutely mad. Poor EJ they must have tortured him and now I am next." Robert, seeing his mother all alone in Richard's room as she waited for him; decided she might have need of a little help to get Richard in there. Remembering what it was like for him and EJ.

Robert knocked on the bathroom door. "Richard it's just me," and opens the door. "Ma is waiting for you and we do have a lot too do today," he said.

Richard looked at Robert dressed in his Indian clothes. "That's easy for you to say you're not the one stuck here with nothing to wear," as he pointed down to his borrowed shorts that are just a little big for him.

Robert laughed. "Richard that's nothing, don't sweat the small stuff. Me and Will have been through worse than that so has EJ, you'll be fine. Besides there's nothing Ma not seen already, so let's go, she's waiting," and hands him a towel. Robert and Richard head to his room where Ma is and Robert sat on the bed beside her.

"Thanks, Robert," Ma said.

"No problem Ma."

"Alright Richard, this won't take long," as she pulled out her measuring tape, pencil, and pad, "now hold still," she said.

"That tickles," he replied.

Chapter 19

"You boys are all the same" as she smiles. "Your mother is right you could use a little sun, you been in the house too long." Ma said shaking her head. "Need to do something about those shoulders and arms. Get some muscles into them. Maybe we should make you an Indian," as she looked at his long white legs.

Richard looked from Robert to Mrs. Downing. "No ma'am! I will not be an Indian!" He said more determined.

She smiled. "Alright Richard, how about just a young farm boy," she asked.

"Do I have a choice?" He asked.

"No," she said.

"No Indian!" He gave her and Robert a hard cold stare.

Ma and Robert laughed. Ma reminded him again. "It's ok, we have enough of those," Ma hands him another pair overalls. "The lotion is on the table. I cut off and sewed up the pant's leg a little so you won't trip."

"Ma'am I can't find my shoes," he said.

Sorry, Richard, she took those with her to, so you won't run off too far. Now change your clothes I've got some sewing to do. It will take me a few days to make you a shirt, but I'll have something for you by lunchtime," she said as she closed the door.

Richard falls on the bed mad, talking to himself. *"And they want me to relax, and have fun. How when I'm stuck here in the middle of nowhere? Mother!"* Looking over toward the table where the lotion is a note was left behind from his mother.

Eric Shepherd

* * *

"Richard"

"Dear Son: By now you have realized that I have left you and Danny here with the Downing's. I'm sorry I tricked you, but I did it out of love. You have forgotten what's like to be young and were gowning up too fast. Ever since your father passed away, you have forgotten what it is like to be the little boy inside and have fun.

I don't want you to be like your brother Jim who is so unhappy with his life, but more like your brother Steve who has found a better life who is happy and full of life. So stop moping, and make the best of things. I've gone to my sisters to be with my granddaughters and will be gone for two weeks.

I've locked the house and will return your shoes and clothes in a couple of weeks. Mr. Downing will get you some overalls from the store in a few days and your brother Steve will check in on you in a couple of days. Take care of EJ and Danny and mind Mr. and Mrs. Downing and get some fresh air, some sun and try to have some fun, love Ma."

"P.S. Sorry about your car.

The nearest parts store is Provo, which is 50 miles

But I also have your wallet too, sorry."

* * * *

"Just great!" As Richard fell back onto the bed with a note in his hand, "I am screwed!"

Wayne knocked on the door, "Richard?" He calls as he knocked on the door again.

"Yes, sir?" He replied.

Wayne entered the room and sits on the bed next to him. "It could be worse," he said.

What's Behind the Looking Glass?

"Worse than this? You got to be kidding! Everyone around here is dressed as Indians as if it is perfectly normal. I am stuck out here in the middle of nowhere with nothing and mean nothing. While my mother," showing him the note. "Is visiting her sisters and my brother thinks it's a great idea!" He said as he rolled his eyes shaking his fits in the air. "Tells me to relax and have fun."

"Richard you are not as bad off as you think," as Wayne rubbed his chin. "EJ now he was bad off, we had to rebuild him and look how he's doing. Now the boys are outside so hurry up, we are burning daylight son," he said standing up and walked down the hall and out the front door where the boys are waiting for them.

"Yes sir," he replied and gets off the bed and follows him as if it was a death sentence and he was about to be hanged.

"Ma?" Julie asked washing her hands at the sink and turned seeing her mother come into the kitchen setting down her sewing basket on the counter as she tacks Richard's measurements to list of things to do today.

"Yes, Julie."

"What's going on? Richard looks so miserable and angry. Did his mother do something?" she asked.

"Yes Julie, she felt he needed to unwind a little bit and have some fun. She says all he does is stay in the house, never laughs anymore. Like all the fun has just gone out of him and was afraid he was becoming like his brother Jim, EJ's father. So she thought we could help by giving him a chance to unwind, try something new. Give her a chance to visit her granddaughters before they went back home in a couple of weeks. So she left Danny and Richard here with us."

"I have to say one thing for Grandma. She no dummy when it comes to her boys, they're all the same." As she watched Richard and Pa go out the door and shook her head. "Poor Richard I bet his feet are going be sore," Julie said.

"I just hope he remembers to put on the lotion or that won't be the only thing sore," Ma replied. Placing her apron around her and begins cleaning the house, starting with floors and Julie and Anna dusted.

"Well, boys have you finished your chores?" Pa asked.

"Yes Pa," they answered as they sat on the swing with EJ.

"Then let's get started. EJ, I have a new job for you son." Handing him the list, "I need you to put a checkmark on every item, making sure that it goes where I want it to and we have everything we need. While at the same time you are working on your wooden blocks. That way we keep everything organized. Richard, have you ever driven a wagon before?" He asked.

"No, sir." Caught off guard as he stares at all the empty space of nothing besides field and orchard as far the eye can see. It was if he had dropped off the earth with no signs of city life or the noise of it at all.

"Well it's about time you learned," Mr. Downing said.

"Pa?"

"Yes EJ?"

"Wouldn't the pickup be easier?"

"No son it runs on gas, the wagon doesn't and we can do a lot more with it and horses need the work to. Ok Robert take Richard and go get the wagon and let's get started," Pa picked up EJ and sets him over in the corner in the shade where he can observe with his blocks of wood and placed the list in his hands showing him how and where things go and how to count each item as they come in.

Will climbs in the back of the wagon. "This ot'a to be fun," as Robert handed the reins over to Richard, as Will, Robert brace themselves.

What's Behind the Looking Glass?

Robert says. "Richard just lightly flick of your wrist because if do it to harrrrrddd," Robert replied.

The horses came to life with a hard start and a jump leaving the barn then started to gallop, Richard trying to pull back on the reins. Robert, Will hanging on tight as they go past the house and down the road a few paces, Pa and EJ laughing, as they watched Richard and the boys fly past them. Robert yelling back "Pa will be back in a minute." As Richard's face turned white as a sheet, trying to get control of the wagon and the horses. Martha and girls with the boy's right behind her, coming out to see what all the fuss is all about.

Pa turned and chuckles at Ma. "Richard's learning how to drive that's all." As she watched the boys come back to the farm with smiles on their faces.

"Mr. Downing sir, it doesn't drive like a car." Richard said as he wiped the dirt and sweat of his face, "and it doesn't smell like one either." As the horse lifted his tail waving his hand in front of his nose… EJ grabbed the side of his ribs from laughing so hard.

Ma shook her head placed her hands on her hips and said. "You silly boys," and went back inside.

"Richard welcome too farming." Mr. Downing said as he grabbed his knees bent over from laughing so hard and wiped a tear from his eye. "Now let's get to work." EJ counts all the boards before they can cut them, checks off the supplies, they need for the day. Saws, hammers, nails and such placed a checkmark by the item, gives Pa and the boys the ok. Pa and the boys go over the plans laying the new foundation first with picks and shovels as they leveled the ground where Pa indicated with markers and string.

Ma and girls came out checking on the progress after an hour or two." You know dear," Ma said as she looked at the house. "While you are added it, a bigger dining room would be nice since you are already here and all, it's just a few more feet that I can see. Now drink your ice tea," and walked back into the house. Pa watched her leave then looked at the boys and then looked back at the house.

Robert whispered over to Richard. "You think your mother throws curve balls? Sometimes I think all women are cut from the same cloth," he said as they watched Pa.

"Robert?" Pa asked.

"Yes, Pa?" Coming to his side as leaned the rake against the house...

"Looks like we need to make a few more changes." He said as he shook his head looking towards the house and sighed. Taking his pad and pencil, grabbing his measuring tape, "Will can you hold this?" He asked.

"Yes, Pa."

"Robert you stand there, Richard you stand right over here." Pa making some more calculations and scratches his head went back over to his floor plans with his ruler and draws some more lines. "I might as well just build a new house why I'm at. It would be a whole lot easier." He said with a gruffer voice, turning around. "You boys didn't hear me say that," he said as he checks to make sure she was well inside.

"No Pa, not a word... No sir," as they smiled.

"Well it looks like we're going have to get some more lumber, but we're going to need it anyway so what the heck, your Ma's right." He said moving the ropes of the foundation guide, "Alright boy's put your backs into let's get back to work."

"EJ?" Pa asked

"Yes Pa," he said as he looked up from his blocks and wiped the sweat from his brow with his left arm leaving a clean dirt smudge where he wiped his brow.

"How are you doing over there?" As Pa comes over to examine a couple more of the blocks.

What's Behind the Looking Glass?

"It's getting a little easier Pa, but my hands sure hurt."

Pa watched him for a minute. "You are holding the handle too tight, don't force it EJ use it the handle like this don't take out such large chunks at a time," he said taking his hand. "No still too hard. Wait for a second, I got an idea." Pa runs into the house and grabs a few boxes of soap and cubes of wax and EJ Swiss Pocketknife. "EJ I want you to carve me something," Pa said quickly draws a shape of a horse in the wax then one in the soap. "Ok crave me these shapes using your knife," he said then placed his knife into his hand.

EJ looked at the Swiss Pocketknife. "Pa I thought I lost this down at the creek," he said.

"I been holding onto it for you son with rest of your stuff, well except for the stuff you were wearing at the time, of course, Ma had Robert burn that," as he rubbed his hair.

"Thanks, Pa, it would have scared all the fish anyway."

"Everyone else too by the smell," Robert and Will laughed remembering that day when they found him. Richard, of course, did not know what they were talking about, his Ma left out this part of the story out. Robert and Will seeing Richard not having a clue what's going on decided to fill him in as they worked.

Pa watched EJ carve away the horse in the soap and smile watching him. Remembering how his Pa taught him and each of his boys. He chuckles to himself remembering how he himself went through several bars of soap and wax, and how frustrated he got when the legs broke off when carving the horses. It didn't take long before the first bar soap was carved. "Snap" fist leg, then two, then three, then four.

EJ doesn't give up. He just kept on carving the horse. Then sets it down, then picks up the wax and begins the second horse, but this time only one leg breaks and sets it on the table and smiles. Pa walked over to examine the horse and rubbed his chin. "Pa the soap horse was tired so he wanted to rest and the second horse threw his shoe," he said.

"Oh, I see! I was wondering why he only had three legs, that would explain it, son," he said as he chuckled. "Would you like some more?" He asked as EJ smiled.

"Sure Pa," he said.

Pa picked up the horse and the wax and legs and took them in the house and hands them to Ma. "Present from EJ," he replied and grabbed couple more bars of soap and wax. "He says the soap horse was tired and needed to rest and the wax horse threw a shoe. So I need some more soap and wax to make more horse's dear, that's all," he said leaves her standing there as he left with a merry old tune.

Ma looked at the two horses in her hand, puts one wax horse in the kitchen window and smiles and takes her little pen knife and carves EJ name it and puts other in the bathroom by the tub. Julie and Anna take Sam and Danny outside around the back of the house with a tray of sandwiches for the boys for lunch and some ice-cold lemonade. Ma right behind them with EJ's medicine and lotion for the boys and carried a basket full of cookies and a quilt for them all to sit on.

"You boys ready for some lunch?" She asked as she looked at their progress as Ma spreads the quilt on the ground in the shade of a nearby tree. Ma looked at the boy's hands and faces. "Go wash up first, I've placed some soap and water by the door, you silly boys." She said then shook her fingers at them, thinking they were going touch her food with those hands.

Pa picked up EJ and cleaned him up and brings him over and leans him under the tree for Ma. "Now that's better," she said as she turns each of the boy's hands over including Richards. "How's your feet dear?" She asked him.

"Little sore ma'am, not use to not wearing shoes," he replied.

"Oh, you'll be fine. She just wanted to make sure you stay put that's all."

What's Behind the Looking Glass?

"I guess so, but I never thought she would do something like this ma'am. Then again she has always been a...little odd."

Pa and Ma laugh, Ma said. "Your mother odd... Now, why would you say that?" She asked.

Richard looked at them thinking *they got to be kidding if they haven't noticed her odd behavior* scratched his head. Whispered over too EJ, "are they all insane around here or is just me?" He asked.

"Richard I think it's just you," EJ said as he cracks up and slaps him on the back noticing his sunburn and smiles.

"Ouch, that stings," Richard replied.

"Sorry," EJ laughed.

Robert noticing it too didn't want to miss out on the fun; leans over whispered in his ear. "Did you forget to put the lotion on?" He asked.

"I thought you were kidding about the lotion."

Robert said. "Nope..." said a bit louder "So how was your ride on the wagon Richard?" As he slapped him on the back.

"Ouch that stings," he said.

"Sorry," Robert replied laughing.

Will noticing the fun too laughs. "That wagon drives like a car I hear, right Richard?" ... "Slap."

"Ouch!" Richard replied,

"Sorry." Will said laughing along with his brothers.

"Ok I get it, I get it," Richard replied.

"Alright boys," Ma said and handed Richard the lotion. "I've hemmed up your overalls, they are on your bed Richard so go put on the lotion and put them on," and giggled; "you silly boy."

"Yes, Ma'am."

Pa chuckled as he watched Richard run towards the house, Ma stares them down. "Martha the boys here just having a little fun and wanted to make sure he was taken care of before it got worse, right boys?" He asked trying hard not to laugh.

"Yes, Pa."

Chapter 20

Richard ran into the house to his room, racing down the hall with lotion in his hand. Bursting through his bedroom door he headed straight for the bathroom. Racing to the mirror that hung over the sink he stared at his panicked reflection in the mirror. Seeing the red marks on his shoulders where the straps from the overalls have been rubbing he touched them and filched. "Oh, that stings". He looked in the mirror and could see the red hand marks still. His entire body ached. "My feet are killing me, my shoulders are killing me, my sides ache, I can barely move. I'll just lay on the cool bed for few minutes let the sting ware down a bit." Exiting the bathroom he headed towards his bed. He collapsed on top of it. Not realizing how tired he was, he fell asleep from exhaustion, Farm life just wasn't for him.

While Richard slept off his exhaustion and pain the boys started back to work. Pa picked up EJ setting him back into the corner with his blocks and soap horse. "Robert, have you seen Richard come back yet?" He asked.

"No Pa."

"How about you Will?" He asked.

"No Pa."

Pa rubbed his chin and walked into the house and walked down the hall to Richard's room. Finding him there he sighs. "Well at least he still here, but sure is sunburn poor kid. His mother's right, he doesn't get out much, must have worn him clean out." Pa smiled, "we'll just let him rest awhile," turned out light and closed the door. "Martha you might want to help him put that lotion on him in a couple of hours, let him rest for now," he said as he walked out the door. "It's alright boys, he just needed a little nap, let's get back to work," he said.

"Yes Pa," they all laughed.

While the Boys and Pa worked building the foundation. Ma girls sat under the tree watching Sam and Danny play in the yard when a scruffy old man that looked like Doctor Hatfield came around the house. "Hello Doc," Wayne replied.

"Wayne, Martha, boys; knocked on the door out front, no one answered so we heard ya working around the back, so we came back here…. What's you building?" As Doc looked at all the lumber and foundation being erected.

"Oh just adding on to the house," Wayne said looking at his wife. "Martha thought the dining room needs to be bigger and we need to build a room for EJ here and make couple others larger at the same time."

"Well the reason I am here," Doc said scratching his chin then turns to EJ. "EJ, how you doin son?" He asked.

"Just fine Doc." As he set down his work for a moment and rubbed the soreness out of his fingers.

"Glad to hear son glad to hear. Wayne, Martha the reason I am here is." He said watching two people come around the side of the house to join him. "Two reasons," Doc said as his guests come closer. "Wayne, Martha you are about to become parents," as he smiled. "The second reason is I needed to examine him again see how he is coming along…Wayne this is Judge Parker, and Mr. Wells from Family Services, they come to see EJ and you."

"How do you Mr. and Mrs. Downing?" Mr. Wells and Judge Parker said shaking hands. "Some farm you got I must say. Doctor Hatfield sure has told me a lot about you and your boys. Indians I would never have believed it." Mr. Well's comments as he looked at Will and Robert and watching Sam and Danny play. "What do you say we go inside and we can get acquainted and Doc here can examine EJ?" Mr. Wells said.

Mr. Wells was an odd duck, to say the least, and not just by his British accent. Even though it was scorching hot outside, he was wearing a three-piece black suit, while Judge Parker was in short sleeves dress shirt and not even so much as a tie. Mr. Wells was a tall lanky fella, form his legs to his torsos all the way up to his neck that looked like long turkeys neck with Adam's apple in the middle. He had to be over 7 feet tall and had shoes bigger then Roberts size 10s. Short neat brown hair that was graying on the sides, Brown eyes under his steel frame glasses that sat on his straight beak nose that could have doubled as a woodpecker.

Ma said to the girls. "Julie, Anna do you mind watching Sam and Danny for a while?" Ma asked.

"Sure Ma, will watch them for you." Pa picked up EJ and Ma, Will and Robert followed behind him to their room laying him on his bed.

Judge and Mr. Wells turned to the boys. "You boys mind waiting outside, why we and the Doc here examines him," Judge Parker asked.

"It's alright Judge they know everything, we don't keep secrets from them," Pa said.

Judge and Mr. Wells shrugged their shoulders. "Alright boys, I guess you can stay," and closed the door. "I understand you want to be foster parents?" Mr. Wells asked.

"That's right Mr. Wells, we do," Pa said. Mr. Well's sets his brown leather briefcase with shiny golden latches on the bed pulls out a folder and takes it out with EJ's name on it flipped through some pages and shook his head.

"Normally we choose the family first then place these kids ourselves, thus saying this is very unorthodox, but this is a very special case," he said flipping through some more pages. "We just don't create parents out of thin air you know. We have to be careful who we choose," looked towards Mr. and Mrs. Downing. "We wouldn't want them going to a home worse than one they were leaving now can we?" *Too late EJ thought after been in a few that either were worse than home or close to it. Very seldom did he find one that actually wanted him rather than a free paycheck.*

"EJ let's take look at ya; none of this funny business like last time," Doc said.

"I'll be fine Doc with Ma and my brothers here," he said as he lay on his bed while his brothers sat on theirs across from him. Ma sat with him as Pa stood closely by.

"Well, you look a lot better, sight better that's for sure." Docs said while opening his bag and pulling out his instruments and began to examine EJ. "Martha looks like you been doin a good job keeping those wounds clean, most those bruises of healed too. Now let's take look at those stitches EJ; looks like we can take this one out on your leg would you like that?" He asked.

"Yes, Doc!" Grimacing at the thought on how it was going to hurt.

"You might feel a slight tug, it won't hurt none," Doc said as he cuts the knot and some of the threads, taking the tweezers and pulls out the stitches rubbing the wound with alcohol. "How does that feel?" he asked.

"It burns just a little Doc." As he clenched his teeth tight as the alcohol burned.

"Now let's see we can bend your knee and stretch it out. Doc bends back his right leg, stretching the muscle. "Ouch! Hurts just a little Doc," he replied.

"Alright that's fine let's check the rest of you," he said undoing the loincloth looks at his left hip Wayne helps roll him over on his side and slowly took off the bandage. "Tsk, Tsk, Martha I was afraid of that, this wound still got a little infection in it not healing as it should," he said.

Judge and Mr. Well's peeked over. "What a mess Doc, you were right I see." Judge Park said.

What's Behind the Looking Glass?

Doc cleaned the wound and placed a new bandage and reties the loincloth. "EJ we need you to sit you up and look at your chest and your back then will be done," he said.

"Yes Doc," Feeling embarrassed as he reties the loincloth after being so exposed to everyone in the room regardless if they were men and his brothers and his Pa or even Ma.

Ma squeezes his hand to reassure him that everything was all right and placed a kiss on his forehead. He whispered that he was doing fine, and they would be done in a few minutes. EJ could feel the love and care she gave him and was more reassured with her in the room as he smiled up at her. The boys helped EJ sit up and Doc unwrapped the bandage around his chest, knocking the air out of his lungs. He waited for a second for him to catch his breath. "Does it hurt when I press here? How about here." He asked.

"Ooooh!" EJ said,

"And here?" he asked.

"Eeeeeeeeeeee!" EJ said grimacing with pain.

"Tsk, tsk," Doc waited for EJ to catch his breath and ran his fingers through his hair. "Martha I hope you like teaching school because this boy here is going to be needing some. Well EJ we can take couple smaller stitches out," he said looking at his back, as he removes them. Doc placed the tweezers back into his bag and rewraps the bandage around EJ's chest.

"Wayne this boy needs to work those shoulders and arms and I have a pair of crutches for him out by the front door. He needs to start using that right leg, not too much now go easy. I don't want to tear the stitches on the other side. So one crutch to keep the weight off, don't tire your self out EJ," he said as he rubbed his hair. "You got to crawl before you can walk son."

"Thanks, Doc," Wayne said.

"Alright Judge, Mr. Wells, EJ's he's all yours," Doc said as he stepped aside. Mr. Wells looks at EJ then at Wayne and Martha, "Doc before you go can you stick around?" He asked. Mr. Wells looked down at the file in his hands. "It says here in the report at that you have examined and in the investigation where it says it is complete regarding this matter. I just have few questions for EJ on the matter concerning his well being so we can get these procedures done." Mr. Wells replied.

Doc sits back down on the bed next to the boys. "Doc what's he talking about?" Robert whispering in his ear, "what investigation?"

"Legal mumble jumble, that's all," he replied.

"Doc is it your professional opinion that EJ here should not be moved from this home?" He asked.

"Yes, that's right. I do believe that and have given this boy now three examines and will continue to do so while he's here," Doc replied.

"I see. It says here you have also examined the boy's home and parents and his siblings." Mr. Wells replied.

"Yes, I did," Doc said.

"What did you find?" Mr. Wells asked.

Doc getting hot under the collar turns red. "It's in the report man read it," he said.

Mr. Wells flips some pages of the file. "Just tell me in your own words," he replied.

Doc, nearly lose it, puffs air making his mustache twitch. "It is my professional opinion that their loony tunes man and need a shrink. The father would be better off trying to have a conversation with a rock; shows as much emotion as a dried-up old prune. His mother, you could take a horse put into a suit and tie she'd ask it to dance; she wouldn't know the difference between that and a real person going down the street. Heck man, you have a better chance of teaching a cow to fly before thinking they would make good parents. Is that clear enough for ya?"

"Yes, that's' fine." Mr. Wells replied. Wayne boys cracking up Martha giving them a hard cold stare while Mr. Wells made some notes in the file. "And the other children in the home what are their conditions?" He asked.

"So far what I can tell, not nearly as bad as EJ, just some mild bruising and little frightened," Doc said.

"I see." Mr. Wells jotted down some more notes.

Mr. Wells looks back at EJ. "This question is for you; I need you to tell me what happened from the last time you were placed with us, according to your file everything seemed fine and your parents and seemed to have improved enough to go back home. So we would like to know what happened so when to question your parents about it, that we won't make the same mistake again," he said. EJ looked at him turning white and pale all the color goes out of his face, mouth dry, lips trembling. Pa went over to his bedside and looks at Mr. Wells then at EJ.

Ma leans EJ's head against her. "Mr. Wells is this really necessary?"

Mr. Well's looked up from EJ's file; actually looks at them then at EJ. "I am sorry Mr., Mrs. Downing, EJ, but we have to know," he replied.

Pa and Ma whispered to EJ. "We are right here and your brothers Will, Robert are here to. Do you think you can EJ?" She asked.

"I'll try Ma," EJ said starts to tell Mr. Wells and the Judge. It was too difficult for him; they understood and let Pa and Ma finish it for him, while they held him in their arms. Letting EJ getting control of himself and Ma wiped his and her tears away. Mr. Wells made very good notes of that because Pa made sure of that.

"Well I don't see a problem here Judge, that's all the questions I have for EJ. Just a quick note; it says here regarding school, got to work on that." Mr. Wells said looking at EJ showing, Martha copies of his report cards mostly "C's" and few "D's"

"Yes sir," EJ replied as slowly gasped with tears still in his eyes and the fear he felt as remembered all the things he had lived through at home. The pain he felt was easy compared to the memories. Wounds would heal, but nightmares are forever.

"Alright, we're through in here. Just have some paperwork for you to fill out and will be on our way," Mr. Wells said.

"Robert you and Will can take EJ outside now and go back to work," Pa said.

"Yes, Pa." Will grabbing one end Robert the other and so EJ could try to use the leg as they sort of hobble out the door, as they watched to remind him.

"Go easy now?" Ma said.

"Yes Ma," they replied.

"You silly boys," as she watched walk down the hall and closed the door.

"Just need you to sign here and here, and initial here, and over here. Then need the Judge signatures here and here and the Docs on this and one on this one… Now then you'll be receiving a check once a month for EJ's care, food, clothing and what not like medical bills; I will send you a check and a new medical card for him."

Martha looked at Mr. Wells like he just fell out of a tree. "Check for what again?" She asked as if he was some sort of pet rather than her son. Needing to clean his cage or pen-like animal. It infuriated her just the mere thought.

"A check for taking care of EJ of course, to help pay for his expense and cost while he's in your care," he replied.

What's Behind the Looking Glass?

"You are joking right?" She asked looking at Judge Parker than at Mr. Wells. Doc just sits back smiles watching the fireworks about too explode. "You think the government can buy him like just a piece of meat from a store or buy love on a shelf." She replied as her voice turns fiery hot.

Mr. Wells felt like a cornered mouse as he looked at Doc with his hands behind his head just smiling away as if he was going bail him out. *No way, he's been there before, he knows better than to argue with her.* Mr. Wells takes a couple of swallows, "glad you feel that way," he said loosening his tie backing away; thinking how to get back on her good side. "Never the less it's our way," he said taking another swallow. "To say thank you, and want you to spend it on him how you see fit." Thinking best to hurry it along quickly, wiping the sweat off his brow, with his sleeve.

"Now to that there are some guidelines we need to discuss and go over and I'll leave you a copy so you can have reference to them later on. This regards to visitation rights of his parents and guardianship while he's in your care." He replied handing them the document.

"Yes we know about that; we have been informed that they are allowed to see him when they want while they are supervised until un-need… We're not happy about it and we have not told him about it yet." She replied angered by the question.

"I see," as he hesitates… "There is one more thing regarding that rule which has slightly changed in the last six months," he said.

"How?" She replied her hands balled into a fist as she waited for the other shoe to drop.

Mr. Wells takes another hard swallow and loosened his tie some more. "We would like him to spend time in the home unsupervised," he said.

Martha came unglued. Her eyes popped right out of her head, knuckles turned white. "You want me to do what?" She said.

Mr. Wells was nearly in the corner climbing the wall, looking for an exit. Martha paced up and down the floor of the room. Wayne blocked the door of the room, trying himself to control the rage that burned inside him.

Judge Parker seeing he needed to do something fast or this poor man was history; he was looking a hung jury. "Martha it won't be for at least a couple of years, not right away at least," he said. Hoping that would settle her down. "And bedsides, Betty his grandmother and you will have full access to him at all times."

After a few minutes things calmed down a little, but the fire never left her eyes or her fury when she looked at Mr. Wells. "Mr. Wells, I want from you and the state in writing and made clear. Not so much as one hair on that boy's head is to be touched until his ready now write," she said. Quickly turning around to face him, she placed her hands on her hips, with an ice-cold stare that it shivered his very bones right where he stood, taping her foot while he wrote in the file. "Is that everything Mr. Well's?" She asked with a low growl.

"That's should do it regarding EJ." He said snapping the file closed, trying to head for the door. While his briefcase stood open. "Now there's just one more small little tiny matter and I'll be on my way," he said heading towards the door. "Not really worth mentioning really," trying to squeeze his way out.

Martha stopped him placing her foot in front of the door. "I thought you said we were done talking about EJ?" She said growling as her fist tightened. Wells noticing her neck muscles tighten and no longer felt safe as he glanced over at Mr. Downing. He was beginning to wonder if this was such a good idea, but he needs those records and also need to know if they would support EJ through rough times ahead. He had more than one mission as he thought of Morgan and the Council of Light regarding the boy's destiny.

"Oh yes, we are; no more questions there." Mr. Wells said loosens the rest of his tie wiped and mopped the sweat off his face, "it's his brother Danny," he said.

What's Behind the Looking Glass?

"Yes, what about him?" She asked with a very hard growl that echoed in the room.

"Something about making arrangements for him to visit him on every other weekend every month," he replied.

"Yes, we and his grandmother felt it necessary to keep the bond between the boys," she said.

"We feel the same way, except." Losing his tie and wiping sweat from his face. "The time period will only be for six months and then revaluated after that," he said. Then quickly ran out the door and down the hall as quick as he can.

Chapter 20-1

* * * *

"Oooooh, what infuriating little man, I could just strangle him," she said taking her fingers tightens into a fist, shaking it in the air.

Judge Parker turned to leave. "What can I say? That's the government in nutshell. Sometimes I hate my job and other times like these; where I get to make a difference. I guess what I'm trying to say is welcome to parenthood. You have got yourselves a boy," he said as he shook their hands.

"Doc I'll be seeing ya," Judge Parker said as he waved and walked down the hall, "oh tell his grandmother hi for me," he said.

Martha, Wayne looked at each other. "I know she said it was going to be tough, but poor EJ," she said.

"Martha there's nothing we can do about it right now, just hope for the best," he said.

"I know dear. Six months. Danny's going to be heartbroken," she said.

"Well for right now we have them both, so let's do what we can," and kisses her on the cheek.

"I guess I'll be going to," Doc said picking up his bag. "I noticed the car out front, I thought for a minute that Betty was around. Thought I stop and say hi before I left."

"Sorry Doc that's her son's car; he staying with us for a while," Wayne replied.

"Oh, which one?" Doc asked.

"Richard," Wayne said.

What's Behind the Looking Glass?

"Little Richard?" Doc asked.

"Yes," Martha replied, "her youngest boy?"

"Well fry me up in bacon, I haven't seen him since he was knee high to a grasshopper," he replied.

"He's just down the hall with a mild case of sunburn," Wayne said.

"Well, then this calls for house call why I'm still here. I might as well take look or she will never forgive me and I know better to mess with her," he said as they all laugh.

The three of them walked down the hall to Richard's room seeing the door still closed. Wayne opened the door and turned on the light, Richard was still asleep. Doc whispered, "Why is he asleep?" He asked.

"We wore him clean out," Wayne said and smiles.

"Oh my, just look at that sunburn this boy is beat red," Martha said as she went over to Richard and gave him a nudge. "Richard,"

Richard's eyes flash open jumps up with a start. "Oh crap!" Seeing Mrs. Downing standing over him, realizing he was still in his underwear lying on the bed, and Mr. Downing standing in the doorway with another person with him.

"Have a good sleep son?" Wayne asked smiling.

"Sorry sir, I'll be right there," Richard replied.

"Oh take your time son, Doc here wants to take look at ya," he said.

"I'm fine sir really, just a little sunburn that's all."

"I know son," Wayne said.

"Do you remember me, Richard?" Doc asked.

"No, should I?"

"Well you were too young most likely, but I remember you when you were the same ages as Danny. Let me see that was way back. I am an old man compared to you. Tsk, tsk too many years for this old coon. Well, let's take a look at you."

"I told you, sir, I don't need Doctor I'm fine," he said.

"Now listen here boy! I've looked at everyone in this household including EJ's family and since I was in the neighborhood. You are going sit here let me look you over or your mother will skin me alive if she finds out that I didn't!" Doc said as his mustache twitched.

"Yes sir," Richard said not liking the idea at all.

"That's better," Doc said setting down his bag on the table and opened pulling out his instruments as he listened to his heart and checked his reflexes. "Now aren't you little old to be playing Indian with the rest of the boys?"

"I not no Indian sir and I wasn't playing."

"Then where's your clothes and why are you sunburned?" Doc asked as he examined him his sore feet and ears. "Say ah" as he checked his throat poking around with a wooden stick. Shining a light into his eyes as Richard tries to sits still.

"My mother took my clothes with her Doc," he said.

"Why'd she do that?" Doc asked.

"So I'd stay put Doc, that's why," Richard said trying to be sybille.

Doc looked at Wayne then at Martha, pulled on his mustache. "Boy you must have got in the path of the wind, didn't you? Then I would mind your mother and stay put because she on a coon hunt and stay out of her way son," he replied as he finishes up and closing his beg and grabbing the handle.

What's Behind the Looking Glass?

"Martha he'll be fine, just a good old fashion sunburn and some sore feet. Just soak them in some water for a few days to tough him up, he'll be right as rain." Doc paused for a moment remembering yesterdays and smiles. "Just dowse him with cold water take out the heat and put some that lotion on him that you been given to the boys and some that oil to loosen those muscles. This boy's strung tighter than a kite."

"Doc how's EJ doing?" Richard asked.

"He's doing fine, just took a few stitches out and healing up, got long ways too go still. See you in a few days now I would stay put if you know what's good for you," Doc said.

"Doc I don't seem to have a choice do I?"

"Not less she left the keys to your car."

"Doc I tried that, she removed the spark plugs too," he said.

"Then Richard, I guess I'll be seeing you to in a few days because son your not going anywhere it looks like and I know better to stay out of her path," he said and waves them all good day.

"Sorry sir, I didn't mean to fall asleep, guess not used to farming," Richard said.

"Its all right Richard, can't turn you into a farmer overnight. Now let Martha put the lotion on you and come out and join us," Wayne said.

"Yes sir," watching Mr. Downing leave.

"Ok Richard let's put this on you silly boy, what were you thinking?" Martha asked.

"Ooh that stings," he said.

"Of course it does, hold still," Martha said as she rubbed the lotion on his back and shoulders.

"Richard, what do for fun when you are home?"

"Whata you mean?" He replied.

"Do you go to dances? Meet nice girls that sort of thing," she asked.

"No just stay home mostly read, watch TV, like to walk, work on my car. Nothing special," he said.

"How come? Do you get lonely?"

"Sometimes I guess, but somebody had to be there to take care of mother after Pa died and everyone got married and left. She would have been alone, so I just sort figured she needed me to take care of her," he said.

"I see," she said. "Did you think maybe she didn't want you to take care of her and wanted you to have a life of your own? Maybe that's why she thought she leave you here. To see if maybe along the way; just maybe you both can have one before its too late. Now then you finish putting the rest of this on and I got the perfect cure for those muscles. So don't go anywhere, I am not quite done with those overalls," she said, and walked down the hall with his overalls under her arm and walks into the kitchen.

"Julie dear, my hands are tired. Do you mind taking this oil down to Richard and put it on him? Be sure to get those sore feet too and leave the door open," Ma said handing the overalls to her.

"Yes Ma," she said as she giggled, walks down the hall with the overalls and the oil.

"Hello Richard, Ma says you need this," she said setting down the overalls on the table and holding up the oil.

"Oh, no you don't!" He replied.

"You boys are all the same. You are just being silly, you might well get it over with because you are not leaving this room. I want to you know I wrestle with Robert and Will all the time," she said as she springs for the doorway.

"Help! Mrs. Downing, help!" Richard calls out.

"I'll hogtie to this bed if I have to Richard, just relax. Now that's a good boy... relax," Julie said.

"Mrs. Downing... Hel... ahhhhh," he replied.

"That's better, you are tight," Julie said working his neck and back and shoulder muscles, Richard seeing Mrs. Downing in the hallway sitting on a stool, watching Julie and him through the door while working on another pair of overalls. She turned her head and smiles like a cat and winked at Richard picking up the needle goes back to work.

"Now let's take look at those feet," she said.

"ahhhhhhh," he said.

"That's a good boy, now that wasn't so bad now, was it? Ok, you can go now," Julie said, hands him his overall. Richard pink and smooth as baby's bottom blushing red quickly put on the overalls and ran out the back door.

"There you are, Richard, what took you so long?" Robert asked as he watched Richard come out the back door with one strap over his shoulder.

Julie opened the back door came outside. "See you later Richard," she said with the bottle of oil and lotion in her hand.

Will and Robert laughing; "Never mind, we know how you feel Richard, ready to get back to work after a nice long nap." Richard too embarrassed to answer just nods.

Laying the boards along the line the pattern shown; the boys worked late through the afternoon. With the sun blazing high above the sky, hammer, and nails pounding in the wood their bare feet running across the ground. It was like watching a dance as the saws whistling of boards and hammers in the background. The boys would carry the boards two by two upon their shoulders, and then laying them down along the floor of the ground. EJ sat in the corner counting checking off each of the boards and then whittling, sanding a block or carving a horse, every so often.

The girls or Ma would come out to give their opinion and refresh them with water or with lemonade, but most the time just to see if they could make a change or two. So Pa would have to send them away, scooting them towards the door. Pa looked over at EJ, "that's enough of that for one day son. Let's give you something else to do. Doc said we needed to work on those shoulders and arms a bit," he replied.

"How Pa?" EJ asked looking around at the blocks of wood. "I can't do anything but this," he replied.

Pa putting his fingers to his chin and smiles and looked at the wagon." Robert, Will you got yourselves a new cutter," he said.

"Yes, Pa."

"Come get him, boys," Pa said. Robert and Will came over to help EJ with his one crutch so he doesn't fall.

Ma seeing what's about to happen comes dashing out the house. "Pa you put him down right now! He's not ready yet," she said hands on her hips.

Pa just ignores her. "Boys just put him in the wagon, Ma he'll be fine you heard the Doc its time to get him moving. Now scoot, the boys and I got everything under control." He said. Ma gives him a cold hard stare then shook her fingers in his face "if…"

EJ turned around. "Ma I'll be fine; Ma please let me try," in a small little pleading voice. That's all it took to take the fire out of her eyes, as she watched the boys help him into the wagon before she went back inside. Pa cleaned up EJ's wooden blocks puts them into a wooden box sets them on the side, with all his horse carvings

What's Behind the Looking Glass?

and smiles at the fine work he has done. Everyone in their place the works sets in motion once again.

Changing dance partners and doing the dosey doe. Grab your partner here we go, grab your hammer, grab your board. Will and Robert carrying; swing those legs bend those knees, boys raise those shoulders high. Kick those feet off the ground boys; we got ourselves a working ho-down. EJ sawing board on the wagon, Richard and Pa on the ground with the hammer, swing those hammer to the beat.

One saw the wood. Two pounds the nail, Three drops the board. Four, kick those feet in the air. Five, bend those knees. Six, swing those shoulders high, lift those boards in the air. Seven, swing your partner round and do the dosey doe. Eight clap your hand slap your knees return to your partner and do it again.

Pa and the boys outside worked until late in the afternoon on the floor of the new foundation. Pa decided to call it for the day wiping his face. "Alright boys, that's enough for one day," he said as he watched the boys fall to the ground on their backs.

"Yes Pa," they replied.

Pa chuckled seeing how tired they are. "You boys rest awhile then put things away for today," Pa said and helps EJ down from the wagon leaned him up next to the boys and went into the house.

"Man am I tired," Richard said as he rubbed his sore arms.

Robert and Will laid back on the ground, Robert said. "You're tired?" Turning their heads to face him "at least you got a nap today," Robert replied.

"Yea, and it turned into a nightmare when I woke up," Richard said looking towards the house where Julie is.

Will and Robert rubbing their legs and arms to get the stiffness out, "I bet we're going to feel that in the morning," Will said.

"I guess we better get moving or you know who will come to

find us," Robert said. Richard didn't even have to wonder who that was; he was up in a shot before Robert and Will. "Oh, I see you met my sister Julie?" Robert, Will, and EJ start laughing. Robert said. "Let's say she doesn't take no for an answer."

Will replied. "No she doesn't, neither does my sister Anna, It runs in the family; no use running either. Does no good; they will just hunt you down, so just get it over with right EJ?" Will said EJ nods head yes as the boys laughed. "In EJ's cases; he can't run, but Pa showed us they sure can melt and blush."

Richard turned his head towards them pondering. "You got to be kidding, they can melt and blush?" He asked.

"Yep didn't you see how EJ handle Ma too let him be in the wagon? She was mad and about tare Pa into pieces. Just two words and done just the right way. That's right we know secret." Robert replied Richard was all ears. "The secret is..."

"Oh, I see you boys are rested. Let's go ahead and start putting things away then." Pa said opening the back door.

"Yes, Pa...Yes, sir." Richard didn't get hear the secret.

"You boys need to finish your chores for the night," Pa said as the boys were cleaning up, girls were out admiring the boys' work. Dancing on the foundation flooring, giggling like schoolgirls among themselves. It reminded them of a dance floor because was so open. Pa chuckled as Sam and Danny grabbed their hands as young men dancing with them to no music, spinning their little legs in the air as they squealed with laughter. Pa looked over at Richard putting things away on the wagon then over at Julie, with a quick smile, rubbed his chin an idea formed in his head.

"Well boys, that's last of it. You go ahead start on the chores Richard can you help me; I have something special planned for tonight. Richard followed him questioning. *What's he got me doing now?* Help me with this box of lights." Pa said opening the shed door by the barn.

What's Behind the Looking Glass?

"Sir, why are we hanging lights around here?" He asked.

"Oh I thought we have a bit fun that's all," Pa said. Richard not exactly sure just does what he is told.

"If you say so sir," he replied. They hang the lights around the foundation boards, Richard thinking he got to be out of his mind, we can't work in the dark.

"Alright go inside and get cleaned up for dinner," he said finishing the string of lights and plugging them in as they glowed in the dark like little twinkle lights of stars.

Martha comes out of the house to see what Pa's up to, seeing the lights around the foundation. "Wayne, what are you up to?" She asked.

"Oh, I thought we have a bit fun that's all. The girls gave me an idea when they came out with Danny and Sam. I thought we do little dancing of our own. Have little fun after dinner if that's alright with you dear?"

"Wayne dear." She said folding her arms around him as she lifted herself on her toes off the ground to reach him "that's a wonderful idea," kissed him right then and there. "We don't need a full moon. I think he might be busy tonight. Nothing fancy now just girls and farmers, I don't want them melting tonight dear."

"I think they might be too tired; I'll put the Indians to bed early dear," he said and kisses her again.

"Yes dear, the man moon will be too busy tonight," she said leaving him and going back inside to finish dinner. "Girls your Pa has a treat for you so hurry up with setting table because you need to change your clothes."

"Why Ma?" they asked.

"They're taking us dancing, now hurry up." That put an extra spark into them. Things started to fly through the kitchen like a dance of their very own. Swan like; plates in hand curtsying as they placed a plate on the table as they bow. A quick little twirl then placed another plate in its place. One in each place then twirl around, spinning each other placing silverware, then a glass, rolls, butter. One, two, three, spin, curtsy, place, One, two three, spin, bow place, la le, da, la le, da, la le, da. Giggled as they passed each their on the floor in the kitchen to the dining room.

Sam and Danny watching them trying to copy them then laughed at them for being so silly. After they were done Ma scooted them down the hall to wash up and change their clothes giggled to her self. Thinking of poor Richard; *well maybe I was little too hard on him letting Julie chase him around the room, but then again, she did work those muscles out and I think his mother would have approved at his age* as she giggles like a schoolgirl.

"Alright boys go ahead wash up for dinner; I want you to change those clothes too. I told your Ma that Indians are going to bed early tonight, we're taking the girls dancing tonight," Pa said as the boys looked worried.

"Just wear your overalls nothing fancy, we're just going have little fun that's all."

"Yes Pa," they said as they grinned.

Richard was the only one that wasn't smiling; he was worried thinking *"this got to be the craziest family."* Their idea for having fun was not what he had pictured in his mind at all. Things were not going well for him at all, *"what was this fun they keep talking about?"*

First, he was left here in the middle of nowhere with no clothes, his car disabled, chased around the room by their sister Julie, hogtied to the bed. Then worked to the ground, sunburned, sore, tired. Now they want him to dance the night away. What fun is this? They're mad completely mad the lot of them. *"Mother, what were you thinking?"* The boys got washed up and changed their clothes except for Richard. He didn't have any clothes to change into, so he just washed up for dinner.

Chapter 20-2

* * * *

The dinner table was all buzz, girls giggling with excitement in their nice farmer dresses the boys dressed in the farmer overalls. They could barely contain themselves. Richard was sweating every time he looked across the table seeing Julie wink at him. He knew he was in trouble as the night wore on. Dinner seemed to go by in slow motion for the girls they couldn't wait for the fun to start, but not slow enough for Richard.

As usual, Pa brings the table to order by clicking the glass with his butter knife and clearing his throat. "A humm, just a few announcements as you know Richard will be staying with us for a couple of weeks to help on the farm, while his mother is visiting her granddaughters." Then he looked at EJ and then at Martha across the table as she nodded for him to continue. "As of today, we are now EJ's foster parents according to the government of this state. It is now official. Welcome home EJ," he replied.

EJ smiles with some embarrassment as his face turned red. "Thanks, Pa." Will, Robert grab his head under their arms rubbed his head. Ma just smiles instead of getting after them. Pa looked over at boys. "Not at the table boys," he said.

"Sorry Pa," they replied.

Ma looked at him from across the table. "It's alright, let them have a little fun," she said and winked back at the boys.

Pa said. "To celebrate this occasion… I thought we have a night of family fun after dinner outback. How about some dancing, under the stars and kick up our heels for just us farmers?"

"Yes Pa," everyone was in unison. Except for Richard he didn't say a word he rather be somewhere else, looked down at his plate hoping not to be noticed.

"That includes you, Richard," Pa said looking straight at him.

"Sir, I thought I would turn in early if you wouldn't mind?" He asked.

"Sorry son; I think your dance card is full tonight," he said looking at the girls. "Ma everything looks so good and me and the boys have worked up an appetite today," he replied.

"Good Pa, because after that infuriating man left, I had to cook up another storm," she said.

After dinner, everyone helped cleared the table and put the food away quickly and everyone helped do the dishes, while Ma and Pa changed their clothes. When Pa came out of the room he was dressed just like Richard just in his overalls. Richard was shocked beyond belief. "Sir I thought you said we are going dancing?" He replied.

"We are Richard, we are; I said nothing fancy just simple farmers, nothing special, didn't I?" He asked.

"Yes, sir." Not relishing the idea at all and sighed.

"Now come on, the girls are waiting." Richard and Pa went out on the deck of the new foundation, Richard seeing Robert, Will, and EJ all dressed the same as him, just simple barefoot farmers in overalls just like him nothing special. The girls including their mother in simple farmer beautiful dress, that barely cover their tiny bare feet, giggling, waiting for the music to start; Sam and Danny sitting on a stool with their little legs swinging. Yes, sir, Mr. Downing was true to his word; it was a simple farmer dance.

Lights flickered hung by a wire showing the dance floor as it glowed and music began to play. Pa takes Ma's hand starts the first dance on the new foundation floor of the house. Richard tries to find a corner to stand in to watch but was not quick enough before Julie found him first. "Hello Richard, going somewhere?" She asked as she winked at him.

What's Behind the Looking Glass?

"I, I, I thought I, I watch for a while," he replied.

"Oh, I see. It doesn't seem as much fun to watch now come on, let's give it whirl." She said and grabbed his hand and dragged him out on the dance floor.

Every time he tried to escape, she would reel him back in and giggle. She had a firm grip on his hand. She leaned forward close to his ear whispered. "Richard just relax, it's just a dance," and giggles in his ear and smiles. After a while, he stops trying to escape seeing he has no choice and sighs and gives in.

Ma nods to Julie with a smile. "Well done," and whispered in Pa's ear. "Look what your daughter has done."

Pa gives Ma twirl on the dance floor so he can get quick glance seeing Richard dancing with Julie he does little chuckle, "that's my girl, he needs to have some fun."

The music stops, Richard thinks he free at last starts to head for the corner, but not for long. "Hello Richard, going somewhere? I believe it's my turn," as Anna quickly grabbed his hand. Robert takes his sister Julie's hand, while Ma and Pa still dance among themselves EJ puts on another record watching the fun Danny and Sam trying copying some of the dancing among themselves laughing at silly grown-ups.

Richard again trying to escape the clutches of this sister, but not succeeding she to whispered in his ear." Just relax Richard," and had a firm hold on him as well. She giggled as he tries to get away.

Robert leans overseeing how hard Richard trying to get away whispered. "You might well just give in, you have already lost," and laughed.

The music stops Richard thinking here's his chance to get away since they have all had a turn at him. "Hello, Richard. May I have this dance?" As Mrs. Downing grabbed Richard's hand, he sighs not daring to say no. He was caught in a trap with nowhere to run. He nods his head.

"Yes, ma'am." Will steps in taking Julie's hand, Pa taking Anna's, Robert each taking one of the little boys Sam and Danny out on the floor. Soon everyone was dancing except for EJ until Ma came over and swings his shoulders around a bit and the girl's dances around him. Pa was right… Richard's dance card was full that night because every girl in the house danced with him at least 4 to five times that night. He never did make too the corner that night.

Everyone tired from the day; Ma and girls bring the festivity to close with a light dessert. Peach cobbler ice wiped vanilla ice cream outside under the stars. The girl's layout a quilt on the ground passing around the plates. "Nice night out Pa," Ma said as she looked up at the sky with a light cool breeze blowing.

"Yes it is," he said as he looked deep into her eyes for him that's where the heaven lay not in the sky above but in her eyes.

"So Richard did you have fun tonight?" Ma asked handing him a plate.

"Actually I did Mrs. Downing," he replied taking a bite as it melted into his mouth, He wondered if perhaps she was a better cook than his own mother.

"I am glad." She said squeezing his hand and kissed his cheek as turned red from embarrassment.

"But I am sure dog tired," he said trying to recover as he wiped the sweat from his brow and finished off his dessert.

Pa looked over at the stacks of lumber in the corner and the boys. "We need too go, Payson, tomorrow and order some more lumber and I need some more supplies that I can't get from Santaquin. Plus we need to fill up the pickup anyway. Ma if you and girls can put a list together of things you need while we're there, we boys can get them for ya… EJ would you like to come with us?"

"Can I?" He asked.

"I don't think we're going run into anybody there, besides you shouldn't have anything to worry about," Pa said.

What's Behind the Looking Glass?

"What about Richard, Pa can he come to?" EJ asked.

Pa rubbed his chin. "If he promises he won't run off anywhere," he said.

"Sir where could I go, I am stuck here remember?" He said.

"You a got point," Pa said and the boys laughed. Pa looked over at Sam and Danny fast asleep, everyone laughed seeing how tired Sam and Danny are as they fell asleep against each other. "Speaking of dog tired. I suggest we all go to bed. Ma you can do those in the morning we've all done enough work for one day." Pa said picking up the Sam in his arms; Richard picked up Danny and followed him into the house. While Robert and Will helped EJ with his crutch and hobble him back into the house.

The boys' headed towards their room getting ready for bed and girls to head off to theirs while Richard and Pa clean up Sam and Danny and put them to bed. "Thanks, Richard," Pa said watching Danny fall asleep and brushing the hair from his eyes.

"Thanks for what sir?" Richard asked.

"For helping me with Danny; I could have done it, you didn't need to," he said.

"Sir I wanted to." As he and Richard looked at Danny sleeping in his bed then bends down and tucked little Danny in. "After all, he is my reasonability too. I am his uncle," as he smiles brushed the hair out of his eyes again. They closed the door and turned out the light Richard went to his room. "Goodnight sir," and closed the door and gets ready for bed, thinking maybe their not so crazy after all, just a little bit.

Ma and Pa made their nightly rounds before turning in themselves for the night, stopping in the boy's room bending down and tucked them in then softly brushed their hair whispered goodnight to each one of the boys, placing a warm kiss on their cheeks. Then proceed down the hall to Richard's room to make sure that his alright.

He nods his head thanks them, they wish him a good night and closed the door. Then they went into the little boy's room where they are fast asleep laying kiss each of their cheeks and wishing them a good night. Around the corner they turned to the girl's rooms side by side they enter. "Goodnight my sweet devil angel's goodnight and sweet dreams." After making full circle they reach their bedroom they enter closed the door. They wrap each other in their arms.

"Thank you, my dear, for everything, I love you so much." "Thanks for the meal, my house is full; the heart is full and I wouldn't trade any one of them for the world."

CHAPTER 21

MIKES LAST BATTLE

A loud sonic boom would have been heard into the next county and beyond if it wasn't for a simple spell hovering over Mike Cotwellar small four-bedroom home, and a hidden basement concealed by magical runes. Back and forth a battle was fought between two sides, the shadow and the light over a book containing the prophecy of this modern age. Also contained in this book held the key to unlocking the power lost eons ago, and how to find the items known as the five keys needed to open the gate.

Mike and Derrick breathed heavily as Derrick left hand shot forth a flash of green lightning as he watched it cress cross the room towards Morgan and his minions. Two more fell as their bodies disintegrated into fine powdered. Morgan growled as he watched his men die, his staff glowed with power. "You can not hope to win against me, you cowards."

Mike laughed as he stood behind an overturned desk against the wall. "It is you Morgan that should be afraid. I do not fear death, for the White Solan will destroy you once and for all. The light shall remain free as it should be." Lifting his right hand into a low arc said "nas'tandnen." Blue fire circled them as it protected them long enough to breathe as sweat beaded down his cheeks.

If only he could hold on long enough until more help could arrive. He was doing his best for a man of ninety in human years, but over nine-hundred in wizard years, and head of **The Council of Light** for nearly two hundred years. His hair gray or what's left of it anyway. His skin had lost its shine a decade ago now ruff as old leather and blotched with age. Not bad for his age, still handsome according to his wife Margaret. Who just turned seventy this past year and still innocent of his real-life or secret wizard's life. She is also the apple of his eye, wishing he could of at least said goodbye,

But his green eyes were bright and still able to hold all the world and her in his eye.

He coughed wiping blood way onto his left sleeve. Knowing the dark blood would never wash out of his favorite blue cotton work shirt that his wife made him for Christmas last year. He smiled inside as he thought about her. Watched her grumble enough times as she picked up his shoes and placed them back under the bed. As a boy growing up, he hated wearing shoes.

He would spend hot summer days with his father fishing or raising sheep on their ranch or spend time planting sprigs of trees on the lumber mill. Shoes were not made for a man, nor a boy at heart. There is nothing like feeling the dirt shifting between your toes or the cool water as you fish in the stream. Mike nodded to his partner that he was fine, gripped his long pearl white staff, more for support as the magic in him waned a bit more.

Derrick a young man in his early years, the average height of seven feet six tall, born in England during the reign of King George the first, his hair black with some gray, blue eyes and strong build like an Irish man on his mother side. Who he can remember still, the young rascal he was just coming into his own. Strong in magic like his father before him as he watched him turn the world upside down in his spent youth. His mouth tightened into a grin as he remembered his long past youth of drinking at the pub known as the Silvery Dog and getting into a fight over the same woman whom he married later.

Her name Liysa with the golden hair, his first wife at the time whom he married soon after the king died. Such memories forced upon a dying man. Who knew then that they would be best of friends now? Most likely they will die this very night together. "No. it won't end like that if I have anything to say about it." Said, " mer'na los." A burst of light surrounded him as his hand pushed his life's energy towards his friend Derrick. He knew it would soon be his last as his hand gripped the staff hard from shaking. Watching it engulf his friend giving him the last of his strength and power.

Mike held his staff in pain as a well placed lightning bolt shot

What's Behind the Looking Glass?

through him. White smoke drifted towards them with two more arrivals from the calls of help he had sent over two hours ago by the shadow of light known in our world (a dragon wing.) Bowden and Jaydan swung wide casting another ward of protection when Morgan said. "Kill. Kill them all. No one leaves until their dead and the book is mine."

The air crackled with electricity as flashes of red and yellow fire. A loud painful scream filled the air as Mike fell grasping his heart. His last thoughts of his friends and words echoed as his life faded away. His last words were. "May the light always be in your heart? Margaret." His body fell to the cold blackened ground. While his soul departed to the unseen world behind the looking glass. Mike placed a last kiss on his wife Margaret's cheek says. "Goodbye my love, may the light always shine. Until we meet again."

"Now is not the time to grieve brothers," Bowden said with his teeth clenched in anger. His hands and staff conjuring spell after spell. A tear fell for his comrade his friend, as he laid a comforting hand on his partner Jaydan. Knowing they must fight on, protecting the book of prophecy which conceals the gate beyond time where the power of light and hopes and dreams of two young boys. Lay well guarded and hidden behind that door. That will save the worlds (here and beyond) from complete darkness. Bowden was roughly half the age of his long-time partner and friend Derrick. Light build, built for speed having Elvin blood in his veins gave him more dexterity than any normal man or wizard.

He did not retain the pointy ears or drawn down chin like most Elvin folk he had come across, but some would say his eyebrows are arched like his father. He stood tall just over eight feet, which was average for Elvin folk. And he did age slower like most wizards do, even slower with the Elvin blood that binds him. Yet here in this mortal world or in this reality, he looked about a man in his late 20s when in truth he was 300. Silvery hair and handlebar mustache and blue silver eyes that could look through your very soul and a square hard chiseled chin with fair complexion.

Jaydan growled. "Go in peace brother." His hand rose palm side up placing a shielded barrier of glass over his fallen friend. His eyes wet with tears, but his heart and mind strong as he engaged in battle. Jaydan was built for strength, broad shoulders easy enough to hold a two-handed sword if need be, and has done so before the ripe old age of two hundred in wizard years, but he looked to be the age of thirty among the human population. He stood almost eight feet tall.

He had been accused of having big feet like his father size thirteen and a half from ankle to the tip of his big toe. Jaydan had one feature he inherited from his grandfather, unlike his sister. He had twelve toes, quite natural if he thinks about it as they wiggled in his hard sole shoes. He also had a strong stout nose and his mother's greenish-blue eyes and his father's square jawline. But he got his caramel white hair from his grandmothers' side.

Jaydan fought hard as he swung his staff hard to the left crashing down another barrier shield on Morgan's side of the room. He had just ducked in time as another well placed lightning bolt missed where he was standing a moment ago. "Eirn'na 'tan' ta" A green ball fire rolled towards two more of Morgan's minions bursting them into flames. Jaydan swung his staff hard to the right with loud crack breaking a knee of another. A quick twirl of his staff with an arc to the left, " yandan' far'drag'nas. The words of wind burst forward the air in front of him into a fire-spitting dragon." He had always liked the extra flare of images, it makes the magic seem more real to him.

Bowden growled. "Show off," while Jaydan smiled back with gritted teeth. Bowden swung hard to his left, a sword of fire in one hand and staff in the other as he made his way towards Morgan. Slowly the three battled making very little headway. Each would turn long enough to glance down towards Mike now at rest. The years seemed to have faded from his face as if he was merely sleeping, Bowden spoke. "Sand fey nor' ass,'" from his left-hand white fire shot from his hand taking down three more of Morgan minions. With hard spin and thrust of his right hand, the sword slipped clean as butter poking out the other side of a man's chest. He barely had time to pull it out and sidestep to his right before being hit with a deathly bolt of lightning.

Derrick and Jaydan followed through by placing both their staffs together, their words echoed. " To noss heydon' maw' say

What's Behind the Looking Glass?

degornen." In a flash of brilliant white light spread across them and their comrade Bowden and the body of Mike. Morgan and his followers shield their eyes from the bright light. When they were able to see, everyone was gone, including the locked chest in which the book was believed to be held in.

Morgan screamed with outrage his staff fell to the floor with a loud crack as it splintered and turned to dust before his very eyes. "This is not the end of this," he shouted. "We will win and the worlds will be mine to control forever!" Morgan reached in his wand pocket says "Notor' na dos enoss.'" A doorway opened in front of him allowing him to leave this reality and leave this world behind for now, for he was not in the fight to win the book. Which he had stolen long ago, leaving a fake in its place? His goal had been to kill Mike Cotwellar and render **The Council of Light** useless without its leader. As he moved forward with his plans to deal with the boy EJ which so far has eluded him because of Mike Cotwellar and his wife Aunt Margaret.

Now all that remains is for Morgan to capture the boy from this world and be placed out of the way from **The Council of Light**. To be able too neither changes his destiny as he takes his place by his side as the Dark Prince, Now that the White Solan can never be nor rises since Jeff was dead. But also remove the boys Aunt Margaret from this world and her meddling in things that are way beyond her. Morgan sneered with thoughts of Margaret, hoping she would be crushed along with the house as he watched the walls and the roof collapsed when he walked through too the other side. "No. We have just begun to fight."

The light winked out around them as Jaydan. Derrick and Bowden breathed heavily, their hands on their knees as they gasped for air and tired. Derrick fell to the ground with blood spreading across his chest. Bowden having some skills in healing magic mumbled. "Raw near' a 'noss,'" with his left hand over Derrick's chest. Slowly the blood seeped back into his body. Derrick gasped when his eyes flew open. Jaydan helped him to sit up and helped him remove his gray cloak and a green button-down shirt. Bowden ripped the cloak into bandages and wrapped it tightly around his chest. Many centuries have passed since a true wizard healer has emerged among its people and none will be chosen among them according to the Oracle of Senta if ever and if Morgan wins this war.

She quoted. 'A healer among men you shall find and his heart pure and made of light, yet he is not a man at all. His destiny converges among finite realities some are not of his own. This is where you will find him, unto him he must choose and the chosen shall choose him. If things remain the same, Darkness will gather and the Coming of the Storm will never end.'

Derrick cringed from the pain as he watched Jaydan take some herbs from a pouch around his belt and casts a spell with his wand bring forth clean cool water into a shallow hole he had scooped out beside him. He then mixed the crushed herbs into a small wooden bowl from his conjured traveling pack hid deep inside his pocket. It always amazed him what magic can do as he mixed the simple healing herbs.

Derrick whispered thanks taking the bowl and tilted back his head swallowed the tonic. Feeling it work in his body as it replenished his strength. It will be weeks before he will be healed completely and leaving a well-earned battle scar. Bowden sat on the chest as they gathered strength as they decided their next move. None of them wanted to discuss the loss of their dearest friend Mike, his body lying next to them and their new duty's as it has left the leader seat empty once more. It would be months before a new vote could take place to install a new leader. For now, they have to say goodbye as each one placed a hand on his shoulder, whispering words of comfort. For them it not really goodbye, just moving on to a new seat that awaits him.

The chest was placed with the award of magic which would be locked away deep into some forgotten cave for now. In a world that not even Morgan would not think to look twice. The birthplace of both the Dark Prince and the White Solan, with a hope for peace and a quick end of Morgan and his reign, Derrick sighed longingly. Just thinking of all the work they have to do now and not too mention returning Mike's body to Margaret as is their tradition of the mortal world. "For now that's all we can do, Morgan has won this battle for now. Now we must prepare ourselves for war. Hunt down his followers and strengthen our bothers and most of all protect the boy and his guardian. The shadow will not win this fight. Fare thee well my brothers until we meet again." Derrick said with a wave of his staff over the golden chest and watched it fade away.

With a heavy sigh, he said goodbye and waited alone on the hill for Mr. Golden Eyes, aka Nathanial, Death walker in the realms of the dead. What better man could he have placed Mike's body into? After all, he was very much a dear friend as he. "Rest in peace brother, may the light always burn within your soul." He said with his hand on Mike's shoulder. Derrick drifted off beyond the horizon. Back too his home town known as Springfield as Mayor and the New Judge of Time the keeper of the gate behind the looking glass, to gather strength and decided his next move. For the war is coming to all men and kingdoms beyond the walls of time. "Have courage my brothers and find strength in the light."

Chapter 22

The house was quiet, everyone asleep from a hard day's work on the farm. Boys are nestled in their beds, not a sound except for one. EJ screamed in his sleep as he tossed and turned. "No! Stop! I must get away! No!" A cold sweat poured down his face as he yelled "No!" Somebody help!"

Robert and Will jump out of bed run to his side to wake him from the nightmare. EJ jumped up with a start with fear in his eyes shook like a leaf. Ma and Pa ran into the room to see what the problem was.

Robert sitting next to EJ as he looked up." He's having a nightmare that's all Ma," Robert said.

Ma and Pa understanding considering what he has gone through today. She went over gave him a hug and a kiss on his forehead, tells him everything going to be alright and brings in a glass of milk. Pa and Ma re tucked in the boys into bed, "try to get some sleep EJ," she said and closed the door.

Robert whispered. "What were dreaming about?"

"Oh you'll think it was stupid," EJ replied.

"Come on, tells us," Robert asked.

"Alright, I was dreaming about Mr. Scarecrow and he was chasing me because I still had his clothes," he said.

"You mean those clothes you were wearing when we found you?" Will asked.

"I had to wear something didn't I?"

"No wonder those stunk so bad," Will said and Robert laughed.

"Alright boys, go to sleep," Ma yelled from outside the room.

"Yes, Ma." Boy's laughing at EJ little nightmare of Mr. Scarecrow.

The house asleep the crickets chirping of a summer lullaby until the morning sunrise "cock doodle do" of Mr. Rooster sitting on the fence next to Richard's window he jumps off the bed with a start. "What the heck?" Ma enters. "Good morning Richard, breakfast is almost ready, there are clean towels and shorts in the bathroom hurry dear." Then closed the door and walked down the hall to the boy's room gets them up ready for breakfast.

Richard looked outside seeing Mr. Rooster walking back to his pen and could have sworn it winked at him." It's barely even daylight you stupid rooster, does he even know what time it is?" Richard stretched trying to work the kinks out and the aches out of his sore muscle in his shoulder and back. "Ouch, that hurts, man I'm sore." Then heads on into the bathroom to get cleaned up, "well at least were going to town today; won't have work as hard that something at least." The hot bath felt so good and having a nice pair of shorts that were his size and were his was good too.

Richard heard a knock on the door. "Richard, can you please hand me those overalls please and those shorts." Mrs. Downing said.

"I have a clean pair of overalls on your bed dear," she replied. Without a question because he knew she would try to come in. He pops out his hand gives them to her and finishes up in the bathroom. "That's a good boy, now hurry breakfast is waiting." She said as Richard wrapped the towel around his waist and heads on down to his room then stops. Julie is sitting there in the room waiting with the lotion and oil in her hand. Mrs. Downing just sets up the stool outside the room with a needle and thread and nods. "Go on Richard," and pushed him toward the door.

Richard sits on the bed and sighs. No use running after yesterday and gives in, "Now that's a good boy," Julie replies.

"Hey, that tickles," as Julie rubbed the lotion on and worked the oil in. "Oh, that's cold."

"Just relax, you are so tense Richard," she said as she worked his shoulders and arms. Then he works the rest of him until smooth and soft then hands him his overalls with a kiss on the cheek. "Try to have a little fun today Richard," she said and walked out of the room.

Richard dressed in his overalls went down to breakfast same old routine as every morning except not an Indian in sight unless you count Danny and Sam. Ma couldn't see what the harm was to leave them that way, after all, they weren't going to town; they could stay and play on the farm all day. What was shocking was Will, Robert and EJ they all decide to dress like Richard today.

"You boys ready to go to town?" Pa said looking over at Will, Robert dressed like Richard?"

"Yes Pa, were ready," they replied.

"Don't you think you need your shoes and your shirt?" He asked.

"Why Pa? Richard doesn't have any and EJ can't so we thought we be all the same today," Robert replied.

Pa laughed. "Alright boys, fine by me. Robert pull out the pickup and bring it around the front," throwing him the keys as he caught them in mid-air.

"Yes, Pa."

"Ma, you girls have the list of things you need from town?" Pa asked.

"Just about finished," as she looked through the pantry checking the items off the shelves with the pencil tapping against her lips. Robert pulled the pickup around to the front of the house and then he came back inside a taking seat next to the boys at the table as he waited to leave. "I think that should just about do it," as she hands him the list to Pa and shook a finger to remind them. "Now you be careful with him, I want him back in one piece Pa and you boys keep an eye on him too," she said.

What's Behind the Looking Glass?

"Yes, Ma...Yes, ma'am." They replied.

"I won't leave the pickup, not even for second Ma, I promise," he said

Ma kissed his head. "All right then, have a good time." The boys head out the door helping EJ into the back laying the quilt and pillow for his back. Robert and Richard climb in the back with EJ and Will took the front with Pa driving.

They headed for Payson, Pa taking the long way, so Richard can see how far it is, to and from the farm. In case he decided and thinks he wanted to try and walk to the next town. After all, Pa's not stupid and knows how stubborn these boys can get sometimes. Plus they weren't in any kind of hurry today. "Richard, do you remember what we told you how we found EJ?" Robert asked.

"Yes Robert I do," he replied.

Robert grinned. "Well EJ here had a nightmare last night," grinning some more at EJ. "You want to have little fun?" He asked. "It would mean leaving the farm and we could get caught."

"I guess so." As they passed passing a scarecrow on somebody's farm, EJ shivered with the very thought of it coming alive and chasing after him and wanting revenge.

Richard smiled. "Leaving the farm you say, humm. Robert what did you have in mind?"

"There is a Scarecrow running around out there without any clothes; we need to give them back, so he'll stop chasing EJ," he said as he rubbed his head with his knuckles.

Richard laughed. "So that's where you got those clothes EJ," he said.

"I had to wear something, Richard… I was like you… running around in my shorts, not even my best pair, but of course, Ma burned those to and left me with nothing," he said blushing red.

Robert laughed. "Oh, I remember. So does Will and you still don't have anything to wear." EJ, Robert laughed as he grabs his sides because hurts too laugh. Richard just rolled his eyes looked toward the open field of the middle of nowhere. *Yes, sir, they have lost their minds and EJ has cracked under the pressure, now they want to chase scarecrows.*

Just up ahead Richard could see Payson the deep green mountains filled with oak and pine and high snow peaks that seemed to loom over them as they grew closer to town. He loved the mountains when he was a young boy. He would walk the trails and hunt and fish in the cool streams that flowed along the trails. What happy memories they are when he envisioned him and his brothers and his father laughing around the campfire after a long day of hunting and fishing, knowing those days are gone and so is his father.

The thoughts of his father still greave him as he tries pushing them out of his mind for he could never return to those trails and he could never bring his father back. He wiped an escaped tear as he looked at the mountains. Mr. Downing pulled into town. "Well boys, we're almost there, let's say we that we fill up the pickup first before going in, and give you boys a chance to stretch your legs a bit," Pa said as he went inside the gas station.

"Robert?" Will called sliding out of the truck and stretched his arms and bending his legs back one at a time trying not to lose his balance.

"Yes Will?" Robert jumped down from the back of the truck to join him as they explore their surroundings. Feeling the cool breeze whips through his hair and the warm sun upon his shoulders it couldn't have been a more perfect day for adventure away from the farm. "What were guys talking about? I got bits pieces about something clothing a scarecrow but that's it." Robert whispers a plan he has in his ear. Will's eyes glance back at EJ then Richard standing over by the pickup.

Will raked his fingers through his hair? "You do realize Pa will kill us then skins us alive if he catches us. Then there's Ma she'll have a cow. How are we going to sneak EJ out of the house, he's only one that knows where it is?" He asked.

Will and Robert paced around in a circle for a minute trying decided what to do, waiting for Pa to fill up the tank and the spare can in the back of the pickup. "All right let's do it," rubbing his hands together, "it will be fun," he said.

"We need to start to collect items for a scarecrow to wear," replied Robert. Robert noticed a straw hat sitting on a bench by the window, slowly strolls over to it and looks both ways "Psssit" Will," then tossed it to him whispers "item number 1" and placed it in the pickup in the box. EJ laughed seeing the hat jump into the pickup Richard looked at them as if he missed something.

"All right boys. Let's go into town." Pa said paying the man and returned to the pickup. The boys all climb back into the truck Will and Robert with gleaming mischievous smiles on their faces. EJ grinning from ear to ear, Richard thinking they have all lost their minds again.

Pa pulled into town on the main drag where the shops of stores stood side by side on each side of the road. Compared to their home town only eight stores stood along the main street sporadic until hit the main part of town where Stringum Hardwood & Goods, the pharmacy stood on the corner of town. A town so small; you'd blink and miss it. Pa found a parking spot for the pickup and the boys' jumped out. "Why Mr. Downing fancy running into you." Mrs. Collins said coming out a woman's clothing store with shopping bags in her hand.

"Hello, Mrs. Collins. I just came in to pick up some supplies for the farm. You know my boys Robert, Will and our new son EJ and this young fella is his Uncle Richard and EJ's brother Danny are staying with us for a while," Pa replied.

Mrs. Collins swoons as she looked over at EJ in the back of the pickup. "Did I hear you right you said EJ is your new son?" She asked.

"That's right. We have four boys and ½ if count his brother Danny and our two girls of course, but who's counting?" As he glanced over at Richard, "we are just adding on to the house to make room for more," he said.

"More! Your poor wife, how does she handle it? Poor dear... Heard there were Indians out there too," she said.

"Yes, there, they're all right; it cuts down on the wash I must say, and easier on their shoes too. "When she looked at the boy's dirty bare feet and faces just wearing their bib overalls it sent shivers down her spine at the mere thought of savages and these ilks of lice infected people trying to populate like filthy rabbits, *how disgusting, how revolting* the nerve of some backwoods chanteys with such a limited education. It made her skin crawl.

"I think we might need a bigger spot at the annual picnic this year at the rate we're growing, never know who might turn up, savages every last one of them. Well, we got lots of shopping to do ma'am, see ya at the picnic, I'll tell my wife hello for ya." They turned and watched her run down the street. Pa started laughing watching her go Richard can't believe the show.

"Mr. Downing Sir. Who was that woman?" He asked.

"Oh just the biggest gossip in town," he replies.

"Sir?"

"Yes, Richard?"

"I'm not an Indian," Richard replied.

"I know that, but you are still one of us, that's all that matters," he said as he put his arm around him and all the boys laugh.

"Sir?" Richard asked.

"Yes, Richard?"

"Aren't you worried about what she might tell everyone?"

What's Behind the Looking Glass?

"Why Richard? They can think whatever they like, right boys?"

"Yes, Pa."

Richard looks at Mr. Downing and the boys. *They are plum crazy just like my mother* as he watched Mrs. Collins point at them, talking to another woman down the street. "Now let's go get those supplies, EJ if you want to walk around a bit we won't tell Ma?" Pa said.

EJ smiled just think about all the trouble he could get in and she wouldn't be the wiser. "Yes, Pa."

"Now go easy I don't want you to get too tired." He said as Robert, Pa helped him out of the pickup and stands him up on his crutch.

Robert, Will stay with him while Richard and Pa go into the store across the street get Richard some work clothing to wear around the farm. Watching them leave checking to make sure the coast was clear, "EJ, Robert and I have a plan if you are game? You know that dream you had last night about Mr. Scarecrow? What do you say we give him back his clothes so he'll leave you alone?" He said.

"How?" As he laughed thinking about his dream as it still gave him shivers as the scarecrows long arms reached out to him while he tried to get away, his eyes glowed red with anger as it chased him down the old and abandoned road. EJ gasped for breath forgetting to breathe as he recalls the nightmare.

"Well we have the hat, we just need the rest, and we can get that at home." Will replied standing on the right side of him and Robert on the other as they proceeded with their plan.

"Robert how we are going to get there? I can't sneak out of the house, not like this." EJ said shaking the dark thought of the dream, leaned up against the side of the pickup.

"Don't worry about that, we will think of something that's what brothers are for."

"All right if you say so, but if we get caught. Ma going to kill us right there on the spot," he replied. Robert finding some shade on the sidewalk near to the store Pa and Richard or in. Letting Will help him over and out of the way of other folks on the street that barely even glanced at the boys with a nod of their head and a simple wave. Others just simply moved across the street or walked around them, mumbled "bums and riffraff."

"Let's see, this should fit, Richard, try these on." Pa tossing him a pair of overalls and couple dress shirts and a couple of work shirts, go on son, try them on," Pa said.

"Yes sir," he replied.

Pa went over to the shoes picked up a pair of good work shoes for him. "That's better now you are starting to look like a farmer now." Handed him a pair of shoes, "try these on for size."

Richard looked at him, "are you sure sir?" He asked.

"Just put them on. I won't tell your mother. Can't have you go barefoot all the time now can we?" He said.

"No sir," he replied.

"I make Will, Robert wear theirs, so you will have a pair too. EJ will have pair to next time we come into town I recon, actually you try those on." Pa walked outside, "EJ come on in here son, we need to see if we can find and fit you for some clothes too." Robert and Will helped EJ into the store and sit him in the chair near the shoes. "Now then EJ I know you hate shoes, but the times a coming son," Pa said.

"Yes Pa, I know," he replied.

"This may hurt just a little," Pa said as they place some socks on his feet and measured him. They find his size take them off and put them in a box, "these are for later so when you can go to school," Pa said.

What's Behind the Looking Glass?

"Yes Pa," EJ replies.

"Now let's see if we can find you some shirts to wear as well," he said.

The boys helped him in the changing room, bring him different shirts. Sometimes funny ones that were so out this world with bright colors and strange patterns that made you cross-eyed to look at them, that they would crack everyone up. They had to guess on the boxer shorts because the bandages made it impossible; plus Ma was making those and a few overalls they just estimated on those and bought and a couple of pairs of new jeans and overalls so Ma could take them in later do to the bandages.

After everyone had something to wear, including Pa, they put them all neatly in pickup including their new shoes. After all the boys figured it wasn't fair if one person couldn't wear any of it then none would. So they were contented just to be dressed as they were before, as simple farm boys. Pa made stops along the way, checking off items on Ma's list and his and headed for home. Unlike the girls it doesn't take boys all day to shop, they were home before lunchtime. With nearly half as much stuff, of course, most of it is on order and will arrive later, but still, they didn't bring back the entire town with them, just empty stomachs and a good time.

The boys unloaded the pickup and put things away, Ma noticed what Pa had done, pointed her fingers at the boxes of shoes and extra shirts and clothes for the boys. "Wayne, me and girls already went shopping for their clothes for school," she said.

"Yes dear, we know, but you picked them out for them. I thought would be nice they chose what they wanted to wear for a change. After all, it's them that have to wear them not the girls," he said.

Martha sighed than noticed a box of shoes for Richard. "Wayne dear are you sure that was a good idea?" She asked.

"Martha he can't go barefoot all the time," Wayne replied.

"Yes dear, I know. But how is he going to stay put as his mother wants him to?"

"You are just going have to trust him, aren't you? He won't go far not without his car remember. Besides Robert and Will keep an eye on him and he'll be too tired to go too far from the farm," he said.

What's Behind the Looking Glass?

CHAPTER 23

While Robert and Will are putting the things away, discussing ways how to get off the farm they gathered the rest of the items needed for EJ's, Mr. Scarecrow. Not realizing Pa's was right behind them. "Robert we need a pair of overalls and a shirt then I think we got it," counting off the items, one straw hat, Pa's overalls and old work shirt that he never wears. "That should do it." Boys tossing them into their bedroom closet, Pa quickly ducks around the corner. "Robert got any ideas on how we are going to sneak EJ out of the house tonight?" He asked.

"Not yet, still working on it? How about you Will? Have any ideas about how we are going to get there?" Robert asked.

"I got an idea, buts it risky, and kinda gutsy. The pickup would make too much noise and Pa would notice it. I was thinking of busting Richard out too and taking the horses out. But it will take all of us to do it if I can get him to go along with it." Will said.

"Will, you do realize if Ma finds out EJ and Richard are missing she gonna go through the roof, kill us then and skin us for breakfast," he said.

"I know, I know but think of EJ. Let's do it for him, besides. It would be fun."

Pa sneaked back to the bathroom as he waited for his boys to leave the bedroom. Chuckling to himself. *"They are right if their Ma finds out, she will skin them alive. I think they might need a little help from the man and the moon to pull this one off, and better make sure the horses are well rested too."*

"There you are Pa? Ma's looking for you," Julie said seeing Pa hiding in the bathroom.

"Just washing up for lunch," he said as he turned on the water grabbing a fresh towel from behind. "Need something dear?" Pa asked.

"She just was wondering where you went. She had a question about something that's all," Julie said.

"Oh, be right there in a minute." He said as Julie looked at him as if he was up to something, giving him an odd look. Pa turned off the water and hung up the towel went into the kitchen. "Martha was there something you needed?" He asked.

"Yes, Wayne. I was just wondering about the boys," she said. "They are kinda dragging a bit. I think they need to rest from working so hard, take a day off. You worked them pretty hard yesterday." Pa looked over at the boys seeing them rubbed his chin, thinking to himself. *They look like more deep in thought then tired. Not going to let the cat out of the bag.*

"You are right Martha. They do look tired; let's give them a day off, heck lets give everyone a day off. You have been cooking up a storm for two days," he said as he opened up the fridge. "Let's have some lunch and I tell you what we are going to do." He said as Pa went outside to gather all the buckets and potatoes sacks and flour sacks, and sets them by the side of the house. He went back inside the house too changes his clothes to simple farmer clothes removing his shoes, just slipping on his shorts and overalls and walks into the kitchen. "Martha is lunch ready?" He asked.

Martha looked at him from head to toe, "what are you up to?" She asked.

"I told you we are all taking a day off, I'll explain during lunch," he said.

Ma and Pa sat down at the table, everyone stared at Pa, Pa laughed, "I have an announcement to make," standing up. "After lunch today... I'm declaring the rest of the day fun day. We are taking a day off except from our normal chores of course, but those are fair game too as long as they get done and the animals don't suffer," he said.

What's Behind the Looking Glass?

"What do you mean Pa by fair game?" They all asked.

Pa just simply stands and up with a glass of water and poured it over Robert's head. Then takes another and poured another over Richards. "That's what I mean boys, hurry up finish your lunch, the buckets are outside and you might want to change your clothes, you to Ma." As he walked over and emptied her glass over her head as she squealed watching the water running down her face and the back of her neck, everyone laughed at the table.

The boys and girls gobbled their food down very fast, raced down the hall to their rooms to change. It was a madhouse; the only one left in the house standing was poor Richard, but that didn't last long. Because Ma shoved him out the door with washtub of water "Splash." Then Pa picked her up kicking and screaming, "don't you dare" and drenched her good. Then she was chasing him around the farm with a bucket of her own. Pretty soon everyone had buckets in their hands chasing each other drenching each other. Pa carried EJ under his arms Robert with a bucket in his hand. Richard for the first time since he was on the farm was laughing his guts out; chasing Danny and Sam with his bucket of water.

Everyone soaked to the bone, mud in their hair, nobody cared. They were so tired they fell to the ground laughing rolling top of each other. Then the tickling began they laughed so hard they had tears in their eyes, EJ ribs would hurt for days. Pa tied their legs together for the leg races and potato sack races. Then the best part came when he laid out the rules of no rules of chores wars. He separated the girls up with the little ones with buckets and the boys with theirs.

The one that came back the wettest lost if there really was a loser in the game at all and chores hand to be done. So the boys headed off towards barn too do their chores with their buckets in hand keeping a close lookout for the girls. The girls in the opposite direction were doing the same, while Pa and Ma watched from the porch with anticipation on their faces to see who was going to get it first.

The boys did their first chore and did a sneak attack around the chicken coop. Robert climbing on top of the roof, Richard handing him the bucket. Will on the other side of the door, Richard on other. EJ standing up in front so they think he was alone. When they came out as soon as the door opened "hello" Splash" Splash" Splash" and they got them good and ran, Richard grabbed EJ headed back to the barn laughing all the way.

Pa slapped his knee laughing to beat all, Ma turned to him. "Now that wasn't fair, they were tricked," she said. This time it was the girl's turn as they watched them climb the hayloft with Danny and Sam waiting for the boys to come out. As soon as all four boys came out of the barn. They emptied their buckets right over their heads "Splash" Splash " Splash" Splash" Ma punched Pa in the arm, "now that was fair," she said as she squeals with laughter.

All the buckets dry and both sides soaked. Ma and Pa handed them each a towel, with smiles on all their faces. They scoot them into the house to change their clothes for dinner. Pa went out to the barn going over the horses as he checked their shoes and the wagon. Making sure everything is prepared for the boy's midnight sneak out ride. By adding few extra quilts under the seat for EJ and extra hay to soften his ride.

Leaving the barn Pa looked towards the house, he chuckled thinking about what his boys are about to do. Then headed back into the house thinking *how was he going to help them get out of the house without their Ma knowing about it and them knowing he knows all about it too?* He smiles remembering Indian tepee. "They don't have to sneak out if they are all ready outside," he said to himself. He went into the house, "Martha what are you doing?" Watched her start dinner as she washed vegetables in the sink and setting a roast into a pan.

"Fixing dinner dear," she said looking at him like he fell out of a tree.

"I told you we are all taking a day off dear," Pa said as he looked into the fridge. Pa pulled out some steaks some potatoes and rolls and throwing them on the counter and some more leftovers. "Now put that away dear, we are eating out Martha, I'll go start a fire."

What's Behind the Looking Glass?

Martha looked at him. "Have you lost your mind, outside?" She said.

"Why not? Its nice night out," he replied.

"All right dear if you say so." Thinking *what is he up too now?* Pa walked down the hall towards the boy's room chuckled before going in. "Robert, Will how would boys like to sleep outside tonight under the stars? You to EJ," he said.

Robert and Will looked at Pa, "are you kidding Pa?" They asked.

"Grab your sleeping bags and mattress for EJ and set them up out back while I build a fire for dinner. We are roughing it tonight and grab one for Richard too," he said.

"Yes, Pa."

Pa closed the door. "*Three down two too go, now how to kick Richard out the door and keep their Ma in.*" Pa headed down to Richard's room, "Richard?"

"Yes, sir?" Richard said drying his hair as he sat on the bed.

"I need you to do me a favor," he said then sat on the bed next to him.

"Yes, sir?"

"I want you to do whatever Will and Robert ask you to do tonight, I don't care how crazy it sounds, you just do it?"

Richard looked at him for a minute thinking how much fun he had today; things aren't as bad as he thought they were. "All right sir, I'll do it, but if they ask me to be dressed like Indian sir. I won't do it," he said.

Mr. Downing laughed. "Too bad son… I was just about to make you a loincloth," then headed on back down the hall.

Robert, Will sets up their sleeping bags outside the back of the house. "Will, you don't think Pa knows anything?"

"About what?" He asked.

"You know, us trying to sneak out," he replied.

"No way, he just thought we like to spend the night out here that's all. If he knew, do you think he lets us do this?" Robert asked.

"I guess you are right, he'd kill us and ground us for a lifetime maybe two lifetimes," Will said.

"I'll go grab our pillows off the bed and start to bring out the you know what from the closet. While you set up EJ mattress," Will said.

Ma calls around the corner of the house for Julie. "Julie, will you tell the boys that dinner almost ready?" Julie looked towards the table seeing it empty, Ma carrying and setting food on a tray.

"Ma do you need me to set the table?" Julie asked.

"No Julie, there's a quilt outside. We're roughing it tonight around the campfire." Julie looked at Ma as if she had fallen out of a tree. "It was your Pa's idea, now go find your sister and the boys," she said.

"Yes Ma," Julie said and headed on down the hall to find the boys in their room. Seeing Robert with their pillows in his hand, "Ma says dinner is just about ready, we are eating outside tonight. Robert where are you going with those?" She asked.

"Oh Pa told us we could sleep under the stars tonight, the four of us cool ha," he said. Robert walked on down the hall with his loot inside the pillowcase, heads out the door.

Julie smiled. *"Outside, the boys are going to be outside tonight,"* and giggled. *"Need to find Anna. Oh, there she is coming out of the bathroom.* "Anna?" she called,

"Yes, Julie?" She said.

"Are up to having some fun with boys?" She asked leaning against the bathroom door.

What's Behind the Looking Glass?

"Always," she said placing the boys dirty clothing into the hamper and empties the tub.

"I just found out they are spending the night outside tonight," Julie said.

Anna looked towards Richard's room. "Do think he will be out there too?" She asked.

"I think so, Robert said the four of us," she said.

Anna's eyes go wide. "Well then. I still have some those feathers from last time and we can get Danny and Sam to help too," as they giggled. "This going to be fun."

Julie leaving Anna with their mischievous plan of their own heads on down to Richard's room and knocks on his door; "Ma says dinner is just about ready Richard," then handing his pillow. "Take this with you, Richard, the boys and you are sleeping outside tonight," she said giggling and walked out the door.

Richard looked at Julie and stares at the pillow in his hand. *"Now they want me to sleep outside, maybe I was right, they are crazy,"* he said to himself bent down to tie his new shoes.

"Oh good I see you have your pillow, common Richard," Will replied.

"Will what's going on?" He asked.

"We'll explain later; Ma's waiting, we are eating outside tonight." Richard rolled his eyes and followed him down the hall. "This better be good Will, because there's a nice soft bed with my name on it," he replied.

Will smiles then whispered. "Oh giddy up, Mr. horsy, giddy up." Richard looked at Will as if he had been hit in the head a little too hard with the bucket today.

Ma at the campfire frying up steaks and campfire potatoes and leftovers salads spread out on the quilt with rolls and butter, yes sir they were roughing it in style. With pies and cakes, cookies; when Ma cooks up a storm she cooks, you just make sure you bring an empty belly to fill.

Pa still had one more problem to tackle as he looked over at Ma; the boys were on there own from here. The now question is how to trick Martha? Pa stretched his arms as if he was tired after a long day, to see if she would notice… *Nothing. Not so much as a glance.* Pa looked at his girls and poked them in the ribs they just poke him back and giggled. *He sees this going to be a challenge and rubbed his chin thinking how to get her to go back into the house.*

Pa stands up for a minute, looked towards the barn; *everything ready there. Looks towards the house the boy's sleeping bags are lined up.* He poked the fire a couple more times to watch the sparks fly through the air. Danny and Sam are still awake with pie and cake all over their face. Pa chuckled watching them eat it smearing all over themselves "*It looks like their having a good time,*" he thought.

Pa turned to the boys. "I was thinking since the lumber wasn't going be here for least a day or two we could go out too the field cut some hay for the horses. Gives us a break from building for a while and check on the rest of the crops as well. Of course, that means becoming simple farmer boys again. What do say, Robert, Will and I think EJ could help as well?"

"Ok, Pa."

Ma *smiled likening the sound of sending the Indian boys home.* Even Richard ears perked up when hearing the news and gave a sigh of relief… He could handle them being just *being and seeing simple farmers. They weren't nearly as crazy except for their sisters. That's a whole different matter entirely. For every time he looked over at them they give him a wink. He knows their up to something, but the question is what? And he watched them giggle in each other ear.*

Richard stiff from all the work from the farm starts rubbing the kinks out of his shoulders; Pa noticed Richard but doesn't say

What's Behind the Looking Glass?

anything just smiles *to himself thinking how hard it is taking a city boy and turning him into a farmer.* Pa poked the fire a couple more times then does couple more stretches himself, he chuckled then smiles looking over at Martha then at Richard. Pa gets up and yawns, "Richard?" he asked.

"Yes, sir?" He replied.

What do you say we put these two little boys to bed before they fall asleep on us? Danny, you look tired," he said.

"I'm not sir, really I'm not," as he yawns.

"Of course your not son, let's just get you cleaned up ready for bed then," he said.

"All right," and he watches him yawns some more. Richard takes Danny's hand Pa taking Sam by the hand walked them into the house. Pa and Richard cleaned them up got them ready for bed. By the time they were done, they were almost out like a light, laying them in their beds.

"Richard remember what I said, do whatever they ask you tonight, by the way, I put extra quilts under the seat just in case," he said.

Richard looked at Mr. Downing, "extra quilts for what sir?"

"Just one more thing, have fun... now scoot. I have work to do." Richard looked at him, *maybe crazy not the word... Maybe crackers or crackpot farmers might be better words to describe Mr. Downing and his little family.*

Pa whistled a merry old tune watching Richard go down the hall, for he has figured out how to keep Martha in the house and busy and away from the boys. Grabbing some lotion and oil they have been rubbing on the boys. "Now where did she put those candles? Here they are," and sets them up in the corners of the room. "Basin of hot water and clean towels; Oh yes a key to the door. Just in case she tries to get out. Also, need to put Mr. Rooster with chickens tonight. The boys might be a little tired when they get back, me too for that matter." Pa closed the bedroom door with a checklist in his mind. Pa rounded the corner running into his wife. "Martha, what are you doing in here?" He asked surprised.

"Wayne, what do you think I'm doing dear?" She asked. "Putting the food away, are you sure you are all right dear, you sure been acting funny all day?"

"I have?"

"As if you are trying to hide something from me," she replied.

"What on earth would I do that for dear? I just wanted to give you a day off too, that's all," he said. Then thinking quickly took her by the hand twirls around the kitchen… picks her up in his arms and kissed her, knocking her back a couple of seconds. "Oh, my dear. I might have to call the Doctor back to find my husband," she said.

He whispered in her ear. "Not tonight dear, he's busy tonight. Let's go put the children to bed. I have a surprise for you," he said and hums in her ear.

"Wayne dear the moon not out tonight," she whispers in his ear.

"That's funny dear. I thought I was the man in the moon." He said then sweepers her up one more time. The room spins as time slows down just for them.

"Yes dear," as she sighed. "Let's go put the children to bed and the rooster too," she said catching her breath.

"I already did dear."

The boys in their sleeping bags as Pa put out the fire and girls headed off to bed and giggle on their way in. Ma and Pa tucked the boys in before going into the house. Pa giving Richard a final wink… Richard thinking he must be cracked and wondering what's going on.

What's Behind the Looking Glass?

Ma and Pa walked into the house and down the hall to the little boy's room giving them each final tuck and kiss on the cheek and wishing them a good night as they sleep. Making their way around the circle to the girl's room they can hear the girls giggling inside. "All right girls its time for bed," she said.

"Yes Ma, Yes Pa," they said watching them head towards their rooms and climb into their beds.

Ma and Pa know their girls are up to something mischievous and it has something to with the boys. Ma just whispers in each in their ear, "please let them sleep in a little bit, but not too late dear." To each of the girls; *after all, why stop them from having a little fun of their own. Pa's up to something, she knows it. The question is what?*

They tucked the girls into their beds wished them sweet dreams and a good night and closed the door behind them. Making full circle Pa started to hum in Martha's ear as he opened the bedroom door. The candles or lit in the corners of the bedroom. Wayne closed the door behind them and locked the door with the key and set it on the dresser. "Oh, my dear! What did you have in mind?" She asked.

"I heard you needed a little soften dear that's all," he replied.

Chapter 23-1

* * * *

The boys outside and waited a little while for the lights in the house to go out and everything went quiet. "Richard, Richard you are not asleep yet?" Robert asked as he poked him in the ribs.

"Ouch that hurts," he said.

"Sorry..." as they laughed. Will and Robert quickly dress in their farmer's overalls. "Are you ready?" They asked.

"Ready for what?" He asked. Robert pulled out the straw hat they found at the gas station and Pa's overalls and an old work shirt. "To go dress EJ's scarecrow, that's what," he said.

"You got to be kidding and how are we going to get there?" He asked. Robert and Will laughed and poked him again. Richard turns and sits up "are you serious?"

"Yep." They nod their heads.

Then he remembered what Mr. Downing said. Well, I'll be a monkey's uncle he is cracked. That's why he wanted me out here too. "We can't get EJ out any easier," Robert said as he looks towards the house. Richard throws on his overalls they helped EJ's with his. "EJ where is this scarecrow?" Robert asked.

EJ draws a diagram approximate location. Richard rakes his fingers through his hair. "Robert now I know you are crazy. I... we... can't walk that far, not like this, my car won't run and we can't take the pickup," he said.

"Robert and Will laughed. "Who said anything about things like that they use engines and gas and make too much noise," Will replied as he pointed to the wagon in the barn.

Richards's eyes fell right out of his head. "Have you lost your freaking minds," he asked raking his fingers through his hair staring at them.

"Richard if you want to stay here we won't blame you," Will said helping EJ with his crutch. "But we have naked scarecrow to dress, have nice sleep," and they started heading towards the barn.

Richard watched for a minute. "You are serious, you do realize your Ma going to kill ya if she finds out and your Pa. I can't even imagine what he'll do to you when he finds out," he said.

"Richard, that's why if you come with us. You can say we forced you to come. Because if you stay here. They'll just say why you didn't you stop them? And think of the trouble you be in if we got caught." *That was true their Ma would hang him out dry and so would his mother regardless if Mr. Downing gave him permission behind their backs.*

"All right, all right I am coming. I just want to set the record straight. Your nuts, crazy; nuts, now let's go find this scarecrow before I change my mind." Richard and Robert helped EJ into the back of the wagon, Richard seeing the extra quilts under the seat just as Mr. Downing said they would be there; he smiles to himself. Robert and Will hooked up the team of horses to the wagon, handed the reins to Richard. "Are you sure about this? Remember what happened last time," Richard said.

Robert, Will, and EJ braced themselves, Robert said. "Just remember Richard, just lightly flick with your wrist because if you do it too harrrrrddd...." The horses come to life with a hard start and they jump leaving the barn, and then started to gallop... Richard not trying to pull back on the reins letting the horses run free. While Robert, Will, and EJ hanged on tight as they go past the house and down the road.

Ma jumped off the bed, "what was that?" Ma looked out the window seeing her four boys going down the road in the wagon with EJ in the back, Richard driving the wagon. Ma ran to the door finding the door locked. "Wayne, what is the meaning of this?" She asked.

Wayne laughed watching the boys going down the road from the window. "Martha let them go, they'll be fine. They had to find EJ's scarecrow and give back his clothes that's all."

"They what? Wayne, you open this door right now!" She said.

"Sorry, dear. They'll be back when they are done. Now let them have their fun, come back to bed."

Martha sighed. "I knew you were up to something," she replied.

"Yes dear," and kissed her forehead. "Now come back to bed let them have their fun."

"Well Richard, so much for leaving quietly!" Robert said as the horses come to nice even gallop on the road.

EJ and Will in the back cracking up thinking of the look on Ma's face in the window as they passed the house. "You were right Robert she did have a cow most likely two," Will replied.

The boys reached the edge of Santaquin. "Ok EJ, what's the best way to go? We need to find the least traveled roads. Because we look kinda funny having a wagon going down Main Street in the middle of the night." Richard said. Will and Robert help EJ up on the seat next to Richard sitting him in the middle with Will on the outside so he doesn't fall out with Robert in the back supporting his back. EJ wearing Mr. Scarecrow's new straw hat, Richard puts on pa's old work shirt. So nobody in town would recognize any of them. Thinking Richard was their Pa and they were coming home from the fields.

With EJ pointing the way avoiding all the street lights they went past the old cemetery up across the fields every now then a car would come by the boys would just wave at them considering Richard with them, they moved on. "Hey boys?" as a searchlight stops on them… two Police Officers stop the boys as they try not to panic and wiped the sweat of their face. "Evening officer, can we help you?" Richard said.

What's Behind the Looking Glass?

"Aren't you boys out kinda late?"

"Sorry officer was just heading back to our farm, just finishing our chores," Richard said. Officer looks at Richard dressed as an older adult and is a lot older than the younger boys. "All right you can go now, don't cause any trouble boys," they said.

"No sir, too tired, our Pa would skin us live and we're already late from doing our chores."

"Then no since me keeping you then," they replied.

The boy's watched the officer drive off and took a deep breath. "That was close... we better hurry before they come back... EJ how much further?" Richard asked.

"Not far, just up the road around the corner ways," he said.

"Now remember Richard... Just a...." Will replied.

"I know just a light flick like this." The horses come to life with a hard start and jump then start to gallop. Richard not trying to pull back on the reins. Robert, Will, and EJ holding on tight as they can to their seats as the horse gallop. EJ laughing as they go down the road.

"You did that on purpose," EJ said.

Richard laughing as Robert falls on his butt in the back of the wagon laughing on the soft hay. "I did!" And lightly pokes EJ in the ribs.

"Ouch," he said.

"Sorry." Richard smiled.

Will laughing as he hanged on to the seat of the wagon. The horses now steady clipped clop, clip-clop down the dirt road towards Mr. Scarecrow. EJ can see the old barn just up the road and points to where the scarecrow is. "He's in that barn," he said looking at his brothers. Robert can see a farmhouse of the owner of the scarecrow and smiles. "EJ I've got an idea. Richard, how close do you think you can get to that house without being heard?" He asked.

"Why Robert? I thought we are going to give back Mr. Scarecrows his clothes?"

Robert laughed. "We are Richard." And whispers in his and Will's ear what he wants to do. Will laughed and Richard cracks up. "You got to be kidding? Oh why not, we come this far," he said.

The boys pulled up closes as they could to the barn to where Mr. Scarecrow was. Leaving EJ on the wagon and taking the lantern so they can see what they are doing. Went into the barn, it didn't take long to find Mr. Scarecrow; he was still there right where EJ left him. Naked as a jaybird nothing, but old gunnysacks and straw. Robert, Richard, and Will picked up Mr. Scarecrow and took him out to the wagon. The boys quickly redressed him with his new clothes and his new straw hat with one additional item in which they decided to pin a note to his chest.

Gone for walk down by the creek and went for a swim, went to town, saw some Indians, got some sun, now I'm back, Mr. Scarecrow is not leaving home again.

The boy's loaded him on wagon started for the farmhouse. After all, they figure they might as well return him home too where he belonged in the first place. They decided Robert being a little more experienced with a wagon could get closer to the house without being heard. The three boys picked up Mr. Scarecrow started to head for the house; Richard holding the shoulders and the head, the boys each holding a leg to keep him together. It being so dark, the boys not seeing the ditch full of water; they fell right into it. Mr. Scarecrow went flying just a few paces in front of them and the boys fell right on top of each other nearly soaking wet laughing.

EJ in the Wagon cracking up at the sight; nearly falls right out of the seat until the lights of the farmhouse come on. Everyone quickly ducked into the weeds, EJ fell backward into the wagon into the soft hay so he's not seen. The old woman of the house came out, looks around for a minute with her scattergun. "I know someone's out there," she said waving the gun in the air.

The boys didn't make a sound; Robert whispered over to Richard whose sweating bricks watching her wave the scattergun in his direction, Robert said whispering. "I heard she's as blind as a bat from everyone in town." After few minutes the old woman went back inside and turned out the lights, and the boys quickly and quietly left Mr. Scarecrow sitting and propped up near the door of the house, where she can find him in the morning. Covering their mouths as they zig-zagged back to the wagon so they are not heard laughing on the way back. The boys quickly jump into the wagon and Richard with a quick flick of the reins the horse gallop down the street a few paces away from the farm.

Robert and the boys realizing it's going to be harder to get back, due to the late hour stop to think of a plan. Because now the three boys are soaked and wet and if they get caught again, what story could they tell? Plus they lost their disguise. The boys paced for a couple of minutes then looked at Richard then back of the wagon and hay in the back, Robert said. "What we need is some cover." Richard trying to ring out some of the water out of his overalls, "Richard do you think you could find the way back to the edge of town that leads to our road?" Robert asked.

"I guess so, why?" He asked.

"Hello stranger," Will said looking at Richard and wagon. "Those officers would remember four boys, but not one and you lost your disguises, plus we live in this town and you don't."

Richard cracked up and slaps his knee and slaps Robert on the back, "It looks like we're going for ride boys." He said pulling back the hay from the wagon and laying a quilt for EJ to lay on and the three boys get in back of the wagon cover themselves up with the blanket and Richard toss the soft hay on top of them so it looks like he carrying a pile of hay instead of boys in the back and headed back to the farm.

Richard climbs back onto the seat of the wagon. Will underneath the hay said. "Richard remembers were under here so go easy on those reins," he said.

"You mean like this?" The horses come to life with a hard start and jump then start to gallop. EJ and Robert laughed underneath the hay as they bounced on the old boards as they went down the street.

"He did that purpose," Will said.

"I know," EJ said as he laughed and Will bouncing and hitting the sides of the wagon. After a few minutes, the horses were going clipped clip, clipped clop at an even pace down the road.

Richard turns around whispered. "I think we're being followed," seeing headlights from behind, "so be quiet." Richard kept on going, not paying any mind and waved at the car to pass them by. The car passed them. It was the two officers from before. Richard waved trying not to panic and act like a stranger. They drive on by as Richard turned the corner and takes another deep breath. The officer circled back around and stopped just ahead of him. "Just great," Richard whispered back, "keep quiet, their back," he said. EJ, Will, and Robert cover their mouths not daring to breathe or daring to move. "Is there something I can help you with officer?" Richard asked.

"Kinda late to be out, don't you think?" The officer said.

Richard trying to remain calm and act like a farmer and like Mr. Downing would. "What do you mean?" I've just doing my chores that's all Officers," he said.

"What kinda chores at this hour?" Officer asked.

"Cuten hay, working on the farm." The officers looked in the wagon and shine the light in the back seeing the hay the boys go stiff as a board as it passed over them. "Wouldn't it be easier to use a pickup boy?" The officer asked looking at the horses.

What's Behind the Looking Glass?

"I can't sir; waiting for parts. Plus the horses need to work too anyway." Richard said watching the light passing over the boys in the back of the wagon. "Everything all right Officer?" Richard asked picking up some of the hay in his hands hoping to satisfy him.

"Yes, yes," as the hay falls back into the wagon.

The other officer walked back around to the front of the wagon. Shined the light on Richard and noticed his wet clothes and bare feet. "Why are you wet boy and where are your shoes?" The officer asked pointing the light down at Richards's feet.

Richard thought of something quickly. "Was watering fields and I fell into a ditch," he said. Which was true, he did fall into a ditch and it was in a field.

The two officers laughed in spite of themselves. "What's your name boy?

Richard almost panicked, "Richard Crow officer." Robert, Will, and EJ underneath the hay tried not to crack up when Richard announced his last name as "Mr. Crow." The boys covered their mouths trying not to rattle the wagon. Richard looked towards the movement knocks on the boards whispered, "quiet" to the boys and to distract the officers from the wagon movement. "Well, officers I need to get back to the farm. It's been a long day. If there is anything else I can help you with," he asked hoping they will let him be on his way.

"So boy where is this farm?" They asked.

Richard points in the general direction hoping it will satisfy them. "Just up the road a piece." Richard said as he climbed back on to the wagon and waved them on, "goodnight sir's," headed on down the road. With a very slight flick of the wrist to start the horse like an old pro, While Robert and Will gritted their teeth and braced themselves.

Richard looked over his shoulders could see the officer were following him whispered back. "Stay down. They are right behind us," he said.

Will and Robert looked through cracks whispered back. "Just keep going Mr. Crow," Robert said. When they reached the edge of the old dirt road that led to their farm. The officers turned off. Richard and the boys not taking any chances went on a little further until they could see the farm before they uncovered themselves. Robert slapped Richard on the back for a job well done as Richard mopped his face. "How ya doing Mr. Richard Crow?" As Robert and Will laughed hysterically, Richard smiled as he grabbed the reins of the horses and with a flick of the wrist, "like this." They started to gallop with a start and Robert and Will fell back on their butts in the soft hay EJ grabbed his ribs from laughing so hard all the way back to the farm.

The boys entered the farm quieter than they left; hoping their parents were still asleep, but not realizing that Pa and Ma were just waiting for them in the kitchen as they looked through curtains counting the boys, one, two, three, and four. Ma gave a soft sigh of relief. "They are all back safe and sound where they belonged, what silly boys they have been." Ma said her eyes glared at Pa and her boys chasing after scarecrows. For Ma and Pa have been busy while the boys have been chasing their scarecrow. They made each boy a scarecrow of their own and placed him next to their sleeping bags prior to their return, including Richard.

The boys put the horses and the wagon away, realizing it was *no use trying to hide their ride since Ma and Pa were going to skin them alive, "oh well,"* Robert thinking how much fun they had, sighed, *"it was worth it."* As they try to sneak back to their sleeping bags, checking to make sure the coast was clear. Richard was grinning from ear to ear because he had a secret about tonight's ride of his own. That Robert and Will did not know that their Pa already knew about it. And it was fun watching them suffer, as they got closer to the house.

The boys reached the house peeked around the corner where their sleeping bags are Will and Robert gasped at the sight. Standing right by their sleeping bags a scarecrow boy for each one of them waiting, Richard lost it right there and then slapping the boys on the back. "Now look who chasing who boys," he said laughing his guts out.

Will and Robert stood bewildered. "How? When?"

Ma and Pa came out of the house. Pa gave Richard a wink and the boys. "Did you enjoy your ride tonight boys?" He asked as Ma raced over to EJ trying still to be mad as she checked his stitches making sure he was alright then giving each kiss on the head and each stern look.

"Yes sir," and they all laughed.

"Alright you silly boys," Ma said giving them each hug. "Now get to bed."

"Yes, Ma. Yes, ma'am." The boys removed their wet clothes and climb into their sleeping bags and Ma and Pa re tucked them into bed. Ma shaking her finger at them. "Now stay put where you belong… you silly boys." As she picked up their wet clothes and returned to bed. The boys are tired they quickly fell asleep.

"I told you, Martha, they'll be fine," Pa said.

"I know, but can a mother worry?" She said.

"Yes dear," and turns out the light. "Now my house full and again thanks dear by the way thanks for the meal and the laughter in my heart today to, even though you nearly worried me to death letting them off the farm," she said.

"Yes dear," he replied.

Martha socks him in the arm. "Chasing after scarecrows," and giggles like a schoolgirl at her silly boys.

Chapter 24

Early morning raises the girls are bright and rested with feathers in hand waking up Sam and Danny. "Hello, Ma," seeing her in the kitchen hiding the feathers behind their backs Ma smiles. Knowing they're up to something, but doesn't say a word regarding the feathers. "Where are Pa and the boys?" Julie asked.

"They are still asleep," she replied.

"Oh!" Julie said giggling.

Ma grabbed a feather herself from the cabinet winked at the girls and smiled at Sam and Danny. "I was about to wake them, want some help?" She asked. They pulled their feathers from behind their back and headed on down the hall finding Pa still asleep starting with him. Ma gabbing his foot Julie taking the other starts tickling him with the feathers. Danny and Sam pile on top of him using their feathers; Pa laughed busting a gut until tears rolled and started tickling all them.

Pa grabbed a feather as they all headed for the boys outside sneaking up one at time one in front of each boy then slowly uncovering a foot. Starting with EJ, Will, Robert, and Richard. Taking their feathers then starting at the bottom, working their way to the top and down each of their backs and long their necks and sides until they cracked.

The war was on, pillows flying through the air, feathers dropping from the sky. Richard swings his pillow, Will swing his. Danny and Sam dog pilling on top Robert then Richard then Pa, Then Ma rolling on the mattress tickling EJ with Julie and Anna… it was a circus of feathers, pillows mangled. Everyone laughed until it hurt, the poor chickens scrambling because they lost all their feathers. Oh well, they'll grow back, after everyone could no longer stand because they were all out of breath from laughing so hard.

Ma wiped the tears of laughter from her eyes. "Alright girls, let's get breakfast ready. Boys go get cleaned up it will be ready in a while."

"Yes, Ma. Yes, ma'am." The boy's headed on down the hall to change their clothes. Richard now familiar with routine just sets the clothes outside the bathroom door for Mrs. Downing. Knowing that when he came out that Julie will be waiting for him in his room. Richard just sighed opens the door. Richard throws the towel over his shoulder seeing Mrs. Downing on the stool sewing another pair of overalls and Julie in his room waiting. He hands her the towel and walked in and sits on the bed. "Julie there's this one spot just right here can you get that for me just a little higher, yea." "Ahhhhh that's better thanks… hey, that tickles… Oh, that's cold."

"Sorry." Julie giggled.

It was nice to see the boys all dressed at the breakfast table in farmer clothes and having the Indian boys sent home. The boys dressed in all their new work shirts including their brand new work shoes. Except for EJ of course, but least he had a new shirt and pair of overalls just like the rest of the boys. Ma even made him a new pair of shorts to fit over the bandages with extra tie string so they wouldn't be so tight around the waist.

With the Indian loincloths, all put away for now. Ma was happy as a clam. She glowed at the table when she looked at her tan boys, for each one was a farmer son again. Finishing breakfast, Ma hands each boy a sack lunch and kiss on the cheek including Richard shaking a finger then reminding him, just because he has a pair of shoes not to run off.

He smiled. "Don't worry ma'am. Will, Robert, and EJ will watch me so I can't," he said as he winks back at her and laughed. Then he swings little Danny into the air. Danny squeals with delight. "Plus leave Danny here by himself. What would my mother think?" As he rubbed his hair with his hand.

Pa and the boys all loaded in the wagon heading for the fields for the day, Pa hands Richard the reins, and the boys all brace themselves. Pa laughed. "Richard just a light flicker of the wrist son you'll be ok," he said.

"You mean like this sir?"... Pa leaned back and laughs holding on to his seat watching the boys fall back on their butts as they galloped toward the hayfields to cut hay for the afternoon.

Ma and the girls watched Pa and boys galloping down the road, "what silly boys we have every last one and I wouldn't trade them for the world."

The boys worked hard in the hayfield with the hot sun blazing down on their backs as the boys cut and tossed the hay into the wagon. Pa helped EJ in the back of the wagon as they tied the bails of hay and then pushed them off to dry in the hot sun. They worked up quite a sweat wiping the sweat off their brows. After lunch, they decide to go down by the creek for a little swim too cool off before going back to work. They even found a spot for EJ so he could cool off to without getting his bandages wet because Ma would skin them all-alive.

When they returned home later that afternoon, they found a visitor sitting on their front porch with Ma and the girls. It was Richard's brother and EJ's other Uncle Steve and his wife come to see how he and Richard were doing. What a surprise as Richard drove in on the farm with the wagon all dressed as simple farmer boy coming out of the fields with EJ and Will and Robert in back swing their legs off the back of the wagon with a load of hay for the horses.

Steve married young right after he served an LDS mission to a gal named Loraine. Had made his money designing and building houses and was a brick mason on the side when things were slow. He looked a lot like his father, dark brown hair or what's left of it and brown eyes which seemed to turn gold when the sun hit him just right. Steve worked out a lot from carrying lumber and bricks and large wheelbarrows of cement, which in turn gave him the broad shoulders. And stood tall like his father, reaching the height of five feet nine inches, his face and skin hardened by the long hours in the sun, he had hard jawline like the rest of the family.

What's Behind the Looking Glass?

Loraine was Steve's better half and always let him know it. She stood just a few inches taller with her long nimble legs reaching six feet one and a half. She was three years older than her husband of six years and been hoping for children, but so far hasn't had any and not for the lack of trying, times have been hard when they discussed the idea but there is still hope more so now considering she found out she is pregnant and hasn't yet told him.

She had high cheekbones that set off her green eyes and short brown hair hiding the gray when she ties into a bun and has been known to be stubborn or just as stubborn as her husband when it comes to getting her way. Her style of dress wasn't that much different from Martha and her daughters even though she might not be in a woman's fashion magazine. It was comfortable and yet plain. She was a stay at home wife taking care of children in her home extra income to help pay the bills.

Steve couldn't believe his eyes. *"Was this same Richard he once knew?"* Richard jumped down from the wagon laughing as he sprints over to see his brother giving him a big old bear hug. Then picking up Danny and swing him into his arms. Steve looked at him from head to toe, "you were right, mother did take your shoes, Richard," he said.

"Oh, she did. I have a new pair now. They are in the wagon; we just went for a swim during lunch today. I just didn't feel like putting them back on, that's all," then laughed. "Come inside while I get cleaned up, just need to put the wagon and horses away." Steve watched with amazement seeing Richard drive such a thing, Richard yelled back. "It doesn't drive anything like car brother, that's for sure!"

"Mrs. Downing is that my brother Richard?" Steve asked. Martha laughed. With shock on his face, "my mother is in for quite a surprise," he said.

"Not really Steve, she was hoping for it," Martha said as she smiles looking towards the barn. "This is my husband Wayne Downing and my boys Robert and Will you have already met Sam and my girls," she replied.

"Please to meet you, sir," Steve said shaking hands.

"So what brings you down to these parts Steve?" Wayne asked.

"Well I was just going to give Richard a call find out how he was doing, but heck a picture worth a thousand words and it was too good to pass up. And I was right it seems. I would have never believed it with my own eyes." Steve looked at Richard in simple farmer clothes playing with Sam and Danny on the floor as if he was a kid again.

Steve and his wife stayed for dinner and visited before returning home. Promising they would be at the annual picnic with Downing family in about week. Yes, sir, they will be needing a bigger spot this year. Pa laughed as he waved them on down the road, but there is always room for one more.

Ma and the girls put away the rest of the dishes the boys out on the farm finishing the nightly chores, the phone rings in the kitchen. "Hello Martha, this Grandma. How are things down at the farm?" She asked.

"Just fine Grandma," Martha replied.

"Richard behaving himself?" She asked.

"Yes Grandma, he and the boys are out doing the chores as we speak. Would you like to speak with if him? I can have Wayne call for him if you would like?"

"No Martha, that's alright just wanted to makes sure he was having a good time." She said as she watched her two granddaughters fighting over a doll and wringing her hands. "In fact Martha, I thought if it would be alright if I could stop by tomorrow if you wouldn't mind and bring my granddaughters with me to see EJ and Danny? I realize it might be an inconvenience for you and they are not due back until next week, but Grandma here is at her wit's end could use a little break and visit with you awhile," she said.

"Not all Grandma. We would love to have you and I'm sure EJ would love to see them too," she said.

What's Behind the Looking Glass?

"Thanks, Martha, you are a dear, I'll see you in the morning then. Goodbye dear."

* * *

"That's enough girl's!" Grandma said trying to rein them in as she hung up the phone while standing the kitchen her husband had built all those years ago. The only thing that had changed was the paint on the walls that were painted a dark salmon color and speckled tiled floor. She never really cared for it then and still doesn't as it really doesn't hide the dirt, but he liked it even though he was colored blind.

Peggy said. "But she started it Grandma!" Peggy replied punching her sister as she tries to grab the doll away from her.

"How would you girls like to go and see a farm and see Danny and EJ?" Grandma asked taking a seat at the table, knowing it was no use getting between them when Peggy had decided she wants something she just takes it away anyway.

"Do we have too?" Peggy whined hitting her again and taking the doll away.

"Don't you want to see your brothers?" Grandma asked.

"Not really...That's mine! Give it to me!" Peggy screamed as Dona takes it back as they fight over it one grabbing the head the other the legs as if was a tug a war. Grandma was getting more and more depressed as she watched them fight day after day. Sometimes shouting from one room to another, but Peggy always seemed to win. Never in her life had she thought it would be so much work after raising three boys. But her mind was not on the girls these days since receiving a telegram from Margaret regarding her husband Mike; letting her know that he had passed away a few days ago, the fond memories of him while she was growing up flood her mind as she grieved for the loss. But how could she go with two girls constantly at each other's throats?

"Why Grandma? All they do is get into more trouble... It was mine first," Dona replies back tugging the doll away from Peggy.

"Sounds boring and dull, there's nothing to do on a farm... No, it wasn't!" Peggy yells back to her sister grabbing the doll.

At last, grandma couldn't take it anymore, reaching down and taking the doll away and throwing it down hard on the kitchen table and yelled letting her temper flare. "That's enough girls. Go to bed!" She tried very hard to control her anger feeling the pain in her chest she gasped and sat back down in the chair feeling dizzy and breathing hard and gritted her teeth as the pain finally subsided. "I am getting too old for this," she mumbled rubbing her chest.

"It was my doll...." Peggy lashes out hearing Peggy scream in the next room.

* * *

"Martha, who was that on the phone?" Wayne asked watching her come back into the living room taking a seat next to him on the couch.

"That was Grandma she's stopping by tomorrow with her granddaughters to visit EJ and Danny," she replied.

"That's nice dear. I'm sure they would like to see them. Martha, you look a little worried. What's the matter, dear?" He asked.

"Oh just something she said on the phone that's all," she replied.

Martha deep in thought Wayne could see something is bothering her. "Martha, what's the matter?" He asked.

"Wayne I was thinking about Grandma, she sounded worried. It was something she said. I could hear it here voice, she's at her wit's end and she still has a few more days left before they go back home."

"Martha sounds like Grandma is in need of some help and she running out of option and fast for two little girls," he said.

"Wayne, we have two girls that would love to show them the way how to be sisters and I think we can keep them busy enough.

What's Behind the Looking Glass?

They won't have enough time too get into trouble and give Grandma a break," she said.

"Sounds like we're going to do some more shuffling again," he replied.

"Thanks, dear. Leaning over and kissed his cheek taking his hand in hers calls for her girls. "Julie, Anna, can you girls come in here please for a minute?" Ma asked.

"Yes, Ma?"

"Grandma is arriving in the morning with her granddaughters and we want you girls to show them how to be the best sisters you know how to be before they go home. Do you think you can do that? Show these poor miss guided sisters how to be sisters?"

"Yes Ma," as they giggled. "So how bad is it Ma?" Julie asked.

"Well, the way I understand it is they hate each other and can't stand to be around each other for long periods of time. They constantly fight and bicker all the time when they are together. The only time they even are reasonable when they are by themselves and not in each other's presence, according to their grandmother and their aunts. Together it is a living nightmare for them and everyone else around them," she said.

Pa rubbed his chin and smiled. "Martha I have an idea," thinking of the potato sack race, leg race. "Let's join them together," he said.

"What?" She thought as he if was insane, "didn't you hear what I just said. They can't stand each other Wayne?"

"Yes dear, I did. Now hear me out. Think of it this way; in a leg race, it takes two people to work it as a team tied together. If one person does all work the other person falls and you both fall. You both go nowhere, but if they both work together you both win the race. So glue them both together and make them work together as a team. Sooner are later they'll get the message or lest kill each other in the process, either way, problem solved," he said.

Pa gleaming from ear to ear, Ma giving him one her icy cold hard stares wiped the smile right off his face. "Dear I like your plan. It just needs a woman's touch; they're not boys you know. Girls this is what we are going to do. I want you to share a room with each of the girls, that way they least can have some pace at night while they sleep. But they will work side by side every day glued together," giving Pa a hard glace with her eyes. "I want you girls to take them under your wing and show them how to treat their brothers especially Danny since he going home with them in a few days."

"Yes, Ma."

"Alright off to bed, we have a busy day tomorrow… Wayne, sometimes I wonder about you; glues them together so they can tear each other apart. I wouldn't be surprised if you tide them together as if they were stuck together like glue," she said.

"Martha?" Wayne seeing that icy look knew better to mess with her when she was not in the mood. Wayne smiles "Yes dear," and leans over and gives her a kiss on the head. Whispered "you know what' is best dear," leaves it alone for the man and the moon.

Richard leaned over the fence. "Robert, I have an idea how to even the odds back into our favor again?" Richard said.

"How Richard?" He asked.

"You guys were telling me how you wined and dined the girls that night to melt the ice. Well, how about we surprise them with morning breakfast before they get out of bed. I'm sure I can get your Pa to help us to. I think your Ma put him in the doghouse again for letting us sneak out the other night. Even though it was fun and Mr. Scarecrow did get his clothes back. It would be a scream to see the look on the girl's faces when they wake up seeing breakfast ready for them for a change. They would all be in a panic," he said.

Robert laughed. "And right under their very noses too." Will nodded in agreement with EJ leaning against the fence.

"I'll go find your Pa and see what he thinks, why you finish up here," Richard said as he walked back into the house seeing Mr.

What's Behind the Looking Glass?

Downing in the living room. "Mr. Downing sir can you help me with something out in the barn?" He asked.

"Aren't Will, Robert, and EJ with you?" He asked.

"Yes sir, I would like to show you something out in the barn sir," Richard said trying disparately to get him to come out there with him.

"What would you like to show me, Richard?" Wayne asked.

Richard starting to get a little frustrated. "Sir" Mr. Downing nodding to his wife then Richard whispered in his ear. "We have a plan too even the score," he said.

"Oh!" looking at his wife. "The horse threw a shoe and you need me to show you how to put it back on, I'll be right there. Martha the boys need me out in the barn. One of the horses lost a shoe," he said and winks at Richard. Wayne and Richard head out to the barn, "boys I hear you have a plan too even the score again."

"Yes Pa, Yes sir." The boys tell Pa their plan of early surprise breakfast for the girl's right under their nose. "Humm… Yes, boys that could work," as he chuckled. "They would never expect that, not from you boys and I'll help. So that means you boy's better to get to bed because you are going to need an early start in the morning," he said.

The boys quickly finished their chores with smiles on their faces. "Ma we're tired," doing a fake yawn. "I think we will just go to bed early tonight. It has been a long day," they each said as they all head down the hall. Ma watched her boys with questionable look just for a moment then not giving any other thought. *Well, maybe they are still tired from staying up most of the night chasing that foolish scarecrow the other night, silly boys.*

"Their right Ma, it is kinda late. You said we do have a big day tomorrow, with company coming and I haven't told EJ that his sitters are coming yet." Pa said and he too does a stretch and fake yawn himself. "I think we should turn in to. What do you say Ma?"

Ma and Pa head down the hall making the rounds like they do every night. First, to the boy's rooms where Robert, Will and EJ sleep, tucking each boy in their beds with a warm kiss on their cheeks and wish them all a good night's sleep. Down the hall, to Richard's room, they tuck him in bed wishing him a good night as well and making sure that he is all right.

Opening the door to Sam and Danny's room brushing their hair away from their eyes kissing them gently on the forehead wishing them goodnight; making the circle to the girl's room stroking their hair gently and with a warm kiss for each one; "sweet dreams my darling's sweet dreams and a good night." Then down the hall to their bedroom, they embrace each other like they do every night. Thanking each for the meal, for our house is full so are our hearts as they climb into bed, and waited for the dawn.

Chapter 24-1

* * * *

Except for Pa and the boys beat the dawn that morning and Mr. Rooster out of bed. Pa sneaked out of bed while his wife was sound asleep. Entered the boy's room gave each boy a quick nudge then quickly tiptoes down the hall to Richards room so he doesn't make any noise to give him a nudge for the breakfast surprise.

All the boys in the kitchen and Pa gave the orders passing out recipes, telling them what they needed to do. Because he had to sneak back to bed too Ma or the gig would be up. She is a very light sleeper, leaving Richard in charge of the menu. Pa will be back to help with the hard stuff when time is near.

Will gathering the eggs from the chickens, EJ peeling the potatoes for the hash browns. Robert will make the biscuits and EJ started squeezing the oranges for the orange juice. Then Pa will come into help with the flapjacks, brown the hash browns and fry up the eggs. Richard can fry up the ham and the bacon. While the boys set the table.

With the plan in motion, the boys scramble about the kitchen in their bare feet peeping around the corners down the hall, tiptoeing throughout the kitchen so they don't make any noise, wearing little aprons around the waist.

Pa sneaked back to the bedroom before Ma starts to stir. Waiting for the moment for Richard to crack the door open with a signal for Pa to come help. The boys busy in the kitchen, Richard left in charge and guarding the door. Richard followed the recipes Mr. Downing left him and remembering the things he learned from his mother.

The boys were amazed at the things Richard knew. Richard just quietly laughed at them. "What did you think I did; starved to death when my mother was away?" Finally, it was time for Pa. Richard sneaked down the hall and gave Mr. Downing the signal. That way if his wife did wake up, she still would be surprised seeing her boys all in the kitchen with breakfast nearly finished. Pa sneaked out of bed quite as a mouse into the kitchen. The boys set the table, Pa whipped up the flapjacks.

Richard frying up the ham and last of the beacon while EJ set the golden brown hash browns and hot biscuits on the table with apple butter, homemade syrup and warm honey. Will and Robert put fresh daisy on the table for Ma and the girls with freshly squeezed orange juice made from EJ, just in time. Ma walked into the kitchen seeing Pa flipping flapjacks in the air and Richard frying the ham and the boys setting the breakfast table. It took her breath away when she rubbed the sleep out of her eyes; "Morning Ma."

"Morning Mrs. Downing, breakfast will be ready in a few minutes so if you would like to get cleaned up there are fresh towels in the bathroom," Richard said as he winked at her, while Wayne flipped another flapjack in the air. Martha's eyes nearly fell to the ground and swooned from the shock. "Martha I'll be in later to work on some of those tight muscles," and gives her a silly grin. "Now scoot dear, we have lots to do today," and pointed her down the hall.

Pa walked down to the girl's room and knocked on the door. "Girl's breakfast almost ready its time to get up." Turning the corner he woke up Sam and Danny and got them ready for breakfast while the girls get over their shock. Pa waited for Ma in the bedroom, *after all, fair play is fair play.* Ma seeing Pa in the room, Pa closed the door. "Martha I understand you need a little softening today before breakfast."

Martha just sighed and nodded her head. "Not too much Wayne," she said.

Ma and girls at the breakfast table, Pa at the head and the boys on one side, Sam and Danny on the other next to the girls. Ma and the girls are in shock once more as they looked at the table and the boys. Ma started off the conversation. "I have a surprise for you boys today, but first thank you for this wonderful breakfast," girls each gave each boy hug and smile.

What's Behind the Looking Glass?

"The surprise is Richard your mothers coming back early and she is bringing with her EJ's sisters and they are going be staying with us for a little awhile." EJ and Danny don't look all that thrilled knowing *how much their sisters like them or should we say hate them.* Richard knowing this as well *thinking his mother must be at her wit's end with these two and feels sorry for EJ and Danny, but thinking at the same time maybe. Just maybe these two bad apples might get something they deserve. And Danny, EJ will get to watch them suffer and get some fun and pleasure and a little payback for what they put them through.*

Grandma was true to her word when there was a knock at the door that morning as little Danny and Sam climbed down from the breakfast table raced to the door. Seeing Grandma they gave her a big hug. "Grandma, Grandma," she bends down gives them both a great big kiss and great big bear hug.

"Just what Grandma needed," she said as she wiped the tears from her eyes. Danny tried to give each sister's one. Peggy wasn't in the mood, neither was Dona as they just stepped aside, folding their arms frowning at their little brother Danny.

Martha glanced over at Grandma and the two girls. "Well just don't stand there, come on in. We were just going to have breakfast that the boys made this morning… Wayne grabs some more chairs and I'll get some more plates." Grandma shoved the two girls through the door.

Richard sees his mother went over and kissed her right on the cheek. "Come Ma, come have a seat." His mother looked at Richard dressed as a young farm boy in his bright yellow shirt and workman overalls. She looked up at Wayne and Martha then back at Richard and looked deep into his eyes. There was a new twinkle in his eye that wasn't there before, he has found that little boy again she once knew. As she wiped the tears from her eye, she knew he was going to be all right now.

Martha busy setting places at the table, Pa placed chairs for everyone. Grandma feeling antsy because she needed to leave the girls here, hoping she could; knowing she couldn't stay with them even thou she would like to. *Oh how she would like to spend more time here on the farm, but she needed to be in Salt Lake City, she had import business and it can't wait. A death in the family and she needed to be there for the next few days.* Martha could see her fidgeting though out breakfast, not acting like herself even though she tried her best to be her loving grandmotherly self. Martha and Wayne could tell something was a miss.

"Boys why don't you go head do your chores before we start doing the shuffle," Pa replied.

"Yes, Pa. Yes, sir." The boys replied back as they gave Grandma one more hug and a kiss before leaving out the door.

"Julie, Anna why don't you take Peggy and Donna out to see the farm, your Ma and I will clean up the table and do up the dishes," Pa said.

"Yes Pa," they said.

Watching the children leave the house. Martha, Wayne and Grandma get up from the table together and go out on the porch to enjoy the morning air. "All right Grandma something bothering you, you can't hide it from us," Martha said. Grandma pulled out a telegram she just received letting her read it. "Oh, that's terrible!" Martha said.

Grandma nods. "He was old and sick for a very long time, 94… it was his time. The problem is, I have to go to Salt Lake City and I could be gone for a few days and the girls have to be back home by then. They are such a mess and I am at my wit's end." She said looked towards the barn where Richard was and at his car. "You have done so much for me already. EJ, Danny and I can't get over just looking at Richard," she said wiping the tears from eyes. "Martha, Wayne what I am going to do? I can't take them with me. They'll tare each other apart if I left them alone for five minutes. They're fine by themselves, miserable like their mother, but fine. But stick them in a room and with little Danny, I even hate to think what's like at home."

"Does Richard know this person?" Wayne asked.

What's Behind the Looking Glass?

"Not really, he was too young at the time when he was around. I think he's better off staying here if he wants to. I'll leave his things in his room in case he wants to come home, but I'm sure I'll make it back in time for the picnic," she said taking a good strong breath of clean farm living. It seemed to give her energy and relaxes her feeling her tight muscles give way with each breath and the warm rays of sunlight upon her... a strange song echoed in her mind putting a grin on her face. *"Green Acres is the place to be..."*

"When do you have to leave Grandma?" Martha asked.

"This afternoon... that is why came so early, I really hate to be a bother," she frowned.

"Nonsense, I was just telling Wayne. We have two girls that would love to help them and I'm sure we can keep them busy enough around here. They won't have a choice but start to get long," Martha said.

Grandma eyed Wayne for a minute. "Not unless you plan to tie them together you won't," she said.

Wayne laughed. "Grandma you took the words right out my mouth." He said Martha just gave him a hard stare. "What Martha, she said it, I didn't," and laughed.

"Well let's go back inside and clear the table and see if we can find us a solution to our problems and two little girls," Martha replied while they cleared the table and do up the dishes. Martha filled Grandma in on the things that happened around the farm while she has been gone; about how the boys sneaked off the farm to chase down EJ's scarecrow.

Grandma nearly busted a gut giving her a hard time. "Martha the boys were just having a little fun, you should go easy on them. I still can't get over Richard driving a wagon."

Martha filled her in about Mr. Wells that infuriating little man from social services. Six months for Danny and the new rules for home visits after two years. That didn't make anybody happy. "I think a strong cup tea is in order Martha after that news," she said as Martha puts on the kettle." It's so good to see EJ again. I just wish he would take it a little bit slower." Grandma said watched him through the window with his one crutch hobbling around the farm; sat at the table while Martha handed her a teacup and took a seat next to her as Wayne leaned against the wall as he watched the boys out the window.

Wayne laughed. "Grandma we've tried slowing him down, he just crawls out the door following after Will and Robert. They just pick him up and carry him with them when he gets too tired. They are inseparable those three boys," he said.

Grandma looked at Danny and Sam outside playing in the yard together, Martha shakes her head. "It's going to be so quiet on the farm without him and Sam going to feel lost not having Danny. He's been such a joy, six months," Martha said.

Grandma pats her hand. "We will work something out dear, the wars not over yet; Grandma's got a few tricks up her sleeve to dear," she said. "You know Martha, Wayne does have a good idea. A little harsh maybe but I like it, and I think its time for a little intervention. Why not glue those two girls together and I mean it, side by side so tight they can not move without the other, like two peas in a pod," she said.

Wayne, Martha looked at her. "Are you nuts? I was kidding Grandma, they can't work like that," Wayne said.

"Why not? Worth a try isn't it? Just for a day or two. What can it hurt? They might even respect each other a little more if nothing else. Wayne, you said it yourself, one person does all the work nothing happens they both fall. If they work together they reach the finish line. Well, they need to reach that finish line and soon." She replied taking a long sip. "Martha they may not be boys, but they are just as tough trust me, they'll be fine. If it doesn't work just try something else, now times a wasting. Now I need to spend some time with Richard and EJ before I have to go," she said.

Grandma went out to the car and opened the trunk and pulled out the box with Richard's spark plugs and wires and sets them in

What's Behind the Looking Glass?

the back of his trunk and walks out to the barn. Richard sees his mother walked over to her. "Need something mother?" He asked.

"Yes Richard, walk with me a moment." They walked over by nearby fence where they could see the endless wheat fields and trees of orchards. "I put your things for car in the trunk, Richard you can go home if want to son," she said.

Richard looked at the house and watched Will, Robert, EJ, and the two little boys together laughing playing in the yard, "Ma if it's all right with you I like to stay," he said.

"Of course you can son. I was hoping you would say that… Son, I am so proud of you. I just wanted you to know that I couldn't ask for a better son," she said. Richard could see something was wrong, he knew his mother when something was wrong.

"Ma what's wrong?" He asked seeing her wipe an escaped tear from her eye.

"I have to leave son this afternoon, we lost somebody I once knew. You most likely don't remember him you were too young at the time, it was your great Uncle Mike," she said.

"You mean that guy that always smelled of sardines?" He asked.

His mother laughed. "Yes, he did smell bad didn't he? Which means son if you went home. You be alone and I'll be gone for a few days, That's why I brought the girls over… bad timing too, not they making life miserable, bless their little wretched hearts," she said as she tried to laugh.

Richard laughed. "I bet Ma," seeing that twinkle in his eye makes her smile. "Ma I wouldn't worry about them. I think those girls will have a whole new set of problems by the time Mr. Mrs. Downing gives them something to worry about. Bickering with each other and Danny will be least of their problems." He said as he laughed, "trust me I know their sisters personally," as he laughed even harder; then gave her a kiss on the cheek and a great big hug. "Ma I love you so much, thanks," he said.

"Are sure you are my son?"

"Last time I checked I was." Ma sees that extra twinkle in his eye and smiles looking around the farm and back at him and wipes her eyes. "Now then let's go find your two grandsons," He replied giving her an extra kiss on the cheek.

Grandma visited for awhile with EJ and Danny before going into the house. Grandma hasn't told the girls yet they were staying here as Richard unloads their suitcase's from the car sets them by the door. She only packed things they would need on the farm. No nice dresses a couple of dolls that's it, she left everything else at home for later. She knew better watching Julie and Anna, she gave them clues about what to wear out here and Martha was a good seamstress herself.

Plus little hard work is what these girls needed. Before a suitcase entered the house Martha insisted she went through them again, "said this won't do out here." Grandma wasn't about to argue with her after seeing Richards transformation she was grinning, she had her boy back again. Watching him swing Sam and Danny around in the air he was a kid again. She just had one more thing to do as she walked on down the hall to the girl's room. Wayne and Martha followed her.

Grandma took two scarves from her purse and entered the room. "Peggy, Dona I want you to know first that Grandma loves you very much." She said taking their hands tying one of the scarves and wrapping around them tying them together. "And second that I want you to do everything that Mr. Mrs. Downing says."

Then taking the second scarf and wrapping around their legs tying them both together. "I'll be back in a few days." then gave each hug and kiss on the cheek and wiped her tears away with the back of her hand, closed the door behind her. Martha, Wayne asks Julie and Anna to watch the girls while they walked Grandma to the car. Martha and Wayne gave her each one more hug and a pat on the back told her not to worry and watch her go on down the road and wave goodbye for now.

"Well Wayne," she said.

"Yes, dear?"

Martha looked towards the house. "I rather have Indians or few scarecrows because those two girls worry me," she said.

"Come on Martha. Remember you got the man and the moon and four little Indian boys that can help you. You'll be fine, not mention two daughters that are the spitting image of a certain wife I love so much." He said as he swings her up into his arms to kiss her as she giggled.

"Thanks, dear I needed that," she said as she looked into his eyes and smiles.

"Now let's go see about those two mischievous girls, didn't you say you had some work for them to do?" He said.

Martha and Wayne headed down the hall back to the girl's room with their suitcases, Ma said. "Julie, Anna will you go and find everyone please and have them sit in the living room?" Ma asked.

"Yes Ma," they said closing the door behind them and walked down the hall and rang the dinner bell to get everyone's attention.

Chapter 24-2

* * * *

Wayne sat on the bed next to the girls. Martha sighed then looked them straight in the eye. "Ok girls, it looks like we need to have ourselves a little chat. Your grandmother has filled us in what has been going on. Oh yes, we know everything down to the smallest little detail. Don't look so shocked girls, EJ and Danny have been here for some time so has your grandmother. We know everything about you," she said as she pats their little hands. "Now then you are going to be here for a few days while your grandmothers away on business."

Martha sighed again. "There are some rules that I'm sure you are not going to like, but you left us with no other choice." Martha getting serious stands began to pace. "Rule number-one; you will wear these at all times until you have learned to work together and learn to behave yourselves. Meaning since we live on a farm there are chores to do every day, if you like to do them or not they still have to be done," Martha said as she paced. "Unfortunately for you girls you are stuck together like glue. So that means you have to find a way to do them together until you go to bed at night?"

Martha paced and stood in front of them. "Rule number-two; this may be hard and it is a must; you will learn to work together and learn to be nice. Meaning; no fighting, no bickering. If and I mean it, if you can't follow this rule then more chores will be added. Trust me, girls, I do have plenty of things you can do. Rule number-three; after chores are done I want you to have fun and play with your brother Danny." The girls looked at them as if they have lost their minds.

Martha stopped pacing and sat on the bed next to them. "Now then my two girls Julie and Anna are wonderful girls. They will be helping you while you are here and have agreed too take you under their wing and show how to be sisters. So let's go down and meet

What's Behind the Looking Glass?

the rest of the family," she said and gave them each warm hug and welcomes them to the farm.

"Wayne dear mind helping these girls on to their feet, I would hate to have them fall and ruin those nice dresses... Oh, that reminds me," as she pulled out two dresses out of the closest. "When you girls get back, you can put these on," holding them up to them.

Peggy and Dona were appalled seeing those dresses, that weren't as fancy or nice as the ones their parents buy them. They were homespun, and something that might have come from a second-hand store, just like their brother's clothing, maybe slightly better considering they weren't exactly threadbare, just plain ugly in their opinion.

"I'll have to adjust the sizes a little, but they'll work just fine I think," Ma said. "Wayne dear please help me with these girls down to the living room," Martha on one side and Wayne on the other. The girls weren't happy as they glide along the floor with one leg tied together and one arm and they slowly went down the hall.

Everyone was in the living room as requested. Pa pulled up to two chairs for the girls to sit on and Ma cleared the air. "Everyone as you know, this Peggy and this Donna, EJ's and Danny sisters." EJ boiling red with anger inside with hate for all bad treatment and for the way they treated Danny and him. Just got up and left the room. Pa understood walked out with him on the porch, put his arm around him.

Danny hid behind Robert, Will, and Richard for protection, even thou the girls couldn't touch him. Martha understands and took charge of the room as Wayne nodded too her from outside to go ahead without him.

Peggy and Donna not looking up from their chairs they knew that their brother left the room and could only guess why. Not that they cared really because they didn't. It meant nothing to them. "*They are the ones stranded in this hick place tied to each other. Why should they have to suffer when their stupid brothers are the ones that have all the problems in the first place? It's those bad genes, nothing but trouble, as they glanced at Richard in the corner. "Just great, they got to him too. The next thing we need is men in white coats, lots of them and big patty wagon and throw them all in and haul them all away and throw away the key before it's too late."* Man this scarf itches," Peggy whispered. Pulling her arm away from Dona

"Hold still..." Dona replied, pulling her arm back as if it was a tug of war.

"No, you hold still," Peggy argues.

"Girls what did I say?" Martha intervenes.

"Now then as I was saying," as Ma cleared the air. "These girls will be staying with us for a few days, before returning home while their grandmother is away on business for a few days. Their circumstances are a little bit different than Richard or Danny, but not much. They are just a little bit misguided that's all and have lost their way." As she bends down and placed a motherly kiss on each of their heads.

"They have just forgotten or just haven't been taught how to be sisters. So be kind to them and treat them nice, I am sure they'll come around, won't you girls?

"I wouldn't count on it," as they whispered so she couldn't hear them beneath their breath. But Martha wanted answer she could hear so she taped her foot beside them waiting patiently then bend close whispered between them in each of their ears. "I want answer girls, a yes or no will do nicely girls."

"Yes Mrs. Downing," even though they didn't mean it.

"That's better, all right now you girls you can help me with lunch, but first we need to look at those dresses. These won't do out here." Martha unties the scarves. "Julie, Anna will you help these girls with those dresses I put in your rooms? Then we can start lunch."

"Yes, Ma."

What's Behind the Looking Glass?

Martha watched Peggy, Donna go down the hall with her daughters right behind them. "Don't get too comfortable girls," waving the scarves."

The girls hung their heads low pushed each other down the hall. "This is your fault," Peggy said.

"No it's your fault," her sister pushed back.

"Girls what did I say?" As Martha rolled her eyes and shook her head. "*Yes,*" thinking "*I will need lots of strong cups of tea, watching those two girls*. Ma went out to the porch where EJ and Pa are; she sat down next to him."EJ I know it's going to be hard having them here," she said.

"It's not that Ma, it's just that every time I look at them, I just want to scream because I know they feel nothing. They just want to destroy everything they touch and there is some part me as if I don't even know them. I have been gone for so long, but every time I look at Danny knowing he will be with them, I wonder how long before he to...?" as the words drifted off.

"I know son, I know," as they try to comfort him.

Pa looked towards the barn. "EJ my son, what you need is something to keep your mind busy to releases some that frustration. Because it looks like son you are going to need to let it out when you get mad. Your Ma here she cooks up a storm when she gets uptight and angry." Pa laughing "how do you think I got these huge arms son? By chopping a lot of wood, building things and farming. We just need to find you something that's all so it doesn't keep building up then blows the wrong way."

EJ looked up the road. "Your right Pa." Puts his arm around him, "we need to find something because I just want to be just like you someday," and puts the other around his Ma and kissed her on the cheek. "Thanks, Ma," he said.

Julie and Anna returned with the girls, Peggy and Donna seeing EJ on the porch with his arms around them, their eyes burned with hate for him. Despised everything he represents in their path. Peggy's mind plotted how to get out of here. *"Oh yes" seeing him and Danny; she could feel herself losing control, that will change when she gets back home and soon. "They think they can get away with it."* Peggy looked right at them eyes burning *"if I have my way. How dare, they think they can hold me in this hick place, think again sister. You can rot here if you think I care, think again,"* she plotted with a smirk on her face.

"Ma we're ready," Julie replied.

"Thanks, Julie, Anna." Ma getting up from the porch and rubbed EJ's head. "Wayne you boy's better go ahead get started with the shuffle. Lunch will be ready in about an hour…All right girls let's go inside we have work to do," Ma said.

"Yes, Ma."

Martha took the girls by the hand led them into the kitchen. Martha took a strong long sash tied it around the girl's waist so they can work side by side. Then took one of the scarves and tied both their wrist so they could both move freely about the kitchen without killing themselves, but still remain glued together at the hip. Watching them and seeing that this wasn't going to work at all.

After a few minutes made a few minor changes. She called it half a bear hug placing each girl's arm around each other's waist. Then strapping them down the side with the sash, and then tying it again in the back to keep them in place. After all, they were stubborn girls as she smiled at them. This left one hand free for each of them and both legs. It was never said two heads are better than one when came to these girls.

Pa, on the other hand, had a whole new set of problems of his own, looking at the girl's rooms. The problem was beds and the rooms were filled, small and packed. Boys were easy. Give them a sleeping bag, mattress or cot they would be fine, even nice soft hayloft once in a while as long it was dry.

The other problem is the boy's rooms. They just started to build them and Martha wants to separate the girls at night to give

What's Behind the Looking Glass?

them some peace. Pa ran his fingers through his hair sat on the bed thinking. Walked down the hall to the boy's room, looked into their room shook his head. "This room is getting smaller and smaller every time," rubbing his chin. "It might be easier to start piling up beds on top of each other," he said to himself.

Pa looked at the ceiling then the floor. "I wonder; Richard, Robert." He called seeing them down the hall, "boys come in here for a minute," he said.

"Yes Pa, yes sir."

"Richard I want you to stand right here." Robert moving him a little over to left, "stand right here." Pa grabbed his tape measure and pad and pencil, measured the ceiling to the floor, then each of the beds. "Richard, how tall would you say you are? Never mind," he measured him and then Robert and then wrote it down. "Thanks, boys… Richard, are you partial to that room down the hall?" He asked.

"No, sir. Why?" He asked.

"Good. I have a need for it I think. You mind if I have you boys empty it and Sam and Danny's room thanks boys, Richard you'll be staying in here. Come see me when you are done."

The boys watched Pa, but he just kept on figuring on the pad. Robert just nudges Richard. They have seen Pa like this before, knows he's already gone far off into another world and best to leave him alone. "Robert, what do you think that was all about?" Richard asked him.

"Richard, knowing Pa. We have work to do and something else to build," he replied.

"Robert he sure likes to build things," he said.

Robert laughed. "Yea that's Pa, Ma cooks and Pa builds and we farm."

"And I help with the chores and run from your sisters," Richard said.

"Hey now, they are not so bad," Robert replied.

"No their not; just kidding," taking his head under his arm rubbing with his knuckles.

By the time Robert and Richard emptied the room, EJ and Will joined them. Helped Richard to move his things into their room, Pa was just finishing up his new plans for the boys. "Boys" as he smiles, "are any of you afraid of heights?" He asked.

"I don't think so, why Pa?" They replied.

"Well, we need mattress and beds and space for you boys. It seems you are getting a little crowded," as he looked around the room. "Even though it may be temporary, but I have an idea that is going to solve a lot of problems now and for the future, I don't know why I didn't think of it before. Where going to build bunk beds for you boy's then put two small boys in the same bed for now until we can build another bunk bed for them later," he said.

So Pa showed his plans to the boys on how to make the shuffle. Putting Sam and Danny in Richards's room and the room Sam and Danny were in they are going to turn it into a dressing room for the four girls since now they have fit two beds in each room. And they weren't quite big enough to hold everything comfortably, that still left them with an extra mattress as a spare and cots for any visitor. After all, there was always room for one more at the farm as long they can find a corner or two. Pa and boys started shuffling things around again. Ma checked on the progress. "Well, Wayne how you and the boys making out?" She asked.

"We're just about finished moving things around," he said.

Ma watched the boys running out this room and that room, securing around busy as beavers. She looked at Richards's room then at Sam's room with a puzzled look on her face. Walked into Roberts Will and EJ room, seeing mattress against the wall, and waiting for

What's Behind the Looking Glass?

something to be placed there. "Wayne dear, I'm just a little confused," she said.

"Well dear, you wanted the girls all together so that's what you got," wiping the sweat from his brow. "Two beds in each of the girl's room and a dressing room for the four of them to share is the best I can do," he said.

"I see that dear," she said, "but that wasn't my question."

"Oh, you want to know about the boys?"

"Yes, dear?"

"We will just put some hay and straw down for them and they'll be fine."

Martha wasn't laughing gave him a hard cold stare. "Not in my house dear and they are not sleeping in the barn either."

Wayne grins and just leans over and puts his arm around her. "No dear. Why would they sleep in the barn, they have beds right here?" And kissed her, "now scoot, I have another bed to build," he said.

"Not until after lunch dear. I'm sure the boys are hungry and would like a break," she said.

"Yes dear, well be right there."

Pa and the boys stopped for lunch as they gathered around the table. Ma untied the girls to give them a break. They have been working hard as they all sit at the table. Pa only thinks it's fair that he should give a warm welcome to their new guests. Pa stands and clears his throat; EJ won't even look at them. Peggy and Dona's eyes stared at them as they burned with anger and kicked each other under the table not caring about the toast. Will, Robert just watched them back, putting their arm around EJ shoulder whispering. "Don't worry about them. They can't touch you here, Pa's right here Will and I are watching," Robert said.

EJ turned his head towards his brothers and whispered. "Thanks."

Robert whispered back. "That's what brothers are for; plus your sisters Julie, Anna got them on a very tight leash. They wouldn't dare come near you or Danny without them," he said.

If that didn't make them mad enough watching Will and Robert; Julie and Anna just realized, Julie said. "Pa, we never did get to thank our brothers this morning for the breakfast they prepared for us before Grandma came and we would like to thank them now if that's all right?"

Pa gave them a nodded." Julie and Anna each got up and gave each brother a hug and kiss on the cheek including Richard who didn't seem to mind, he just smiled blushed a little. Pa got two extra kisses of course for being extra sneaky before returning the table. Peggy and Donna were appalled by the sight, thinking they have lost their minds. There was no way in hell were they going to hug or kiss their brothers like that, more or less show them any sort of affection.

Pa telling the girls their rooms was done and they now have their own personal dressing room for the four them. *Julie and Anna were thinking how exciting a dressing room just for girls* felt Pa and the boys deserved and extra kisses and huge bear hug that nearly knocked the wind right out Will, Robert, and Richard. They gave EJ a small one bear hug but gave him extra kisses instead to make up for it. "All right girls let the poor boys breathe," Ma said.

With one more little squeeze. "Yes Ma." Then returned to their seats whispered to Peggy and Donna. "Your brothers are just so cute," watching their eyes fall out their heads.

Pa cleared his throat. "As I was saying your rooms are done so if you girls want to go down and do whatever you girls do down there that's fine," he said. Pa glanced over at Sam and Danny. "You two boys are going to be bed partners for awhile … Not that you aren't all ready," as he smiled and rubbed each of their heads. Considering they find them sometimes sleeping on top of each other when they check on them, having to re tuck them in sometimes at night.

What's Behind the Looking Glass?

"Sounds like we have work to do," Ma replied.

Julie and Anna smiled. "Yes, Ma." Peggy and Dona didn't answer they just looked at their hands. *"Great more work, is this nightmare ever going to end?" Peggy said with barely a whisper and kicked her sister under the table, "oh that feels so good."*

Then she kicks back. "Stop it," Dona replied.

"You stop it!" Peggy replied.

"Girls..." Martha said looking in their direction.

EJ and Danny smiled as they watched their sisters go down the hall with Julie and Anna right behind them. Pa gazing over at Sam and Danny; "well boys, I guess you're coming with us unless you want to go with them?"

"No way sir, they're boring," Danny said.

Richard laughed picked up Danny. "Then let's go and have some fun," taking Sam by the hand. With Richard watching the two boys while Pa, Will, and Robert started to build a bunk bed for them to sleep on. It was fascinating to watch him work the design.

Pa took the frames from the two beds, he was able to make the beds taller then join them together with a new post. Then he made a small ladder from the tepee posts. Then strapped them together with strong bolts and wrapped with a corded rope to bind them together. He was a master craftsman Pa left nothing to chance.

Chapter 25

They rocked the bed, bounced on the bed. Pa himself as big as he was climb on the top bunk made sure it didn't budge an inch before he was satisfied. In his book safety first when came to his boys. Pa rubbed his chin decided to add to it just in case, add extra braces here and there thought it could never hurt. He planed on later to change the design making notes in his book.

Ma had to see what was all the racket the boys were making. "I told you dear," as she looked at new beds in the room for the boys. "They won't be sleeping on straw from the barn," he said with a silly grin.

"Wayne what in the world is that contraption." Ma said as she looked at the two beds as one.

"I call it a bunk bed like army uses in their army barracks, but a little more comfortable." Ma glanced at Will on the top Robert on the bottom.

"Don't you think its neat Ma?" Will asked.

Ma putting her hand to her mouth gasping. "Will get down from there," she said.

"Ma it's safe," Will said as he bounced up and down on the bed, her eyes nearly fell out of their sockets as he jumped down to the floor; she almost fainted right there on the floor, trying to catch her breath by putting her hand to her chest.

Danny and Sam raced into the room climbed the ladder jumped on the bed that nearly does her in right then and there. "Oh no!" She said picked the two little ones off the bed. Martha giving Wayne another look and at that bed closed the door, reopens grabbed his shoulder. "Wayne! In the kitchen NOW!" She pulled him through the door leaving the four boys in the room.

What's Behind the Looking Glass?

Richard turned towards the door. "Robert, I think your Pa might be in the dog house again," he said.

"Looks that way," as they all laughed. "And I thought we had sister problems. Except for you Richard you just have a problem with our sisters," Robert replied.

"Ha, Ha," as Richard took his pillow and threw at Robert everyone started throwing pillows.

Ma letting the boys play outside for a while and poured a second cup of tea to settle her nerves. "Now... Wayne... Dear!" Ma said sitting down while girls are down the hall. "Do you mind, explain to me about that mess in there?" As she tapped her fingers on the table.

Wayne calm as a cumber said. "Martha you wanted me to find a solution to the problem so I did. The boys were getting crowed so I fixed it. Their rooms weren't ready yet, we're farmers not Indians, there's no tepee in the yard. Now everyone is under the same roof where you can keep an eye on them," he said pausing only for a minute.

"For as that bunk bed goes, it safe; I've jumped on it myself several times on the top bunk and you know I'd never let anything happen to any of my boys or my girls." Then he bends over and kissed her then leaves her sitting there.

She stopped him and grabbed his hand. "One more thing Wayne could tell them for me to be careful," she said.

"Yes, dear."

"And one more thing, the little ones, no bunk bed and not up there dear, oh no!" She said in a shaking scolding voice.

"Yes dear," Pa replied almost disappointed.

Ma drinks another cup of tea still shaking a little with nerves. Wondering if this tea is strong enough before going back down the hall to the girl's room, adding some more with little extra lemon to take the bitterness out.

Pa walked back into the boy's room looked at the bunk beds against the wall and sighed "room looks little bigger now that we can now fit four twin beds in here; still little crowded, but it works fine for the boys." After finishing up the room, setting up Richard's bed, "Pa took another look around and laughed. "Alright go see if your Ma needs any help, other than that boy's I think we are through here for today," he said.

"Yes, Pa." The boys walked down the hall to their sister's room and knocked on the door "Ma need any help we are done?" They said.

Ma looked at the four girls. "Nope; I think we are done to for a while," as she untied Peggy and Donna. "Alright, time to have some fun girls, now scoot. We will start dinner in about three hours," she said.

Donna turned to Anna." how can you have fun out here?" She asked.

"Oh you'll see," taking water glass from the sink filled it up with water then dumped it right on Robert's head; Julie in turned found Will, Pa and Ma laughed, watched the boys run to their room; Julie and Anna running outside dragging Peggy and Donna.

"Where are we going?"

"To get buckets silly," Julie said.

"For what?" Peggy asked.

They didn't have to wait long as they watched all six boys come charging out of the house headed for the barn, grabbing a bucket, filled them up with water. Ma and Pa sat on the front porch and watched, waiting as the six boys chased the girls around the farm with their buckets of water, to pounce on each other.

* * *

"It's nice of you to come, Betty," Margaret said as she greeted her when she arrived at the funeral home.

What's Behind the Looking Glass?

"I got here as soon as I could Margaret. Has anyone else arrived yet?" Betty asked looking around the room.

"Just a few people," Aunt Margaret said dots her eye with a tissue.

"Well let's go inside and get reacquainted, it's been a long time," she said.

"So how are all your grandkids, Margaret?" Betty asked taking a seat against the door a few feet from a stained brown casket lit by lights on each side as flowers of every kind sat around it and around the room. Right away you could see he was well-loved and will be sorely missed. Margaret new differently that in some ways he was not really gone nor had his life truly ended according to the man called Death aka Derrick and his new partner Nathanial. Members of something called **The Council of Light**. That watches over our world unseen by most deep in the realm known to some as behind the looking glass.

But this was not important as the realization that she to could be hunted according to Derrick as he and his followers stood nearby mixed in the group of people. As they pay their respects as it custom in her world giving her reassurances. That he still lives on, not just in her heart or her memory. How? She could not understand. How a person can die and still remain leaving his body behind. No, she could not believe it nor could she as she watched Derrick stand in a nearby corner with his staff leaned against him while he watched over the room and protected her from harm day and night.

"Fine, all of them married now and have kids of their own. I'm a great Grandma, can you believe it? And to think I'll be 70 this year, how about you Betty?" She asked her mind coming back to the conversation sighed heavily and wiped a tear with the back of her hand.

"Well I still have hopes for one," she replied wiping her own tears as she looked over at Mike lying so quietly as if he was merely asleep.

"You mean you finally got that son of yours out of the house?" Margaret asked.

"Yep!" She smiled. "I tricked him, but he might still have a chance," she said.

"You did what?" She replied. Betty told her what she did to her son Richard. She nearly busted a gut right there in the funeral home. The director had to come over give them both a glace. "Betty, you didn't?" Margaret replied.

"I did and now he is the happiest boy I have ever seen. Practically begged me to stay when I left this morning… I was glad to because I need him there."

Then Betty got real quiet as she looked at Mike over in the corner. Betty's sisters were just arriving through the door with her other son Steve and his wife Loraine behind them. Steve walked over to his mother and gave her a hug and a kiss on the cheek then makes his way around the room. Afterward, he comes and joined her with her sisters and Aunt Margaret. "I saw Richard a couple of days ago mother, I must say. "WOW!" When he came sprinting off that wagon. I nearly fell right off the porch. I just can't believe it," he said. Aunt Margaret looked as if she could not believe it her self. "She did it all right, I have seen it and it was a gas," Steve said slapping his knee.

Marry looked around the room. "Betty where are the girls?" She asked.

"Let's just say their fine and leave at that Mary," Betty replied looking for a way to try to change the subject. Betty seeing someone she wanted to talk too gets up and walked over to them to visit.

"Steve?" Asked Mary.

"Yes, Mary?" Taking a chair and pulled it across and turned it around while he sat on it the wrong way resting his arms on the back of the chair. His wife more ladylike took a seat next to Margaret wiping an escaped tear.

What's Behind the Looking Glass?

"Did she say anything to you about the girls?" She asked Mary and Lizy taking chairs around place them around their little group so they could speak more privately.

"No why?" Watching his mother talking to someone else.

"How about you Aunt Margaret?" She asked.

"No nothing. Just about things about EJ and farm life, Richard, grandchildren, now that you think about it, there was something wrong. I just can't put my finger on it. She got real quiet about it just before you came in. Oh, look is that Doctor Hatfield that old sawbones," she replied watching him make his way over to them before going around the room.

"Well hello Margaret, it's been a long time you old warhorse. I see they haven't kicked you out the pasture yet," he said shaking everyone's hand and giving a hug to Margaret.

"Oh Doc, you know me... I still got a few races still to run in these old legs of mine," she said.

"Ladies, charming as last time I saw you last.... Steve, how long has it been? You are the one person except," counting on his fingers. "That I haven't seen under my step-a-scope now why is that?" He asked Steve standing up and shaking his hand.

"Wrong neighborhood I guess or you just can't catch me Doc," he replied.

"Well sooner or later boy you and your mother too she the wind you know. I can't seem to pin her down long enough to see her," he said.

"Well if you are looking for her she right over there," Steve said.

"Well she not going anywhere, mind if I sit awhile, my legs need a rest and you ladies look like you need someone to talk to you a while. I would like to talk about something that's been on my mind why you are all here in one place if you wouldn't mind me spreading a little gossip Margaret that is?" Doc said. Steve grabbed a chair for Doc and as he joined their little group. Margaret gave a nodded to Derrick that he checks out and is not a spy.

"Oh please do tell I'm all ears." As Doc was giving some the news of the happening around town and filling in some of the details Betty left out about the farm and Downings and everything else. Of course, he does not know the current events or the aware about of the girls, that's no shock. But Steve and rest were eating it up like candy. Aunt Margaret nearly lost all her faults teeth a time or two.

Grandma said. "He looks so peaceful lying there that old stubborn goat," Betty said as she looked upon his face and talks to an old friend of heir's. "He was the one that gave me my first knife. In fact, he could shave a sheep faster than any person alive when he was young," she said looking down at his hands. "I remember the days at the dinner table he would come home taking fish from a pond, skin them slicker then whistle and smoother than butter. I am going to miss him," as she wiped a tear from her eye…"

* * *

"Splash," the water hits the boys and girls scream as they chased the boys around the farm. "You wouldn't dare?" Julie screamed with laughter as she in return and splashed Robert. EJ comes hobbling along with his. EJ raised his small bucket of water to splash Anna. Instantly his face turned white as the color drains from his face, pain shocked, stricken, eyes closed and fell to the ground and the bucket fell to the ground with water spilling all around him…

* * *

Betty's hand started to tremble as she swoons near the open casket reached for her chest started to faint to the floor. The room was in a panic as she started to fall to the floor. Doc and Steve and her sisters raced over to her… knocking over chairs and pushing everyone back.

What's Behind the Looking Glass?

* * *

Ma and Pa ran off the porch with shock as they watched EJ fall to the ground not sure what just happened. Richard and the girls stood over where EJ is lying in shock...

* * *

Doc down on the floor near Betty checking her out, Steve cleared the way so they can have some room and helped his mother up off the floor. Betty pushed him away. "I'm all right, just tired, been a long day that's all."

Steve and Doc helping her to a nearby chair cleared the way fussing over her. "Betty, stop it! You can't fool me," Doc said

"Me neither mother," Steve said taking her arm as he guided her to another chair close by. The room was in a panic as others tried to see what was going on. Derrick and his followers quiet the room and bring it back under control.

"Or me," Margaret replied, "Doc's been telling us what's been going on and so has your sisters," she said. Margaret could have sworn she heard strange words of power and thought she saw Derrick's eyes glow bright, *but that just not possible or is it? But she had seen or thought she saw Mike's eyes for time to time glow like his. Could it really be possible?*

"I tell you I'm fine," Betty argued as she tried to get up they just sit her right back down in the chair.

"Not you to Margaret?" She asked.

"Yes me too; the wind here has blown her self out and this warhorse is going make sure that you see some more races. Instead of going off half-cocked out of the starting gate like young stallion of twenty which you are not anymore. Now then let's get you out of here so Doc here can take look at you." Margaret argued.

"I told you I'm fine. There is something wrong at the farm, I know it." Betty said as she tried to get up one more time but is just too weak to move.

"Mother you are not fine," Steve said and her sister nearly picked her back off the floor.

Betty almost in tears; "Steve, Doc please if I promise to sit here, will you just call, I have to know then I'll go anywhere you want me to." Seeing nobody taking her seriously she tried to get up again.

"All right mother. Margaret sit on her if you have to, but there's probably nothing wrong. She's worrying over nothing," Steve said shaking his head…

* * *

Ma and Pa seeing EJ on the ground noticed the stitch around his waist is soaked with blood. Pa quickly picked him up dashed him in the house. Yelled too, Richard. "Keep the girls and little one outside please." Will and Robert followed EJ into the house, Pa setting him on the bed, Ma taking a knife that Grandma gave her, Pa watched her. "Martha?" he said.

"Wayne, be quiet dear. I need to concentrate," she said as she cut off a good pair of overalls and threw them in a corner without care. "Will run that tub, Robert find some ice" feeling, EJ's head, "Pa go find my kit." As she takes off the bandages, I was afraid of that. Doc was right that wound of his has gotten worse. He doesn't need any more problems poor kid," as she brushed his hair wiped her tears.

Pa in the kitchen grabbed Ma's kit the phone rings. "Hello… Steve … kinda busy, make it quick … EJ's hurt, don't know how bad yet. The stitches torn… Ma says the fevers back… Oh, Doc he's there, send him back, need him quick bye…" Pa hung up the phone and grabbed Ma's First Aid Kit and returned down the hall.

What's Behind the Looking Glass?

* * *

Steve returned back to the main party whispered to Doc in his ear. "Doc seems we have a problem," he said.

"Another one?" Doc replied

As Steve gazed over at his mother? "You are wanted back on the farm, EJ just collapsed and torn the stitches and is running a high fever, not sure what else. Mr. Downing said just happen a few minutes ago," he said.

"Man when it rains it pours cats and dogs around here," Doc said Steve and Doc looked at Mike in the casket, his mother nearly on the floor again and now back on the farm.

Chapter 26

"Doc I don't think she can take anymore?"

His mother looked over at Steve standing by Doc whispering his ear. "Steve do I need to call myself or are you going tell me because I'm not going let three old maids stand in my way." She said as she starts to get herself up and off the chair and they sit her right back down again.

"Betty you are not moving, you promised," Doc replied.

"Yes I did, so far I haven't heard word one. Expect air; like I'm getting old and need to take it easy, well I did that, look what happened," she said, getting madder as she sits in a chair feeling helpless.

Doc laughed. "Steve your mother is a spark plug has still spark, I'll give her that.... All right, Betty, you simmer down. There's nothing you can do about it anyway and I'm sure he'll be all right," Doc said.

That got her goat now she was boiling over like a steam engine. "Doc if you don't tell me," Betty looked over at Mike. "You two are going to get reacquainted real fast," she said.

"He just tore that stitch and the infection I been worried about, well it festered went off like a firecracker. He has a high fever and what else I am not sure. Now then let's take look at you then I'll go and head back to your grandson," he said.

"We can look at me later Doc after you take look, my grandson. But right now Doc I also need to take care of Mike," Betty gazing over at him over in the casket.

Aunt Margaret puts her foot down and stands up. "Betty you are the most stupidest horse around," pulling her up out of her chair, dragging her over by Mike. "I want you to take a good look at him.

What's Behind the Looking Glass?

What do you see? I'll tell you what you see, a tired old man, a happy 94 old man who has lived his life; well that's what you see? Now scoot he's dead there's nothing more you can do for him that hasn't been done all ready… Steve, Mary, Lizy glad to see you, but I think you have more important things to do than sitting around here with me," as she placed Betty into their hands.

"Yes, Aunt Margaret?" They all replied. Betty turned opens her mouth shocked about to protest, Margaret just shoves her out the door.

"Betty you never did tells us where the girls are," Lizy replied walking back towards their cars. With a firm grip on her sister's arm, too keep her from escaping or falling down.

"Oh they're safe, not happy I'm sure but safe," She replies with a frown on her face as they walked beside her. But in her mind, all she could think about was Mike and her grandson EJ. "*What has he done now?*"

"Betty, you didn't?" Mary replied. She just smiles not saying another word about it.

"Doc I'll make you a deal if you want to look at me, you look at my grandson first. I'll stay put and mind that's what I'll do. Doc if you are looking for a bargain now's the time." Betty said.

Doc rubbing his chin starts counting on his fingers. "Betty I want something more this time, I know how well you are going to mind," he laughed. "After all the years I have known ya. Heck, I'd have better luck teachen a possum too dance a square dance," he replied following their little group back to the cars.

"Let's see. I have looked at both your sisters and all your grandkids from head to toe and one that got stitches from here to breakfast; we have'ta keep putin the stuffen back into him. Oh yes did I tell you about your son Richard one with sore feet and nice red beat sunburn, he could almost glow in the dark. Then let's see now, there's your other boy Jim and his wife," as he rolled his eyes. "Let me see that's," counting on his fingers… "I think, oh yes," he looked over at Steve. "Steve and his wife, of course, theirs one more now after the news I just heard today, she doesn't know it yet… So Betty dear, your price might be a little bit low… Marry, Lizy, Steve can you make sure that Betty here makes it back to the farm and oh Steve please bring your wife. Just to make sure your mothers all right and tries to blows away." Steve drives his mother back to the farm with everyone following behind him…

* * *

Pa carried the First Aid Kit under his arm as he ran to bedroom Robert with the ice in his hands. EJ on the bed began to come around. "Ma, it hurts real bad," he said.

Ma stroked his hair behind his head on the bed. "Shush, I know." She replied watching the sweat pouring down from his face. Pa seeing EJ waking up feels relived, Ma turned to Pa. "He just fainted from the pain and is little dazed… EJ you are burning up son we need get you cooled off. The girls are our outside ok." She said as she removed the rest of the bandages. She can see the blood oozing through, she knew this isn't good and tries to calm him.

"Wayne we have a bigger problem." As she stands up as she looked at EJ trying to sound calm. "EJ I'm going get something for the pain… Robert, Will can you watch him for a minute," and taking Robert's hand. "I want you to hold this bandage here and don't move it." Taking Pa outside the room, "We can't put him in the tub, he'll bleed too much and the infection around his waist on his side has spread…"Doc was right about that last rib, I think it snapped. We have to find another way to cool him down and fast."

"Martha, Doc on his way, but it will be a while, Steve just called," he said.

Martha looked at him. "What? How did he know?" She asked.

"He didn't say… anyway Doc is on his way back to the farm."

What's Behind the Looking Glass?

"Ma, EJ needs you he's burning up and we are having a hard time holding him still," Will said.

"Wayne grabs some towels and ice and buckets of water," Ma said and ran back into the room. "Will, go get Richard I think we're going need some help…Tell Julie… oh, those girls." Ma *thought about Peggy and Donna and how tired she was. I need hands and their tied up with two girls that are useless that need to be watched. What do I do? She wondered gazing at her little boy on the bed?* "EJ?"

"Yes Ma," he replies.

"Do you trust me, son?" She asked.

"Yes, Ma."

"Good. Because I need Julie in here with me and I can't do this alone and I can't just throw a sheet over you to hide you," she said.

EJ swallowed hard he looked over a Will and Robert standing in the room watching him with concerned faces. "Just Julie, Ma you promise. None of my other sisters, well maybe Anna, but not those two no way Ma, no deal!"

"I promise, besides who would keep eye on them? Will run, I need Julie and Richard."

Richard and Julie outside on the porch paced back and forth as they watched the girls sitting on the swing, making sure they didn't move a muscle. Anna was keeping eye on Sam and Danny busy out by the horses. Will nearly runs them over opening the door. "Julie, Ma needs you and Richard where's Anna?" He asked.

"Watching Danny and Sam," she replied.

Will pulls Julie aside "Ma needs your help with EJ, but I don't know what to do with the girls," he said.

"Will that's easy; Richard can you grab that sack of potatoes for me, thanks," hands the girls each a peeler. "Now then girls I want you too peel every last potato and put them in these buckets." Will only stared them down at them. "Will here he'll be glad to sit here and watch you do it...Won't you?" Will, nods in their direction and took a seat on the porch. "Come on Richard, Ma and EJ need us."

Pa brings in the ice and buckets of water from the tub sets them in the room passing Julie and Richard in the hallway. "Heard Ma needed some help Pa, how bad is it?" Julie asked.

"Well it's not good, we need to cool him down and we can't put him in the tub this time. Ma having a hard time getting the blood to stop so she can re-stitch it closed, but he's awake and in a lot of pain."

Julie seeing Ma and EJ on the bed, "Julie I need your help to re-stitch him do you think you can help me?" She asked.

"Yes Ma," she replied.

"Robert, I need you to go into the kitchen heat some water and bring some of those pain killers that Doc left."

Pa brought in some towels and hands them to Ma. Ma and Julie dip them in the buckets place them around EJ waiting for the pain to subside a little bit. "All right EJ, now your going have to trust me, Robert and Richard are here, but Will is watching your sisters. So can you trust me and Julie?" She asked.

EJ looked over at Julie. "If I don't, she'll tie me to the bed anyway Ma then tickle me to death like she does Danny and Sam," he replied.

Ma laughed. "You got a point," as Julie lightly grabs his foot tries to tickle it.

"Ooooh that hurts." He replies so she settled for a kiss on his cheek. Ma wiped some more of the sweat off his face. Ma and Julie removed the bandage and the towel around his waist.

What's Behind the Looking Glass?

Julie faces nearly turns green seeing the puss and blood-forming around the wound; "Ma you are right, that is nasty," trying not to look away.

"That's not worse of it," as she whispered in her ear. "Look toward his lower ribs see that last rib where that bruise is, I think it snapped clean through and infected the inside. That's why his burning up so fast due to all the infection raging inside around his side," Ma said.

"Robert, Richard I need you to hold him still, Pa you need to hold his legs down... EJ this going to hurt and I'm sorry we can't wait any longer, but we have stop this bleeding," she said. Robert placed the stick between his teeth, "now bit as hard as you can." Ma taking the needle and sticks it into his side and into his leg with thread, stitching. EJ jerks off the bed screaming while boys hold him down. The stick falls out of his mouth as he passes out from the pain. Julie dabs and wipes and Ma re stitches the wound closed. The girls outside no doubt most likely were smiling. Until Will gave them a hard cold stare, daring them to even blink as he stands to stare them down to the ground.

Ma and Julie clean EJ up, putting on new bandages and covered him back up with a light sheet. Pa moves him to Richard's bed so they change EJ's bed set him in it, with a light dressing covering him with another clean sheet keeping cool towels and ice by the bed not leaving his side. "All right boys," she said after seeing EJ tucked into bed sleeping.

"Ma I'll stay here why you go and get some things done around the house," Julie said. Washing her blood-soaked hands in a bucket of soap and water and wiped them on a clean towel while she removed her apron lying in the pile of dirty towels.

"Thanks, Julie," she said.

"Me to Ma," Robert replied.

"Thanks, Robert, but Pa needs you, Will and Richard. "I need some help to watch the girls and to watch Danny and Sam. Dinner still needs to be done," she said as she looked at EJ, she felt just a little wiped out.

Cars started pulling into the farm, Will screamed into the house "Pa we have company and I mean company." Pa rushed down the hall with Richard and Robert rushing outside prepared for war. "They are not taking him, not without fight boys," Pa said Richard and Pa barreling out the door; Ma closing the bedroom door behind them with Julie barricading the door with a dresser. One, two, three, four cars pulled up to the farm. Pa and the boys loaded for bear. Pa holding the shotgun full of buckshot.

Steve and Grandma got out of the car first. Pa and boys nearly killed over laughing at themselves, Pa and Robert seeing two more women with Doc plus Steve's wife getting out of the fourth car. Pa breaths sigh of relief and aim the gun down towards the ground.

Grandma saw the look on their faces and laughed. "Scared ya didn't we? Well, you are not the only ones." Grandma said as she introduces Mary and Lizy to them. "Let's go inside," she said.

"Grandma you decided to come back I see," Wayne said. "Will, run tell your Ma she got that help she needed, just in the nick of time to," Pa replied unloading the gun and placing the shells into his pocket and puts the gun back in the closet high enough to keep it out of reach. "Doc what we like to know is how you knew about it and when you did?" Wayne asked.

Mary and Lizy noticed Peggy and Donna on the porch peeling potatoes. "Well Mary, she did say they were safe, just not where," Lizy replied.

"Yes, Lizy that's what bothers me," Mary said as she looked at Richard in his simple farmer clothes which he hasn't had a chance to change since the water fight. In fact, none of the boys have been kinda busy for some reason?

Peggy and Donna smiled at their aunts, hoping they see the light at the end of the tunnel and stop peeling the potatoes and got up from their spots. "Girls" Mary and Lizy stopping them and shook their fingers. "Not so fast, we're going need those potatoes for supper so just keep peeling," Mary said.

"But... I? We?" They replied.

"Sorry girls."

Will running down the hall to their room yelling through the door. "It's ok, Grandmas back and she has the Doc with her and Steve and more people I don't know who they are," Will said through the door.

Chapter 27

Ma sighed with relief hearing that Doc was here. "But how in the world did they know anything was the matter in the first place?" Shrugging their shoulders Julie and Ma moved the dresser away from the door and open the door as they watched a whole gang of people walk down the hall. "I must say you are a sight for sore eyes," Martha said as Grandma and Martha give each other a hug.

As they all gazed over at EJ sleeping and watch him open his eyes, staring at all the people in the room, checking to make sure he was covered. Ma and Julie laughed as he blushes bright red. Grandma rushed over to him and kissed him on the head. Cussing him out; "Don't ever do that to me again EJ, if you need something just pick up the phone." She said taking a dime out of her purse putting into his hand. Martha not understanding a word what they are talking about neither does he for the moment. Grandma gave him a kiss on the cheek?

"But Grandma I didn't," he replied.

"Shush now," as she wiped the sweat off his face.

Martha looked at Steve and Doc. "What is she talking about? Did something happen up there?" She asked.

Doc pushed everyone out of the room except for Grandma and Martha sends everyone down the hall to visit. "All right EJ let's see what you have done shall we?" Doc said removing the sheet and pulling out his bag. "Tsk, tsk… " Saw the crutch in the corner. "I guess you know where you are going to be for the next couple of days don't you son?" Taking his temperature and watching Martha wipe the sweat from his head cooling his chest with a cool towel. "That's right in this bed," EJ all ready hating the idea. "No Indians either I am afraid not this time," Doc said looking around his waist.

"EJ does this still hurt when I press here?"

What's Behind the Looking Glass?

"No," he said.

"What about here?" He asked moving down the side of his ribcage where has mostly healed.

"Just little Doc," trying not to make face.

"How about here?" He asked.

"Ouch that really hurts Doc," the pain nearly sends him clear to outer space Doc watched the rib slide back from the rest. "Yep clean through," as Doc rubbed his chin looking at the nasty bruise. "I knew it wasn't healing right, darn it to. You got to be the tough's kid to put clothes on I swear. If you were a girl it might be easier, than again maybe not."

EJ didn't think it was funny at all neither did Martha. "Sorry Doc, but I like my boys just the way they are," kissed EJ on the cheek.

"Oh, I didn't mean anything by it. Just that if he was a girl you could throw a dress over him he'd be fine and cover everything that needed to be covered. Of course, I wouldn't suggest that, that would be silly now. The problem is Martha this boy here can't have anything near that waist and around his chest except bandages and he has to get out of that bed or we are back to square one. It has to be lousy, goosey, airy clothing. No ties, no strings, nothing heavy either It has to breath be light and move freely," he replied.

"Well another problem for another day not that we had our share for one day," Doc said looking over at Betty and EJ. "All right Betty. A deals a deal," looking her straight in the eyes. I've looked at your grandson and I'm going to write another prescription," taking out his pad giving it to Martha. "And will see EJ in two days if not sooner… Now than Martha, I need to borrow a room for a while, I have four more people to see… Starting with this young lady," he replied grabbing Grandmas arm.

"Doc who are the other three?" She asked.

"Oh didn't you hear the news?" Doc said grabbing Grandma by

the arm. "You, her and her other son plus his wife," and closed the door behind him.

Pa walked into the room seeing Grandma being escorted down the hall by the Doc. "I've come to relive you dear," he said watching Doc closes the other door behind them. Pa seeing EJ, "how are you doing son?" He asked.

"Better I think, just hot," he said as Ma wiped him down again.

"Well, then how things out there?" She asked

"Oh interesting would be an understatement," he replied.

"I just heard the news,"

"Which part?"

"About me seeing the Doc," Ma said not too thrilled about it.

"Oh that, I got even more news than that?"

"There's more?"

"Tons more; that's why I come to relive you, you're missing all the fun, now scoot"

"What about dinner?"

"Oh, that's another thing you are not going to believe your eyes. I had to put the table outside on the foundation to make room for everyone. You wanted help dear they come in, droves, now scoot." He said with a kiss on the cheek.

Martha walked down the hall towards the kitchen, people securing about left and right, women she never seen in her life. Julie and Anna were working beside them, talking up a storm; Peggy and Donna scrubbing carrots and washing dishes in the sink side by side not daring to even move from the spot. Kettles were boiling, food being prepared; boys setting the table, everything humming along; Sam and Danny playing with both their Uncles squealing. Martha walked into the kitchen. "Hello dear; dinner will be ready soon, can we get you anything? Oh, by the way, my name is Mary and this is my sister Lizy and you know everyone else I think," Mary said.

"Hi, Ma," the boy's wave she waves back.

"So how can I help?" Ma asked.

Mary looked around the kitchen. "Let's see," Lizy pulled Martha up a chair handing her a cup of tea. "Just sitting right there in that chair dear that's how... Now then as I was just about to tell my sister how?"... Mary going on with the conversation with Julie, Martha sits and watched from the corner of her kitchen listening to all of the events taking place.

She heard all kinds of things about Grandma and other things that nearly shocked life right out of her. Wayne wasn't kidding about the news of the day, but that's not what she really wanted to know. When she heard Doc's voice from around the corner? "All right Martha," seeing Doc come out with Grandma down the hall; "It's your turn," Doc said turn turning to Grandma. "Now remember what I said... No more, you are not as young as you used to be Betty, you take those pills and I'll check in on you in a few days."

Martha looked at Grandma waiting for her to explain more. "Oh. He just being cautious that old goat, I'm fine dear really," as she struts into the kitchen as if nothing was wrong.

Doc takes Martha down to the room where the girl's new dressing room was. "Doc will somebody tell me what's going on and stop this nonsense?" She said as she watched Grandma walk away.

"For some strange reason call bad timing or I like to call it twining thinking of word a twinkling instance. They both collided at the same moment in time. The thing is it was bound to happen sooner than later, why at that time who knows?" He said.

"Doc you are making no sense," she replied.

"Humm," Doc paused thinking how to explain. "All right EJ infection and wounds were bad some not healing; he was trying to hurry it long."

"Yes, we know that."

"What you don't know is his grandmother in there was in bad shape too. She was wearing herself out, spreading herself too thin. It was catching up to her. The farm was helping out and gave her way out, reliving the stress and she was doing what she loved, bringing some that spark back. The problem is. She took on too much at once. Then when Mike died everything came tumbling down. Worrying about the girls and everyone… not let anyone carry the load. So her heart started to give a little. Saying 'listen, I need to rest a minute.' Those two little girls Peggy and Dona were driving her crazy as much she loves them."

Martha had a better word for it and wondered if his real mother felt anything. She doubted it thinking about EJ and Danny and the girls. "Tell me about it Doc I had them for nearly a day. Things started to unravel here; I thought I was going lose my mind," Martha said.

"That's why it's time to get you checked out and before that happens dear… Now than! Handing her a dressing gown and stepped out of the room so she could change.

"But Doc I feel fine, really. Just a little stressed but fine?" She replied before he could close the door.

"Now listen here Martha a bargain is a bargain so don't argue with me," Doc said.

"But Doc! I didn't make that bargain," she replied.

"I know, that's the best part. Now than gown please." *Martha thinking I'm going have a serious talk with Grandma as she puts on the gown.* Doc closed the door and grins from ear to ear *knowing he has finally gotten the upper hand for once over these two women.* Doc examined Steve and his wife with a kick of his heels and bows to the ladies. "Now then if you don't mind? Now that I have seen every last one of you, good day and goodnight and I'll see some of you, if not all you of at the picnic in a few days… Oh please try not to get sick because you all wear me out for being a simple country Doc."

Everyone waved to Doc thanks him and laughed and tries to promise to behave for a day or two at the least as he goes out the door. Continue to go on about the visiting of the day. Martha goes back into the boy's room down the hall seeing Wayne and EJ. "How are you doing son?" She asked as she wiped him down again.

"Still hurts Ma, I am really hot," he said seeing the sweat pouring from him.

"Doc says we can stick you in the tub for a few minutes, but we have to keep those stitch's dry as much as possible. Wayne can you run some cold water put some ice in it, not too deep," she said feeling EJ head with the back of her hand. "He is really hot, I'll get some more medicine," she said.

"Thanks, Ma," EJ replied watching her close the door so he could have some privacy.

Ma went into the kitchen seeing Julie and Mary still working on dinner. "Mind keeping eye on things for us a bit longer?" She asked.

"Martha you don't have to say another word, we are here to help… what do you need?" Mary asked.

"EJ's burning up and we need to cool him off so just keep everyone here why we take him down the hall. Julie, I need some of that broth dear; can you make some for me?"

"Sure Ma," she replied as she hands her a cup. Pa picked up EJ with Ma and headed down the hall to cool him off, while Julie and Mary blocked the way giving them their privacy.

Grandma seeing the doorway blocked. "Julie, what's going on?" She asked.

"EJ's still burning up so his Ma and Pa are cooling him down in the tub," she said.

"How?" She asked

Julie shrugged her shoulders. "Doc said she could as long she didn't get stitches too wet," she replied.

Grandma starts to go down hallway Mary blocked the way. "Betty they can handle it without you. I think you have had enough excitement for one day. They are just giving him a little bath if they need your help they know where to find you." She said shoves her back into towards the living room back to her other grandchildren.

Ma slowly pouring cold water over EJ, Pa taking a towel folding it over the stitches keeping them as dry as possible his temperature starts to drop a little. Ma gave him the broth to drink sits by the tub. She wiped the sweat and water from his face and chest. EJ breathing deeply more relieved as the pain subsides and his temperature drops. "Thanks, Ma, that's a lot better, Ma I'm a mess and I can't even be an Indian, nothing… not even a farmer according to Doc," EJ said.

"EJ that's not true son," Pa said placing his hands on his shoulder. "It's not the clothes that make the person. It's what inside what counts." And brushed his hair away from his face, "who told that?" He asked.

Ma kissed his cheek. "Don't worry, will think of something. I don't know what yet but something. Right, Pa?"

Pa nodded his head. "You bet."

Ma leaned down placed another kiss on his forehead. "And it won't be no dress either," as she checks his temperature again. "Pa I think we take him back to his room now I believe dinner about ready," she replied.

"Pa, do I have to go back to my room? I'm tired of being alone and it's not fair for you and Ma too sit with me and I do feel so much better, I'm just hot that's all," he replied.

What's Behind the Looking Glass?

"Ma sighed. "You don't have anything you can wear son, not yet anyway. Let's think about it son for now let's get you back to your room for now."

EJ disappointed hating being left alone when all the fun is out there sighed brokenhearted, him being stuck in a room. "All right Pa. I guess I don't have a choice do I?"

Pa took EJ back to his room and tucked him back into bed. "All right now rest awhile we will come in give you your dinner." Leaving him alone they both walked down the hall to their guests and the rest of the family.

Grandma paced the floor seeing them enter the room. "Well, how is he?" Giving Martha a hard look and the third degree *imagine keeping me out* she thought.

"He's better Grandma just needs to be cooled off a bit that's all, gave him something more for the pain."

Wayne laughed. "Grandma, your grandson is something else," as he puts his arm around her. "After all, he just went through, he rather be in here with us than in that room. He doesn't have a stitch to wear; he says 'why do I have to stay in here when all fun in here?' After we just stitched him up cooled him off, he's ready to go out do some more. Now, who does that does remind me of?" He said *as he looked at Grandma after hearing about her little adventure of the day from her sisters and son Steve.*

Grandma turned to Wayne. "Is there any good reason why he couldn't come out here? He's not contagious, he just hot, we can keep him covered well enough I think. Just put him on the couch or a cot for now… Heck Wayne, the boys been Indian's most the summer, he'll be fine. Besides all that are here are just his aunts, uncles, brothers, sisters. They're not going to care. Let them see him. We're not going anywhere," she said pointing to the suitcase by the door. "Now then where do we want to put him?" She said looking around the room "I'll clear a path."

"Grandma, Martha will skin me alive," he replied.

"Shush now, oh look there's a spot." Grandma starts heading for the couch, yelled over at Robert and Richard as they sat on the couch. "Boys clear the couch, EJ's coming through." Martha turned around in mad dash hearing the ruckus. Grandma shoved Wayne down the hallway "now move it dear, he wants out of that room I want to see my grandson."

Martha ran over to Grandma. "What are you doing?" She asked.

"Clearing spot dear for EJ, what do you think I'm doing? Wayne says he wants out of the room so he coming out here," she replied.

"Grandma he can't! He has to stay in that bed, you heard the Doc.

"Yes I did, one bed is good as another dear," she said.

"Grandma he doesn't have anything wear," Martha replied.

"I know that and so does everyone else, I don't think they are going care at the moment. I can ask if you like?" Grandma whistles to get everyone's attention. "Does anyone care if boy we all know comes out in sheet because he has nothing to wear?" Everyone laughed except for Martha and two girls and goes about finishing dinner. "I guess not, sorry Martha. Oh look, here comes my grandson now." Martha raced over draping the sheet over him, EJ beaming as he passed by everyone. Pa gently sets him on the couch.

"Thanks, Pa," he said.

"Are sure EJ?" He asked

"Yes Pa, I'll be fine," he said as Pa tucked in the sheet around his waist. Ma seeing the sweat starting to pour from his face again begins to worry about keeping him cool. "Ma I'm fine," seeing the worry in her face. "Just really hot again that's all," he replied.

"How's the pain?" She asked.

"All right, not any worse if that's what you mean, just hot Ma," he said.

What's Behind the Looking Glass?

Ma bends down and kissed his warm forehead looked over at Pa then smiles at EJ. "Are sure you are going to be all right here?" She asked.

"Yes Ma," nearly panting.

Ma whispering Wayne's ear "His burning up again," Wayne nods and goes over and fills up another bucket of water with more ice with towels and brings them over to Ma, so she can place them around EJ to make him more comfortable.

All the boys and men in the living room visiting amongst themselves with women in the kitchen were finishing up dinner; the sweat just pouring off EJ, EJ whispered to Robert standing over him. "Robert, I can barely breathe. It so hot in here I need some air," as if he going to pass out due to the heat in the room.

Robert nudged Pa. "We have a problem." Pa and Robert seeing EJ's eyes starting to glaze over due to lack of air and the heat in the room. "He can't take the heat in the room needs some air and quick." Pa can see EJ about to pass out with sweat pouring down him, his breathing slowing down a bit and began to get raspy.

Pa quickly jumps into action yelling picked EJ off the coach headed for the door. "Will grab the door, Robert meet me on the other side of the house!" EJ's head lolled behind them.

Ma and Grandma staring in shock as the room goes into panic watching Wayne and the boys run out the door with EJ in Pa's arms. "What in tarnation?" she said. Mary and Liz watched gasping seeing the sheet flying through the air over Pa's shoulder, Richard right behind it picking it up off the ground. Grandma barred the door from the girls. "I think the guys of got this one ladies, he just needs little fresh air that's all," she said.

Pa laid EJ down around the side of the house as Richard covers him with the sheet, EJ comes back into focuses. Breathing more deeply still sweating

"Thanks, Pa I need that," taking in couple more breaths. EJ breathing more regularly, he looked down seeing the sheet barely covering him. "Pa? The girls, they didn't see anything, did they?" He asked.

They just laughed. "Do you want me to go ask?" Pa asked as he blushes red.

"No," EJ said and tucks the sheet around his waist takes a couple more breaths blushing red.

Pa looked at the table around the corner, seeing dinner almost ready. "Robert go grab a cot and setup over by Ma in the corner. EJ since we have you out here you might as well be out here with us."

Robert runs back into the house passing Ma and the girls standing in the room nods his head, picking up a cot from a nearby corner. Ma follows Robert watching Pa with EJ. "Pa? What do you think you are doing?" She asked.

"EJ's joining us for dinner dear," he said.

"Out here?" She asked

"Yes dear, he needed some fresh air, he couldn't breathe and was too hot in the house. Plus dinner was ready so we thought what the heck we were already here. Oh, he'll be fine dear," swinging EJ's legs. "He'll be right by your side the entire time." Robert sets up the cot and Pa placed him on it and Pa making sure the sheet covered his waist. "See dear, his fine… Now then let's eat."

Everyone gathered around the table outside on the new foundation, EJ over in the corner by Ma as she placed a tray for him for his dinner, Ma fixes him a plate. Ma glanced over at him, EJ smiles as he listens to the conversations around him. Ma sees the sweat pouring down from his face and he just whispers "Ma I'm fine, just hot," takes some bits of his food.

Thing is he was not fine at all; he just didn't want Ma to worry. The conversation at the dinner table was astounding, to say the least with news from all different sorts. Of course, Ma had some news of her own with a little extra surprise. "Wayne dear I was thinking about the boy's rooms." She said as causally passed down the mash potatoes to the boys and the gravy. "I was thinking we might have to add a couple more rooms. The ones we have just won't be enough dear." She said as she glanced over at the boys and blinks at the girls. Wayne looks at her for a minute not realizing what she just said then she smiles. Martha looked at Grandma and winks with a grin with a warm glow on her face.

Grandma knife hits the plate first then it happened. "Oh My... Your Not?" Martha nods and grins again looking at the boys than at girls. Next thing you hear across the table on Pa's plate "Clank, Clank"

Ma blinks at him. The table goes silent you could hear a pin drop. Everyone waiting, looking at Wayne across the table he smiles, then grins with a twinkle in his eye. Gets up from his chair goes over to Martha kisses her right then and there as he looks into her eyes. "Are you sure dear?" He asked.

"Doc says he thinks so by next spring, he thinks we should have another," she replied.

Pa stands right there and shouts." Folk's, looks we are going have another girl or boy added to or a little family."

Julie and Anna sighed. "ahhhhh, I hope it will be another boy he would be so cute. Course another sister would be nice to, to help even the odds." Anna said.

Pa returned to his seat nearly dancing back. Pa looked at the house and the new foundation started to laugh. "Boys?" Looks at Ma across the table, "I guess we better hurry get those rooms done or I will be in trouble," he said.

Steve and the boys laughed. "Now he thinks he's in trouble."

Strange words echoed in the air, attached to a light breeze as it encircled EJ as his body heated up from the strange infection. With a simple word "nes' a noth'" EJ eyes drew heavy and begin to faint as the strange man with red glowing eyes and scar down his right cheek waved his black bone staff; stood watching in the shadows watching the family around the dinner table.

Dinner conversation carry's on with more advents of the day. Ma glanced over at EJ watching him starting to slump over and breathing haggard as the sweat just pouring off his little body nearly falling off the cot. Ma jumped, racing out of her chair to catch him as he fell to the ground with his head in her lap. Pa raced over from the table next to him. "Wayne he's really is burning up and fast," she said.

Pa yelling to Robert; "Fill the tub quickly; Will, go grab the bucket of water from the living room." Everyone dashed about as fast they could, Pa taking the bucket of water throwing it over EJ while Ma tries to cover what she can of the stitches with a table napkin and kitchen towel. Pa picked up EJ in his arms running down hall soaking wet placed him into the tub, with Grandma on the phone calling the Doc back.

Things always seem to go wrong, but nobody predicted or saw the strange wisp of smoke that stood by near a tree as he watched them. Morgan grinned while he watched the panic strike fear into the family, for he could no longer wait for his prize to heal like a normal boy as he drew staff and whispered words of healing that would heal the boy within a months time instead of six months when the boy would come of age and his power would begin to manifest. "Soon my Prince soon we will rule the worlds together," dissipates as he retreated once more into the shadows.

Derrick watched as Morgan dissipates as he clutched staff and protects the boy with every fiber of his being lifting the dark shadows around him and fell to his knees. Gasping for breath, grandma turned as their eyes met. Derrick gave a quick wink and shimmered before her eyes before she could even blink, he was gone.

Look for Book 2 Masks Behind Shadows
of What's Behind The Looking Glass series
Coming soon.

CPSIA information can be obtained
at www.ICGtesting.com
Printed in the USA
BVHW071010170521
607542BV00001B/14